Sophie's Sister

NINA PAINE

This is an IndieMosh book

brought to you by MoshPit Publishing
an imprint of Mosher's Business Support Pty Ltd

PO Box 147
Hazelbrook NSW 2779

indiemosh.com.au

Copyright © Nina Paine 2020

The moral right of the author has been asserted in accordance with the Copyright Amendment (Moral Rights) Act 2000.

All rights reserved. Except as permitted under the Australian Copyright Act 1968 (for example, fair dealing for the purposes of study, research, criticism or review) no part of this publication may be reproduced, stored in a retrieval system, or transmitted in any form or by any means, electronic, mechanical, photocopying, recording or otherwise, without the written permission of the publisher.

 A catalogue record for this work is available from the National Library of Australia

Title:	Sophie's Sister
Author:	Paine, Nina (1963–)
ISBNs:	978-1-922368-32-4 (paperback)
	978-1-922368-33-1 (ebook – epub)
	978-1-922368-34-8 (ebook – mobi)
Subjects:	FICTION: Literary; Family Life / Siblings; Action & Adventure.

Sophie's Sister is a work of fiction, a fusion of events and characters both real and imagined. Those that were real have been used fictitiously without any intent to describe actual conduct.

Cover design by Nina Paine and Ally Mosher

Cover layout by Ally Mosher at allymosher.com

Cover images from Shutterstock

For my parents

About Nina

This photo was taken before I wrote *Sophie's Sister* – probably before I wrote anything! I've dedicated this book to my parents, because they gave me life, they gave me love, they gave me two fantastic brothers and they gave me the foundations for a good life.

My work has always revolved around words. And pictures.

www.ninapaine.com

'The mass of men lead lives of quiet desperation.'

from *Walden*, Henry David Thoreau (1854)

PART ONE

Getting There

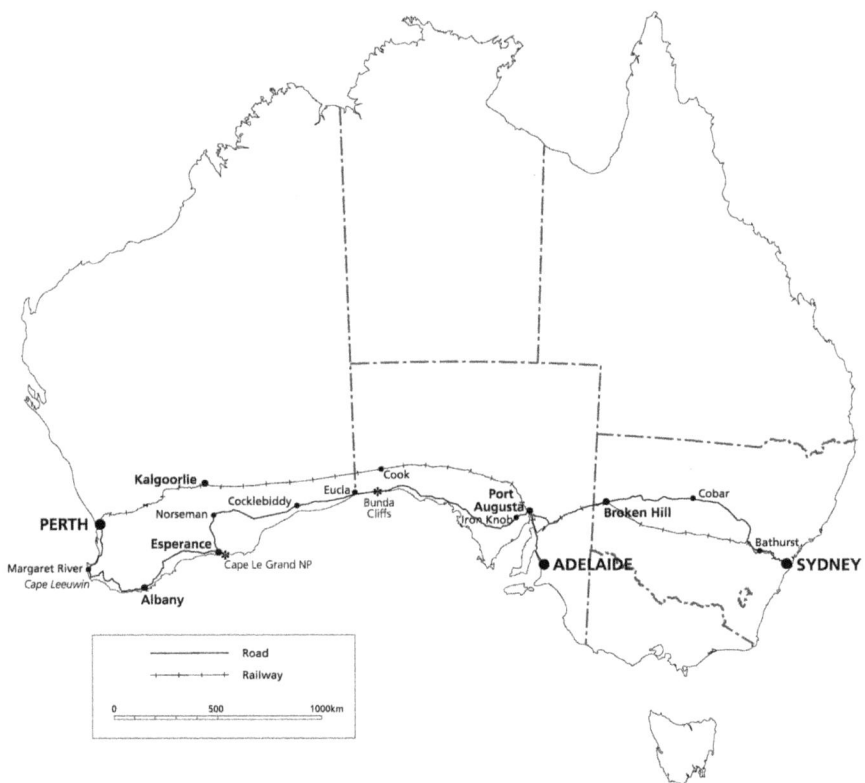

Cartographer: JOHN CLEASBY

The Catalyst

'*Owww*, shit!' Sophie cursed under her breath as she tripped over a branch.

You have *to go*, I said to her.

Piss off, Georgia, she whispered back in anger.

Sophie's stubborn – Taureans usually are. We'd argued a lot over the years, many times. But that's my job. Everyone has some kind of inner voice – Sophie's just happened to be me, the twin sister she almost had.

I'm Georgia. Sophie calls me that because I'm always on her mind. I guess you might think of me as like an aura, drifting along with her all the time. Mostly I hang around just outside her ear, but for maximum impact, I go in! I try not to do that too often though – it's this thing about being in an enclosed place. I hate it. Memories of that fateful journey still haunt me when I can't feel the fresh air around me. Water's the same. You won't ever see me in water, but then you won't ever see me at all!

Fateful journey, you're wondering? I first met Sophie almost forty years ago when we were no more than a single cell, floating through the miraculous gunk that was to nourish us for nine months before we made our grand, though incredibly messy, entrance. Thing is, I never quite made it. After we split, I wanted to explore a little, so I took a more adventurous path and landed myself in trouble. No-one ever knew there were two of us, and there's a belief among many that you don't miss something you never knew.

But I made it out, in my own way, and ever since then I've been hanging out with Sophie. Everywhere she goes, I go. Everything she reads, I read too. And just about every thought she's ever had is one I've heard. Of course there are times I can and do need to make myself scarce – I'm not entirely insensitive.

I've also been known to be a little on the outspoken side – okay, sometimes a lot. Too much. When Sophie senses I'm there, she can find me really annoying, like a mosquito while you're trying to sleep. I don't mean to be like that. Truly. My intentions are always good. At least *I* think they are. On the other hand, when I'm a comfort I'm like a well-worn and much-loved beanie on a cold winter's night, there when she needs me. Sadly, though, I don't think she's aware of me at all when I'm a comfort. That's the thing with good stuff – it's often overlooked.

Since our split, I've seen it as my job to tempt Sophie with alternatives – to open her eyes to things she may not otherwise see, to push her in ways she doesn't think she wants to be pushed, I've wanted to challenge the way she thinks, the way she lives. Why? Because I know that if *I'd* survived those gruelling nine months, I would've approached my life with so much more vigour than Sophie's always displayed.

It's hard being a twin. There's a protective element in the relationship that's normally reserved for a parent, combined with the push and shove of a sibling who wants the best for you but wants to give you a hard time while you're getting it, and then that's all mixed with the love and encouragement a best friend is always there to give. You want them to have it all.

It's even harder being a twin who isn't there, not physically anyway. It's been particularly hard lately, because things have been going a little haywire, and I've been starting to admit defeat. Getting really frustrated with Sophie is probably a more accurate way of putting it, and that, in turn, is pissing her right off. I'm beginning to realise that after all these years I've been pretty ineffective. Sophie has rarely paid me any attention, which is a shame because I think if she had, she'd have had a happier time for many years when life wasn't all she hoped it would be.

I'm also beginning to wonder – I hate to admit this – if I might be partly to blame, that maybe after all this time I've started to become a little resentful that she survived the pregnancy and I didn't. All these years I've had a window to the world through Sophie, and that's always been enough. But for some reason it's not anymore. I've been getting so frustrated living *her* life when it always seems so beige. I want colour and excitement before it's too late. Life's too short, or it could be. Our dad died before he turned forty – that certainly makes *me* stop and wonder how long we've got, and I'm surprised it hasn't done the same for Sophie. And maybe I'm wrong, but I've always assumed that my time will be up when Sophie's is, but I don't know. My existence isn't what you'd call normal.

And so on that overcast Saturday morning towards the end of May when she tripped over a branch, that was me in action. I was messing with her head – at least that's what she always accused me of doing. I prefer to think of it as a gentle kind of nudging, although it's fair to say that on that day I didn't feel much like being gentle.

Why was I doing it? Because she'd been offered an extraordinary opportunity – a chance to cross the Nullarbor, something she's wanted to do for ages. She's always thought that crossing the Nullarbor is like a rite of passage for Australians, that it has to be one of the country's must-do and yet least done travel experiences, definitely one of the least appreciated. She'd just been given her chance.

୧଴୨

Sophie was bushwalking in the Ku-ring-gai Chase National Park, north of Sydney, with a few others from Gedup'n'go. It was a regular monthly outing that Cath, their photo editor, had instigated, and autumn was about the best time of year to take to the great outdoors in Sydney.

Sophie had been working on and off with Gedup'n'go for a few years. It's a well-established, independent and unusual sort of publishing house with a very strange name – at least Sophie thought it was strange, until Cath set her straight the day she started working there.

'Equal emphasis on each of the syllables,' she said. 'Ged-up-'n'-go. You know, Strine!'

'Strine?'

'Australian! Get-up-and-go!'

The offices were situated on the edge of the bush, far from the suits and the stress of the city. They produced a small range of Australian adventure publications, but their main one was a quarterly magazine, *Gedup'n'go Today*, and Sophie was on their list of freelancers, called on to work in-house on occasion if the deadline was approaching and they were feeling the pressure. She's a graphic designer and illustrator. Her first commission for them had been to provide an illustration for a feature on camels. However, in the time she'd been with them, she'd become a bit of an all-rounder – or at least a part-of-the-way-rounder. Some of that was no doubt because she lived so close to the office and could get over there easily and often at short notice, but it was also because she was so keen and loved being there.

One of the other publications they produced was a little activity booklet for children – *Gedup'n'go Kids*. It was a fairly new venture that had been doing well, with short articles and interesting bits of information for younger readers. Sophie often helped the *Kids* team with illustrations and, from time to time, short stories. She could also lend her hand to basic admin work if it was required, be it in the editorial, photography or accounts department, or relieving the girl on reception when she needed to go to the loo or wanted to grab a coffee, but perhaps her greatest interest outside her own work was that of the cartographers. Sophie loved maps. Whenever someone she knew was away, anywhere, she'd look out a map and follow the route they were travelling, and it was Frank, Gedup'n'go's chief cartographer, who she would approach before anyone else if she had some time and was able to help out.

The bushwalkers always met in the car park at the Gedup'n'go offices in Duffys Forest, and when Sophie pulled in that day she thought, as she did every time she drove through the gates, what a great place it was to work. The others were already there and checking the contents of their combined backpacks as Sophie was deciding which spot to park in – it was usually such an easy decision because there was always little choice when she arrived for work. Not today though – it was the weekend and today she could park almost anywhere.

The near-empty car park allowed her focus to be drawn to the gum tree that grew mischievously across the path of entering vehicles. When she first started working at Gedup'n'go she wondered why it, and a couple of others like it that encroached on valuable car space on busier days, had not been cut back. She was silently moved when she learned that the man who originally planted the trees still tended them, and it was his wish that they be left to grow in whatever direction they liked. How nice it was, Sophie thought, that one man's gentle wish had been respected.

୧୬୦୧

Make up your mind, Sophie. How hard can it be to choose a car spot?

She ignored me. We were off to a good start.

Sophie had straight shoulder-length light brown hair that was tied in a ponytail and poking through the back of her cap, accentuating her square face that today, as every day, wore no make-up. She was looking like Jodie Foster. People had often told her that, but I didn't always see it. She'd also been told she looked like Diane Keaton, and it's true, Sophie's dress sense could be a little unusual, but I'm pretty sure the person who thought she actually looked like Keaton was optically challenged.

As she stepped out of her car and said hello to her friends, the easy smile that always lit up her face also created just one adorable dimple. I'd often wondered if the other one would have been on my face.

Sophie had always considered herself average, in every sense – average height, average weight, average looks, average intelligence – but I think she undersells herself, and I'm not the only one. That said, she is a little clumsier than most, and she's not a great decision-maker, but she really does have so much going for her, not least of all her loyalty. I have no idea why she has so much self-doubt, but her unawareness of everything that's good about her can be endearing. Even I'll admit that.

The girls said their hellos but wasted no time getting into Cath's car and driving off. I'd always loved the fact that Sophie could drive for literally only minutes – out of suburban St Ives, past the Wildflower Garden and a little bit beyond Terrey Hills – and we'd be in a national park. If she went a little further still, we'd reach Tumbledown Dick Hill, where the panoramic view of the ocean appeared suddenly and would tug at my heart. Well, that's what it felt like. I'm sure a heart factored into my being. Somehow. Sydney is such a beautiful place to live. Sophie and I both know that. We also know that Australia is a fantastic country, but it's been Sophie's work at Gedup'n'go these past few years that's opened my eyes to all the amazing travel opportunities we have right here. Lately though, while she's been happy to simply daydream, I've been restless, and it's hard to not let that restlessness get the better of me. Like when she's sleeping.

I don't need much sleep, but it's always been fun to invade Sophie's. It's especially fun when I hear her telling people about the weird dreams she's had, knowing I had a part to play in how they unfolded. But occasionally she wakes up in tears and that's when I know I've either been in her head at a bad time, or I've gone too far and needed to back off for a while.

But that's as far as it went with Sophie. She's a dreamer, and my impatience with her to make at least one of those dreams a reality – to get out there and do something exciting – was escalating.

ಸಾಂ

They hadn't been on the road long when Cath pulled up just beyond the Number 8 post on West Head Road. They all grabbed their packs and made their way over to the Bairne Track, a world away from the routine Saturday morning activities they'd escaped. There were plenty of cars around when they set off down the track, but for the next few hours I didn't see anyone else.

The track was mostly even and broad, without too many obstructions. They'd been chatting as they walked, and came uncomfortably close to stepping on a small snake that was stretched out across their path. It was an unexpected curiosity, not to mention a great photo opportunity. Cath was quick to pull out her camera and get as close as she could. I, on the other hand, kept my distance. Creepy, slimy snakes. Ugh. I hated them. Even Cath admitted afterwards that she wasn't sure what sort of snake it was, and had moved towards it a little too quickly.

I was much more excited about what we saw next – a rock wallaby! It sauntered onto our path a few minutes later and was a much nicer, far less aggressive and definitely less threatening distraction. It stayed a while. This time the others kept their distance, not wanting to scare it off, but I went right over to it, slid down the curve of its back and along its tail like it was a slippery dip.

But then the girls made a move and it hopped away. I followed it and jumped into its pouch, then went with it for a little way – this was *the* best way to travel – but before long I realised I couldn't see the girls anymore so hopped out of that pouch to catch up with them.

The walk took us through bush that was alive with birdsong, and along ridge tops to a point where we could enjoy the interrupted but lovely views over Pittwater and the Basin. It was an overcast morning, so the water didn't sparkle like it would on a sunny day, but even so it was a picture of isolated tranquillity.

We stopped for about half an hour, the girls resting on a couple of well-positioned rocks as they soaked in the view and caught up on things from both in and out of the office. Then it was time to head back the way we came. I was enjoying the voices of the bush that took over as conversation between the girls thinned. Each of them was now lost in her own thoughts.

༄༅

Sophie was the first to break the silence that had descended upon them as they neared the top of one of the steeper slopes.

'What's coming up in the next issue, Cath?'

'Ooh, we've got a piece on the Larapinta Trail, which I'm really excited about, and another on places to go to learn how to rock-climb. Our main feature though will be on cave-diving.'

Immediately Sophie thought of Jack.

'Sounds interesting. Where does that take you?'

'We're focusing on a particular cave under the Nullarbor, called Cocklebiddy.'

'I've heard of it.'

'Have you? Not too many people have.'

'Yeah, someone I used to work with dives. He's told me about Cocklebiddy.' Sophie thought back to the days when she and Jack were more than simply work colleagues. 'I've always wanted to drive across the Nullarbor, but until this friend told me about them, I had no idea there were flooded caves out there. Hard to imagine.'

'Yeah, they're extraordinary. We've got a photographer and journalist lined up to meet the divers out there.'

Cath paused for a moment, thinking something through. 'Are you serious about that, Soph? About wanting to drive across the Nullarbor? Because we've been thinking of getting someone to join the photographer, someone to do a little feature for the *Kids* mag. You'd be perfect.'

'Tell me more,' Sophie said.

∞)CR

I wasn't going to let this one pass her by without giving it my best shot. I could almost feel Sophie's heart skip a beat with the excitement she felt at the thought of an adventure like this, and with me in her head she lost all concentration and stumbled over a fallen branch. Yes! Well, it's like I said. I was nudging her in the only way I knew how, because I knew she was about to come up with an excuse not to do it.

'*Owww*, shit!' Sophie cursed under her breath.

You have *to go*, I said to her.

Piss off, Georgia, she whispered back in anger.

'Are you okay?' Cath asked.

'Yeah, fine. When's he leaving?'

'On the 9th, two weeks from today, but he's leaving from Perth, and you'd be away for a couple of weeks.'

Sophie's mind was racing, and I knew she was thinking it all through – the pros and the cons, why she'd like to go but also why she couldn't or, more to the point, wouldn't. Her first thought was Celia, and how she'd worry.

Ah, Celia – that's our mum. I call her Celia because, well, that's her name, and it never felt right calling her 'Mum'. I'm sure if I'd had a normal relationship with her – *any* relationship with her – 'Mum' would've floated off my tongue as easily as it does Sophie's. But I've had no relationship with Celia, except as an observer. That's something I've always been totally bummed about. Sophie and Celia are so close. I'd love some of that closeness, some of what Sophie has. Or even to be able to share it in a real way with Sophie, because Celia is a beautiful, gentle soul. And although Sophie can be grumpy at times, she's more like Celia than she realises, something that's as clear as day to anyone who knows them both.

So yeah, if Sophie was out on the Nullarbor with a stranger, Celia would worry – about her with him, about his driving, and about the trucks. The road trains. The Eyre Highway would have plenty of them and one thing Celia worried about more than anything when it came to the safety of her children – even though they were all fully fledged adults – was them being out on the roads, especially when they were sharing those roads with trucks. But despite all the commotion going on in Sophie's head, and to my enormous surprise, I could tell she was actually thinking about Cath's offer.

She thought it could be great if she got along with the photographer –

And you probably would –

But what if I didn't, Georgia? There would be no escape. I'd be with him twenty-four hours a day, every day for a couple of weeks. I don't even have too many friends I'd want to be with for that amount of time.

Sophie considered the idea for a moment longer before she spoke again.

'I'd love to, Cath, but the timing's no good –'

I knew it! She'd barely even considered it. My frustration was about to boil over.

'I've got a school reunion coming up, and Peggy'll be away that second week in June. I told her weeks ago I'd help out while she's gone. It sounds like a great feature though. Tell me more. Has Gedup'n'go ever done a piece on cave-diving?'

It turns out that the photographer was a man by the name of Clinton West – not someone Sophie had ever come across at Gedup'n'go, and Cath had only spoken to him over the phone a few times so didn't know too much about him. Cocklebiddy is a tiny settlement on the Eyre Highway, midway between Esperance in Western Australia and the South Australian border. Just north-west of the town is Cocklebiddy Cave. Cath said it was one of the world's longest underwater caves, and a team of divers was about to go down.

Silence returned as they walked. Sophie had fallen behind the others, but that wasn't so unusual – she'd always been a bit of a loner, more often by choice as the years went by. No doubt the others were consumed in their own thoughts – Sophie certainly was.

Like I said, Sophie and I had struggled many times in the past. I wanted her to break away a little, to have some of those experiences she'd been daydreaming so much and so often about – the ones I'd missed out on but wanted to have – but she'd led such a sheltered and safe life when she was much younger, and she'd never really shaken that off.

From where I stood, Sophie had a gift I'd missed out on. Life. But she wasn't using it very well. And yet I can't say she wasn't happy. In recent years she'd seemed happier than I'd ever known her to be, which made my job that much more difficult. This Nullarbor trip, I knew it could be one of those life-changing experiences and I desperately wanted her to go. *I* wanted to go. I could feel myself getting so worked up and was almost at breaking point so knew I had to give it another try.

Go on, I said to her as she stumbled again, this time on a rock. *Do it, it'll be fantastic. Forget the reunion – you've never been interested in them anyway – and Peggy would understand. She doesn't need anyone there for her while she's away.*

Yeah, but I said I would be, and I've been helping to get this reunion happening and now I want to go. It's been over twenty years – I'd love to see some of those people I was friends with back then.

Why? You've always said that anyone you've wanted to keep in touch with since then you have, and it's just one night. One night, I repeated. *This is the kind of adventure you've been dreaming of for years, and how often does an opportunity like this come along? You can't* not *go.*

I can, and I've made up my mind, Georgia, so will you GO AWAY!

But I wasn't going anywhere. Not yet anyway. I hadn't finished.

Same old story, Soph – any excuse. Don't you want more from life? Seems you'll do anything to avoid a bit of excitement or adventure.

What's that supposed to mean?

Melbourne, for one. You were offered a great opportunity to work down there, but did you go?

I didn't want to move to Melbourne.

But you love Melbourne.

I love visiting *Melbourne. That doesn't mean I want to* live *there.*

Okay, what about the Overland Track? That never eventuated.

I broke my ankle, idiot – doesn't make for easy walking.

Yeah, very convenient that was. You could have gone, once you were back on your feet.

You're impossible, Georgia. Just shut up and leave me alone will you? I'm not *going*, Sophie snapped, and with that I made the kind of decision I realised I'd wanted to make for a long time. I decided I'd go without her.

৸৹য়

I needed to calm down. Short of tripping her up again and again, which would've been pointless – and I didn't want to hurt her – there wasn't much more I could do. We walked on.

Sophie was preoccupied, thinking about the dive team headed for Cocklebiddy Cave and wondering whether Jack might be going. He'd spoken to her about diving there, but it had been a few years since they'd seen each other and she didn't even know if he was still diving, although it was more than likely he would be. Cave diving had seemed, as Sophie sometimes wondered if she'd also been, the unsuspecting focus of a mid-life crisis – one he should have made it through by now.

In the time she spent with him she thought he was searching – it was as though he needed something else in his life. Diving hadn't been the answer, but it had helped – at least on the surface he'd been so much happier than he had been. He'd taken to it so well, and he'd been good. Really good. Hugely respected among other cavers for his knowledge, wisdom and above all his common sense, for knowing when personal safety was more important than an ill-advised dive.

From the moment he'd taken his first class he seemed to enjoy life underground as much as he did above it.

And then there was Sophie.

Ah, Sophie and Jack. I love them both but wanted to knock their heads together at times. I should start at the beginning.

They'd known each other so long, used to work for one of the big newspapers – she as a graphic designer and him a sportswriter. That was something I would never have guessed, Sophie and a sports nut. She doesn't have an athletic bone in her body! But there you go. She ended up hating the frenetic pace and the ruthlessness of a lot of the people at the newspaper though. But not Jack. She didn't hate Jack at all.

Sophie's never been an easy person to get to know – more often than not she doesn't let herself get too close to people, and certainly not too quickly. She doesn't warm to people easily, either. But Jack was different. She liked him almost immediately, although sometimes she'd wondered why. He could be moody, which meant at times having to tread on eggshells around him, making things harder than they should've been.

Jack was a tall, well-built man with a gentle voice. All that was good. His hair was dark brown with the beginnings of some grey, and it had a bit of a curl – it was usually short, but when it grew a little longer the curls became curlier and suggested a hint of eccentricity. Sophie loved that, and I thought it was cute. But I think Sophie was attracted by his thoughtfulness as much as anything else. Jack wasn't the kind of man who would act first and think later. There were times she'd watched him and could almost see the thought process happening behind his attentive eyes.

He was also a private man, at times intensely quiet. And maybe that had something to do with it, too. Sometimes when I hear people talking just for the sake of talking I'm reminded of the quote attributed to Jorge Luis Borges – 'Don't speak unless you can improve the silence!' Loud people can often be the most boring. But Jack wasn't loud and he certainly wasn't boring.

He came across as a serious man at work, always focused. But he wasn't like that all the time. The first time Sophie had spent any time with him out of work was at the company's Christmas lunch, and she learned then how he could shine in social situations. Away from work he was animated and witty, at least he could be. Their first non-work conversation hadn't started out with too much humour at all.

At that stage Sophie knew almost nothing about Jack, but what she did know she was both attracted to and a little intrigued by. She was already seated with an empty chair beside her when he'd arrived late and his choice was limited. Sophie wanted him to come and sit next to her, but at the same time she hoped he'd walk right past and find somewhere else because, as was always the case when she found herself in the company of someone she didn't know, or didn't know well, she didn't know what she'd talk to him about.

'Mind if I sit next to you?' he asked.

'Sure,' Sophie replied before she'd been able to come up with an excuse to slink underneath the table and disappear from the function altogether. There was some general chatter at the table of eight, and drinks were soon ordered, but by the time their drinks arrived, she and Jack were talking to no-one but each other. Something Sophie *had* heard about him was that he was a diver, and something she suddenly remembered about coping in social situations was to ask a person about something you knew them to be interested in – chances were they'd be happy to talk about it for a lot longer than you'd want to listen.

'I hear you dive?' she'd said, and instantly the ice had broken.

'I haven't been doing too much lately,' Jack said. 'We've had some problems at home with Charlie, one of our kids.'

Sophie's face gave her question away.

'Leukaemia,' Jack said.

Sophie felt a sadness she was unable to express in words. 'I'm so sorry, Jack,' she said gently. 'How old is he?'

'He's six, diagnosed when he was only two. It's been a rough few years.'

Sophie sat listening in silence, trying to imagine coping in that situation.

'Relationships are hard enough when it's just the two of you, as you'd know,' he'd said.

That's interesting. Do you think he's trying to find out if you're in a relationship, Soph? I think he likes you!

Not now, Georgia.

'They become infinitely harder to keep together when children come into the equation,' Jack continued, 'and when one of those children has a life-threatening illness, there's enormous pressure.'

Wow, he's really opening up to her. I was all ears.

'We both wanted what was best for Charlie, but our ideas of what was best were different.'

I'd heard this before and knew that although many couples made it through the hard times, a lot of them didn't. What I was hearing was that Jack and his wife had reached a crisis point in their marriage – the fact that he was telling Sophie so much, though, was curious. Maybe he needed to offload, and maybe that was easier with someone he barely knew. Or maybe he really liked Sophie and felt comfortable talking to her about this stuff. Whatever his reason, there was something nice happening between them.

Can't you feel it, Sophie?

Shut up, Georgia.

Well, I could feel it, even if Sophie was numb to it.

'That must be so hard,' Sophie said. 'How's Charlie doing now?'

'That's the good news. After all the treatment – and the difficulties we had deciding what that treatment would be – it's looking good for a full recovery. We've been told he should be able to enjoy a long and healthy life, but I doubt whether I'll ever be a hundred percent sure. Not for some time, at least.'

'I'm sure he will be, if that's what the specialists have told you. They'd be pretty upfront about things like that.'

'Yeah, they have been.'

'So, tell me about your diving. How long have you been doing it?'

Jack paused for a moment.

'Probably over ten, but by necessity – becoming a dad first of all, and then Charlie's illness – it's been off and on for some time. I've been scuba diving since I was a teenager though. Cave diving is a much more recent interest. I was just about to go back to one of my favourite caves, out on the Nullarbor, when Charlie got sick. I couldn't spend so much time away from the family after that. It would've been selfish.'

'You have other children?'

'Just one, and that was another factor. She's a couple of years older than Charlie, and in perfectly good health, but she missed out on a lot of our attention while Charlie was so sick.'

'But now Charlie's doing so well, you might be able to get back into it?'

'Maybe soon. I need to focus on my family for the time being, try to get us all back to something that resembles normal.'

I gathered, from what Jack had hinted at, that it was his wife holding him back – that perhaps that word 'selfish' had come from her. But I also got the feeling that something very strong was pulling him towards more cave diving, and it was likely that any problems in their marriage would only escalate, not only if he went ahead with it but also if he ignored it.

☙❧

I was both surprised and disappointed that, when Sophie and Jack returned to work the following year, it was like they'd never had that conversation, and it wasn't long until the job she was doing had started to get Sophie down. Disillusioned with the place, and imagining it was much the same everywhere, she made the decision to start freelancing, and handed in her resignation.

There were people she was sorry she'd be leaving, and Jack was one of them, despite him being strictly back in work mode whenever their paths crossed. She'd thought a lot about him over that Christmas break – about his son, and his diving. About how lives can change so unexpectedly. About how she'd always found him not only interesting, but interested in what other people had to say, even her! She hadn't met too many people like that. *Such a nice man*, she'd thought. *But a good man with a wife and children, and he wants to do the right thing by all of them, especially after all the problems they've had.* She couldn't believe that her thoughts had started wandering, but she made them stop, because one of the things she most admired about Jack was that she knew he would never stray.

I really liked Jack, too, and even if Sophie hadn't been able to see it, she'd also been in his thoughts. I think I can even take some of the credit for the closeness they eventually succumbed to, because for Sophie the decision as to whether or not she'd ever get involved with someone else's husband was easy. She put herself in that woman's shoes and it was a clear 'No'. She may have held a deeply cynical view of marriage, but at the same time she always hoped that some of them survived unscathed.

Once Jack had made it known he *was* thinking about her that way, however, Sophie's world turned upside down and she learned how hard it can be to say that one little word. How easy it can be for all thoughts of and consideration for a wife to be obliterated, at least in the moment. I'd discovered a weakness I didn't know she had, and Sophie discovered she wasn't as strong as she thought she was.

Sophie still believed Jack was a good man, despite the path they went down all those years ago and the lesson she and I both learned from it all – you never really know anyone. Even good people are capable of destructive acts, acts that can have far-reaching consequences and create a pain that runs every bit as deep as the love.

Sophie and the others made it back to the Number 8 post, back to the car park at Gedup'n'go and back to their respective homes to pick up where they'd left off with their Saturdays. For Sophie, there was nothing much she needed to do, except get her dog Cujo out for a walk, and I always loved our walks together, especially in autumn. I loved seeing the beautiful soft shades of Cujo's blond fur melting into the colours of the leaves that had fallen from the liquidambars lining so many of their local streets. I loved how those leaves crunched beneath their feet, and paws. I just loved being out there with them.

Today was different though. Sophie was cranky with me, and she wasn't my favourite person at the moment either. Her life wasn't enough for me anymore and I knew if I didn't do something about it, we weren't going to last much longer. It was like Jack and his diving. Sometimes what you have is never enough.

Life Divided

It's impossible not to wonder what my life would be like without Sophie, and hers without me. We've been together almost four decades. It's not that I'm concerned about me – I know I'll be okay – and at the moment I don't care how she'll be, but if I'm honest, it did sting a little when I announced I'd go away without her and she didn't try to change my mind. I know in life a lot of things have a natural course to run – certainly a lot of relationships do, and that's what ours is, just another relationship. But it's not. It's more than that.

I should be happy for her – she's settling into a good life, one she seems perfectly okay with, even if I think it's pretty dull. Age must have a lot to do with that, because with age comes strength. She's got the strength now not to care so much – if at all – what other people think, or spend time doing things she doesn't want to do. She's also become good at simply avoiding anyone who has a negative impact on her life. Well, anyone except me! *I* don't think I'm a negative impact, but there are times she does.

I'm sure that's why she loves freelancing so much – work environments can be toxic. A lot of people wouldn't like the isolation that comes with freelancing, but she's fine with it, which is why I know she'd love the Nullarbor trip, and I don't get what's holding her back. The places she's always been drawn to aren't the big crowded cities but the wide-open spaces – she loves the lack of enclosure, the sense of isolation and, most of all, the lack of people.

Just quietly, I think a lot of people might envy the lifestyle Sophie has – the enormous freedom and the huge variety of work she does. Her days have an oddly distinct routine within a fantastically flexible framework. No two days are ever the same. That said, some things *are* the same, day after day, and most days start with Cujo.

I love Cujo. Sophie usually wakes up between about six and seven when she hears him stirring beside her bed. She'll open her eyes and smile as she watches him stretch. His front legs reach as far as they can in front of him, while his bottom reaches for the ceiling. That's when I start to play. I like to position myself on his tail end and jump onto Sophie's pillow. Then I watch as he sits looking at Sophie with his deliciously big, round brown eyes, waiting for her to get up and give him breakfast, then play with him for a while before she has her own.

I think Cujo knows when I'm there. I like to waft past his nose sometimes, trying to tickle it like a feather. More often than not he'll twitch or reach a paw across to rub his nose. It's so funny. I could do that for ages, but I know when to stop.

Sophie hasn't always had a dog, but Cujo's been the light in her life these last few years. The small number of men she's been involved with have left scars that have built on one another rather than heal, and she doesn't seem to want to be with anyone anymore. All she wants is a simple life, and she doesn't see people, with all their complications, fitting in to that life much at all.

She also no longer trusts her own judgment, not where people are concerned anyway. But a dog? Sophie thought a dog might be the answer. I wish *I* could've been the answer. We would've been so close, I'm sure of it. But I have to agree, Cujo is the next best thing. They enjoy their days, their daily rituals, and getting up, having breakfast and a play are just the beginning. They also walk together and – if she doesn't have any pressing work to do and the weather is okay – they go out late in the morning.

The walks are good for Cujo, and they're Sophie's responsibility, but they're good for her, too. Outside she can clear her head and enjoy a break from whatever she's working on. She always switches her phone off and we have some of our best conversations while we're out with Cujo. At those times it's just us. But sometimes, when she's been down, the fog in her head has been too thick to penetrate and walking has only given her more time to dwell on things. That's never good. I remember one time in particular, when our quiet walk had dragged her back to a past she didn't want to revisit.

It had been a perfect November day – jacaranda trees were in full bloom, their fallen blossoms of lilac-blue blanketing driveways and front lawns with a mass of unmistakable spring colour. It was my favourite time of year.

Cujo was a fully grown Golden Retriever back then, but still very much a puppy at heart. He was also strong and easily distracted – a friend of Sophie's had once referred to him as a Renaissance dog because he was always stopping to smell the roses. On this walk, however, his attention was drawn to a highly energised and annoyingly small dog that had dashed out of a neighbouring house as soon as it heard them pass. Once the two dogs saw each other there was nothing Sophie could do to get Cujo's attention back to their walk. She tried – she even struggled – but no matter what she did, Cujo had found a playmate and he wasn't going anywhere. I wasn't thinking about Sophie – I was having way too much fun pretending to be a ball between the two dogs. When I think about that, in retrospect, I probably wasn't helping.

And it hadn't been the day for this to happen. Sophie had been consumed with thoughts of Jack and she was fragile. They'd seen each other again when common friends from the newspaper had met for lunch, which wasn't unusual, nor was it something she minded at all, but these catch-ups were always bittersweet and this time it hadn't been long since they'd ended their relationship. It had been on good terms, but it was still achingly difficult.

It was the change in her voice that made me stop and look at her. Her words had softened and then broken into a sob, and as she realised there was nothing she could do to get Cujo's attention, she crumbled.

Sophie, what's up? They're just playing, I said gently. But she didn't hear me. *Sophie?* I repeated. I watched on helplessly as she sat crying in the gutter, having given up on getting Cujo away from his new friend. I'd never seen her so overwhelmingly and absurdly distressed. It was like a wave of physical and emotional paralysis had taken hold of her, and it was ages before she could find the strength – and before Cujo had tired of the unexpected company – to pick herself up and get going.

It was a morning I knew I'd remember forever, without any loss of clarity, because apart from being heartbreaking, it seemed so pathetic – *she* seemed so pathetic. I was so saddened by what I'd seen that day because Sophie was usually so much more together than that. But somehow it ended up being a turning point for her. If her relationship with Jack had been causing her so much inner turmoil, ending it had been the right thing to do.

※

That bleak November day is such a far cry from Sophie's current frame of mind. She doesn't have to work in-house anywhere this week, but she does have a trip to Melbourne coming up, and she's looking forward to it.

'Time for our walk, Cujo.'

That four-letter word did it every time. Cujo led Sophie towards his lead and they were off, ready to enjoy another day and whatever or whoever might appear in it.

Despite not being someone who generally went out of her way to talk to people – particularly people she didn't know – there were many times Sophie actually enjoyed the encounters she and Cujo had on their walks, and found herself intrigued by the differences among people at this most basic level. Some would simply smile, some would add a 'Good morning', some even stopped and chatted for a while – they were generally other dog people.

'Morning. Beautiful dog! What's his name?'

'Cujo.'

'Cujo?' Wasn't tha–'

'Yep, Stephen King.'

'How could you name your beautiful dog after a literary monster?' some would ask.

Those familiar with Stephen King's novel of the same name knew that Cujo was a once lovable family pet who, in the pursuit of a good time, chased a rabbit into a cave that was infested with bats. The Cujo of King's fame – a monstrously large Saint Bernard – was bitten by one of those bats and turned rabid, which in turn triggered a series of events that would linger in the minds of those who read the book, or saw the movie, long after they'd finished it.

Sophie had endured much good-natured criticism over the years about the name she had given her dog, but to her it seemed perfect. And most of all, she knew that her Cujo would be the antithesis of the one people had read about, and she liked the contradiction.

'Well, it's a good strong name for a male dog, and I've always loved King's novels. We both like it,' she continued, 'and you'll be pleased to know I keep a strong hold on his lead whenever we see rabbits!'

Conversation over, they'd move on and, as always, Sophie would say to herself, *One more who asked what Cujo's name was, but not mine!*

There was one other type of person they would encounter on their walks, a type Sophie couldn't understand – Cujo, too, was put out by them. These people didn't tell Sophie she had a gorgeous dog – they didn't speak at all, nor did they make eye contact. As they passed within arm's reach of one another, not a single muscle in their faces so much as twitched. *How hard is it to smile and say hello?* she would ask herself. To her it was one of the many tiny events that would combine to make each day a good one. It was the next bit – thinking of things to talk about after that – that she always found more difficult.

While the reactions of most of these people meant nothing to her, there was one man Sophie found a little bit more interesting. She saw him from time to time, out with his black Labrador, and he always wore a broad-brimmed hat under which he kept his head bowed and his eyes hidden by dark glasses. There was nothing exceptional about him. He was average in height and build and he dressed as casually as people do when they walk their dogs. Sophie recalled the first time she had seen him. He completely ignored her, but that wasn't the only reason he'd caught her attention. It was early one morning, mid-summer. Sophie and Cujo had set out before seven as they usually did at that time of year – any later was too hot.

This man with the black Lab was wearing a well-worn and faded dark blue singlet that emphasised the strength in his arms – strength that had no doubt developed from sheer hard work rather than hours spent in a gym every day. His boots, scuffed and brown, and his lightweight, mud-stained grey pants also suggested a man whose work was physical and kept him outdoors. Already the air was thick with humidity and he'd started to sweat. But he hadn't noticed Sophie back then and he continued not to notice her now. He was always as caught up in his own private world as Sophie could be in hers and maybe – apart from that sizzle of attraction she felt – maybe that's what sparked her curiosity.

౭౦౧౩

Sophie and Cujo were almost home. They hadn't seen the man with the black Lab, but they'd passed a boy on his way to school. *He'll be late*, Sophie thought and then remembered her school reunion, now less than a week away.

She reached her door and switched on her phone, and as she was topping up Cujo's water bowl, the beeps started up. *Geez, I'll be glad when this is over*, she thought. I looked over her shoulder to see a couple of new emails waiting for her, and three missed calls. Seems there was still heaps to do before the night.

Remind me to call Jodie back later, will you, Georgia?

Sure, Soph, I love being your secretary, I mumbled back.

Sophie put her things down and wandered over to Celia's place. When she wasn't with Cujo, or working, they spent a lot of time together. Celia had been retired for a few years and Sophie's studio apartment was at the back of her place, so we never had to go far to see her. Sometimes this was hard for me, because they always found plenty to talk about and never seemed to tire of each other's company. I wanted to be part of that.

I think, with our dad not being around, Sophie developed a much stronger relationship with Celia than she otherwise might have done. Over the years I'd seen people – men – shrug her off, believing she lacked independence because she was so close to her mum, both geographically and emotionally, but I knew that wasn't it. It was an abundance of love and caring, and it was going to have to be someone pretty special to accept that about her and want to be part of it. That was fine with Sophie, and I loved that about her, that she didn't care and wasn't about to change who she was for anyone. She was as protective of Celia as Celia was of her, more and more as the years went by.

It was times like now, however, when Sophie called in to Celia's for that much anticipated cup of tea after her walk with Cujo, that I would think about what it might be like if the three of us were enjoying those cups of tea together. How it would be if Celia was sitting there with her two daughters, her twins. She'd told Sophie ages ago that she'd wanted four children – they just ran out of time. But there almost had been four of us. Life would've been so different. If only.

'Helloooooo. Is the kettle on?' Sophie called as she walked in Celia's back door.

'Hello, darling, how are you?' Celia greeted her with a kiss.

The kettle boiled and Sophie made the drinks.

'What's on for you today, Mum? No, don't tell me, it's patchwork day! I almost forgot. Won't stay long.'

'That's okay, plenty of time. Tell me, what's the latest with the reunion?'

'Ugh. At the moment it's a constant flood of emails and phone calls. I hope it's all worth it.'

The two of them chatted for a while before Sophie glanced at the clock and realised how much time had passed.

'Better get to work. Oh, I won't see you tomorrow, I'm heading down to Melbourne with Frank.'

'Want me to feed Cujo?'

'Please,' Sophie smiled.

'What's happening in Melbourne?'

'Frank has to meet someone about the next issue and check some stuff while he's there, and he asked if I'd like to go down with him for the day, which is fantastic!'

'Are they paying your fare?'

'No, but it's not that much to Melbourne and back. I don't mind.'

'I guess it'll be an early start for you?'

'Yeah, we've got an Uber picking us up from Gedup'n'go at 5.30.'

'That's the worst part of a flight – the ride to the airport. I hope you get a good driver. Some of them shouldn't have their licences.'

'You worry too much!'

'Well it's true. Remember the last time we went to the airport in the shuttle bus? They're just as bad. He was on his phone most of the way in.'

'Yeah, but we got there.'

'That's not the point.'

'We'll be fine. I'd better go.'

'Well I hope it goes well. Give me a ring when you get home, or call in if it's not too late. Oh, are you still okay for Friday – Uncle Russ's?'

'Yep, looking forward to it!' See ya!' Sophie kissed her mum goodbye.

25

※

All children mean a lot to their mothers, of course, but Celia had always been overly protective of her children – especially Sophie, being her only daughter. But there was something more to it with Celia, and decades had passed before I could even begin to understand what it was all about. Fear. Celia's was the fear of loss, and when I was younger I'd been too self-absorbed – too Sophie-absorbed – to see that.

※

Sophie had warmed to Frank during her time at Gedup'n'go, and her warmth was always reciprocated. He was an older, fatherly type – or that's how he was with Sophie – and she loved hearing him talk with such devotion and affection about his wife and family, and what they were up to. They were close, active and adventurous, and even though Sophie wasn't, she genuinely loved hearing the stories people told.

Frank was also a conscientious and decent man who loved his work and was always more than happy to impart his vast knowledge on anyone like Sophie who showed an interest. Even when he was at his most busy, Frank was never too busy to treat people well, or take the time to explain things to them, and Sophie would soak it up. When she was at Gedup'n'go, her desk was in the same area as Frank's, and in the time they'd worked so closely they'd established the beginnings of a lovely, trusting friendship.

Their day in Melbourne came and went fairly quickly, and without incident or much excitement. What Sophie would remember most from that day were the flights there and back.

'Looks like you might be the only passenger with an empty seat beside you,' Frank said as they buckled up and waited for the plane to leave Sydney. 'Nope, spoke too soon!'

Just as the plane was about to take off, one of the flight attendants brought the missing passenger to the empty seat. Straightaway this young boy introduced himself – his name was Jethro – and was chatting away like he'd been wanting to meet Sophie his entire short life. He was instantly charming and in the distance between Sydney and Melbourne cut through to any maternal instinct Sophie thought she might have had.

As they started to taxi, Jethro asked Sophie if she would help him adjust his headphones so they would sit comfortably on his head. After that he wanted her to change the station on the radio and then get the volume just right. But it was as they watched the video describing how to put on their seatbelts and make sure they were fastened tightly that Jethro's arrow pierced Sophie's heart. He was an expressive and delightfully funny child and was taking the instruction very seriously. Sophie watched as he pulled his seatbelt as tight as he possibly could, his face distorting comically as he did so. The wondrous expression on his face was surpassed only by the one he then pulled as they took off. His talking had ceased. It was as though he had never flown before and was anxious about what might happen next, but he later told Sophie and Frank this was his third time in the air.

Once the plane had levelled and Jethro relaxed again, their conversation resumed.

'Do you know why people like me so much?' he asked Sophie.

Strange question, she thought. *Funny, but strange.*

'No, I don't. Why do people like you so much?'

'Because I was named after Jethro Tull.'

'Is that right? Are you sure it wasn't Jethro Bodine?!'

Sophie and Frank – and even some of the passengers nearby – thought that was funny, but Sophie's humour was altogether lost on her young travelling companion.

Jethro was six – and three-quarters, he'd made a point of adding – and Sophie thought about him many times after that day, wondering how he was getting on.

୫୭୦୪

The flight back from Melbourne was more subdued. Frank had been talking to Sophie about the colleague they'd met for lunch, and the next issue, and before long, the conversation turned to Sophie herself.

'I hope Jethro's mum was there to meet him this morning,' Sophie said. 'I lost sight of him when everyone was getting off the plane.'

'He was quite a charmer, wasn't he? See what you're missing out on?'

Wow, wasn't expecting that, Sophie thought.

'I'm so sorry,' fumbled Frank. 'I had no right to say that. You were so good with Jethro though, and I've often wondered why you don't have kids of your own. But it's none of my business.' Frank tried to change the subject, aware he'd crossed a line. 'Tell me, freelancing must be difficult sometimes, not knowing what the next job will be, or where it'll come from. You wouldn't have a typical day like us nine-to-fivers, would you?'

'No, that's true, but that's one of the things I love about it.'

'But there must be so much uncertainty. You don't mind that?'

'No, not at all. For better or worse, it's just me and Cujo. As you know, I don't have those normal sorts of responsibilities like kids and a mortgage.'

'Sophie, I really am sorry, I didn't mean –'

'It's okay, Frank, truly. I know your intentions are always kind!'

Frank lowered his eyes for a moment and then spoke again. 'Cujo's your dog?'

'Yeah.'

'At the risk of saying the wrong thing again, do you mind if I ask you something personal?'

'Go right ahead. I might not answer you though!'

'Why aren't you married?' Frank said. 'You're a lovely lady, great with kids, even if you like to pretend you're not. Jethro took a real shine to you.'

Sophie paused for a moment. It wasn't the first time she'd been asked that question and yet she didn't have an answer.

'I don't know, Frank. When I was a kid, I always assumed I'd get married and have a family. I guess I never met the right man – or haven't yet. I don't think I'm an easy person to get to know.'

'I wouldn't agree with that.'

'Yeah, but you're you! It's different if I like someone enough!'

'Isn't there anyone else you like – not an old fogey like me but, well, you know …'

'Fraaank! No offence, but I don't think of you that way!'

'Oh, no, of course not, I didn't mean that.'

'Well yeah, there is,' Sophie softened, as she thought of Jack. 'Or there was. I guess it wasn't meant to be. One of my friends thinks I don't want it enough, and maybe she's right. I like my life, Frank. I love the people in it, and I enjoy my own company. There's not much I'd change about it. Not now anyway.'

'That's a healthy attitude, Soph, but don't feel you need to shut the door to the possibility, will you?'

Sophie laughed. 'Okay, Frank! But you know what? Someone else once told me that men look for women who are like their mothers, and girls go for men who are like their dads, and so I don't know what it is I'm supposed to be looking for!'

'Wasn't your dad around?' Frank asked.

'No, he died when I was really young.'

'Oh pet, I'm sorry.'

'It was a long time ago, Frank.'

'Your mum never remarried?'

'No, we were – are – her life.'

'You have siblings?'

'Two older brothers.'

'She must be very proud of you.'

'Of us all.'

'Can I ask what happened to your dad?'

'He had cancer.'

The 'C' word – so often it's a conversation stopper, but Frank was genuinely interested and wanted to know more.

'What sort of cancer?'

'It was bowel cancer. If it had happened today and been detected early enough, chances are we'd have had him in our lives a lot longer, but –'

Sophie paused.

'Are you okay?' Frank asked.

'Yeah, but are you sure you want to hear all this?'

'Only if you want to tell me. I'm interested in you, Sophie, and besides, we've still got almost an hour before we land!'

'Okay, where will I start?'

Sophie told Frank about both her parents – how they met, what their lives had been like before they met, and in the short time they had together.

'It's hard to imagine the difficulties so many people go through, when my own life feels so blessed.'

'She's the best, Frank. Selfless, independent. I'm so lucky to have her.'

'How old was she when your dad died?'

'Thirty-one.'

'Thirty-one,' Frank repeated, 'with three young children, and no parents or parents-in-law around to help. How did she manage?'

'I don't know, but we became her sole focus.'

'Sometimes I wonder how anyone – especially someone with a young family – keeps going from day to day once they've been told they have a terminal illness. Life can be cruel.'

They were both silent for a moment before Frank spoke again.

'Well, we can only be thankful that he and your mum met, and that they had the time together that they did. *And* that he got to have that family of his own, even if he was only with you for a short time. It makes me feel so lucky.'

'Yeah, me too. Can I show you something?'

'Of course.'

Sophie took out her wallet and removed a worn piece of paper that she unfolded carefully so as not to tear it. It was a copy of a page from one of the last letters her dad, Robert, had written to her mum, and she passed it to Frank. He read it quietly.

> *I thank you from the bottom of my heart for the love you have given me, for the home you have made for me when I was so much in need of one, for the children you have given me and for nine years of companionship. I do love you up to the sky and back again, to the bottom of the sea and back again and all the way around the world and back again.*

As he read it Sophie noticed a tear fall from his eye. He wiped it away and then folded the paper back up as carefully as Sophie had unfolded it.

'I don't know what to say.'

'You don't have to say anything. I haven't shown that to anyone before, but it's been so nice spending today with you. Thank you for asking me along.'

'It's been my absolute pleasure.'

'You know what? That's what I was always hoping for – the incredible love and devotion my parents must've had. But I've never come close, which is why I gave up and got Cujo!'

'Don't ever give up, Sophie. Someone's out there for you.'

'But that's the thing, Frank. I don't feel like it matters anymore. I'm okay. It took a while – too long – but I'm okay.'

Frank had that concerned fatherly look on his face, one that Sophie loved but also one that made her laugh, if only for a moment.

'I'm so glad you came with me today,' he said, 'and I want you to know I'm always here for you.'

Frank noticed Sophie looking a little melancholic. *Not surprising*, he thought.

'I'm sorry, I've brought up some really personal things for you. You're looking tired all of a sudden. Are you okay?' he asked.

'Yeah I'm fine thanks, Frank. The early start must be catching up with me. Actually no, I haven't been feeling that great all day. No, that's not it either, I feel okay, just not quite right. A bit distracted, perhaps, like you feel when you've forgotten something. I'm sure it'll pass.'

Frank squeezed Sophie's hand, and felt her squeeze back.

ಸಿ)ಲ

And so Sophie's week had started very differently to mine. I'd always felt that her freedom paled in comparison to my own, but since that bushwalk it had become obvious to me how little I'd actually exercised that freedom. *Am I any better than Sophie when it comes to living life?* I didn't *have* to be with her all the time, but I'd wanted to be. I genuinely liked being with her and I honestly thought I could make a difference. But now that she's feeling so content and settled, I'm feeling like I've achieved nothing all these years, that I've wasted my own second chance at experiencing life – whatever that might mean.

I've been starting to plan my great escape. My Nullarbor adventure. The good thing is that no-one but Sophie knows about me, so I can move around unseen and unnoticed. Most of the time Sophie doesn't even know I'm there – we've managed to live together in relative harmony. It was only once she turned thirty that I started giving her a hard time, and that was because I thought she needed to get a move on and start enjoying herself. *Really* enjoying herself. But that's going on for ten years ago. Time for me to get a move on, even if I can't talk her into doing the same.

So today, while Sophie was with Frank, feeling like she'd forgotten something, that was me. After she left for the airport this morning I slipped away, taking the opportunity to go in to Gedup'n'go. I wanted to find out as much as I could about Clinton West, the photographer heading out to the Nullarbor.

It was a fantastic morning, and I was learning all sorts of things. In all the years I've been with Sophie, I really have just been *with Sophie*. I haven't ventured more than a few metres from her at any time. Ever. So my little trip to Gedup'n'go was a bit of an experiment. It was nerve-wracking, and I felt exposed without Sophie there with me, but I was determined.

I headed off in the direction of the office. Gedup'n'go isn't that far from home, but I soon figured out that I couldn't go any faster than Sophie could on foot, and it was too far.

So I stopped at the next set of traffic lights, thinking I'd drift through the open window of a car that had stopped on the red. But did any of them have an open window? Of course not. Bugger. Instead I waited for a ute so I could grab a ride on the back, and fortunately I didn't have to wait long. After only a few minutes I grabbed my ride, and within about ten minutes I hopped off again at lights near the office and took off from there. I was feeling so independent and free, even brave, but I had to admit it did feel strange being out on my own.

The next thing I learned after I arrived at Gedup'n'go and made my way from the reception area into the corridor was mind-blowing. I could pass through people. Awesome! All these years I had no idea. I could see, I could hear, I could even smell things. And although I couldn't *be* felt, I was able to feel. I could feel Cujo's beautiful soft fur, the warmth of the sun, the movement of the wind. If Sophie had been with me and she hadn't seen this guy coming the other way, they'd have bumped right into each other, but I went right through him. This was so much fun! Maybe I could pass through a car window too – I'll try that on my way home.

Then a thought. *What if Sophie can still hear me?* I needed to be sure one way or the other.

'Sophie!' I called.

Nothing.

'Sophie, can you hear me?'

Still nothing.

'SOPHIE! Your feet look like the hobbit's!' An ex-boyfriend had once told her that, and I knew if I were to say anything that would get a reaction from her, that would be it.

But again nothing, so I was confident that if I wasn't actually with her, she couldn't hear me. I'm not sure how I feel about that, not yet anyway. This is such new ground for me. It's already feeling like I'm on a fantastic new adventure, and it really hasn't even begun.

As it turned out, I didn't learn much about Clinton West. In the time I spent with Cath, only once did she have cause to open the file containing his details and there wasn't much there when she did. All I was able to find out was his number plate, which was attached to a blue Kombi. This was his mobile home, the van he apparently lived in more often than not. Mr West, I discovered, was a man of no fixed address.

So there wasn't a lot I could do until I arrived in Perth. I tried not to think about how hard that might be, which was easy because I was still so excited about being able to pass through solid stuff. Next question – how am I going to get to Perth? I'd been curious about long-distance train travel for ages. By flying you miss so much, and we'd be driving back from Perth so something different would be good. Plus, there's always been a certain romance associated with long-distance train journeys. Whether there's any truth in that or not I have no idea, but this is my chance to find out.

Oh. My. Goodness. I'm taking the train across this massive continent, Sydney to Perth, Pacific Ocean to Indian. On. My. Own. *Yippee!*

It was all coming together. Sophie and I had watched a documentary on the Indian Pacific and the Ghan a few months ago, and I remembered that the Indian Pacific leaves Sydney only twice each week – Wednesdays and Saturdays. I needed to be in Perth by Saturday because that's when Clinton was leaving, so I'd catch the train from Central Station on Wednesday. That didn't leave me much time. Already I was feeling so excited about the next couple of weeks, and by the time I was home again I wondered why I hadn't done something like this long ago.

I was also feeling incredibly bold and liberated! But at the same time I couldn't help but feel a little sad, because Sophie wouldn't be coming with me.

You can't have it both ways, Georgia, I told myself. *And maybe this is what we both need.*

Wednesday

Today's the day. I'll get the bus from across the road at about ten, because I'm not sure exactly what time the Indian Pacific leaves from Central, but I know it's this afternoon. The bus will take me to the station and I'll get a suburban train into Central from there. I've done that plenty of times with Sophie.

Sophie. She's totally ignored me since that bushwalk, and I haven't felt much like talking to her either, so things have been quiet between us. Sometimes we just need a little space when we're angry, and I had a feeling if I tried to make peace with her we'd end up arguing again. I didn't want that. So I played with Cujo for a while before I left, but that only made me sad. I'm going to miss him. Miss the rides on top of his head when Sophie takes him for a walk. Okay, I'll miss Sophie, too. Of course I will. But it's only two weeks, and I know if I don't go I'll regret it forever. I have to do it. Have to see what kind of difference it will make, to me and to Sophie.

Just before 10 o'clock, I slipped away.

ഓൾ

I arrived at Central Station in plenty of time. The Indian Pacific wasn't leaving until mid-afternoon. There'd been no problems getting here, but I was feeling low. Would Sophie miss me? Even a little bit? I needed to find a distraction.

One of the things I've always enjoyed doing is watching people, and train stations are a great place to do it. I made my way across to the interstate platform and was gazing at the people waiting over on the other platforms – the suburban platforms. Boring! Looks like they're waiting to go nowhere in particular, nowhere exciting anyway, and it shows on their faces. For them, waiting for and catching the train is probably something they have to do to get from home to work and back again. But on my platform – the interstate platform – everyone's about to take their first adventurous step away from the mundane and into the unknown.

And then I spotted an elderly couple, waiting on a wooden bench seat on my platform. They grabbed my attention in an instant because they looked so much like a matching pair that I could imagine them as life-sized salt and pepper shakers! They had to be husband and wife. Sitting side by side they were dressed alike, and very sensibly for travel. They were both grey, probably about the same height, and a little on the round side, but comfortably so. Both his feet were flat on the ground, so were hers. He was totally immersed in a book that sat open on his lap, so was she. He was a few pages into his book, she was too. And he was wearing a hat. Yep, so was she.

I imagined him to be a fisherman – all that was missing was his rod and a river into which he could cast his line, and I imagined his book was transporting him to such a place. I made my way over to see if I was right.

Yes! It is a fishing guide, to Western Australia. Her turn next. She looks like a devoted wife, loving mother and adored grandmother, and I imagine she's reading a nineteenth-century romance novel.

Wrong. She was reading about the wildflowers in Western Australia. Oh well, one out of two's not bad. But her hat's fantastic! Unlike the rest of her outfit, it's a kaleidoscope of colours. It's crocheted, and I bet she made it herself. Doesn't matter who made it though, I decided I'd make myself comfortable on top of it for a while. They look so nice, unassuming and content, my salt and pepper couple, and I liked them straightaway, so I planned to get to know them as well as I could over the next few days, as we travelled across to Perth.

As I waited with them, a young guy in baggy jeans and an oversized T-shirt hanging even lower than his oversized sweatshirt passed us by. *Likely a student from Sydney Uni*, I thought, because slung over his shoulder was a heavily laden daypack and he was fiddling with his phone as he walked, rather than watching where he was going. Okay fair enough, it could've been any young guy, not necessarily a student. Muted sounds of Jethro Tull were seeping from his headphones and, for some reason, it made me think of Sophie.

I shook thoughts of her away as the music disappeared into the murmur of Wednesday afternoon commuters and started to feel the excitement building among all these total strangers on the platform. But it was only when my salt and pepper couple got up to go that I realised passengers had started to board. It looked like the Indian Pacific would be departing on time.

No doubt everyone had read about the journey, maybe even heard stories from friends who had done the trip. They'd have some idea what to expect, but it's never going to be just as we might imagine. Better for some, probably most, but perhaps not all. I was willing to bet that for many, like me, we were about to live a dream. *Bring it on*, I squealed, as we made our way towards the train!

I'd watched as people checked in their luggage earlier. Now they were forming a queue and looking out their tickets as one by one – or couple by couple – they were welcomed and then directed to their carriages. Some of them could've done with their hiking gear – this train was so long! It was clean, too. Must've taken someone all morning to get it looking so shiny.

I was going to travel Gold Kangaroo, a decision based purely on the direction my salt and pepper couple was headed. Their names were Jim and Clare – I'd seen it on their tickets as they were welcomed at the gate.

They passed carriage after carriage after carriage. The earlier ones were marked Red Kangaroo – they were the cheaper ones – but every carriage had an iconic and freshly polished wedge-tailed eagle on its side. *Fitting*, I thought. *They're Australia's largest bird of prey and they love the open country. I hope I get to see some.*

Jim and Clare stopped at car L, their home for the next three days and three nights, along with the lounge and dining cars I'd been reading about. I'd get to know them soon enough. There was plenty of time – we had four thousand, three hundred and fifty-two kilometres to cover.

Already I was missing Sophie and wished she was here with me. I was feeling a bit like a child who had run away from home after a tantrum. I was sorry I'd been so aggressive on that bushwalk. Sorry too I hadn't said goodbye before I left. I felt ashamed, but I couldn't help it. I've been trying so hard and for so long to get her to do something exciting, or even something just a bit different, but she wasn't budging. Nope. I'd made my decision. She wasn't here and so I tried again to push all thoughts of her aside in favour of having a good poke around inside the train.

❧☙

I followed Jim and Clare into their twin-share cabin. It was small but it looked okay, and they seemed happy with it. Most of the space they had was filled by a couch – it was roomy enough to seat three by day, and by night it would become the sleeping quarters for one, with a bunk bed for the second passenger hovering overhead. Securely, I hoped. There was a narrow cupboard that provided a teensy bit of storage room for no more than a few hanging items, and a tiny fold-down table was fixed below the window and would hold a book or two during those times when the couch was a couch and not a bed.

It was when Clare opened the door to the bathroom that I laughed. A fold-down toilet was built in below a fold-down sink, both of which needed to be folded up in order to take a shower. It was cramped and the lighting was dim, but Clare seemed pleased that it was theirs and they didn't have to share it with anyone else.

No sooner had Jim and Clare put their things down and explored what little there was to explore in their cabin when there was a knock on their door.

'Welcome aboard, Mr and Mrs Bradley. My name is Simon, I'm your steward.'

'Jim and Clare, please,' Jim said as he shook the man's hand.

'Jim. Clare. Thank you. I wanted to let you know we have a welcome reception in the bar later this afternoon –'

'Oh, how lovely, dear,' said Clare.

'It's a chance for you to meet some of your fellow travellers. We have people from all over the world riding with us on the Indian Pacific. You'll have other opportunities to meet people over the next few days, during journey information sessions and at mealtimes when we encourage you to sit at different tables, but this is to help everyone make that first step. Then, after a drink, we'll give you a rundown on the train itself and what you can expect over the next few days.'

'That sounds wonderful,' said Clare. 'We'll be there, won't we dear? What time, Simon?'

'Excellent,' Simon said. 'It will be at four o'clock, and the bar is two carriages towards the front of the train. Do you have any other questions for me?'

'Oh yes,' said Clare. 'Do we need to vacate our room at any particular time for the beds to be made up?'

'Not at all, Clare. That all happens while you're having dinner, and then your cabin will be returned to its sitting-room status during breakfast in the morning.'

'Well that sounds very efficient,' said Jim. 'Jolly good.'

'Oh, one thing I need to ask you,' said the steward. 'We have two sittings for all your meals. Do you prefer earlier or later?'

ಬಂಡ

During this first afternoon on board, and before the welcome reception, I was happy to watch suburban Sydney disappear behind us from the lounge car. No-one much was there – I guess they were getting settled in their cabins – but it had been such a big day, and I admit I was feeling a little melancholic. Had I done the right thing? My thoughts were soon interrupted by a few uplifting notes that came through the lounge's intercom, followed by a voice that was as soft and smooth as velvet. It was the first of the information sessions.

> Well hello everyone! My name is Vince, and I'd like to welcome you on board the Indian Pacific. I'll be talking to you from time to time as we make our way across to Perth. I'll tell you about the places we're passing through, the towns we're about to reach, as well as the history of this magnificent train and the railway itself. Some of you might know much of it already, but for those who don't, I hope what I'll be sharing with you will be of some interest.

I wonder if Vince is real, or if he's a recording.

> The beautiful views we're seeing at the moment will be familiar to many of you, but for the rest of you, this impressive natural barrier we're forging our way through right now is known as the Blue

Mountains, and we're coming up to Katoomba. After that we'll pass through Mount Victoria and, after that, Bell. At Bell we'll be at the highest point the train will pass through on its journey between Sydney and Perth.

The rest of the afternoon passed quickly, probably because I slept through most of it. I'd been so tired after I got on the train. I put it down to the fact that I'd just made the biggest and boldest move of my life. Or since my death. Whatever.

Now I was rested and feeling excited, but a little nervous, too. It hit me as soon as I woke up that I was further away from Sophie than I'd ever been. A lot further. But I was feeling good. I'd woken to the sound of people moving about, and given the fantastic smells coming from the direction of the kitchen, it must have been dinner time, so I moved along to the dining car where I again saw Jim and Clare. They were sitting at a table with a couple from New Zealand – David and Julie – and I made myself comfortable as I read the menu over Jim's shoulder. It was headed 'Blue Mountains Dinner', so I was guessing that each meal would be different, and would come with an appropriately named menu, depending on where we were.

The two couples placed their orders and were starting to get to know each other over a Sauvignon Blanc from Orange, in the New South Wales central west, when their entrees arrived.

'The soup for you, madam. And yours was the salad. Enjoy, ladies. I'll be right back with the others.'

'Thank you,' said Julie. 'The soup smells delicious, and isn't it all presented beautifully.'

'Indeed it is,' said Clare. 'Crisp white linen and polished silver cutlery –'

'Not to mention how excellent the service has been since we boarded. What a lovely young man that was.'

'Delightful,' agreed Clare. 'And if what I've heard about the food on this train is correct, we're about to enjoy the first of many culinary delights. Cheers.'

'Cheers,' they all echoed as the men's entrees arrived. But no sooner had they all started to eat than something grabbed Clare's attention.

'Oh no, Jim dear. Something's wrong with that lady.'

'What lady, love?'

'The one at the table behind you.'

I turned around as the attention that was focused on this woman grew, from her husband to the couple they were dining with, then to a steward, other staff members and a broader audience of passengers, one of whom was, fortunately, a doctor.

The woman's eyes had rolled to the back of her head, something I'd never seen before.

'She's diabetic,' her husband told the doctor. 'In all the excitement she must've let her blood-sugar level drop.'

'When did she last eat?' the doctor asked.

'I'm not sure. We missed lunch, so she might not have had anything since breakfast this morning.'

While the doctor attended to her, the steward organised a call through to Bathurst Hospital – they'd have an ambulance waiting to pick her up when the train pulled into the station there.

I had to get myself out of this dining car, get some fresh air – this wasn't the sort of excitement I'd been looking for. I left Jim and Clare, and their new friends, and found myself a quiet spot between two of the carriages, looking out into nowhere, dreaming.

That's better. After a few minutes I knew I wanted to stay out there all night. It was beautiful outside. Clear. Peaceful. But I also wanted to see Jim and Clare's transformed room. *I'll go back in, soon*, I told myself. *Then I'm coming back out.* If I'd been sleepy this afternoon, I wasn't anymore.

☙❧

Their room looked really good. It was amazing what could be done with such a small space. But when two adults were added to the mix, as happened a few minutes later, there were plenty of head-banging opportunities. There was almost no space for Jim and Clare to do anything. I could see the makings of a bedroom farce right in front of me, so I settled into a corner and waited for the show to begin.

'I'm going to take a shower, dear,' Clare said.

'I might give my teeth a quick clean before you get in, love, if you don't mind.'

'Yes, go ahead. It will take me a few minutes to sort myself out here.'

It was so funny, watching them try to do the most basic pre-bed rituals in such a small area, but they managed, and when Jim emerged from the closet space they called the bathroom, Clare took his place.

Once he'd changed into his pyjamas and had climbed the small stepladder to the top bunk, Jim listened for the shower, noticed Clare's giggling had stopped, and called out.

'Are you okay in there, love?'

'What's that, dear?'

'How's the shower?'

'Oh, not bad. It's a pity I'm not more flexible. There isn't much room in here, and the light isn't good. Will you be coming in after me?'

'Not tonight, love, I'm already in bed! It sounds jolly inconvenient if you ask me.'

'Oh no, it's not too bad. The pressure is excellent, and the temperature is perfect. What's the bed like?'

'Well, it's plenty long enough, but it's narrow. I'll have to be careful if I turn over through the night. Wouldn't want to fall to the floor!'

'Let's hope that doesn't happen, dear. I'm about to get out. Are you sure you wouldn't like a shower? It might help you sleep.'

'Quite sure. I'm very comfortable here.'

When Clare emerged from the bathroom, she looked refreshed and soft.

'Well, that was rather invigorating. I'm sure you'll feel better tomorrow after a shower. I do, despite the difficulties. But it's not like home!'

ఎంఇ

I'd been seduced by the night sky earlier in the evening, so I quietly wished Jim and Clare a good night's sleep and slipped through their window, floating to the roof of the carriage. I'd been thinking about train-surfing – seen people on TV who were travelling on the top of a train in Bangladesh when it was too crowded for them to travel inside, or maybe they couldn't afford the fare. I *never* imagined it was something I might do, because there was no way Sophie would try something like this.

Okay, fair enough. If she was here and she did do this, she'd be arrested, that is if she didn't fall off and kill herself first. But out here, without her, there was nothing to stop me. And it was *awesome*. I'd heard people talk about riding a motorbike without a helmet, or driving in a convertible with the top down, and they loved the feel of the wind through their hair. I didn't have any hair, but I'm betting what I was feeling was way better than anything anyone else had *ever* experienced. I felt completely free, for the first time in Sophie's life, and I couldn't get enough. Not only did it *feel* sensational, but to be out there, with nothing between me and the sky as it dazzled with its simplicity, was something I felt so lucky to be experiencing.

Once my initial and overwhelming awe subsided, and I made myself comfortable up there, the words of a poem Sophie had immersed herself in years earlier were trying to come together for me. It was Bob Dylan's '11 Outlined Epitaphs', and it went on forever, much like this train. But the bit I always loved was about Al's wife. I wish I could remember it, but I can't. She – Al's wife – was telling Dylan he couldn't possibly be happy. He asked her how *she* could know how he was feeling. She said it was because all his songs were so depressing, and he tried to explain to her that that didn't mean he wasn't happy.

I had a feeling Al's wife was never going to get it, and out here, tonight, as I gazed up at the stars in the bulging night sky, I realised Sophie had never got me either. But then maybe it had worked – or not worked – both ways. I had no right to assume I knew whether or not she was happy, or what it was she needed to make her happy. And as I thought about that, I knew that coming out here was the right thing for me to do, for both of us. She really does drive me to despair at times – doesn't seem to matter whether I'm with her or not. But I'm not ready to let go yet, not entirely. Selfish I know, but I'd miss her heaps.

But look at me! Here I am, *on top of the Indian Pacific. Yippee!* If I could pinch myself I would. Those stars – I can't believe how many there are, and how clear the sky is. I thought of that woman, who'd be in Bathurst Hospital now, and of Clare as she'd watched on helplessly. What a beautifully caring face she has. I like Clare.

And I thought of Sophie, because her sky is so much smaller than the one I'm in awe of tonight. Then I remembered the little prince, from

Sophie's favourite book by Antoine de Saint-Exupéry, and felt a familiar twinge. Sophie is with me now. I can feel it. And I can picture her at home in her yard, Cujo by her side. It's time they spend together every night, so I know she and I are looking up at the same stars and I can feel our thoughts become one. It all looks so calm and peaceful up there. And Sophie is feeling so calm and peaceful.

She'll be listening for the little prince, for that sweet laughter of the stars. And as the comforting smell of indoor fires burns thick in the night air, her head will fill with warm winter thoughts that she'll share with no-one as she says goodnight to another day.

Thursday

The day's new light was creeping into the dining car as I slipped back inside the train. I'd stayed out all night so I could watch the sun rise from my personal vantage point, and it was unbelievable. There was nothing to get in its way as it floated above the horizon, and it was beautiful seeing the countryside come alive as it was touched by this first light.

But it was strange not being with Sophie. It was like part of me – almost all of me in fact – was missing. At the same time I was feeling invigorated. Not hanging around with Sophie meant I could go almost anywhere. Do almost anything. I can't believe it took me nearly forty years to work that out. There was so much to think about, and my head was spinning – at least I'm sure it would've been if I'd had one! I felt like a tiny tuft of tumbleweed, somersaulting with joy as I thought about the night I'd just had.

Exciting and incredible as it was, however, it presented me with my first disappointment. Before I left Sophie it hadn't occurred to me the train would be travelling through the night and that I'd miss seeing so much of the country. I crossed virtually all of New South Wales from the roof of the train, in darkness. But then I suppose if we didn't travel through the night, it would take a whole week to get to Perth. Maybe doing the return trip would be one way to catch up on some of that missed scenery, but for me it was a matter of being patient. Once I arrived in Perth I'd be tracking Clinton down and with him I knew I'd see it all.

Breakfast wasn't far off. As I listened to the familiar clanking of pots and pans, and smelled those wonderful kitchen smells again, passengers were starting to appear, and I was all ears. Despite being so narrow, the general consensus was that the beds were comfortable, and I'd been wrong – really wrong – about something. I'd imagined that the train's gentle and rhythmic motion as it passed over the tracks would create a soothing mantra for a good night's sleep, but from what I was hearing, that wasn't the case. I'd been oblivious to it up on the roof, but passengers who were arriving bleary-eyed to breakfast spoke of being acutely aware of every bump. It had been a rough ride, with constant creaking, rocking, grinding, squeaking, rattling and jerking, and no rhythm whatsoever. It had made for a dreamless night and, for some, a sleepless one.

The welcome news, compliments of old Velvet Voice, was that the track between Bathurst and Broken Hill was the country's worst. In other words, it had to get better from here.

Ah, Broken Hill. Our approach to this town was dry, flat and dusty, but the closer we rattled towards it, the more the colours were exploding, just as they had done in *Priscilla, Queen of the Desert*. I'd watched that movie with Sophie and knew I wanted to see Broken Hill some day. That day had arrived.

ಲ಄ಃ

If the weather reports were to be believed, Sydney's big dry was about to come to an end. Almost a year had been and gone without rain. Autumn had come to an end and the mornings and nights in particular were becoming noticeably cooler. Some days were still magic. Others hit with an unexpected and startling chill. Today was one of those days. *I hope I'm not coming down with something,* Sophie thought. She was cold and had just walked back in her door to grab a jumper when her phone rang.

'Hey Soph, it's Jodie, how are things?'

'Jodie hi, not too bad. I was going to call you tonight. How are the reunion plans coming along?'

'Not that great – we've only got thirty-two who've said they'd come. We need to get more, at least sixty or it's going to be too expensive. It shouldn't be that hard – there were about 150 in our year group.'

'So what are you going to do?'

'Keep trying.'

'But the RSVP date passed ages ago. If any more were going to come they would've been in touch by now.'

'Not necessarily,' Jodie said. 'People are busy, they forget. We need to contact everyone again and get as many as we can.'

'You can't do that!'

'Why not?'

'Because they're supposed to be adults! If someone hassled me to go to something I didn't want to go to, I'd be even less likely to want to go!'

'Yeah but you're weird, Soph!'

'Thanks, Jodie.' Sophie had long since given up caring too much what other people thought of her and wasn't in the mood to argue this point. 'So what's the plan?'

'Noomi and I are going to ring around. Will you help?'

'No way! If they can't get themselves organised, I'm not going to do it for them.'

'Go on, Soph. Don't be such a grump.'

Sophie didn't react to that, but she knew she was being grumpy. She sighed.

'Okay, but no phone calls. I'll send out a group email to everyone, but I'm sure if they'd wanted to come they would have let you know by now. They should've, anyway.'

Sophie had been torn about the reunion, wondering if she'd made the right choice. She'd been thinking a lot about the Nullarbor trip, and whether Georgia had been right, because at the moment, crossing the Nullarbor was looking a lot better than trying to inject some enthusiasm into her old classmates to attend a reunion she wasn't even too sure she wanted to attend herself. Maybe she *had* used it as an excuse to avoid going away.

I don't know why I agreed to help them, she thought as she typed the email and hit 'Send'.

The others followed Sophie's email up with their calls, and in doing so they proved her wrong. Their perseverance paid off and, in the end, with the reunion only a couple of days away, they were approaching their target figure. Sophie was pleased for them. Jodie and Noomi had tried hard, which was more than she'd done. She felt bad and hoped for their sake it would be a great night. *And*, she told herself, *as I'm not heading out to the Nullarbor, I might as well try to have a great night myself.*

༄༅༅

It was an early breakfast for everyone, and it wasn't that long after sunrise when we arrived in Broken Hill, or the Silver City, as it was apparently also known. I should've been excited, but instead was hit with another disappointment. We weren't going to be seeing as much of it as I hoped. We'd travelled more than a thousand kilometres since we'd left Sydney, but because of our emergency stop in Bathurst last night, and because the train's arrival time in Perth needed to stay fixed, the off-train tour of Broken Hill had been cancelled. Instead, we only had about twenty minutes to wander aimlessly around the few main streets that radiated from the station and were still an hour or more away from coming to life.

You're here though, Georgia, I said to myself. *Make the most of it.*

The station at Broken Hill was much like a small suburban Sydney train station, but that's where any similarities between the two places ended. Straightaway I knew I'd never forget the colours out here. The soil for a start – it was an incredibly rich red. And the sky, not a blemish. Before I left Sydney I thought Broken Hill might've been as famous for being *where* it is as much as for *what* it is. It's outback New South Wales after all. But I was wrong. Its mining history is huge, something that was evident all around, with a lot of the streets named after minerals.

As soon as we were off the train we were right there, with the town in front of us, and everyone, including me, scattered. Lining the streets were some beautiful old buildings – some ornate Victorian, others classic Federation. The main street was Argent Street, where the old post office, town hall, police station and courthouse were. Everything had such a peculiar beauty. *No wonder lots of eccentric artists have called this place home.* Art galleries seemed to be as big a drawcard as pubs.

Pubs. There must've been one on every corner. But the one that caught my attention almost immediately, and held my interest longer than any other, was the Palace Hotel. Its cast-iron balustrades and long verandahs were straight from *Priscilla*, and although it wasn't open, that wasn't going to stop me!

Inside, the walls were completely covered in murals, with not a drag queen in sight. No-one in sight, for that matter. But that staircase was just as I remembered from the movie, and that's why I was here. They always keep these things polished, so even if I can't feel it, I can pretend it's adding that little bit of extra whoosh as I slide down. Again. And again.

It must've been about my twenty-seventh time when I heard the train's whistle and knew I had to get out of there, fast. The train had started to pull away but I made it. Just.

It was only then I noticed the enormous, eye-catchingly ugly mound of mining waste on the other side of the train. The slag heap. Velvet Voice had told us about that, but I must've been looking the other way as we arrived, planning my visit to the Palace! It certainly helped identify the town, though I'm not so sure that was a good thing.

It had been all too quick, but I'd felt Broken Hill's magnetism, and knew I'd been touched by just a hint of its unsophisticated enchantment. Unsophisticated. Yep, we had that in common!

ଛଠ

In no time at all the train was heading west again, snaking its way towards Adelaide. We were headed for Port Augusta and had to go via Adelaide because it was a major terminal, not only for the Indian Pacific but also for her sister train, The Ghan.

It was a fantastic detour. The scenery was really changing and I'd settled myself up on the roof again. Our early morning taste of the Outback had given way to a much prettier, far less dramatic kind of landscape. South Australia's wheat and dairy had taken centre stage in the gently bulging countryside south of the Flinders Ranges. I loved watching it all pass me by. Even the many cancerous splashes of Paterson's Curse were exquisitely attractive, as were the spectacular pink lakes. I'd seen pictures of pink lakes that were so strangely beautiful I'd assumed the colour must have been fudged during the printing process, but that wasn't the case. I could still hear Velvet Voice's announcements, just, and apparently the pink is a result of the high concentrations of a salt-loving algae. When the light is just right, like now, these lakes are eerie.

I was back inside the train by late morning. Lunch passed by and my lazy morning was looking like it could easily turn into a lazy afternoon as the tracks led us towards Adelaide, but I wanted to explore some more. I wanted to see some more of the passengers, and their carriages, having spent most of my time so far with Jim and Clare.

I suppose some people catch the train if they need to get from Sydney to Perth, or vice versa, and they don't want to fly or drive. Maybe others have to do it more than once in a lifetime, in which case they might go for the cheaper option – reclining seats rather than their own cabin, and a cafe rather than a restaurant. Whatever their reason or motivation, I wanted to have a look around. My motivation had been Sophie – I'd been missing her overnight and wasn't going to let myself dwell on her. I had to keep busy, so off I went, to see what I could find at the other end of the train.

The good thing was that the already impossibly narrow corridors hadn't got any narrower. People here were getting to know each other just as intimately as they were closer to the front of the train.

After that, the first thing I noticed was how messy it was. These carriages had reclining seats for the passengers but there were no doors they could close around their own space, so they had no way of hiding their untidiness from the world. Clothes, pillows, blankets, food wrappers, all sorts of rubbish and personal stuff was cluttering the little bit of space they had. Some of them were reading, others were listening to music, and a few had their laptops open. Working perhaps? Maybe, but I saw a couple of people playing computer games. I even saw someone writing in a journal – with a pen, on paper! *Another dinosaur like Sophie*. But I loved that about Sophie. One day she'd wake up and find she'd been left behind, but I don't think she'd care.

The people at the back end of the train were a younger crowd – single men and women, students and backpackers maybe? Young families too, maybe on their way to visit relatives in other states, or coming home. The noise they were making, just by talking to one another, came and went in waves while I was there, but there was always movement. People were getting up and down from their seats, coming and going from the cafe or their own lounge car, or waiting outside the toilet. Restless children were running along corridors, squealing until a parent grabbed a wrist or spoke a quiet but firm word to try restoring a little discipline.

I made my way further on down the train to see if all these back carriages were the same. In layout they seemed to be, and their windows weren't any smaller than they were up Jim and Clare's end, where there was clearly more money. But the individual dynamics of each carriage varied a lot more than they did up the other end of the train. Retirees and travellers up there were a much more restrained mix.

As I exited that first red car, I heard music, and as I emerged in the next, I felt like I'd arrived at a party. It was another lounge car and the atmosphere was alive. Everyone was talking and singing as one of the passengers strummed on his guitar. No-one was watching the passing scenery. Instead they were either sprawled across the chairs or each other. They were loud, but they were having a good time, and that's what it was all about. But I passed through this carriage as quickly as I could because I was feeling a bit unsettled among all the commotion. Sophie was no party girl, and avoided crowded spaces, and so I wasn't used to it. Maybe in time I'd be more relaxed in that sort of gathering, but I was still finding my way on my own.

I passed through the next car just as quickly when I encountered a screaming baby and all the paraphernalia that a parent travelling with a little one has to carry with them. I felt for the young mum, but I also felt for the others around her, and hoped for everyone's sake the baby wasn't going to be crying all the way across the country.

Next carriage, instant sensory relief. There was chatter, but the volume was down low, and once I started paying attention, I realised a group of them were asking each other who'd be at the top of their list if they could invite any famous person – famous dead person – along to a dinner party.

'Fred Hollows,' was the first name I heard.

'Oh, that's a good one,' said her friend. 'I'd ask Martin Luther King.'

'Van Gogh,' came the voice of a young man I'd seen sketching. He'd been quietly shading the contours of the face of the girl beside him while she slept. His girlfriend perhaps. She was pretty, and would be happy with the drawing, I'm sure.

'Paul McCartney,' came another.

'He's not dead yet, you idiot,' his friend said as he threw a pillow in his face.

I would always remember Sophie's reply when she'd been asked the same dinner party question, many years ago. 'My dad,' she'd said, and my heart had broken. I wanted to tell her that he was always with her, in her heart and her soul – that the man who'd won her mum's heart all those years ago was a beautiful, caring and devoted man who had loved her so much. But my memory of our dad was no better than hers and I think she knew all that anyway.

I think, had she known she was meant to have a twin sister, Sophie would've opted for the whole family reunion at that dinner party. My heart aches when I think about that, too. I wish I'd been part of my own family. Imagine if Sophie knew I was her twin sister, rather than just the voice she so often shrugged away. I loved how close they all were, and I craved some of that closeness. To be able to feel the love from Celia and her brothers that Sophie feels, and to be able to give it in return. To belong. But these dinner parties were just a game, and that was never going to happen.

I remembered almost nothing of the time our parents were together, and Sophie and her brothers wouldn't remember much more. To grow up not knowing your parents as they should be – together – was rough. And as Celia had never remarried, they hadn't had the chance to see any of that adult sort of togetherness at home – the sort most children would take for granted. Sophie was too young to understand anything of relationships in those first few years before our father died – sometimes even now she thought she was every bit as clueless.

She never knew what it was like to see Celia and Robert having a conversation, or an argument. She'd never heard their more tender moments late at night when she should've been asleep. She didn't remember seeing them hug, or laugh together, or dance. She remembered none of that. She didn't even know what Robert's voice was like and, more than a lot of things, she wished she did. Celia had such a gentle voice, but what was the voice like that had won her heart so very long ago? I was little help there. All I could try to tell Sophie was that it was a warm and compassionate voice, and she would've loved it. Loved him.

Maybe there is something in the theory that women look for men who are like their fathers, or maybe for Sophie there was a fear of real intimacy – a fear of the unknown and of what she too might someday lose if she were to get too close and fall for someone she might have a future with. I knew she'd thought about it, a lot, and like her I couldn't begin to imagine that kind of loss and the pain it would bring.

I'd seen something inside her die after her last relationship had crumbled, but I couldn't work out what it was – not for ages. At first I thought it might've been desire, but I know she was still capable of feeling that. No, it was hope. Everyone is taught that hope is a good thing, but for Sophie it only ever led to disappointment. Hope had died for her all those years ago, but I have to admit, she seems to be living happily without it.

So much for Sophie being a dreamer. I'm as bad. The pillow fight around me had escalated, and anyone who'd been sleeping wasn't anymore. I couldn't understand why anyone would be sleeping on a trip like this – didn't they want to see the country as they travelled through it? That said, it would've been so easy even for me to drift off in the sun-soaked carriage during the afternoon. I didn't need as much sleep as Sophie, but I needed some, and I hadn't got any last night. I couldn't resist the pillow fight though – I'd never been in one and to me the pillows were like clouds. Very fast-moving clouds. I jumped from one to another as they flew past, but it all stopped suddenly as someone called out, 'Steward!'

In a heartbeat it looked like everyone was back asleep, trying not to laugh at the same time. And then I heard a ping, and another, and suddenly the entire carriage seemed to be waking up to the individual tones and rings of a room full of mobile phones. We were in range again. Adelaide must be close.

As I made my way back to the front section of the train, I noticed that there were also sleeper cars in Red Kangaroo. Each had a large common bathroom, and a dining room, and when I snuck a peek inside one of the rooms I saw a man snoring away happily while his wife sat doing a crossword puzzle in a room that didn't appear much smaller than Jim and Clare's cabin, if at all. An in-between section. Personal space, but minus the element of luxury. Seems the Indian Pacific catered for everyone.

ಬಿ)ಅ

When we arrived in Adelaide we had a few hours to make the most of the train's scheduled stop with the next of the off-train tours – one that went ahead without a hitch. I was in Adelaide about twenty years ago with Sophie, so it was a little bit familiar, but back then we'd been met with a week of dismal weather, whereas today the sun was out.

Adelaide was green, even though Velvet Voice had told us it was the driest city in the driest state on the second driest continent (after

Antarctica). It had nothing of Broken Hill's roughness, which I'd loved. It was far more elegant. There was a lot to like about Adelaide. I liked its uncomplicated street layout and its broad avenues. I liked the nice green parks that surrounded it on all four sides. And I liked that it was built around the sleepy Torrens River. I liked a lot of its architecture, too. I think, had my life been a normal one, I would've been an architect. Adelaide had lots of beautiful old colonial buildings and heaps of churches. Still, it wasn't a patch on Sydney.

Back on the train, I returned to the lounge car. It was all mine for a while, but people were starting to come along for their pre-dinner drinks, and to reflect on a day that was now void of any sunlight. During the day, the big windows in here were a real drawcard – you could soak in much more of the passing scenery than you could through the windows in the cabins, and with Velvet Voice's commentary, this special carriage was a magnet.

It had a few single-seat leather chairs that the passengers would rearrange, depending on their own particular social requirements, and between these were small but heavy round tables. I knew they were heavy because I'd watched people try to move them. They were too small for anything much apart from a couple of drinks, which is all anyone in there generally had with them anyway.

The day was drawing to a close and the lounge was filling up with early diners. They would've known dinner wasn't far off, but I'm sure the smells wafting along the corridors from the kitchen would've helped get them moving. That and the promise of a Barossa red with dinner. Big sigh.

It was smelling so good. I always wished I'd been able to taste things, but not being able to was something I'd learned to live with. Out here though, with all these strangers, it was different. Everyone was going gaga about all the food that was put in front of them. I wouldn't have believed train food could ever get that kind of reaction, so I knew I was missing something special.

ಸಂಚ

'– very proud of them all, even the next generation, who are getting to that age where they're leaving school behind and flying the coop. Yes, life's been good to us, hasn't it, love?'

I was snapped out of my taste-deprived misery by Jim's storytelling voice, and so opened up my eavesdropping ears. Jim and Clare were once again with the couple from New Zealand – so much for dining with as many different people as they could!

'Well, yes, but it didn't start out that way, dear.'

With their dining companions appearing curious to know more, Jim continued.

'We'd only been married a short time and knew we wanted to live in the Blue Mountains –'

'And that we wanted to build our own home out there,' said Clare.

'Yes, it was one of our big dreams – that and a family. We bought a block of land and found a place to rent just around the corner while we were building, so we could watch its progress.'

'I remember those mornings so clearly. Jim would make us both a coffee and we'd walk around to the site. He'd wrap his arms around me and we'd watch the men as they made the mud bricks before Jim left for work. Sometimes he'd get his hands dirty and help, if they came on the weekends, didn't you, dear?'

'It was a wonderful time of life for us, and an insight into what goes into building a house. Each of the bricks was painstakingly positioned –'

'And the fun part for me was making it a home, once the building was complete. We didn't have much money, so relied mostly on hand-me-downs, but we felt so lucky, and were so happy.'

'Our second summer in our new home was a terrible one though,' continued Jim, 'and before it was over we'd lost everything.'

'What happened?' Julie asked.

'Bushfire,' said Clare. 'All that mismatched second-hand furniture that we'd been given from an assortment of relatives and friends, our wedding gifts, all our photos, some old but very special books and a few dolls. Everything. Gone.'

'That fire destroyed our home, along with five others. We had to start all over again. But we got past it – we had youth on our side – and life's been good to us since then.'

Oh my goodness. I can't even begin to imagine what that would be like. It seems to me that, at some stage, everyone has to live through hard times. Maybe not me, things don't get much harder than being dead, but

I thought of Celia, who had also been starting out on a whole new life with Robert when their lives were turned upside down. Problems strike when they're least expected. But that wasn't the end of Jim and Clare's story. Riding the Indian Pacific had been another dream they'd shared, and Jim said it had come about as the result of good fortune.

'Tell Julie and David about our shop, dear.'

'Ah, yes. Well, I'd always worked in the book trade.'

'He just loves books,' said Clare. 'There's almost nothing he doesn't know about them, and publishing.'

'Well, I don't know about that, love, but we had a shop in Katoomba, dealing in rare and second-hand books. Clare worked there with me.'

'I loved the books, too, but I had a lovely little corner of the shop, full of old toys.'

'And dolls,' Jim added. 'She's always loved dolls. It was a modest shop, but for most of my working life it had been a successful little business for us.'

I didn't get the impression they had measured its success by the wealthy lifestyle it had afforded them. If anything, just the opposite. 'We loved everything about that little shop, didn't we, dear.'

'Yes, we did,' continued Jim. 'Not only its contents, but the endless historical tales that lay beneath the surface of each and every item –'

'The interesting strangers it brought into our lives –'

'Yes, we met some wonderful and interesting people over all those years.'

'And we were in it together,' said Clare.

Jim and Clare looked at each other and I could see that the love they must have felt for each other all those years ago when they were first married hadn't dimmed. Moments like that made me ache for what Celia and Robert had been denied, and for what I always hoped Sophie would find.

'Over the years we'd also accumulated our own private collection of books and toys, a collection which, once we sold the shop and retired, seemed to be more of a burden than a joy,' said Jim. 'I suppose it was just us moving on to the next stage of our lives.'

'Some things we would never have parted with, but others we knew had to go.'

'How was your meal?' a voice I didn't know asked unexpectedly.

Damn. Unfortunately Jim and Clare were interrupted when another couple stopped to talk to them on their way out of the dining car, but there was more to this story, I knew it. I only hoped I'd be around when they told the rest, because I liked them and was interested. People in general interested me and, given my limitations, observing them was something I'd grown accustomed to doing.

It had been impossible not to get swept up in their story. It also helped me snap out of the mini-slump I'd dipped into. I reminded myself that I was having a fantastic time, and not just because I was eavesdropping on the passengers. That staircase at the Palace Hotel in Broken Hill had been the best, and train-surfing last night – awesome. I didn't have much to complain about. And tomorrow is another day. A day closer to the Nullarbor.

Friday

I was learning a lot in the lounge car from Velvet Voice as we moved slowly west, but again, as Thursday had fast turned into Friday, I missed seeing a great big chunk of Australia. As the sun had been coming up this morning we were six or seven hundred kilometres west of Port Augusta.

But the day was just beginning, with its own stories about to unfold. Velvet Voice told us that the Nullarbor Plain is one of the world's most remarkable landscapes, and that the train runs across the 'true' plain, not like the Eyre Highway that skirts the coastal fringe of it. It was dead flat, he said, and over an area of about two hundred and sixty thousand square kilometres, it appeared to be swept clean of everything but the exceptionally hardy blue bush and saltbush. I suspected this alone would be enough to turn a lot of people off doing the trip, either by train or by car – they'd find it boring and dull – but then some people manage to bring their boredom with them.

But having spent so much time with Sophie and her workmates at Gedup'n'go – heard them all talk about it and seen so many photos from all around Australia – I'd grown to love the stark and hostile beauty of these remote parts and couldn't wait to see it for myself. I knew it had to be seen with an appreciative set of eyes – eyes that didn't just look, they saw. Far from being as dead as it might appear, it holds its own unique kind of fascination and surely a person's senses – all of them – would come to life out here. I know I can't experience it like everyone else, but I'm going to give it my best shot.

According to Velvet Voice, the Nullarbor Plain is a limestone plateau that was once under the sea, and it extends six hundred and seventy-six kilometres from Ooldea in South Australia to Rawlinna in Western Australia. He said that the world's longest straight stretch of railway runs for almost two-thirds of its entire length. *That has to be something those wedge-tailed eagles appreciate more than those who are earthbound ever could.* Then I had an idea. I hadn't yet seen the front of the train, so today I planned to cross the Nullarbor with the driver.

Everything I'd been seeing inside the train, and outside, was new to me, and I felt like a sponge as I soaked in as much as I could. And while it wasn't all that far to get to the front, I couldn't believe how long this train really was.

It's fun watching people so early in the day – some are morning people, others definitely not. But as I passed the steward delivering cups of tea and coffee to various cabins, I suddenly felt a bit flat, because sharing a few moments over a comforting cup of tea was reminding me of Celia's kitchen and the last time I was there with her and Sophie. It seems so long ago but it's only been a few days.

When the steward knocked on a familiar door, it opened to reveal Clare's gentle face. She was wearing a floral pink nightie and fluffy slippers and looked full of hope and optimism for the new day. Jim was standing behind her, staring out the window. The sun was up but the sky still cradled the softness of the dawn, and the land beneath it was yet to feel the harshness of its full glare.

I couldn't wait to hear the rest of their story from last night, but before that happened we had to travel about two thousand kilometres, and we'd be crossing the Nullarbor Plain. I'd heard it said that some people would prefer a road train reverse slowly over their limbs than to venture across the Nullarbor, but already I could feel the excitement on board, most of which was my own.

As I pushed on towards the driver's cabin, cloud cover was beginning to replace the beautiful sunrise and the day was starting to look surprisingly overcast. For some reason I'd assumed if it was dry, it would be sunny, too. But we'd been told it was unlikely to rain. I should've known. Velvet Voice said that the Nullarbor was one of the driest places on earth, with an annual rainfall that rarely exceeded two hundred millimetres.

෴

As I made my way to the front of the train – through the even more exclusive and quiet Platinum class – the mallee country that had given way to red sandhills was now giving way to the Nullarbor. I couldn't believe it was so barren, even though I expected it to be. It was mesmerising, too, this treeless plain. The reddish-brown earth was so dry, baked beneath kilometre after kilometre after kilometre of knee-high bush scrub that extended in every direction to the horizon.

Already my thoughts were largely focused on my return trip across the Nullarbor, and Sophie – the endless flat dry landscape had been particularly conducive to drifting off. I had a strong feeling that Jack might be involved in the dive at Cocklebiddy – although I had no real reason to think this – and if he was, that was one good reason for Sophie not to be here. Stirring up the past has a habit of stirring up unnecessary heartache.

I remembered the start of their relationship. They were heading out to hear some music. They could've been going to hear a reading of the *White Pages* and Sophie would still have gone. She was hopeless when she liked someone enough, and I know I was as excited as she was. I knew something was going to happen long before she did.

Had I survived, we generally wouldn't have had any problems when it came to falling for men. Our tastes were usually different enough – a bit like our taste in clothes! I would've worn bright colours and looked like I'd given some thought to what I was going to put on each day. Sophie likes a more thrown-together-at-the-last-minute kind of look, and earthy colours. But when it came to Jack, well, let's just say I could totally get why she liked him so much. If nothing else though, I was a realist, and there was no point me feeling even a hint of jealousy when things started heating up between them.

They went first for a meal and then headed to a club where they found themselves a table and a couple of seats right in front of the performing duo, whose music and humorous banter created just the right atmosphere. The unexpectedness of the whole evening left Sophie feeling like a figure from a Chagall painting, floating weightlessly above an otherwise normal snapshot of life, and I was happy for her.

Okay, maybe I *was* a teensy bit jealous. I kept quiet that night though. This was one area I always promised myself – promised her – I'd stay out of. Relationships are hard enough. So all I could do back then was watch on as Sophie tried to navigate her way through it, because after the gig, it all went pear-shaped. The happiness she felt, mixed with all the uncertainty and anticipation, led to her complete meltdown when she and Jack left the darkness and emotional neutrality of the club.

❧☙

As Georgia was recalling that night, so too was Sophie. She and her mum were driving home, having had lunch with Celia's aunt and uncle on the Central Coast. Through roundabouts, along narrow, windy roads. Winter had arrived, but it could easily have been another perfect autumn day. The air was crisp but still, the sky without a trace of cloud, and a gorgeous shade of jacaranda blue that teased of a spring still an entire season away. But as they headed south the skies darkened, and the leaves that had been anticipating that fatal push were clinging desperately, many taking flight in the wind and dancing a peculiar autumn twist as they made their final descent.

Sophie and her mum had done this drive together dozens of times before. Celia didn't have too many surviving relatives, but her uncle had moved to a sleepy little beachside town up north some thirty years earlier, long before the Central Coast was considered to be on the outskirts of Sydney. Back then the drive may have taken longer but the traffic was less daunting and the drivers less aggressive. No-one was in any great hurry. Sophie could never understand why they were now.

Although Sophie was older now than her mum would have been the first time they made this trip, she had always loved going up there with her, largely because of the drive home. Celia's uncle, well in his eighties, had always enjoyed talking about his past – their past. He recalled people and events still strong in his memory, and it never failed to trigger things in Celia's mind that she would then talk about to Sophie as they made their way back to Sydney.

For Sophie it was a window – a window into a world that her mum didn't talk about a great deal, nor did she dwell on it, so Sophie used these occasions to piece together a life that she knew to have been clouded with sadness in its younger years. *I wonder if she really doesn't remember a lot of it,* Sophie thought, *or whether she chooses to forget.*

Sophie glanced across at her mother as the sky darkened with every click of the odometer and she saw a gentle, soft soul, a lady who had once possessed enormous inner strength, the kind that only seems to come to people when life has knocked them around too much. But most of that strength had now gone.

It was fair to say that the anxieties her mother felt, more and more as she grew older, were at the root of a good many cautious decisions Sophie had made over the years. There had been times when Sophie was much younger when that had given cause for the occasional disagreement between them. Despite that, however, she only ever felt love towards her mother. And very protective.

They drove on in silence. Sophie needed to concentrate as the conditions were becoming treacherous. It looked as though the weather forecasters might have been right after all, but Sophie's mind was wandering to the Nullarbor trip she'd passed up, and Jack, back in those very early days.

She had been quietly thrilled, and enormously surprised, to hear from him after she left the newspaper and had begun freelancing. They'd been little more than workmates before then, but he suggested they meet for drinks sometime, and although she still wouldn't let herself believe there might be something in it, she was starting to dream along those lines.

It had been lovely seeing him again – they talked about all sorts of things, like the people they both knew from the newspaper, and what had been going on there lately, but he was interested to hear how things had been going for her, whether she was getting enough work. He was also trying to dig a little deeper, to learn more about Sophie and what she liked to do.

'I love to read, of course!'

'Of course!'

'And I spend a lot of time with my dog, Cujo.'

'What sort of dog is he?'

'The best! He's a Golden Retriever.'

'And …'

That's interesting, Sophie thought. *He didn't mention the Stephen King connection. Maybe he's not a fan.*

'And I take a lot of photos, mostly if I'm away somewhere. I use them as references when I paint.'

'Ah, so you're an artist?'

'Well, no, I wouldn't call myself an artist, but I love to paint.'

'Sport?'

''Fraid not.'

Jack looked disappointed.

'I know, you were just starting to like me, weren't you?'

'Oh well, maybe I can change your mind about that. How about music?' he asked.

'Oh, I love music, but doesn't everyone? And theatre. I love the theatre.'

So apart from sport, which Sophie had assumed was Jack's everything – along with his family – she found out that evening that he was also into the arts. Theatre and music in particular. It was the next time they met for drinks, however, that their relationship changed, turning from lovely to heart-achingly difficult.

'I thought I might go to hear some music tonight,' Jack said as they were finishing their drinks. 'Would you like to come?'

Oooh, Sophie thought. *This is it!*

'I'd love to. Who is it?'

'Sea of Hands.'

'I don't suppose you'd be surprised to learn I've never heard of them.'

'They're an English folk duo.'

'Oh, okay. Weird name – but sounds good!'

They'd parked the car a couple of blocks away, and were enjoying a short walk back together in the chilly June night air after the gig and before the night took its first step towards being over. They walked in silence. Sophie was thinking about what a lovely time she was having, but that there wasn't much of it left. When they reached the car she felt the gentle touch of Jack's hand in the small of her back. It was so soft a touch and yet that's all it took. Once they were in the car he reached across and kissed her, and under the forceful softness of his lips she felt the strength of their desire and the joy of this unleashed passion burst right through her.

The moment was intoxicating, but in no time she was feeling its sting. Sophie had managed to lose herself for only a few seconds before she felt herself turning numb. *He's married.* She knew she had to pull away. She hadn't been at all surprised by his kiss and yet it rendered her incapable of even a sound. An excruciating silence followed. This had become so real and she had no idea what to do. She couldn't bring herself to say anything for fear of it being the wrong thing, or even worse, being told something she didn't want to hear. But she assumed he wouldn't be going down this path unless there were problems, serious problems, with his marriage, and he wouldn't be going down it with her unless he'd developed some really strong feelings for her.

It's Jack, he's one of the good guys, isn't he? Everyone knows that, she tried to convince herself. *But what if they've all been wrong?'*

He finally broke the silence. 'Is it inconceivable?' he asked. 'Us?'

'No, of course not,' she replied gently, moved by his self-doubt.

In the weeks – months – that followed, they both struggled with the situation they'd created and the fact that they'd allowed themselves to create it. They were caught up in something that was harder to deal with than either of them had ever anticipated. They obviously cared deeply for one another, and maybe they really were falling in love. They'd certainly been walking a destructive path, but they hadn't been doing it lightly – perhaps just a little naively.

Eventually it would be over, but before then they would be again and more intimately drawn together.

ಸಾರ

My thoughts were disturbed by another information session, an announcement that the train would soon be stopping in Cook.

Cook was a virtual ghost town but remained an important town for the Indian Pacific because that's where it took on water, fuel and a change of crew. It also delivered the much-anticipated weekly supplies to the town's residents – all two of them.

Damn, I missed Watson and the start of the straight section of tracks. It was so easy to get caught up in thoughts of Sophie.

I moved as fast as I could up to the driver's compartment, and as soon as I saw the view from his window, isolation took on a whole new meaning.

Velvet Voice wasn't joking when he said Cook was one of Australia's most isolated towns. He'd said it was 1100 kilometres from

Adelaide, 1500 kilometres from Perth, and a bit more than a hundred kilometres from the Eyre Highway, which ran across the country just south of the railway line. From up here with the driver it wasn't hard to imagine how remote and lonely a town with only two residents must feel.

The driver himself was a jovial-looking man with a beer gut, gingery grey hair and a matching beard. His skin was tanned and deeply lined, his hands coarse and stained, and I was willing to bet he knew this train as well as a mother knows her child, and every inch of the tracks as well. As I arrived to join him, he was doing his best to educate a much younger man sitting alongside him, a man with a trainee badge pinned to his shirt.

'There was a time fifty-two of these settlements existed for the railway workers,' he said. 'They're all still marked on maps but Cook and Tarcoola are the only two that still exist. Back then they needed on-site maintenance crews – this was in the days of steam locomotives.'

'Geez, that's going back a while,' said the trainee.

'You're not wrong, son. Cook survived longer than most. It was really something back then, but the change to private ownership of the railway's infrastructure – now let me think, when was that?'

The trainee had no answer.

'Ah yes, it was back in the mid-1990s. That's when Cook experienced a massive change. It had been known as the Queen City of the Nullarbor up until then.'

'Yeah, I've heard that before.'

'Back then there was a population of around three hundred. Cook was full of character, and characters. They lived comfortably in those big bungalows – see them up ahead – and it survived well with a post office, general store, a school, locomotive workshop, airstrip, cemetery, swimming pool, a hospital –'

'Oh yeah, someone told me about a sign they have there, really funny it was. Can't remember what it said, though.'

'Our hospital needs your help. Get sick!'

'Ha, yeah, that was it!'

'Things were tough for a while there. Did you know they even had a golf course!'

'Fair dinkum?'

'Yeah, that's the truth. No grass though. Not a single blade! But as you know, the people who live in remote areas learn to adapt very quickly.'

It was incredible riding up in their cabin, seeing the country pass by from the front rather than the side. For one thing, this country is *so* vast. And the tracks – wow. Unflinchingly straight – one moment I'd be watching them disappear under us as we sped along, the next I followed them as they converged way ahead of us on the horizon. I'd been looking at those tracks for ages as we were getting closer to Cook and thought it's no wonder they call them sleepers. Watching them was making me drowsy. But I snapped out of it when the driver sounded the whistle. We were pulling into the station, and it was no Broken Hill. Suddenly that didn't seem so remote anymore.

The driver had been telling the trainee that Cook is the only place left on the Nullarbor where the train stops and passengers can get off to reacquaint themselves with the concept of walking on a surface that is blissfully still beneath their feet. Portable steps had been positioned exactly where each of the train's doors would open once the train stopped – clever! – and when passengers stepped from them they stepped immediately on the hard dusty ground that carpeted Cook as it did much of the Nullarbor. The station itself, once a welcome sign of civilisation, was instead bashful, hiding behind overgrown trees and offering little more than a bench seat for those whose brief visit to Cook wasn't brief enough.

I was out even before the train had completely stopped, and as I watched everyone else come down those steps it was clear that the most memorable characters left in town – and there were gazillions of them – were the flies. Everyone was doing the great Aussie salute the moment they disembarked. They were even getting to me. Ugh. Up until now I'd been enjoying passing through solid stuff – not having to wait for doors to open – but it also meant solid stuff could pass through me. I know flies are only small, but it was the weirdest feeling. They were driving me nuts. *At least everyone else has hands to swat them with.* And just like that my thoughts were back with Sophie. It occurred to me that there might have been times – back on our bushwalk for one – when I irritated her every bit as much as these flies were irritating me, and everyone else out here.

What a confronting thought. I felt ashamed. I only ever wanted the best for her, but maybe she didn't see it that way.

Despite the flies, Cook was an interesting stop – and probably my only opportunity to explore such an isolated, strange little town. But we were soon on our way again, leaving Cook behind with its cheerful everlasting daisies, bluebush scrub, and flies, and I was back with the driver.

'How far are we here from the Great Australian Bight?' the trainee asked.

'About a hundred kilometres.'

'Cool. Wish we could see it.'

'Son, it's spectacular. The Plain ends abruptly with limestone cliffs that plunge straight down – a hundred metres in some places – and the white waters of the Bight are savage. You would've seen pictures, surely.'

'Yeah, but it's not the same.'

I knew what he meant. This, perhaps more than anything else, was something I also wanted to see. And I would see it, in not much more than a week. I couldn't wait.

We crossed over the border into Western Australia, and while I can't say I'd seen any evidence of a bend in the tracks, we were about to reach the western end of the record-holding stretch of straight railway track, and the western boundary of the Nullarbor Plain itself. This also meant we'd passed by Cocklebiddy, and I tried to picture the divers as they made their way from who knows where to what I imagined was yet another isolated, small and strange outback town.

So that's how I spent Friday afternoon. Watching the tracks and lost in thought as a landscape of blurry Australian green continued to be sucked under the train. It was only once the sun began to sink low enough for me to catch a blinding glimpse of it – before the driver drew the shade – that I became aware how easy it is to be hypnotised by these wide-open spaces. Trees had returned to the picture and were illuminated by the late afternoon light, capturing and displaying it so beautifully, their long shadows creating a picture postcard. Sophie and I had been to many art exhibitions and galleries in Sydney, and there were times I'd look at paintings by some of Australia's better known painters and assume that the passing of time and a lack of care had allowed the colours to fade. Either that or the artists simply hadn't got it right in the first place. But the more I saw of this country the better I understood how incredibly skilled those painters were, how their eyes could really see and their souls could truly identify with the spirit of the land. It was a gift.

※

I wanted to join Jim and Clare for dinner, hoping to hear the end of their story, so I left the driver's cabin. I wondered if I'd find the Kiwis with my salt and pepper couple again, and sure enough, there they were. But all they seemed to want to talk about was Cook, and the flies. *Come on guys, you can do better.*

Then just as I was about to give up and leave to do some more train surfing – it would be my last chance tonight – their drinks came along and they made a toast to their time on the Indian Pacific.

'So, Jim,' David began. 'You were about to tell us last night how you and Clare came to be here, riding the Indian Pacific. There seemed more to it than simply the realisation of a retirement dream.'

'Ah yes, that's right. We've never told anyone this – well, except for family – but it's a most interesting story. We're here because of a doll.'

'A doll?' Julie looked puzzled.

'Yes. As I mentioned last night, Clare and I ran a shop – I dealt with the books, Clare sold old toys. But when we retired we sold a lot of our stock.'

'We would like to have kept so much more than we did, you understand,' said Clare. 'Or at least passed some things down to our children and grandchildren. But they didn't want them. The young ones today – their interests lie in books they read from a screen and toys that don't come with an ancient musty aroma! Go on, dear.'

'Clare had come across this small carved wooden doll, long ago,' Jim continued. 'It was as old a doll as either of us had ever seen. Its clothes were intricately embroidered, but unfortunately they were also badly tattered and its face was very shabby.'

'It was so pretty, though,' said Clare.

'Yes, it would have been beautiful once. But this is the interesting thing. It also appeared to have had a severed head, as there was a clear cut through its neck where a strong glue had been applied.'

'I had to have it,' said Clare. 'It wasn't cheap. I had to pay around eight hundred dollars, which was a lot back then for a doll, but being in the business it wasn't all that surprising. This little doll had been exquisitely crafted, and her age alone – they said she was from the Tudor period – made her something of a mystery. You go on, Jim, dear.'

'Well, in the process of reducing the volume of our personal collection, and thinking ahead to our years in retirement, Clare had decided this was one doll she could part with, and so, along with boxloads of other once-loved toys and precious editions, I contacted a reputable auctioneer. We were both staggered when they told us this doll could bring up to twenty thousand dollars, and then they said they were giving it a reserve price of fifteen.'

Julie and David looked as surprised as I was.

'But blow me down, if I hadn't heard it for myself, I wouldn't have believed it when they rang and told me how much the doll had actually sold for. Apparently this little doll was one of only two such dolls that were known to still exist, and despite its damaged condition –'

'In fact because of it,' Clare interjected.

'Yes, *because* of its specific damage – the severed head – it was an extremely precious item. Some English collector with a passion for the history of the monarchy had paid forty-six thousand dollars for it. The doll, it was believed, had belonged to a very young Henry VIII. Can you believe that?!'

'*We* couldn't believe it,' Clare said. 'And so we booked ourselves a ride on the Indian Pacific! It's our fiftieth wedding anniversary next month, and we've always wanted to do this trip but never had the time, or the money.'

Like their dinner companions, I was gobsmacked by their story and so happy for them. Too often the good things in life pass right by those who can seem most deserving – those who quietly let their lives unfold, accepting the good with the bad. But not always. And as they continued their 'Goldrush Dinner' we were only hours from Kalgoorlie, which made this story perfectly appropriate.

I was looking forward to wandering around Kalgoorlie – an after-dinner visit was to be the last of the off-train tours. Velvet Voice had told us that it was known as the 'Queen of the Golden Mile', that it was the heart of the gold mining industry in Australia's West and had lost little of the atmosphere it held in those gold-rush days. Prostitution, he'd said, continued to be accepted as part of the town's unique atmosphere.

The promise of seeing some of Kalgoorlie's famous 'ladies of the night' outside the many beautiful old pubs that lined the town's wide streets was all that many on the train needed to keep them waiting up, no matter how late it was. But it wasn't to be. Again. This time there'd been a problem with refuelling, the train was late arriving in Kalgoorlie and the tour was aborted.

If nothing else, this trip had taught me that things don't always go as they should, and even the best planned adventures will have their setbacks. I'd only thought about the good stuff before I left Sophie, and of course no-one tells you that tours don't always happen the way they're meant to, but apparently this wasn't so unusual. It's a big country to cross and a lot can happen over a few days to delay things. We'd been unlucky missing out on two of the off-train tours, but that's the way it was. It was almost midnight before they knew whether or not the tour would go ahead, and by then a lot of passengers had given up and gone to bed. But it was our last night on the train, and that's how I was going to spend it. On the train, surfing under the night skies!

Saturday

At around five this morning I made my way back to the lounge car. I was alone except for the quiet shuffle of staff preparing for the final leg of the journey. We'd crossed a substantial part of the nation's stark interior, and I'm sure I wasn't the only one who was feeling pleased with myself for doing so. We were only a few hundred kilometres out of Perth, travelling through rural country as the sun woke with a stretch and a yawn above the horizon. It was the most peaceful and perfect backdrop to what I could feel was going to be an exciting day.

The last meal on board, like all the meals these past few days, was aptly named. The Avon Valley Breakfast was served as the train passed through Northam, a little town at the heart of this picturesque valley. *Wow, I thought as I saw two brightly coloured balloons float by in the distant sky. It looks fantastic up there. Maybe one day Sophie will give that a go.*

Sophie again. No matter how many new things I was distracted by, I was still thinking about her, and wondered if I'd ever be able to stop. But maybe I didn't want to, not really.

Good morning passengers.

Ah, these interruptions always helped. It was Vince again. Velvet Voice of the Indian Pacific, coming through loud and clear.

> I hope you enjoyed your last night on board and are looking forward to your arrival in Perth. We have just passed through Northam, the last major town before Western Australia's capital city. Many of you may know not know this, but Perth is Australia's most remote city and long regarded one of the most isolated cities in the world. In fact, our Asian neighbours up in Singapore are closer than our fellow Aussies over in Sydney.

I'd never been to Perth with Sophie, so would've been happy to look around a little when we arrived, but today was Saturday, the day Clinton West would be leaving to cross the Nullarbor, and I had to find him for my return trip.

ಬಿಀ

It was a big day for Sophie, too – the day of her school reunion. It had been on her mind for the last several weeks, but until last night when she'd received a call from an old school friend, her thoughts hadn't extended too far beyond the organisational side of it all. Sophie and Jane had spent many entertaining hours together back in the days when they sat side by side playing oboe in the school's orchestra, but Jane had all the talent and had gone on to make music her life.

'Hello, Sophie speaking.'

'Hi Sophie, it's Jane, from high school!'

'Hey Jane, what a nice surprise! How've you been?'

'Really good. It's been a while!'

'Yeah, twenty-one-and-a-bit years!'

'I wanted to let you know that I'll be at the reunion. Sorry I've left it so late, but I wasn't sure what was happening with our schedule.'

'That's okay, it's great you can come.'

'How many are going?'

'Almost seventy.'

'That must be about half the year. That's not bad.'

'Yeah, considering there were only about thirty when the RSVP date kicked over.'

'So I'm not the only one who's pretty slack with that sort of thing!' Jane said. 'Look, I can't talk now, but we'll catch up tomorrow night.'

'Yeah, great, see ya!'

'Oh hey, Soph, are you still there?'

'Yeah, still here.'

'Why twenty-one-and-a-bit?'

'You know our year group! It should've been twenty, but it was already twenty when the idea of having a reunion first occurred to anyone, and it's taken this long for it all to come together.'

'Why am I not surprised! Better go. See you tomorrow night.'

Sophie was starting to look forward to the night, despite her long-standing reservations about reunions. Her old friend Kelly was coming up from Wollongong and staying with her overnight. *I hope this peculiar feeling goes away before tonight*, she thought. She didn't feel sick, just not quite right. Maybe it was a few nerves about the reunion and being among her old year group again. But she'd also noticed that Georgia had been really quiet since the bushwalk the other weekend. *Maybe she's sulking*, Sophie wondered. *Or maybe she meant it when she said she'd go to the Nullarbor without me. It's weird, whatever it is. Nice, but weird.*

ಸಂಚಾ

The train pulled into Perth around 9.30am, after one last information session and with everyone ready to find their land legs again.

> Ladies and gentlemen, we are almost at the end of our four thousand, three hundred and fifty-two kilometre journey from Sydney to Perth, but I want to let you know about one final off-train tour – and this one will definitely be going ahead. For those of you who are staying tonight in a hotel, you will probably find that your rooms won't be ready for you. Anticipating this, we have lined up a city tour, which will help fill in a couple of hours while you're waiting for your rooms, should you choose to join us. The coaches are waiting at the station and will show you many of Perth's attractions. My personal favourite would have to be Kings Park, many hundreds of hectares of spectacular native parkland with wonderful views across to the city …

Yes! This, I knew, was the ticket I needed. With a little luck (okay, a lot, but it was all I had) I'd be able to spot Clinton's blue Kombi somewhere along the way.

I'd only ever heard good things about Perth, despite tales of one or two business tycoons who made names for themselves decades earlier through not altogether admirable activities, and if first impressions were anything to go by, I had to agree. Lots of water, most notably the Swan River, parks at every turn, and gardens that were so well cared for, bursting with gorgeous seasonal flowers. It was clearly an affluent city with lots of development going on. I wondered if it would be able to stay so nice and uncluttered. Sydney hadn't.

I wanted to take it all in but had to keep my eyes out for my ride. When we were about half an hour into the tour and making our way through the streets of Perth's laid-back CBD, I saw it – a sky-blue Kombi about to pass through a crossroads a few blocks ahead of us. It could be my ride, and if it was, I needed to act fast, something I'd become unaccustomed to doing over the last few days. This was important though, and fortunately the time I lost while we'd been stopped at lights was time I was able to make up while the Kombi was also stopped at lights, and its driver was clearly a cruisy kind of guy, in no hurry to speed off when the lights turned green.

But all that energy was wasted. When we caught up to it and I left the coach, I could see its number plate wasn't the one I was after. Bum. I decided to stay with that Kombi for a while though, as it made its way through the shopping district and down to the Swan River, which was a hub of weekend activity. The Swan Bells Tower that had been pointed out to us earlier on the tour sat on the edge of town – it was striking and looked ready to lift off into the endless blue sky, and I wondered whether I'd have more chance of spotting Clinton West's Kombi if I made my way to the top. I had to think of something, because the driver I was with had stopped down by the ferry terminal and parked his van, then just stayed there, staring out at the river.

But I had to keep moving, so I found another car that was headed back towards the centre of town. I was really liking Perth with its old colonial buildings, so carefully and lovingly restored, edging on to the streets. I was trying to see as much as I could but I was getting more and more anxious about finding Clinton's van, and then the car I'd jumped into pulled up in front of a shopping arcade that branched off one of the main city thoroughfares. Three teenage girls hopped out of the back, leaving the driver – a woman – with a young boy in the front passenger seat. I was getting so restless. Although it was Saturday morning and busy in the streets of Perth, it was nothing like the busy Sydney would be if I was there, and I was sure I could find Clinton's Kombi if I didn't have to keep stopping like this. The trouble was, I felt as though too much time was slipping away. As this woman was about to pull back into the traffic I heard the sound of a siren fast approaching, and so as she hesitated to let it pass, I jumped, right on to the roof of a fire truck as it sped through Hay Street, passing what would've been many interesting landmarks were I not seeing them in a frenzied blur.

The fire truck was heading towards the WACA when I saw it – another blue Kombi. *Please don't be the same one I caught a ride with earlier.* It was pulling out of a service station, and a quick glance at the number plate was enough for me to know for sure – this was my ride. Yay! With all the will I could muster, I jumped from the fire truck, eased myself through the driver's open window, passed above the tanned arm that rested on its sill and through the smoke that wafted from the cigarette he held between his fingers, and settled myself in for the ride. I was here at last, with Clinton West, and we were off.

He was a curiously nice-looking man – not handsome in the golden age of Hollywood way, or a male model kind of way, more in a good-looking but aged Aussie surfer sort of way. A greying beard framed the lower portion of his tanned face, making it hard to say how old he might be – beards could add years to a man – but I put him in his mid-fifties. His hair, once blond I assumed, was greying like his beard and yet it hinted of a sun-bleached youth.

Something I knew almost immediately – I was going to enjoy the soundtrack to this road trip. Clinton's collection of chipped cassette covers – *cassettes!* – with their faded labels, had been haphazardly thrown together in a box and left on the front passenger seat. They suggested a man who was a child of the post-war era – a baby boomer with a taste for rock and roll, and right now he was playing Van Morrison, one of Sophie's and my favourites. I wanted to think of a name for Clinton's van – after all it was, along with Clinton, to be my closest companion for these next couple of weeks. And right then, as 'Here Comes the Night' boomed loudly through the speakers, it came to me. I'd call this big blue van of Clinton's 'Morrie', in honour of Van the Man. *Perfect. Our first song together and there could be no more uplifting music on a road trip.*

I made myself comfortable and took a few moments to look properly at this man. I thought the lines around his eyes might've been evidence of someone who had enjoyed life, but to see him as I was seeing him now, alone and deep in thought, they also spoke of something much harder to pinpoint.

But there'd be plenty of time to get to know Clinton over the next couple of weeks, and as we headed out of Perth I noticed we were going south. It was only when I caught sight of a surfboard in the back of Morrie that this made sense. We'd be following the coast.

I told myself Sophie would be doing fine back at home. I'd found my ride, Clinton had the music up loud, and I was on the road. Life was good.

෩෩

It was around the middle of the day and our first stop was Busselton. Clinton pulled up a short walk from the jetty at Geographe Bay, took the key from the ignition and headed towards the town centre to buy himself some lunch. I stayed behind because the jetty had grabbed my attention – more so than a milk bar was going to. It was incredible, and beautiful. It stretched so far out into the bay, and according to the sign we'd parked in front of, it was the longest wooden jetty in the southern hemisphere, reaching out almost two kilometres. I bet it was one of the most photographed, too, with those four quaint little blue houses hugging one another at land's edge.

Clinton had only been gone a few minutes when I saw him returning from the shops and was able, for the first time, to take a good look at him – how he held himself, his gait, the kind of things it was impossible to determine when he was behind the driver's wheel.

He walked with a casual but distinct confidence and I wondered if, as a younger man, he might've been a little too sure of himself. I was glad to have struck him at this later stage of his life. Most people take themselves a whole lot less seriously as they get older. Men, in particular, tend to mellow into more likeable human beings. I'd often wondered why so many of them felt they needed to impress people when they were younger. It's such a turn-off.

When Clinton reached the van, he pulled his camera from its case beside the box of cassettes, spilling a bundle of papers beneath it at the same time, and took it, along with the bottle of Coke and sandwich he'd bought, to the jetty. I was going to go with him, but as the papers shifted on the front seat I noticed a list of names – names of people expected at Cocklebiddy for the dive a few days from now. And that's when I saw it – Jack Murphy. He *was* still diving. Fantastic! It was a few years since he and Sophie last saw each other, so it would be great seeing him again.

I'd already been feeling the excitement and anticipation of what lay ahead, but knowing Jack was going to be at Cocklebiddy made me feel even more so. I left the van and followed Clinton along the jetty. There must've been hundreds of pylons stretching out to forever, and I tried to imagine what it was like below the surface of these blue–green waters. The water looked so calm, but the sign had said the pylons created an ideal home for the abundance of sea life down there, and had I not been afraid of the ocean, beautiful though it may be, I would've gone in for a look. My water phobia had to be about that detour I took almost forty years ago, the one that ended my chance at a normal life.

As I was catching up with Clinton, I was thinking about Sophie and Jack. I'd been so sad for Sophie that the two of them hadn't worked out. Timing could be everything sometimes. And of course other commitments, in their case his. But it was a beautiful day out over the ocean, and for the first time since I'd decided to leave Sophie and come on this trip I felt completely relaxed. And very pleased with myself! The sea breeze was blowing gently and I was able to drift along with it until I reached Clinton. As soon as I did, I realised how curious I'd become about this man in just a few short hours. People were always interesting to observe. Some, however, could be intoxicating. And as I looked at those lines around Clinton's eyes it came to me. They were thoughtful eyes, etched with a deep sadness though, just like Celia's.

I was so lost in thought as I followed Clinton along the jetty that I hadn't realised we'd got to the end and turned back, and so was startled when I heard the door of his van open and saw him returning his camera to the front seat.

෨෬

It was mid-afternoon by the time Clinton started up Morrie and drove out of Busselton, but he didn't go far. I'd imagined we might drive into the night, but I'd been forgetting something. Clinton was a surfer, and we were approaching the Margaret River region where some of the world's best surf can be found, especially at this time of year. There'd be none of this once we left the coast to join the Eyre Highway, so he'd want to make the most of it while he could. Surfers were like that. Sophie's first great love had been a surfer, which is how I came to learn a little about what makes these guys tick. I'd sit there with Sophie, watching him and others like him, lost in their hypnotic trances as they sat on their boards, bobbing up and down on the water, waiting for a wave. To them, the lure of the ocean was as powerful as the surf could be. I was sure it was something inherent – a connection with one of the greatest forces of nature. I never quite got it, but had put that down to my fear of water.

Sophie's first great love had also been her first great mistake, and it was a first for me, too. It was the first time I really understood how little help I could be to her. I had tried, really tried, but perhaps a broken heart is something everyone has to work through in their own way, and their own time. Being with Sophie as she lived through it all, the good and the bad, made me realise I'd never have that. Some things never bothered me – like missing out on a normal school life, or friends – because I felt like I had all that, with Sophie.

But finding someone to love, like having a family, was different. So too was Sophie's love life. I had to admit though, this first time, I'd still been learning …

A definite and weird tension had been building between them one night soon after they'd met, and after a moment's quiet, he spoke with a softness that made everything inside her turn to marshmallow.

'Did you feel that?' he asked.

'Yeah, I felt it.'

Something had passed through the air between them – and it wasn't me. I wasn't sure what it had been, but they were both savouring the moment and it was the first time I'd really wanted to know what something was like, to have something all my own. But I was never going to have that. Maybe I was jealous, but I didn't want to be. I wanted Sophie to be happy. And she was, but it wasn't forever.

They were still young but had been together over a year when she was at the beach with her friend Kelly and saw him arrive with someone else. Another girl. Together. Sophie stopped mid-sentence, looking both hurt and puzzled, and then he saw her. He simply shrugged, then turned away.

'Bastard,' Sophie whispered under her breath.

'What?' Kelly replied.

'Look over there.'

'Oh shit, the bastard.'

'That's what I said. Can we go?'

That was it for Sophie. She didn't want to see him again, or even talk to him, which was easy because he never called again after that. A bastard *and* a coward. She'd been so upset for so long, and I'd wanted to help her through it when I could see how heartbroken she was. She was my sister, and when she was hurting it was like I was hurting. But it was Celia who helped pick up the shattered pieces of Sophie's heart back then. Celia was there for Sophie in a way I could never be, and I was glad for that, glad Sophie had someone. But at the same time it had felt like I didn't belong anywhere.

Ugh. It's impossible not to think about Sophie so much. I've been with her forever and it's weird not having her with me. I'm trying to convince myself I don't need her, and I have to keep reminding myself how annoying I'd become, that this trip was what *I* wanted. It *should* be easy to think about all sorts of things now I'm not in Sophie's head. It wasn't.

While I'd been reliving Sophie's first real heartbreak, Clinton was driving towards Gracetown and I started to pay more attention to the world outside the van. *I need to stop getting so distracted.* This section of coastline is stunning. We passed so many beaches between Cape Naturaliste and Cape Leeuwin, with their huge swells rolling in from the Indian Ocean. So many surfers out there, too. To a non-surfer like me it looked spectacular, not to mention spectacularly frightening and dangerous – and no place for the faint-hearted. Surfers are a different breed though, especially the experienced ones. For them, the awesome size and staggering power of the surf is as magnetic as it is hypnotic. I'd heard that these waves crash consistently on to the reefs and beaches around here, luring surfers from all over the world, and a few photographers at the same time.

Views worthy of captured moments were there in every direction, and when Clinton pulled up high on a headland and we had time to soak it all in, I was mesmerised. It was a place of incredible contrast, from cliffs to reefs to white sandy beaches. Fierce winds were blowing directly off the sea, and huge fragments of granite boulders had crumbled into the sea over many years. But at the same time there were wide and gentle slopes covered in shrubs and grassy heath, and masses of wildflowers rolled slowly towards the coast.

We were here for the night, on this remote, rugged coastline. I couldn't have been happier, and as I glanced across at Clinton I thought I'd see a face that was feeling the same. But he had a faraway look in his eyes. It was like he was worlds away, somewhere intensely private, and I hoped he was okay.

We were both brought suddenly back to the here and now when Clinton's phone rang. It took him a moment to find it. I watched as he stretched behind him into the cabin of his van and dug it out from beneath an old beach towel that spilled sand all over the place when it was disturbed.

'Clinton West,' he said. 'Yep. Yeah mate, I'm well, how about you? Margaret River. Left Perth this morning. Yep. Yep. Yeah, it's been ages. No worries, I'll be there in time for Wednesday night's briefing.'

Then a longer silence, before a distinct change in his tone.

'I'm okay. No really, I'm doing okay. It's been almost five years, can you believe it? Sometimes it seems like I saw her only yesterday but other times I try to picture her and, those finer details, you know, it feels like they're slipping away. I don't want to lose her like that. It's bad enough she's not here. Yeah, I know. Listen, we'll talk more in a few days. Thanks, mate. Bye.'

It was the first time since I'd joined him earlier in the day that I'd heard Clinton's voice, and it was somehow reassuring. Although he hadn't said anything earth-shattering, there was a lot of love in his voice. A lot of pain, too. I watched as he tossed the phone back behind him, closed his eyes and leaned his head back hard. He was hurting, but I suspected he never let too many people know how much.

I knew I'd have to wait until we arrived in Cocklebiddy, when he met up with whoever it was he'd just been speaking to, before I'd learn any more. I also knew that was going to make the next few days seem excruciatingly long, but there was nothing I could do, nothing except stay with him. Times like this I wished I was like everyone else, able to offer some kind of comfort. But then if I was like everyone else I wouldn't be here, and before Clinton allowed himself to be swallowed up in grief, he turned the key and headed down to the beach where he grabbed his surfboard from the back of the van and took those familiar steps towards the foaming waters where I suspected he'd find solace.

I was happy to watch him surf for a while, because it had been such a big day. I also wanted to watch the sun set. It was a strange thing for me, the idea of seeing it go down over the ocean instead of coming up. But as it was being pulled towards the horizon that gripped Australia's west coast, Clinton returned to the van with his board and did what any photographer would do when presented with a sample of Mother Nature's finest work. He pulled out his camera and started shooting.

And in the silence of the moments as day turned to dusk, the only sounds to be heard were two of my most favourite – the crashing of the waves and the release of the shutter – both sounding their best when all else is still. I became lost, unexpectedly, as I thought about Clinton – a man I barely knew but one who had already touched my heart.

༺༻

Kelly arrived from Wollongong with not much more time than allowed her to dump her things, quickly change and put on her make-up, then stop in at Celia's to say a quick hello. It had been a cold day in Sydney, overcast and gloomy, and as she and Celia were talking, the rain started falling heavily.

Kelly was tall and thin and was wearing a brightly coloured kaftan under a knee-length coat. She had sandals on her feet. Not great in the rain. Her hair, which she dyed a deep auburn colour, was short. She looked fantastic. Sophie was in jeans and boots, with a long floral shirt hanging under a beige coloured jumper. She had a scarf around her neck. The rain was getting heavier, and Sophie wondered if they should leave quickly before it got any worse or wait a few minutes to see if it would get any better.

'We'd better go,' she interrupted.

'Okay, have a good night,' her mum said. 'Bye, Kelly. Nice to see you.'

'Bye, Celia,' Kelly said as she kissed Sophie's mum on the cheek.

'And drive carefully,' Celia called out as they were making a dash for the car.

Sophie had been looking at her mum as she and Kelly were talking. Celia looked much as she always had – a little more grey hair, a few more kilos, but not a lot had changed about her over the years since she'd retired. She worried way too much, but that was the way she was made, and Sophie knew it was never going to be any different.

'Yeah, yeah, I always do,' Sophie called back.

'No, I mean it. It's not what *you* do I'm worried about, it's what the others on the road might do.'

As Sophie turned on the ignition, the words her mum had just called out – the words she always said to her when she was heading out in the car – echoed in her mind. *Drive carefully.*

ಸಿಂಚ

Sophie's reunion was tonight, and I knew Kelly was coming up from Wollongong and staying over. I sometimes wondered if Sophie and I would've been as close as the two of them were. They'd been friends for almost thirty years – really close friends for most of that time. Even after Kelly married and had kids, she and her husband always made Sophie feel like she was part of their family. They could've been sisters, they were that close.

Kelly was always able to make Sophie laugh, and I loved that. It was always fun hanging around when the two of them were together. Sometimes though it just hurt. I loved that Kelly cared so much about Sophie. But it should've been me. I could've made her laugh, too, and I certainly cared about her. Just as much. More even.

Right then, as I was watching Clinton recover from a sad reminder of his past, and picturing Sophie leaving for her reunion, I felt a sudden bolt of something pass through me, and as it did I finally realised what was at the core of Sophie's being. It was her concern for Celia. How did I not see that? How could it take just a short drive with a complete stranger to open my eyes to what had been in front of me all these years? For so long I hadn't understood the very thing that made Sophie who she was. Now I was beginning to.

Sophie and Kelly didn't have far to go – just a couple of suburbs away to the pub they'd frequented back in the days when they were all still living near to where they'd grown up and been educated – but it was a bleak night and Sophie felt relieved once she'd parked the car. Getting from the street into the pub was their next hurdle, but they took advantage of a slight break in the downpour and dashed across the road to the shelter of the night's venue.

'Just as well it's our twenty-one-and-a-bit-year reunion and not just our five,' Kelly said.

'Why's that?' Sophie asked as they made it inside and shook the rain off them as best they could.

'Heels!' she laughed. 'Remember how high we were wearing them back then? God it was awful!'

It was true. A lot had changed over the years, not least of all a desire to be comfortable rather than have a well-defined calf muscle and a little added height. But they would see how much had really changed in a few minutes when they walked into the private room that had been set aside for them that night. As Sophie and Kelly made their way along the corridor towards that room, Sophie's eye caught someone else's just inside the main bar. It was the man with the broad-brimmed hat and dark glasses, the one who never made eye contact when she saw him out walking with his black Lab. He was sitting on a bar stool, facing in her direction. At least she thought it was him. It was a little hard to be sure, as he didn't have his dog with him, and this time she could see his eyes. They were nice eyes too, she thought as they met hers for an all-too-brief moment. Soft and dreamy. They seemed to sparkle, which surprised her when she thought of how he did such a good job of hiding them most of the time. But she was sure it was him. It *is* him, she realised as he got off the stool. *Shit, he's coming over.* But then he took the drink a mate had brought over to him and they walked off. *Definitely him,* but it was all so quick. The moment was over in a heartbeat and forgotten in another as the girls walked into a room that Sophie swore was full of strangers.

Kelly grabbed her name tag from the desk at the door and was off to mingle without hesitation. Not Sophie. She stood there for a few moments, trying to find a place for herself among these people as she had done relatively effortlessly all those years ago. It was hard not to stare, but in that she was not alone – there was a lot of staring going on during the evening.

Shit – who are all these men? I'm sure I'd remember if I'd spent six years of my life with them. No, these guys have to be the fathers of the boys I knew!

It was a thought that stayed with her for much of the night as she greeted and was greeted by a roomful of people as though they were long-lost friends, which of course some of them were. Most of the women, she thought, looked much the same as she remembered, although in all fairness to the blokes, bottles of hair dye, lots of make-up and dim lighting could have all been working in their favour. But the guys. They could do little to cover their expanding waistlines and balding heads – and there were a lot of those.

Her thoughts were interrupted when someone cupped their hands over her eyes from behind. Sophie pulled them off and turned around.

'Jane!'

The two girls squealed, hugged and then both spoke at the same time.

'Next little lamb to the slaughter!' That was all it took – they were sixteen again. Their oboe teacher used to say that each week as one of their lessons was coming to an end and the other was about to begin.

'How have you been?' Jane asked once they'd stopped laughing.

'Really good, how about you? Tell me about the orchestra. And your parents. How are they?'

Sophie had never been all that comfortable talking about herself, and so it was a tactic she often used when it came to conversations – she'd answer the question about herself briefly, then ask one or two of her own.

They talked for a while about Jane's life as part of a professional orchestra, and all the travelling it entailed, then Sophie asked Jane if she'd just arrived.

'Yeah, just been here long enough to wonder who a lot of these people are.'

'Me too,' said Sophie.

But as the night wore on, some strange process of metamorphosis had been happening, and the faces that Sophie once knew finally began to emerge on these imposters. The overall package may have changed – physical change was inevitable – but the essence of these people was formed way back then, and in a sense they remained the same young people she once knew. All any of them had been doing in the ensuing years had been adding layers, creating characters whose slant on life had developed enormously, but the core of their being remained reassuringly familiar.

'Let's go mingle,' Jane said, and in no time they'd both been pulled into separate clusters of nostalgia.

'Kate! Sam! Wow, great to see you. I think the last time was –' she paused while she tried to remember – 'would've been English, with Mrs Freeman. Geez, was there *anything* that woman didn't know.'

'One of the few good ones,' Sam concurred. 'Made me want to be a writer.'

'And succeeded, from what I've heard and read over the years. Good for you. And you two – still together I see!'

Sam and Kate hadn't been the only two from their year group who had ended up together. There had been one other couple. Sadly though, there had also been two deaths – one from a childhood illness that he never fully recovered from and another in a car accident – and tonight those old schoolmates were remembered warmly during speeches made an hour or so into the evening. But the sombre mood during those speeches didn't last long.

'Hey Soph!' Another hug from someone's dad. *Oh no, who's this?* Sophie hoped it would come to her quickly because he clearly remembered her.

He sensed her vagueness. 'Music class. Mr Clark. The piano –'

'Ross! Hi!' How he'd changed from the small boy who, with his mate Andre, had pulled off one of the funniest stunts Sophie had ever been witness to at school.

'Are Andre and Nick here?' The three boys had been inseparable at school, mucking up at any opportunity. Nick had been the ringleader.

'Andre's over there,' he pointed. 'Nick –'

'Don't tell me, he's in jail!'

'Yeah, he is.'

'You're kidding me? I wasn't serious. *Really?* He's in *jail*? What did he do?'

'Didn't you see it on the news? It was huge.'

Sophie looked vague.

'He'd been living in country Queensland with his old man, this is a year or so ago. There'd been a sign on their front gate that read "Trespassers will be shot. Survivors will be prosecuted." Didn't stop the cops!' Ross laughed. 'They'd been growing dope in epic proportions for years, and finally got busted. Cops reckoned that even after the clean-up there was more weed left lying on the ground than they'd ever found in any of the big busts.'

Sophie's surprise was not so much that Nick's life had turned out the way it had, but how her own had been so relatively uneventful. *Not such a bad thing all the time,* she thought.

'We all knew he was going to end up either in jail or dead, right?' Ross was still talking. 'What a wasted life.'

'Glad he didn't drag you down with him.'

'Yeah, me too. Come on.'

Ross led Sophie across to a group where Andre, ever the ladies' man, was with some of their old classmates. All drinking, all laughing, all having a good time.

'Hey, hi guys! Ross just reminded me of that music lesson when he and Andre wheeled the piano out of the room without Mr Clark noticing.'

'You what?' Charlene said. 'No way!'

'I remember that,' said Gill. 'Well done, boys!'

'How come I never heard about that?' Charlene asked. 'How did you do it?'

Ross told the story as the others who were there remembered the mucking up they used to do in that poor teacher's class.

'I don't know how we all kept a straight face,' Gill said.

'You were probably thinking about the shitload of trouble you were going to get into,' said Ivett.

'And we did. But we'd had worse, it was no big deal. I think Mr Clark had been embarrassed that he hadn't noticed, and didn't want the other staff to know, so it was kept quiet. He wasn't such a bad dude. How about you Soph – still doing your Kate Bush impersonations?'

'You remember?'

'How could anyone forget!'

Just then, the Beatles' 'Twist and Shout' came blaring across the room and before Sophie knew it, her old mate Stu had appeared, taking her hand in his.

'What are you doing?'

'Dance with me, Soph.'

'I can't dance!' she laughed.

'Neither can I, but who cares?'

Who cares indeed, Sophie thought. There was a time she would never have danced, not in front of all her old schoolmates, but tonight she almost felt like a completely different person. A more liberated one.

So it was a fun night, a lot more so than Sophie expected, but then she knew that at the settled age of thirty-nine she was up for it. Fifteen, even ten years ago, there was no way she could have been talked in to going – too many insecurities and too little faith in people's ability and willingness to accept others as they find them. She wasn't completely sure they did now. She just didn't care anymore.

෩෨

It was around 2am when the girls arrived back at Sophie's place. Once the pub had booted them out, a few of them had moved on to Rachel's house for coffee before calling it a night. And when their heads hit their respective pillows they were both swarming with thoughts of the hours just spent.

'Hey, Kel – twenty years just passed us by in a few hours. Weird, huh?'

'Yeah, but it was great fun. And hey, how about you? I saw you dancing. You never dance!'

'Well there you go – something must have come over me.'

'Stu came over you! He always liked you.'

'He always liked everyone,' Sophie laughed.

'True. Hey, who was that guy in the pub when we arrived? He seemed to know you.'

'No idea,' she responded. Over the years Sophie had kept pretty quiet about a lot of things, especially any love interests, until they were somehow cemented in reality. 'You know, I'd never thought about it before tonight, but these people we almost never see – the kids we were at school with – they've probably helped build the foundations of our lives.'

'Get real, Soph!'

'No, I mean it.'

'Well I hope you're wrong. The thought that Nick might have had anything to do with how I've turned out is a thought I'd rather not have.'

'Well no, okay, not him – not all of them. But the ones we spent time with. And our teachers. I reckon they've helped create the framework we've needed to become who we've ultimately become.'

'Maybe you're right, Soph, but that's way too deep for me.'

Sophie was quiet for a moment, then said goodnight.

'Not so fast,' said Kelly. 'You haven't told me if you enjoyed it – you looked like you did, but I know you were a bit hesitant about going at one stage.'

'Yeah, I did. I'm glad you talked me into it. But I'm not sorry I didn't go to the last one. Ten years out of school, I couldn't have handled seeing everyone pulling out their phones or their wallets. They're like display cabinets for photos of their other halves and their kids. And they would've all asked to see mine and thought what a loser I was when I didn't have anything to show them.'

'Oh, Soph.'

'I would've hated every minute, and gone home feeling worse than I did before I went.'

'So what made tonight different?'

'I don't know. Maybe it's acceptance – I've grown to love my life, regardless of the things I don't have. And maybe it's because I'm learning that a lot of that stuff doesn't matter. No, that's not right – of course it matters, but it's not necessarily for everyone.'

'Did you notice that for all the talk of happy marriages, gifted children, exotic holidays and fancy houses, darker stories were beginning to emerge?'

'Yeah, I did.'

'Separations and divorces, problem teenagers, crippling mortgages, ageing parents. It's not all a bed of roses. I reckon there'd be plenty of them who'd love to be single and childless again.'

'Maybe.'

'You might not have what a lot of us have, Soph, but you don't have the bad stuff either. And there's a lot you *do* have. It's just different.'

As the girls drifted off, Sophie thought back to her old school days, and how Kelly had been such a constant through the years. She treasured their friendship. But friends like that were a precious few. When they were all younger, they had the time to get to know their friends so well. As children they didn't hold much back, if anything. Their main focus every day would have been having fun, hanging out with their friends. Back in primary school, study wasn't something anyone was terribly committed to, although that time would come soon enough. And then once they became adults there was another complete shift in their priorities, when they worked not to make friends but to earn a living – at least that's what most people seem to be driven by, by necessity as much as desire. Perhaps they don't take the time – don't *have* the time – to spend on friendships like they did when they were kids.

Sophie hoped that, more than any of her old school friends, Kelly would be the exception. But it's impossible to know. Friendships can fall apart, and sometimes as easily as they come together. Old friendships can shatter without warning, while the thread that connects the newer ones can somehow withstand greater pressures. Humans are such complex creatures, and friendships – any relationships – are curious things.

These connections, however, aren't generally the result of a few hours spent catching up at a reunion or two over the years. They're the result of untold and precious ties. Sophie and Kelly had been there for each other since their school days. They'd supported one another through the good times and the bad. Tonight they'd snatched a glimpse into the lives of many familiar and now almost middle-aged faces at the reunion, and they might have thought they'd caught up with all that had been happening for these old friends in the passing years, but if getting older had taught Sophie anything, it was that the faces people present to the public can often bear little resemblance to the lives going on beneath that veneer, and that even the most precious of friendships might not be forever. Time can change so many things.

'Are you still awake, Kel?'

Nothing. *Good,* Sophie thought. 'Georgia, are you there?'

Nothing from her, either.

'Georgia,' Sophie whispered a little louder.

Still nothing.

Maybe that's it. Maybe that's why I'm feeling a little off-colour, dizzy even, in a good way. I can't believe I danced! And that I had such a great night. Maybe Georgia has *gone away.*

❧☙

Life. It was a lesson I thought I might only now be starting to learn much about myself. I looked around me – it was dark outside except for the warm glow of the moon over the Indian Ocean. Clinton had climbed into the back of the van, pulled a blanket over him and gone to sleep. I felt strangely at peace again. It had been quite a day. There was a lot I didn't know about this man, but he seemed to be one of the good guys.

Sunday

Clinton's scream ripped through the still midnight hour, sending a chill right through me that I sensed would stay with me forever. He was saying her name, Wendy, over and over, hugging his pillow tight as he struggled to contain his sobbing.

It must've been a nightmare, and the kind of nightmare that disturbs a man's sleep so violently doesn't just go away when the sun rises. I wanted desperately to comfort him, this man who was now sitting bolt upright, dripping with sweat and weeping uncontrollably. 'Why did you have to die, Wendy?' he whispered. 'I miss you so much.' But I couldn't do anything. I was helpless. Useless. And I knew, if in a single scream I could feel the effects of this woman's death so strongly – a woman I didn't even know – he must be living with an unimaginable sadness.

Clinton didn't get back to sleep. I wondered if he woke from nightmares every night or whether the earlier call had set off memories that, most of the time, he was able to keep at a more comforting distance. Wendy must've been his other half, but how she might've died I had no idea.

In the dark of the night, death seemed to be consuming me. I couldn't shake it from my thoughts. Sophie was in her thirties before the impact of our own father's death seemed to hit her the hardest. She'd had this fear that one of our older brothers might die at thirty-six, like our dad had. But no-one did. It was an irrational fear, she knew that, but it was real. She'd even mentioned it to Celia after that and was surprised to learn she'd had the same thoughts about all three of her children.

Even I'd felt it, which was weird because I, of all people, knew death was nothing to be afraid of. Not if it's anything like mine. Seems to me that most of the difficulty is in dying, not death itself, and mine had been a lot of fun, at least to begin with.

I wanted to tell Sophie, tell everyone, that death is a peaceful thing, and that the hardest part about it is the effect it has on those left behind.

They just need to remember the love, because that's what will carry them through.

What happened to me all those years ago was really strange, but I was an anomaly. I don't know when my time will be up, but for everyone else the transition is immediate. All that remains, and it's no small thing, is that love.

In a sense I was glad my family wasn't also scarred by the knowledge of a child lost in utero, but I also wished more than anything they'd known *something* of me, and that Sophie would take me more seriously. I knew all about them. It didn't seem right they had no idea about me.

Sophie's always had a bit of a preoccupation with death. She puts it down to our dad, but I've always hoped that maybe there's some part of her – some obscure little part, perhaps – that remembers me, and not just that I can be an annoying voice in her head. I wish I could work that one out. I've tried. I'm comfortable with death. It's my constant companion, my life, strangely enough. And for Sophie, death has been a part of her life for as long as she can remember, but she's never had to endure the sadness of the death of someone really close to her, as both our parents had done, as Clinton has obviously done. She didn't know any of our grandparents, and she was too young to remember anything of our father. For so long she's been one of those people who think you can't miss something you never knew, and in that, she's always felt blessed.

And yet strange as it may seem, because we're both dead, I've always missed our dad too. Heaps. I never saw him after he died. I don't see anyone once they've died. I think my afterlife is different because of the twin thing. Maybe the inner voice Sophie hears – me – happens for all survivors of multiple births, if one or more doesn't make it. I don't know.

When Sophie was younger, I'd seen her looking with envy at how close some of her friends were to their dads, and she'd get inwardly angry when others spoke badly of theirs. I always felt that way when I saw *any* two people who were so close not getting along. They don't see how transient life is, how futile it is to waste irreplaceable moments. They'll get to the end and wonder what it was all for, so they might as well make the most of it while they can. I wish I'd survived to help Sophie through the hard times, to really be there for her, as a normal sister would be. She would've been there for me, too.

I spent a lot of time over the years thinking about what Sophie's life might've been like if I'd survived. I also thought about how different *our* lives might've been if Robert had lived longer. I've tried to imagine us being a family of six, rather than the four they became. The entire family dynamics would have been so different. Life would've been so different. Sophie and I would've had so much fun, I know it. Twins always do.

∞⋈

It was still a few hours until sunrise, and the darkness of the night was suffocating my thoughts. Death. I started to think about the many ways a person can draw his or her final breath. My own path had been quite exciting. It just ended badly. But what about those poor souls who die without anyone, their bodies found days, even weeks, after they've died – by an unsuspecting neighbour who starts to notice a horrible smell, or a stack of local papers around the letterbox. They die alone, but once they're found they stir the conscience in so many sad and guilty souls. Their deaths become so public, and everyone struggles to come to terms with how it could've happened, how these people could have had no-one. But then so do the deaths of those whose lives are deliberately taken by someone with a reason that so few of us can begin to make sense of, or for no reason at all.

Death has such far-reaching effects. Any death. It might be dignified and peaceful, drawn out and painful, sudden and unexpected or calculated and heinous, but the effects are enormous. The end of a life that has given and received love touches so many, and each death has a way of making people stop and think. And reflect. It's a chance to consider the things that really matter. But it so often comes too late.

As I looked again at Clinton, I couldn't imagine that anyone would reach the end of his or her life – even middle age – and not have been touched by a death that was too close.

∞⋈

Sophie made herself a cup of tea, grabbed a book, and went outside with Cujo. Celia was already out there, reading the paper.

'Hi, Mum. What's news?'

'Hello, darling. Nothing. It's only ever ads and rubbish in Sunday's paper. I don't know why I still bother getting it.'

'The TV Guide!'

'Yes, I suppose that's it. Kelly left early.' Celia sounded surprised. 'She came and said goodbye on her way out, said it was a great night. Did you enjoy it?'

Sophie laughed. 'It's not like Kelly to get such an early start! She had some family thing on at lunch time so had to get going. But yeah, it was good, much better than I expected it to be –'

'But?' Celia looked into her daughter's tired eyes, a puzzled expression on her face.

'But when I think about the whole reunion thing, it's just so weird.'

'In what way?'

'Well, I barely knew many of the people from my year group, but we all had such a good time, reliving the past for a few hours.'

'But that sounds good.'

'And that's what I find so hard to get my head around. So many of them never gave me the time of day at school, nor me them. So why is it we're compelled to greet one another all these years later with smiles and hugs as though we've been wanting to see each other for ages? If we had been, surely we would have. *I* would have.'

'I don't know, darling. Maybe that's why I've never gone to any of mine. I never settled in at school, or made any lasting friendships once we moved to Sydney.'

'Yeah, but your situation was different. Your mum had just died, you were uprooted from the country to the city – your life had been turned upside down.'

They were both silent for a moment. 'I don't know,' Sophie continued. 'Do you think it was our teenage insecurities that stopped us from getting closer to each other back then, or our learned insincerity that makes us try to now.'

Celia rubbed Cujo's tummy. 'Oh, Soph. It's probably a bit of both, but we all change throughout our lives, mostly for the better, I hope. You wouldn't have wanted them all to snub you at the reunion, would you?'

'No, of course not, but most of them were like strangers, at least at first. Everyone was so nice, and made the effort to find out how life had been in the years since we left school, but – I don't know – what's the point, really? And how much can we genuinely learn about anyone in a situation like that? Not much, I don't think.'

'Try not to overthink it all, darling. You had a good night, that's the main thing. We're all here for the long haul, so we might as well make the most of it while we can.'

Sophie drank her tea. *Mum's right. I shouldn't go looking for a point or meaning for it all. She told me years ago that we're simply here to do our best for ourselves and each other, and to give and find great experiences. And it* was *a great night. Making more of it than that is a waste of time.*

Celia looked down.

'Is Cujo alright?'

'Yeah, I think so. Why?'

'He seems a bit listless.'

'Maybe you're right.' Hearing his name, Cujo had got up and moved from Celia to Sophie, his tail wagging.

'I think he's okay! We might go for a walk. Do you want to come?'

'Love to.'

Sophie attached Cujo's lead, grabbed a bag, and they headed out.

'So tell me, who was there that I would know?'

'Hmmm. Oh, Jane came! Remember, from orchestra?'

'Yes, of course I remember Jane. What's she up to these days?'

'She plays professionally, lives in London and travels the world.'

'And she came just for the reunion?'

'Nah, it was just good timing. They had an unexpected break so she came down to see her parents. A few came from interstate and overseas – don't know that I would've done that. I have to admit I didn't think Noomi and Jodie would pull it all off as well as they did. It was a great turnout,' Sophie conceded. 'Oh hey, do you remember Stu Croft?'

'I do. He was always so nice and polite when he came over. I'm sure he had a thing for you. He seemed to be here all the time!'

Sophie laughed. 'Yeah, well he went. Funny you say that because Kelly said the same thing last night. I thought he was coming over because you fed him so well! He was such a big goofy sweetheart then and he still is! We danced!'

'You didn't! Good for you! I suppose he's married?'

'I did! And yes, he is.'

'Sophie! You never dance!'

'I know, I surprised myself! He just asked. Actually he didn't even ask, just grabbed me and the next thing I knew – I'm no dancer, but then neither is Stu!'

'Good for you. What a pity he's married! I hope you didn't tread on his toes!

'Ha! I did, but he stepped on mine, too. You know, I'd looked out my old school uniform a few days ago and was reading what everyone had written on it on our last day. Maybe that was it. The things he wrote – he really did seem to like me back then.'

'Well *I* knew that.'

'So how come I never saw it? Oops, nature calls!'

Sophie waited for Cujo to do what he had to do, then picked it up and tied the bag.

'Watch this, Mum.'

Sophie handed the bag to Cujo, who gripped its ears in his teeth.

Celia wasn't sure whether to laugh or be disgusted. 'When did you teach him to do that?'

'I didn't. It was just the way he looked at me a couple of weeks ago when we were out walking. I knew he was telling me he wanted to carry what I was carrying, so I gave it to him. Just like now. He took it and carried it. Neat, huh!'

'I wonder how long before he realises what it is he's carrying!'

'I don't know, but it's nice not to have to carry it myself. It catches peop–'

'Great trick!' someone yelled from a passing car.

'See what I mean – it catches people's attention!

∞◊

When the sun came up on another day in Margaret River, it brought with it no hint of the darkness from the night before. Clinton hadn't been able to find peace through sleep after his nightmare, but things never seem so bad, nor people so alone, by the light of day. He pulled Morrie's door open and swung his legs out the side. Sitting up, he stretched and took a deep breath before reaching behind him for a can opener and a tin of pineapple. It was hard to tell which he was enjoying more – the sweetness of the fruit or the crash of the waves pounding the shore – but the waves won. I watched as they lured him in. Those waves were there to be ridden. The pineapple could wait.

I was about to follow him when I caught a glimpse of a book in the back of Morrie. It was called *Abandoned*, and on the cover was a photograph of a rusted, broken-down old truck in the middle of the desert – nothing else around for miles. Below the title it read 'Photographs by Clinton West'. *Ooh, he's been published. How exciting!*

So again I was distracted by the inside of Clinton's sleeping quarters. I hadn't looked beyond his front seat back in Busselton yesterday, nor since then, but this was Clinton's home, so everything he owned was probably right here in front of me. There hadn't been much up the front – his cassettes and lots of camera stuff, a pair of thongs on the floor and, stuffed into the compartment inside the front passenger door, more maps than I'd ever seen outside of the Gedup'n'go office.

But in the back – what a mess! He had a mattress, a couple of pillows and an old blanket, about eight tins of pineapple, a pair of jeans, a sweatshirt, an old pair of runners and a broken plastic clothesbasket full of what appeared to be the rest of the man's entire wardrobe, as well as a small bag of toiletries. There was also more reading material – a couple of photography magazines, a book on cave diving, and the notebook I'd seen him scribble in once or twice. Of course the surfboard and towel he'd taken with him would usually be there too, but that looked to be it. He seemed to be a man to whom material possessions meant little, and maybe this had become even more so since Wendy's death. That stuff didn't matter, I had to agree. How many people would love the kind of freedom Clinton has. As long as he isn't hurting anyone, and is able to support himself, the world is his. And then I caught a glimpse of a photo in Clinton's wallet, which was lying open beside his mattress.

It was an old Polaroid – the colours faded by time and distorted by the chemicals used to create instant photos when those cameras were all the rage in the 1970s. Scribbled in barely legible handwriting at the bottom was what looked like 'Pasta Point, 1984'. *He was still using an Instamatic in the mid-1980s?* The photo showed a young Clinton West, clowning around with a girl a little way out in the surf. She was wearing a bikini, had long blonde hair and was sitting on a surfboard – maybe he was teaching her how to ride. They were both laughing and I could tell they belonged together, despite the dodgy image. The girl had to be Wendy – the photo had captured a generous smile and it made me ache for Clinton's loss. I bet she was a free spirit, like him. I looked at the photo for a minute longer, beginning to understand how part of him must have died the moment she did.

Unexpectedly, I was enjoying the solitude and found myself once again thinking of Sophie. I'd always thought of myself as a far more outgoing and social creature than she was – or I would've been – but even so I was feeling good in my own company and the thoughts it allowed me to lose myself in. *She's starting to make more sense to me.* For so long I wished for a different life for Sophie, one that gave her all the things I thought she wanted. But I was starting to realise that maybe they were things *I* wanted – things I'd missed out on – because what she wanted most was love, and I'd never been able to orchestrate that one for her. I was thinking, too, how different Clinton's life might've been if Wendy had still been alive. Maybe that's what he sometimes thought about too, out there riding the waves.

After a while I made my way down to the beach. I felt like being with Clinton as he surfed. I thought about how, if I let myself go *right* in, it might wash away all these thoughts of death I've been swamped in, but the ocean is such a powerful force and I couldn't bring myself to go in the water. Being out there though, *over* the ocean, just me and Clinton and the pounding surf, that was awesome. Every last sad and sleepy sensation I'd been cradling was now wide awake and, if I'd been slowly gearing up for the new day back there in Morrie, I was now in top gear. I even felt, for the first time, what it must be like for surfers – what pulled them towards the drama of this offshore world and let them focus on nothing but catching that next wave. Out there it was possible to forget everything else that was happening in your life, to escape the everyday, much like people do when they're on holidays and don't turn on the TV or buy the paper. Air surfing! I loved it!

The day was still young when I followed Clinton back to the van where he dried himself off and pulled on his jeans, and I couldn't help noticing he was in pretty good shape for a man his age, whatever that was! He finished his can of pineapple, tossed the empty tin in a plastic shopping bag that was hanging from a hook over the front passenger window, and started up the engine. Clinton's Kombi may have been converted into a four-wheel-drive, but it hadn't lost that distinctive coughing and spluttering sound of a VW.

ಬಂಡ

It was today when the extraordinary beauty of this part of the country – this little bump off the south-western corner of Australia – really came to life for me. We left Gracetown, continuing south through the Margaret River region. *Sophie would love it here.* She's always been strangely drawn to wine country. It doesn't matter where it is. In vineyards she sees a peaceful and ordered charm that she likes to imagine going on forever.

I'd heard a lot about this area, and read a lot over Sophie's shoulder, too. And not just the vineyards. But here I was seeing it for myself, and I thought that what made it unique were its contrasts. We'd come from the rugged coastline, where massive swells constantly pounded the shore, and yet unspoilt beaches lay sedately by. Where impressive karri and jarrah forests, some with trees as tall as a skyscraper, stood guard over sleepy pastures and rolling vineyards. Not too many people lived along this scenic stretch – the Limestone Coast – but it had a wild and exotic beauty.

Even along the most unlikely stretches of road I was learning to expect the unexpected. Clinton hadn't travelled far. We were a few kilometres beyond the township of Margaret River itself when he noticed, up ahead on the road, something that made him slow down. It was a moment or two before I could make out what it was. All I could see at first was a big blur – some kind of animal about to cross the road – but by the time he'd grabbed his camera and inched a little closer I saw it was an emu, with something else trailing along behind it.

Oh my goodness, I gasped. *How gorgeous.* Stumbling along behind the emu were three chicks. They weren't small by normal bird standards, but by emu standards they were tiny – except for their feet, which were huge. Their fur was still striped, so they couldn't have been more than about three months old, and how incredibly soft they looked. I wanted to be able to reach out and hold one of them. But even if I could have, it would've been out of the question. That was some consolation. Clinton stopped the van and shut Morrie's engine – far enough away so as not to frighten the emus, but close enough that, with the monster lens he attached to his camera in lightning speed, he'd be able to capture every tiny detail of the magic moment we were both witnessing.

The parent – it had to be their dad because he looks after the little ones – was strolling towards an open field off to the right, where I caught sight of an enormous kangaroo pounding off into the distant trees. I was busting to get out and go for a ride, but all too quickly he was gone.

'Take your time, guys,' Clinton whispered. 'That's it, nice and slow.'

I could see that I expressed my enthusiasm very differently to Clinton, and once I calmed myself, I realised that after his few softly spoken words, everything was so quiet. There was just one sound – the sound of his shutter as he pressed to release it time and time again. How lucky we were that there was no passing traffic while this was going on. Still too early for most people.

I would've been happy if we'd ended the trip right there and then. It was such a precious and unexpected moment. But instead, after the feathered family had safely made it to the far side of the road and was disappearing into the distance, something else caught Clinton's eye.

I followed his gaze and saw it for myself. It was a little blue wren, a male, sitting on a fence post by the side of the road. I'd never seen one before, only in pictures. They were my most favourite bird. Well, second favourite now I'd seen the baby emus. Against the bright green pastures – clearly there'd been no drought over this side of the country – his coat was dazzling. An intensely vivid, almost electric blue, he was flitting about from post to post as Clinton sat patiently and quietly, again taking photographs. I, on the other hand, was feeling an overwhelming urge to play. I often thought it would be neat to come back in my next life as a bird. *If I have a next life that is. Maybe I've been lucky getting to share this one with Sophie, and Clinton.* I couldn't contain my excitement any longer and, knowing Clinton wasn't about to drive off in a hurry, I was out of the van and ready to fly.

I wondered if he knew I was there, this beautiful bird. I tried to get him to move closer to Clinton, but I was powerless. Then he flitted over towards Morrie. I was having so much fun. These birds are all over the place. They never stay still for more than a couple of seconds. *Uh, there he goes!* When I glanced again at Clinton I saw, behind his camera, a look of pure joy on his face. Right there, sitting on his rear-vision mirror, was the little wren. I didn't dare move while he was there, but he didn't stay long. Maybe just long enough for Clinton to take a few photos and for me to feel I'd witnessed something incredible. *What a morning!*

Back on the road we passed the turn-off to Prevelly Beach, where the mouth of the Margaret River opens to the Indian Ocean, and to a non-surfer like me the waves look super scary. Whether our next stop had anything to do with his work or whether Clinton was there purely for his own meditation I don't know, but once he'd pulled up in the Leeuwin–Naturaliste National Park, on a cliff-top overlooking Contos Beach, he grabbed his notebook. At the top of the page he wrote the date and a brief record of what he'd seen. *Maybe for captions.* I knew from Sophie's time at Gedup'n'go that the photographers needed to supply captions with all their work.

Sunday 10/6
Contos

- beautiful, sensuously curved beach
- distant ocean deep sophisticated blue, striking contrast to playful pale blue sky above – matches Wendy's eyes
- water reaching forward in giant curve to powdery white sand clinging to shore.
- Colour of water at shore – exquisite. Gemstone? Not turquoise, but close
- Luminous
- Blanket of heath covering massive limestone cliff like well-worn glove
- sweeping view

Then he put his notebook aside and we both stopped to soak it all in. It was, as he'd written, a sweeping view. And a beautiful one. But when I glanced across at my driver I noticed that although he was staring straight ahead, it was into a world that I suspected was far removed from the one in front of us. I remembered last night, and thought how strange, irrational fears can catch up with people when they least expect them, but so too do moments like these – moments of great calm.

As I had come to expect, Clinton didn't stay transfixed in that moment for too long. Out came his camera and off he went, making his way across the limestone and granite outcrops that punctuated the ground cover like blisters. Although the vegetation was mostly green, I was bouncing around some gorgeous coastal wildflowers, ones that would turn a lot of this area into a blaze of colour a little later in the year. They looked nice but they didn't have any perfume. All I could smell was the ocean.

I was enjoying all these little side trips with Clinton. When he wasn't driving, surfing, taking photographs or deep in thought, he was out walking, and he kept a cracking pace. I loved it.

As Clinton returned to Morrie, I was in two minds about leaving. I was disappointed, because the views all around us were fantastic, but I was excited about where we might be going next.

༄༅༅

We passed Boranup Forest on our way down to Augusta. These forests in the south-west are awesome – it's impossible not to be humbled by trees that have been around so much longer than we have and will be here long after we've gone. They made me wonder again about my own death – my second death, I suppose. And Sophie's. Celia's too. No-one knows what's going to take them in the end, and that's a good thing. I wonder what it will be for these trees? Not a chainsaw I hope. But how boring, being such a majestic tree. Out here with almost nothing but the weather to keep you entertained. Sure, people come along from time to time and think you're amazing, but is that enough? I'm glad I'm not a tree. But then I stopped to look at them some more, and tried to imagine them differently.

I tried to picture them in the early hours of the morning, or as day turns to night – the shadows they cast must be incredible. And I tried to imagine an atmospheric haze wafting through them, or a mist, creating the most intricate shadows and bathing them in such a mysterious light you'd wonder who held such a wondrous paintbrush. But I couldn't do it. I couldn't picture that, maybe because I don't like forests. They make me feel strangely claustrophobic and fearful of all I can't see. It's a bit like being underwater. I prefer wide open spaces – the ones that make Australia the largely unpopulated place that it is. Sophie is the same – I'm beginning to think that maybe I'm more like her than I ever realised.

I was happy we didn't stop to pass some time in Boranup, especially as the unblemished skies of earlier in the day had been taken over by clouds that were threatening to rain down hard at any moment. I wondered if this was typical of the weather down here. This stretch of coastline is, after all, exposed to the full force of whatever Mother Nature feels like thrashing at it, and it didn't develop its rugged, wind-swept profile all by itself.

Clinton's next stop was in Augusta, when he left Morrie and went for some lunch. I went with him.

'A hamburger with the lot, thanks mate, and a chocolate milkshake.'

This man's diet left a lot to be desired, although for a man on his own, on the road, it wasn't surprising.

'Coming up.' The man behind the counter glanced across at a young girl sitting in the corner of the cafe. 'Will you get off that damn phone and make this nice man a chocolate milkshake, for God's sake?' He scowled at the girl. 'Kids today, I give up sometimes.'

'She yours?' Clinton asked.

'No, she's her mother's.'

'*Da-aad.*'

'Well get yourself over here and do some work for a change.'

Clinton winked at the girl as she put her phone in her pocket and got up from her seat. She responded with an apprehensive smile.

'Looks like a storm coming through,' Clinton said as the man made his hamburger.

'Sure does. Where're you headed?'

'Down to Cape Leeuwin, to the lighthouse.'

'It'll be wild down there, but spectacular on a day like this.'

'Just what I'm after.'

'Yeah? Why's that?'

'I'm a photographer. The wilder the better!'

The young girl's ears pricked up. She straightened her blouse and flicked her hair. She thought she was about to be discovered!

Clinton found a seat in the cafe and ate his lunch. *Poor girl*, he thought. *Stuck here in a greasy cafe with her old man when probably all she wants to do is get out there with her friends and enjoy life.* In the background a local radio station crackled songs of love and despair. *That music doesn't help.*

Before the young girl had a chance to quiz Clinton about whether he did any fashion photography, or knew someone who did, he was back on the road. And if I'd thought what I'd seen earlier was wild and remote, I had to begin measuring on a whole new scale. We reached the lighthouse, standing tall at the end of a long and narrow peninsula and surrounded by a low-lying granite outcrop, storm clouds above looking increasingly ferocious. It was hard to imagine this place under anything but threatening skies, and it seemed fitting to see it like this, but no doubt it has its good days. And when it does, you wouldn't have to move to be able to watch the sun rise over one ocean and set over another, because right here was where the choppy waters of the Indian and Southern oceans merged.

There were a few tourists around, all braving the blustery winds and making their way from the car park to the lighthouse. I went with Clinton, but it was wild out there, which made it harder for me than moving had ever been. If I lost my concentration, I'd be blown way across the ocean.

But I made it, and went with him to the top of the lighthouse. Once we'd stopped spiralling, however, Clinton stepped outside again. I followed him. The view was incredible – stark and hostile, but worth it. Looking south there was no way of knowing where one ocean ended and the other began – where they met was one ferocious mass – and to the east and west there again wasn't a whole lot to distinguish these two bodies of water. But I did feel a sense of wonderment being up there, and that same wonderment was on Clinton's face as he started shooting. These oceans have been here, pounding the shore, since the beginning of time. That's even longer than those trees in the forest.

The view behind us was every bit as awesome. Apart from a few cottages and the car park, what we gazed down on looked unnervingly treacherous. It was all stunted vegetation and more lethal looking rocks.

But looking at places from so high up is fantastic. Only the birds get to see it like this most of the time. *Maybe I'll do some more flying of my own, once we're somewhere calmer.*

Photos taken, Clinton was on his way back down when he stopped suddenly on the narrow, winding stairs. In that instant, everything was still. Whoever else might've been going up or down also stopped, as intrigued and captivated as he was. Out of nowhere someone had started to sing. She had an extraordinary voice, and was singing a song Clinton knew – 'Amazing Grace' was a song everybody knew. *Wow, I've never heard it sound like that, or sung in a place like this.*

It was several moments after the last note had been sung before anyone moved a muscle, and when they did it was the sound of applause that replaced the silence. I looked at Clinton and saw moisture in the corner of his eye.

We passed the woman who'd been singing on our way out – she'd attracted a small crowd. Her voice had been like an angel's, and she seemed to have touched Clinton like only an angel could.

'Thanks for the song,' he said. 'It was beautiful.'

'My pleasure. I never hesitate if I'm in a lighthouse. The acoustics are fantastic.'

'My wife used to sing that one – it was one of her favourites. Never in a lighthouse though.'

And at that we were on our way.

ಸಿಡ

It was already dark as we approached Albany. There'd been only a few spots of rain during the afternoon and the wind had died right down not far east of Cape Leeuwin. This corner of the country seemed to be one national park after another. Mother Nature at her best. Old-growth karri trees dominated the landscape around Pemberton, and birdsong greeted passing travellers who were willing to turn off the air-conditioning, turn down the sound system and wind down the window. The raucous and unmistakable laugh of the kookaburras, the sweet twittering of fairy wrens. I felt like I was passing through the pages of a fairytale.

Pemberton looked deliciously cosy. A timber town filled with timber houses whose residents would be burning warm and crackling open fires on these cold winter nights. My imagination was doing all the work, as Clinton didn't stop here. Nor did he stop further in Denmark, but the town looked every bit as alluring – if not more so – with deer farms added to the already enticing picture. We'd passed a turn-off to Peaceful Bay and I thought how lovely that detour might have been. When you've passed signs to beaches with names like the Boneyard and Suicides, like we did back in Margaret River, the name Peaceful Bay has a safe and mellow ring to it.

Middleton Beach, where Morrie, Clinton and I were to spend the night, was a few kilometres from Albany's centre. It would be morning before I saw much of this place, but Middleton had to be one of the city's more popular beaches. I imagined aqua waters would sparkle by day here as they lapped the shore, but now, at night, they were glowing eerily under fluorescent green light that shone not from the moon above but from floodlights that lit the trees on the shore. It was blatantly artificial, but a pretty sight. I was tired. Clinton had wandered off with his towel and a change of clothes and returned a while later with a bottle of Coke and some fish and chips that he ate on the beach before returning to the van, reading for a while and then calling it a day.

Monday

There's a path that winds its way from Middleton Beach up and around the headland and all the way into Albany, about five or six kilometres away. Albany is an old settlement, Western Australia's oldest, and it sits on a stretch of granite hills that overlook sleepy Princess Royal Harbour. Ahead of it, King George Sound glistens under the early morning sun. I would've gone for that walk even if Clinton hadn't. It made a great start to the day. This was the kind of life I dreamed of for Sophie, but she seemed okay just reading about these places, or hearing about them from someone else. She always felt that so much of the joy of travel came from sharing it with someone, someone who would soak it all in and then relive it with her in years to come. For her it was that or nothing. She was a hopeless romantic – one with a spirit of adventure that remained largely unexplored because she had no soul mate and she wouldn't go it alone.

ఎరెపె

The dismal weather had returned to Sydney. It was, once again, cold and wet – the kind of weather that could soon become depressing in its greyness. It was also the week Peggy was away, and Sophie would be spending much of the week at Gedup'n'go, but not today.

As she organised herself for another day's work at home, Sophie paused to soak in the wonder of the changing seasons, never more evident than now. Directly in front of her as she looked out her front window was a magnificent nyssa that grew in her mum's backyard. In the many years she'd been working so much from home, it hadn't just been her walks with Cujo that allowed Sophie to appreciate the four seasons and the individual beauty that came with each of them.

This one, huge tree, with its branches sweeping gracefully outwards and extending well beyond the window's frame, was so often a welcome diversion for Sophie's tired eyes. Tiny lime-coloured buds would develop through the spring into a healthy luscious dress of a deeper summer green by year's end. By mid-May, virtually all that green had been replaced by spectacular autumn rusts, oranges and reds, which gradually – or quickly if there were strong winds – fell to the ground, leaving a blanket of bright red that turned to deep crimson as the life drained from the leaves. Quite a show.

Today the conical-shaped tree showed no sign of colour – almost no sign of life. There was not a leaf to be seen. But the elegant nyssa, its naked branches dripping with rain, was not at all coy about its state of winter undress. Its brittle skeleton was always such a stark contrast to the radiant coat it wore proudly throughout the rest of the year. *Perhaps*, Sophie thought, *it's enjoying the feeling of freedom before the demands of nurturing a new growth begin.* It was hard, though, to imagine any kind of enjoyment in being as exposed to the elements as it was today.

Sophie almost felt that she, too, was enjoying some kind of strange new freedom. She was feeling very much like something was missing – some part of her – but it felt good, its absence providing a strength she was ready to carry.

Through the soaking branches of the nyssa, Sophie could see her mum in the room across the yard, sewing not by the light of the sun that often drenched this favourite room of hers but by an electric light above her that erased the gloom from outside. *She looks so calm and content,* Sophie thought. *Just as she always does. I don't know how she does it. Nothing ever seems to rattle her.*

Celia had lost so much over the years, but she remained forever thankful for all she *did* have. She'd often tried to impress upon Sophie that the other stuff, the stuff that can seem overwhelming at times, isn't usually so important in the scheme of things, that maybe true contentment comes only once we learn to be grateful for all we have, rather than to be forever wanting more.

Sophie's thoughts were interrupted by the phone.

'Hi, Cath. Yeah, just working from home. Sure, no problem, I can be there within an hour.'

Bugger, Sophie thought. She didn't mind going in to Gedup'n'go, but on a day like today it was nice not to have to get properly dressed and go out. A couple of people had called in sick, Cath had said. One of them was in admin, and they could use the extra help.

A couple of hours after she'd arrived at Gedup'n'go, Cath came in to see her.

'Hi Sophie, thanks for coming in. Would you make a call for me please?'

'Sure.'

'It's to a guy called Terry James. He's coordinating the dive at Cocklebiddy. You mightn't get him straightaway, but keep trying.'

Sophie took the piece of paper Cath handed her as she sipped on her tea.

'Let him know that Jack Murphy can't get to the cave until Thursday morning,' Cath continued. 'Problems at home, and with his phone, apparently.'

'Jack Murphy?' Sophie almost choked on her tea.

'Yes, you know him?'

'Yeah, we worked together years ago. He's the guy who told me about the caves under the Nullarbor.'

So Jack *was* going to be at Cocklebiddy. *I wonder what the problems at home are*, she thought. *Hope it's not Charlie. Nah, he wouldn't be going to Cocklebiddy at all if something was wrong with Charlie.*

What a distraction. Sophie wasn't sure whether she wished she was out there or glad she wasn't. A while after she and Jack had first stopped seeing each other – intimately at least, because they still kept in touch – she sensed he still didn't know what he wanted. Knowing this, her own feelings of confusion – the ones she thought she'd managed to overcome – had returned. He'd been so determined it had to be over and yet he still seemed to be thinking about the possibilities.

But then he'd gone quiet again, and that's what she always found so infuriating about him – his silence. It was like a form of mental torture, and always left her feeling the kind of doubt that made her question so much about herself – what she wanted in life, how she would know whether a man was right for her if she were to stumble upon him some day and things seemed to fit, why she let herself get caught up in situations that were clearly so destructive. There were times she simply couldn't work Jack out, but she loved him, and had always tried not to make things more difficult than they already were, because she never wanted to waste a moment of the limited time they had together.

Sophie and Jack had known each other for so long before anything had happened between them, built a solid foundation that had become their friendship and would see them through to the end of their days whether they remained in touch or severed all ties. Difficult times were a part of life, and as far as Sophie could work out, bitterness and anger never solved anything. This is how Jack was – and what did she expect anyway? It was a doomed relationship from the start. He was married. What had she been thinking?

As Sophie tried to get through to Terry, she recalled their first time together. It was a few months after they'd been to hear the English duo, Sea of Hands. Their kiss that night had been followed by weeks of avoiding each other, avoiding the inevitable conversation and what it might lead to. But they could only avoid it so long.

Jack had asked her along to hear an Irish folk musician who was performing one Sunday afternoon that spring. The concert was in a converted warehouse in an uninspiring industrial area near the beach, on the Central Coast. A makeshift cafe sat alongside a space that was decked out with a number of mismatched and well-worn lounges and assorted chairs. It was a surprisingly cosy set-up and, as Jack had promised, the singer's voice was exquisite. They'd enjoyed the performance from the comfort and intimacy of a much-loved couch, his arm across her shoulder and her hand on his lap. It had been a couple of beautifully melodic hours.

'What shall we do now?' Sophie asked as they were leaving the warehouse. She'd thrown a blanket in the back of the car, thinking they might go for fish and chips and watch the sun set on the beach before heading home, but the blanket didn't touch the sand that evening.

'Let's go to your place,' he'd said.

Back at Sophie's they were enjoying a glass of red, listening to Eric Clapton, and as the sweet and powerful orchestral introduction to 'Layla' was building to a crescendo, the nervous excitement Sophie was feeling was becoming impossibly hard to contain. She knew what was about to happen – they both knew. She almost felt she was drowning in this new love and the untold anticipation of all that was to come. But she was also aware that the possibilities weren't endless, that it was likely to be a relationship with only stolen moments, and that she was embarking on a world of uncertainties. It was Jack, after all. It wasn't going to be straightforward.

Jack took her hand and led Sophie to her bedroom. Enormous calm mixed with unmeasured excitement overwhelmed her as she sat on the side of her bed, watching him undress. He let his clothes fall beside him and then lowered her down slowly, tenderly caressing her as he unzipped her jeans and unbuttoned her shirt. Jack was deftly stripping her of all her clothing with a well-practised ease and, to her relief, without her having to stifle even the slightest nervous giggle. Many beautifully delicious minutes passed before he reached it, but the last thing to come off was her scrunchie, and at the moment she felt him pulling it from her hair she also felt him slip gently and blissfully deep inside her.

And in those precious and silent moments afterwards, she recalled a few words William Hurt's character in *Kiss of the Spider Woman* had said – 'The nicest thing about feeling happy is that you think you'll never be unhappy again.'

As she thought about that now, while she was trying to get hold of Terry James, she knew how deceptive that feeling was, because it had only been a matter of time before the strength of their own deception had forced Sophie and Jack to rethink, seriously, what they'd started.

ഓൽ

It was only a couple of days since I'd joined Clinton in Perth, but I'd already grown to like him. *What's there not to like*? I felt safe with him, as I'd always felt with Sophie, which was not only weird – how could *I* come to any harm! It made me doubt the independence I was so convinced I possessed – or would've possessed, had I lived a normal life. *Maybe I do need someone. A security blanket, of sorts, like Linus has in* Peanuts. I tried to make a joke of it, because it was an unexpected admission, and one I didn't feel too good about.

There was something else I wasn't feeling too good about this morning. I felt as though my time was coming, and while I wasn't altogether sure what that meant, I knew it had something to do with Sophie – a strange reassurance that she was okay, which was good. Good for her anyway. For me it was a feeling I didn't want to have to accept. None of us likes to learn we're no longer needed. This trip was shaping up to be so much more than just an adventure for me. It was feeling like a lesson, and lessons are taught for a reason. I wasn't too blind, nor too stubborn, to understand this one.

I stayed a few steps behind Clinton as he walked around the headland at Albany, stopping with him from time to time as he photographed a lizard, or a wildflower, or the wide expanse of ocean. It was beautiful, but the lizards were boring around here. I wanted to see a Thorny Devil – they're the best – but they're desert creatures, not coastal. Or a gecko. They've got great feet. It was a stunner of a morning – looked like a sensational day lay ahead for anyone lucky enough to be outdoors enjoying it. But I was feeling despondent. What if Sophie doesn't need me? If she's better off without me?

After his walk, Clinton returned his camera to the van and went for a swim. The sun had only just come up when we'd set out, but a few other people had since emerged from wherever it was they'd spent the night, and were on the beach soaking in the view and the warmth of the sun, if not the water. Not many were in swimming. I saw a young mum making castles with her toddler in the sand, so went over to them. I tried as hard as I could to knock the sandcastle over, because I felt like I needed to kick something, but it was impossible. I was useless.

No more than about ten minutes could have passed when I saw Clinton walking back to Morrie. His swim had been brief, but his breakfast, a tin of pineapple, was even briefer. I'm sure *he* knew where he was going today, but for me it was another day and another unknown destination. I had to snap out of the mood I was in. *Think about what you're doing, Georgia. You're out here, make the most of it. Isn't that what you'd be telling Sophie?*

And I was right! As far as the travelling went, I was loving it all. It was the adventure I'd been hanging out for. The drive across the Nullarbor probably wouldn't hold any surprises – there's the Eyre Highway and, well, that's about it. But this first section from Perth was something I hadn't considered at all. Seeing so much of the south-west unfolding hour by hour, kilometre by kilometre, one surprise after another, was fantastic. And being with someone who knew what he was doing and where he was going was the best. It meant the whole experience was going to be as good as it could possibly be.

We weren't far out of Albany when Clinton turned off the main road and drove towards a secluded little spot called Two Peoples Bay. He must want to take more photos, because there seemed no reason for heading off the sealed road towards what was more than likely another obscure destination. But then I saw that obscure spot and I knew there were some places people should see, whether they had a reason to or not, and that the best time to see them was when no-one else was around.

It was hard to imagine even one person having ever set foot in this bay, let alone two. The sand looked like it had never known the weight of a footprint nor the blemish of a stray piece of seaweed. Dotting the shore were rocky outcrops of rust-coloured granite. More were nestled at the foot of the rolling green hills, keeping watch over this sublime haven. But the water. It looked purer than the sand and it sparkled more brilliantly than the sun. These colours were like paints squeezed straight from the tube – nothing had dulled their vibrancy and I didn't know how any photographer could do justice to the visual feast I was devouring, but I watched with great interest and enormous admiration as Clinton had a go.

It was only then I realised that although I'd seen Clinton taking photos these last few days, I hadn't been paying all that much attention. I did now. I watched his extraordinary patience at work, his determination to capture just the right shot. Here it was the frothy waters that were pushing boldly on to the beach, then retreating with a whimper. He seemed to be waiting for the exact moment when the patterns they left were at their most playful. And I saw how carefully he handled his camera. It wouldn't surprise me if he knew it as intimately as anything he'd ever held in his hand. This is his one great passion – his heart and soul are in every photo he takes. I didn't think I'd ever see him looking more content than he did right now. Two Peoples Bay seemed to be his nirvana.

We were there for maybe a couple of hours – it was an all too brief glimpse into another gem on Western Australia's south coast. There was a serene and tantalising beauty there, which left me in awe of the contrasts I'd seen in such a short distance. The exposed and treacherous Cape Leeuwin couldn't have been more different to the protected and blissful sanctuary of Two Peoples Bay. But as was so often the case when I found myself lost in a world made for dreamers, I was brought back to the moment with the familiar kicking over of Morrie's engine, breaking those precious sounds of silence. We were, once again, on our way.

The winding, hilly roads that had taken us out of Albany earlier today had given way to a very different, more pastoral landscape once Clinton rejoined the South Coast Highway. Vast areas of flatness took over as the Stirling Ranges disappeared behind us. We passed fields of canola, stretching towards forever. I'm sure I could hear their vibrant yellow residents singing in the breeze! They managed to clear away the last of the grumpiness I'd been feeling this morning. Yellow is such a happy colour – I love it. Beyond the fields we passed a huge dam where cows standing on the rim looked as though they'd been put there by children as if they were little plastic animals on a make-believe farm. Their coats of black, white and shades of brown made them look strangely cartoon-like against the rainbow blue of the sky. I was glad Clinton had seen them too, and had pulled over to the side of the road, because it was a lovely picture to devote a few minutes to.

The road from Albany to Esperance is almost five hundred kilometres, and apart from the occasional photo opportunity, as well as stopping for petrol and a bite to eat, Clinton didn't veer off the highway until we were almost there and the strong light of another day was slowly filtering and fading to dusk. It had been a long, largely silent day after we left Two Peoples Bay. The music was continuous, and from time to time Clinton would sing along, but I found myself deep in thought, as he was, for much of the journey. At times I couldn't help thinking of those familiar but increasingly annoying words uttered by children all over the world on trips with their parents – at first only half an hour from home and still with hours to go, and then with increasing regularity as the kilometres dragged on, and on. *Are we there yet?* And then I had to remind myself of the size of this country. It would be well over four thousand kilometres from Perth to Sydney, going along the Western Australian coast as we were, and we were still a long way from the start of the Eyre Highway which would take us across the Nullarbor. This, I had to convince myself, was only a short stretch. I had to get used to it, to surrender to it and to make the most of it, because I might never do it again, and we only get from life what we're willing to put in. Isn't that what I'd always told Sophie?

ఇఁర

The stretch of road that crawls along the coastline just west of Esperance is part of a circuit – The Grand Ocean Drive. It takes in Pink Lake, exquisite Twilight Bay and Picnic Cove, and it leaves travellers longing for more. I know this because Clinton did the circuit and I couldn't get enough.

I didn't know whether there was a specific job for which he was doing this part of the trip, or whether it was an opportunity for him to expand his personal photo library for a future that was yet to be determined. Cocklebiddy was, as far as I knew, the sole reason for his drive across the Nullarbor – at least that's all he was doing for Gedup'n'go – but this man was a photographer and, like surfers, they grab every opportunity they can to do what it is they're instinctively drawn to. He wasn't being disturbed by many phone calls, nor did he seem to be making any. He was at ease on his own, and content with the ever-present pull of nature.

I was enjoying a beautifully calm end to what had been a blissfully mellow day. Transparent, pale aquamarine waters kissed the granite outcrops that were such a distinct presence along the ocean's edge. They looked so pretty as they blended into a much deeper, denser blue on their way out to meet the dozens of islands across on the archipelago. From there, they simply vanished over the horizon. But as we were coming into the town of Esperance, I saw a few dolphins making the most of the balmy conditions just offshore. *They know how to have a good time.* I'd always dreamed of playing with dolphins and wondered if Clinton might be stopping here – if this might be my opportunity.

Yes! Morrie came to a stop along the Esplanade. Clinton sat quietly for a while, looking out along Tanker Jetty where fishermen had dropped their lines and countless other people were strolling up and down its length. They'd stop from time to time to watch the antics of the seals that were swimming close by, hoping to catch discarded fish heads.

Clinton's photographic interest, in the short time I'd been with him, lay entirely in nature – and abandoned and badly rusted old vehicles that nature was at times burdened with. He hadn't spent much time over the last few days in the company of other people – only those from whom he'd bought food or other supplies – but here was an opportunity to take some wonderful shots of men whose patience must equal his own. Men who didn't chat much with others whose lines reached out alongside their own but who sat quietly, sometimes for hours at a time, waiting for that tug and thinking thoughts as private as thoughts can be. I found the stillness of their faces fascinating, the intent in their eyes captivating, and the pull of the activity itself a little puzzling. Had *I* been able to take photos, this is the sort of image I'd be looking for. But I couldn't, and Clinton, despite wandering off on a stroll along the jetty, had not taken his camera. He looked tired, like he wanted no more than to stretch his legs and then call it a day. But I wasn't tired at all.

    I felt sure he wasn't going to drive off anytime soon, so I took the opportunity to go and play with the dolphins – and the seals! Well, the seals didn't seem too interested in playing – not if it meant missing out on fish heads. Their heads were bobbing out of the water from time to time, and they'd honk for food if one of their mates was getting more than his fair share, but that was about all. The dolphins were the ones having all the fun. I hovered over the water where I thought one of them might appear at any moment, wondering if my presence might have any impact on them, but it didn't. Theirs did on me though! I didn't know if I could make it work, but I concentrated hard and, on the couple of occasions I positioned myself just right, so I was there as they emerged from the water, I pretended I was being booted through the air by a dolphin, somersaulting over the waves. *Yippee!* This was great. The more I did it, the more accurate my timing was getting. But as I was trying to perfect this particular aquatic sport, I noticed Clinton making a move, so I knew I needed to get myself land-borne again.

    I watched as he left the jetty and headed for a toilet block. Five minutes later he emerged looking much fresher. Must've had a shower. He stopped by Morrie to pick up a magazine, which he took with him back to the jetty and read until the lights came on along the Esplanade. I was enjoying watching the fishermen as their day was also drawing to a close. They were a silent breed, entrenched in routine. I had no doubt they'd be back to do it all again tomorrow. And the day after. And the day after that.

    With the light no longer strong enough to read by, Clinton stood up, stuck the magazine in his back pocket and walked until he found the local Chinese restaurant where he ordered numbers 3, 14 and 32 to take away. Then he returned to Morrie, where he dug out a fork from his makeshift cutlery drawer, had his dinner, read a little more and called it a day.

☧

Sophie managed to get through to Terry towards the end of the working day, by which time she'd relived the ups and downs of her entire relationship with Jack. There had been too many downs, and it all stemmed from the fact that he wasn't available. She'd clung to the hope that someday they may be together, but eventually admitted to herself that was never going to happen and she needed to move on. She'd told him she couldn't do it anymore.

Sophie still carried the ticket stub from the night they went to hear the English duo, Sea of Hands, as well as a poem Jack had written for her when his soul seemed to be at its most tormented. When he told her he'd written it, she felt her heart weaken with an even greater sadness at what couldn't be. Kelly had once told her she pictured Sophie with a man who had poetry in his soul. Sophie knew she had found him but the knowledge that she couldn't keep him had caused a kind of pain she hadn't anticipated. The sadness only escalated once she read Jack's poem about the internal conflict he was trying to make sense of. She had felt his pain every bit as much as her own.

Weeks passed. Months. She missed him but she knew she'd made the right decision. It had been a particularly difficult parting because neither of them wanted it to be over, but they moved on with their lives and eventually felt it was okay to resume their occasional lunches. It was lovely seeing him again – it always was. But it was bittersweet. There seemed no way to avoid that.

Jack had bought drinks, sat back down with her and asked Sophie how she was doing. He could see the sadness in her eyes as she responded.

'I'm okay. How about you?'

There was a pause.

'I love you. So much,' he said gently.

Jack hadn't ever said that before – not to Sophie – and to hear him say it now was both heartbreaking and healing.

'I never knew that,' she replied softly, as she wiped a tear that had fallen on her cheek.

☧

As Sophie drove home from Gedup'n'go that evening it was still raining. She wasn't sure how much she'd achieved that day. She'd been thrown when Cath told her about Jack. Then, as she turned the corner into her street, her thoughts turned to her mum, and how together she'd always been. She wished she'd inherited some of that. So much about life, about people, always seemed to have eluded Sophie. She knew she'd spent far too many years trying to work it all out, but life became a whole lot easier once she admitted she was never going to, and decided instead to get a dog.

Unexpectedly, Cujo had been the life-changer she'd hoped for. In him she found a companion whose face never failed to bring a smile to her own – one who was always and overtly pleased to see her, who loved her unconditionally and allowed her to love him. He always responded warmly to a cuddle and he was, above all else, uncomplicated. Sophie was the most important person in the world to Cujo, and for that she loved him to pieces. Life, she realised, is what we make it, and there's no point making it more difficult than it has to be.

Sophie was content knowing that, with Jack, there was nothing more she could have done. She'd been herself, but that hadn't been enough, and no amount of time was going to change that. She'd wanted to be able to help him sort it out, whatever *it* was, but she knew he had to do that on his own. If there was a choice to be made, he had to make it himself, and deep down she knew that choice had been made, long ago. It was, she decided, better that she wasn't on her way to Cocklebiddy.

She pulled into her driveway and smiled as Cujo ran out in the rain to greet her. *Home*, she thought.

Tuesday

I didn't know why he was up so early. It was still dark when Clinton started up the van and drove a short distance from the centre of town where he'd stayed overnight, then parked again and hopped out, camera in hand. But then the sun's rays started trickling through the dawn, breathing new life into the day, and as the sun itself emerged from deep below the horizon we were treated to what I now presumed Clinton already knew would be a dreamy sunrise. There was a little cloud cover in the sky this morning, but it made the 360° panorama from the top of Esperance's Wireless Hill even more memorable. Beneath the scattered cushions of soft wispy grey, Esperance sat silent and still behind a row of Norfolk Pines that lined the Esplanade. The bay could've been yawning with the effort needed to shake off the night's slumber, while the archipelago had been touched by a fresh new light that made me think how perfect the word 'esperance', French for hope, was. From where we were, it was clear that the intrinsic beauty of Esperance lay not in the town itself, but all around it, and I was pleased that my time along the southern shores of Australia's massive western state included a little time here. I would never forget my time with the dolphins and the seals, nor would I forget this morning.

Once the sun had fully risen and the best photographic opportunities had passed, and once one more tin of pineapple had passed his lips, Clinton drove Morrie back down the hill and out of Esperance to Cape Le Grand National Park, only half an hour away. It was now Tuesday. Tomorrow we'd reach Cocklebiddy. It was so easy to forget about the real reason I decided to join Clinton, but the reading he'd been engrossed in the last couple of nights and the fact that we were only one sleep away brought with it an anticipation I hadn't felt since I left Sophie, something that seemed so long ago.

Cape Le Grand National Park. I imagined more intoxicating

scenery, more indescribable colour, more of nature's modest perfection, and it was all that. It also seemed to be a magnet for anyone who loved the great outdoors. Driving through to Lucky Bay, where Clinton stopped and parked Morrie, I saw two camping grounds and plenty of picnic facilities, as well as walking trails, boats, people swimming, surfing and fishing, and enough Aussie flora and fauna to keep a photographer happy for weeks on end.

Lucky Bay was also pretty. Sophie would've loved it, because it had the most lovely, sensual curves, reminiscent of Whiteley paintings where he captured the female form with not much more than a suggestive sweep of the brush. Trees surrounded the bay and offered shade and shelter, but it was the beach itself, or more to the point the kangaroos lazing around on the sand, that took me by surprise. More playmates! They would've been enjoying the area's raw beauty long before people ever did, but they seemed okay with the human intrusion and were perfectly happy to lounge around alongside their two-legged visitors. They'd always have plenty to dine on here, from the coastal heath and dried-up seaweed to eucalypt and banksia groves, not to mention whatever thoughtless campers might leave behind.

So although it didn't look like the kangaroos were about to go anywhere, Clinton was. He took off with his camera equipment, down the Coastal Trail, and I followed him from the start, here at the beach. According to a sign we passed, the walk continued along the coast from Cape Le Grand at one end to Rossiter Bay at the other. But doing it all would take a full day, the return trip twice that, and I knew he hadn't taken enough stuff with him for an overnighter. Not only that, but we were expected at Cocklebiddy tomorrow.

After about half an hour, we came to Thistle Cove. Wow. Dazzling sapphire-blue waters off in the distance turned to a brilliant turquoise colour before they spilled onto the beach by Clinton's feet, but he paused for only a few moments before trekking into the hard tract of wilderness ahead of him. Damn, he's not staying here. Reluctantly I followed, because apart from this spot being so beautiful, I knew the next leg was taking us to a place called Hellfire Bay. I hoped it was nicer than it sounded.

I couldn't imagine much difference in the slice of coastline we wandered along today and the one mapped by the early explorers so long ago. It was amazing, being in a place so untouched and unspoiled, and it made me feel incredibly privileged. I watched over Clinton's shoulder as he pulled out his notebook and started to scribble.

Tuesday 12/6
Lucky Bay to Thistle Cove

- massive outcrops of granite and gneiss
- Ribbons of milk white sand
- isolated coves
- clear water – azure

Notebook away, Clinton walked a little further along the track before he stopped to photograph one of the granite peaks that formed a striking chain in this section of the park. As he did, I noticed a few raindrops falling from a sky that was taking on a menacing darkness. They were scattered, but they were getting really heavy, really quickly. Clinton found shelter just as quickly and made sure his camera was under cover. When it came, the downpour lasted only a couple of minutes, and after it stopped the sunshine returned even brighter than before. It lit up the dripping landscape in a way that transported me back to a time in Sophie's life when Jack was all she was thinking about. It must've been the spider's web I saw up ahead on the track, hanging tenaciously under the weight of the fallen rain.

ℬⳉ

Sophie had woken one April morning after a light fall of rain overnight. It was the time of year when there were spider webs everywhere in the garden, some of them huge, but all of them extraordinary when you stopped to look at them properly and think about not only how they got there, but how they managed to *stay* there. She knew there would be some good photographs to be taken, not only because of the rainfall but because she'd woken to fog, so she grabbed her camera and went outside to discover a wonderland of webs, heavy under the weight of water droplets that hung on every strand like precious pearls, glistening in the rays from the early morning sun.

Sophie is no photographer, just a keen point-and-shooter, but even she'd been able to capture some lovely images that morning, images she later showed Jack. She thought little more about them after that, and didn't imagine Jack would have either, but some months down the track, when they knew it was over, he wrote the following to her.

> *I recall your photos of the spider and the magic of the webs woven in your garden and I see you weaving a web of love around your family and friends and I imagine you, like the spider, being too close to see the brilliance with which it shines and I would weep – if I could – for the mindlessness of the wind that tangles it and rejoice in the instinct that rebuilds it.*

In Sophie's eyes, no-one had ever written a more beautiful sentiment, not for her anyway. 'I can't keep rebuilding it,' she said to herself as she quietly wept. She wanted to reciprocate somehow, to return the sentiment as best as she knew how. Not in words – they were Jack's domain and she felt hugely inadequate alongside him when it came to that – but in a tiny card, a card she made with one of her spider-web photos on it.

෫෬

Sophie had always wondered if her card had meant anything to him, as his words had to her; if he'd kept it or maybe thrown it out. And I wished back then I could help her but I'd seen how this relationship had affected her – wanting someone you can't have is never going to be easy, and Jack was showing no signs of leaving his wife and family. I had wanted it to work – I wanted Jack to be with her, always – but this was one of those times I needed to butt out and let time take over.

It was the gentle release of his shutter that brought me back from days long gone. I looked in the direction Clinton was shooting. Cape Le Grand. It was impressive. Wild. Captivating. With a steady foot and his keen photographer's eye, he was capturing so much of this awesome scenery. I'm sure he'd like to have gone further, but the days are short at this time of year. He made a few more notes before turning back.

Thistle Cove to Hellfire Bay

- sweeping sand plains covered in heath
- rugged granite peaks and fierce rocky headlands
- picturesque bays and clean sandy beaches
- swamps and freshwater pools

ೞාᏣ

Back at Lucky Bay Clinton was entranced, as I was – as all the campers who had returned from their day's activities were – by the gentle friendliness of the kangaroos that greeted them. It was one last opportunity for Clinton to take a few more photos before the light drained from another day, and for me to play with these weird-looking native Australians. There was nothing better than sliding down the back of a kangaroo, along its tail and up into the air, then doing it all again, but most of them were lying down. *Come on, guys.* I tried to urge them. *Get up.* But I was powerless, and they were boring.

I'd lost sight of Clinton, but it didn't matter. As long as I could still see Morrie, I knew I hadn't been left behind. And it was fun, watching all the activity and listening to the conversations going on all around me. I hadn't heard too many different voices since I'd been on the train.

Everyone seemed to be getting along well, talking among themselves, making new friends, lending a hand if it was needed anywhere. If someone discovered they'd forgotten something, there was someone else who was happy to lend theirs.

'Haven't got a bit of alfoil you could spare, have you mate?' I heard someone calling to a nearby camper. 'Ours ran out last night.'

'All yours mate,' the guy responded as he threw the foil across.

But as the foil was midair, another guy who was walking past reached out to try to catch it. He was just having a bit of fun, but he lost his balance and fell.

'Are you okay, mate?' one of the others asked him.

'Moy? Yeah, awl good, oym good,' he slurred as he tried to get up, then stumbled again.

A few looks passed between the campers as we all realised that this guy was pissed.

Someone moved to help him up and, despite his resistance, managed to get him settled on a nearby fold-up chair, where he was able to reach for another beer and keep drinking. *Interesting night ahead.*

Just as things settled, Clinton emerged. He was carrying a portable gas stove – *where's he been storing that?* – and a shopping bag, as well as his camera, which was hanging around his neck. He put that down carefully on a little fold-up table beside Morrie, then set himself up, unwrapped a couple of sausages and started cooking them as he tore open a bread roll and lined it with tomato sauce.

'Looks like you could do with some onions, mate,' someone said as he looked across and saw Clinton had none.

Clinton laughed. 'Forgot to buy one,' he said.

The man scooped up some sizzling onion from his own barbecue and brought it over. 'It's not the same without onions,' he said.

His wife had followed him across with a salad bowl. 'Here, have some potato salad too, love. You look like you forgot more than just an onion.'

I might have been wrong, but my guess was that Clinton hadn't forgotten anything. He kept it all as simple and easy as it could be. That said, running out of essentials or forgetting something seemed to be part of the camping experience – the rule rather than the exception.

As the night wore on, the peace that had settled over the campsite was shattered by the same guy who'd stumbled earlier in the evening trying to catch the alfoil. He'd been singing to himself, which was fine except when he felt he wasn't singing loudly enough and so adjusted his volume, but the collection of empty beer cans around his feet was growing steadily. He'd taken himself off to pee but didn't go all the way to the toilet block. Even more unsteady on his feet now, he wasn't thinking about the others he was sharing the site with, and having done what he set out to do he stumbled back towards the camp, tripping over a sleeping kangaroo as he did so.

'Ahhh! What the –'

The poor roo had woken with a start, whipping its tail up and knocking this guy flat. In its haste to retreat, and no doubt a little disoriented and frightened, it jumped through the campsite. It was so quick but as the roo went past Morrie, where Clinton was sitting on a fold-away chair, its tail smashed against the little table, knocking his camera to the ground. I watched his face, illuminated by the campfire. At that moment, he looked as broken as I feared his camera might be.

It had made a terrible sound as it fell, and I wondered whether Clinton would have words to say to the guy who had tripped over the kangaroo, causing all the commotion. Maybe he'd even start a fight. But his focus was on his camera alone. A few of the campers came over to see if much damage had been done.

'Is it okay, mate?' one of them asked.

'It'll be fine, thanks,' Clinton said calmly as he scrutinised the damage.

The campsite had gone terribly quiet, and at that moment everyone was looking towards Clinton.

'You sure? It took quite a hit.'

'No really, it's okay.'

'Why don't you come over and join us for a while,' the lady who'd brought Clinton some salad earlier in the evening asked. 'Are you on your own?'

'Thanks again, but I'll call it a night. I've got a long drive tomorrow.' Clinton put his camera safely inside the van, tidied up his dinner things and then retreated into the inner sanctum that was his home. He sat cross-legged on his mattress and, under the strong light he used to devour maps by night, I watched as he set about repairing the damage done to his camera. It didn't look to be as bad as it had sounded, but he was meticulous in making sure every part of it was okay.

Just as it had taken me a while to pay much attention to Clinton when he was taking photos, I also hadn't paid much attention to his camera. Until now. It was different to any I'd seen before. For one thing it looked incredibly strong, and as he fiddled around with it, I noticed some writing scratched underneath.

Happy 21st Clint,
Dad

And next to that, JW '83

Oh my goodness. A gift from his dad. No wonder it's so precious to him. The 'JW '83' made me think, too, that perhaps his dad hadn't just given it to him, he'd made it for him. Wow, how fantastic.

Clinton was playing around with his camera, doing some minor repair work – the worst damage looked to be a chip to the edge of the lens – and testing all the settings, almost until the sun rose the following morning. I couldn't begin to imagine how tired his eyes must've been by then. I did, however, start to appreciate a little more about this man and his passion for photography. *I wonder if his dad was also a photographer, or maybe some kind of craftsman.*

I'd seen in Clinton an inherent understanding of the land, and I'd watched his gentle approach as he shot image after image, patiently waiting for hours – as he sometimes would have for days – for the moment when the light projected on his subject would give him the best or most unusual shot. Or when there was extreme weather to capture a scene unlike any other. I'd watched as he translated the poetry he saw all around him into what I could only believe would be unforgettable photographs, and I'd watched how careful he'd been as he took his camera apart, bit by bit, making sure it was okay, carefully gluing fragments back in place on the rim of the lens.

His patience extended well beyond waiting for that perfect picture. It even extended beyond staying up all night taking care of an inanimate object. The drunk last night hadn't cared too much for the others he was camping nearby, and he didn't seem to care too much for the wildlife in the park either. And yet Clinton had said nothing. Had done nothing. Others would've. Clinton could've put this guy in his place in a heartbeat, I knew it, but he'd chosen not to. Silence had never offered me any power, but I knew it was a powerful tool for most people. Earlier tonight, though, I wondered whether, in that man's inebriated state, a smack on the head wouldn't have been more effective.

Wednesday

'Good as new,' he said quietly to himself. 'It's all okay, Dad.'

It was still dark outside, but once Clinton was satisfied his camera could do everything it should be able to do, he took himself for a shower before returning to Morrie and getting back on the road. It was as if he wanted to avoid having to see anyone from the night before, least of all the man who had disturbed the peaceful ambience that had swept over the campsite at the end of the day. I'd heard stories about people like that at Gedup'n'go. Everyone always said they hoped someday those people would learn to respect nature, and other people – even themselves – but they always came to the same conclusion. Some of them never would.

ಸಿಂಆ

Clinton reached the Coolgardie–Esperance Highway before the sun had fully risen. I felt a tinge of sadness as we left the coast, but it didn't last. We'd be joining the Eyre Highway at Norseman – western gateway to the Nullarbor – and were due at Cocklebiddy before the end of the day. I couldn't wait.

We hadn't been on the highway long at all when I saw something up ahead. It wasn't another family of emus, but as Clinton started to slow down I was able to make out a thumb, attached to a distinctly female body. Old blue jeans hugged the curve of her hips, and a loose white shirt fell softly from her shoulders. She had leather boots on her feet, a cowboy hat on her head and a backpack slung across one shoulder. Clinton pulled over.

'Thanks,' she said as she hopped in, careful to avoid the camera equipment and paperwork he quickly pulled a little closer in his direction.

'You've got an early start. Where are you headed?' he asked as he pulled back on to the tar.

'Kalgoorlie.'

'I can take you as far as Norseman, but then I'm turning east.'

'That's great. My name's Mary, and thanks again.'

Mary must've had special powers, because she'd been able to bring Clinton to life with little more than her smile. I had to admit, she was as beautiful as her Irish accent. *This could be an interesting ride.*

'My pleasure,' he said. 'Clint. Clinton West. It's a bit bigger than Ireland, isn't it?'

'Sure, but not as green.'

Judging from his reaction, the Irish accent – particularly when it came from the lips of an attractive woman – was something he responded well to. Last night, as I watched him hard at work, fixing his camera, I'd wondered about Clinton, and what appeared to be his largely isolated life. I wouldn't say lonely – he didn't strike me as a lonely man – but I'd wondered if his memory of Lucky Bay might be scarred by the way the night had ended – whether people had disappointed him a lot throughout his life, and that's why he lived the life he did. It's why Sophie is so happy to be on her own. The more I thought about her, in the context of Clinton, the more I was realising how much of a pain I must be to her.

But today's another day. We're edging our way towards Cocklebiddy, and I'm sure even Clinton would have to admit that it's not a bad day at all that starts in the company of a lovely young Irish woman.

'Why Kalgoorlie?' he asked.

'I'm visiting a friend, Angie. We've never met, but we used to email each other when we were in school. It was something our teachers got us to do, to connect with someone on the other side of the world. Now it's all Facebook of course, but I've always wanted to come to Australia and I wouldn't come all this way and not look her up.'

'Has she always lived in Kalgoorlie?'

'As long as I've known her. Her dad worked in a gold mine, although he died some years ago. Her mum runs a hotel and that's where Angie works.'

'She's not a skimpy, is she?' Clinton asked with a smile.

Mary frowned as she looked at him.

'No, she's not. Why? Do you know some of the girls up there?'

'Wish I did. No. I don't know Kalgoorlie well at all, but it's an interesting place to visit, and I'm sure she'll have nice cold Guinness waiting for you when you arrive.'

'And what's your line of work, Clinton West, if you don't mind me asking?'

I'd been hovering around the rear-vision mirror, watching Clinton and Mary, and I was riveted. They seemed to click. It was so nice. And I was curious to hear how Clinton would respond to Mary's question – to hear how he talked about his work, even himself.

'Me, I take photos, that's all.'

Oh, right.

'Of what?'

'Life, mostly.'

'That's pretty broad.'

Go Mary!

'It's a pretty broad canvas I've got to work with.'

I was enjoying the ride as much as Clinton and Mary seemed to be. Men are always nicer to get to know when they're away from other men, one on one, and I hadn't seen this side of Clinton before. He could be a charmer. He seemed genuinely interested in Mary and her story and I could tell she was feeling safe and relaxed with him.

By the time we reached Salmon Gums, where Clinton stopped for breakfast, I'd learned a little about Mary, her home in Ireland and her family, her adventurous spirit and her travels in Australia so far. About Patrick, the boyfriend whose heart she'd broken when she left for this year-long adventure. And Frederik, the Danish guy she'd met in Broome a couple of months ago, who was planning to join her as soon as his work commitments during the peak holiday season up there had passed.

'One in every port?' Clinton joked.

'No, it's not like that. But I do hope we meet again somewhere. He was good fun and we wanted to see a lot of the same places.'

'Well, then, I also hope you find each other again someday,' Clinton said.

'Aye, but I'm realistic about that sort of thing. It's more than likely he'll change his mind, for whatever reason – most likely someone else!'

Clinton admired Mary's independence. So did I. I'd like to have *been* Mary! She was a good talker, which, with his far more reserved approach, made the two of them a great travel team. Unfortunately it was a team that had a relatively short time together, but it wasn't over yet. Salmon Gums was only halfway between Esperance and Norseman.

'You know what I'm loving so much about this country?' Mary asked Clinton as they tucked into some hot toast. 'Well, *one* of the things anyway?'

'What's that?'

'Place names, like Salmon Gums.'

'You like that one, huh?'

'Well, I didn't at first – it made me think of fish breath.'

'Fish breath?! You're definitely not from around these parts, are you!'

'Well I didn't know about the trees, but they're beautiful.' Mary glanced across at a photograph hanging in the cafeteria as a waitress came and poured them some more coffee.

'That was taken early one morning a few years ago,' the waitress said.

'It's so pretty,' responded Mary.

I went over to take a closer look at the photo and was both surprised and excited to see Clinton's name in tiny print at the bottom. *Tell Mary you took it*, I urged him. But he didn't. And right then I knew that Clinton didn't feel the need to prove anything. That's definitely Sophie's kind of man, and I wish she'd been here, with Clinton. She would've liked him.

'The gum trees around here get that beautiful rich, salmon-pink bark towards the end of summer and into autumn.'

'It's such a pretty name,' Mary said.

'Yes, it is,' Clinton agreed, 'when you're not thinking about fish breath.'

'The place I come from – it could hardly be described as a town – it's called Painestown.'

Clinton laughed. 'Truly?'

'Aye, not much poetry in that, is there? There's not much more to it than a dozen or so houses on a hill. Massive corn fields surround one side of the hill and vegetable fields the other. Dublin is forty minutes away, and I went to primary school between the two places, in a village called Curragha. It was big compared to Painestown – it had a church and a pub as well as the school.'

'Did you like growing up there?' Clinton asked.

'Aye, I loved it. Loved everything about it. We lived on a farm and had donkeys – I love them.'

I'd never seen a donkey, not a real one anyway.

'Did you know they all have a dark band across their shoulders?'

'No, I didn't know that.'

Mary had taken off her hat when they walked into the cafeteria and, as she did, her long black hair had fallen softly around her face. As she talked about the things that meant so much to her, her green eyes widened and lit up her entire face. I was glad Clinton had picked her up. He was great, but another face, a bit of conversation, it was a nice change.

'My mother was a dance instructor in Curragha, so I had to go to classes after school with all my friends, but I hated it. Never could get my feet right. When all the other girls were dreaming of joining the ballet, I was dreaming of seeing the world. I would talk to my dad about it all the time as he worked the farm. I adored my dad, still do. He'd take me on the tractor with him, and sometimes when I was a kid he'd even let me drive it, though at the time I was barely tall enough to reach the pedals. My dog Conan would run alongside.'

'Conan,' Clinton repeated. 'Great name!'

Mary spoke warmly of her family – her parents, as well as her older brother and two younger sisters. It was clear they were a close family who shared a lot of laughter, and I wondered if they all had smiles as big as hers, and whether they all shared her enthusiasm for life.

'Have you ever given much thought to parallel universes?' Mary asked after they'd finished breakfast and Clinton was paying the bill.

'Where did that come from?'

'Oh, just wondering. Have you?'

'Sure.' He held the door open for her and they walked back to the van.

'Wouldn't it be great to be able to follow a few of our most treasured relationships through to their natural end – my ex back in Ireland who I love so much, but I knew I had to go away and he wasn't prepared to come with me; Frederik up in Broome who I may never see again; maybe one or two others. How good would it be to be able to enjoy every one of them, each existing without any knowledge of the others. I think it's possible to love a number of people, very much. Do you, Clinton?'

The more she talked, the more I wanted to hear. She was so open about things. It was hard not to make comparisons with Sophie, but I felt mean thinking that.

'Sure, I do.'

'But we have to make choices and how do we ever really know we've made the right one? It was so hard for me to walk away from what I had in Ireland, but I knew I had to travel. It was like something inside me was pulling me away from all I knew and loved and was comfortable with. Patrick couldn't understand it. He said all he needed was me. How can anyone be so sure, and want so little?'

Wow. Patrick sounds like Sophie. No wonder he and Mary parted company. Could easily be Sophie and me.

'Some people have dreams that seem even larger than life, Mary, and that's great – they need to be followed. But others get great pleasure out of simple things, and sometimes those with the simplest of dreams – the dreams that are within easy reach – find contentment way ahead of the rest of us,' Clinton responded.

Ouch. That was like a kick in the guts. I thought immediately of Celia. And then Sophie. How alike they were, and how frustrated I'd got with Sophie so often, because I wanted her to dream big. Big *had* to be better. Didn't it?

Clinton had crushed that belief in a couple of sentences. I felt so small.

Then everything was quiet. The two of them had become as lost in their thoughts as I was in mine. I wondered if Clinton might be thinking of Wendy.

Some time passed before Mary at last broke the silence, and I lost all thoughts of Sophie.

'Who's this we're listening to?'

'Jackson Browne.'

Mary giggled. 'You must be older than you look!'

'How old do I look?' he asked. I could tell he enjoyed being teased.

'Oh, I don't know,' she said. 'But you haven't told me your plans. Where are you going from Norseman?'

'You didn't answer my question.'

'Seventy-three,' she laughed. 'Now where are you going?'

'That's not very nice, Mary.'

'Oh, I'm sorry, you big sook. I'm kidding. You don't look a day older than fifty-three. Is that better?'

'Much better,' he said. 'And pretty close.'

'Well?'

'Well what?'

'Well where are you going?'

'Oh … Cocklebiddy.'

'Cocklewhatty?'

'Cocklebiddy.'

'Another wonderful Aussie place name! What's there?'

This road trip was getting better and better. I was starting to hope Mary would change her mind about Kalgoorlie and stay with Clinton.

'A hole in the ground.'

'And?'

'And down that hole is another world. Underwater caves.'

'No.'

'Yep. The Nullarbor, as you might know, is a vast limestone plain, flat as a pancake and dry. When most of us think of it we probably don't think it ever sees a drop of rain – it lies there day after day, under the searing sun. But it does get rain, and that rain can be so unexpected and heavy. Frighteningly heavy. These holes in the ground – and there are loads of them – have come about when the earth collapses into sinkholes after heavy rains. The limestone it pounds is weak. Did you have an ant farm when you were a kid?'

'No.'

'Kids in Australia often did. They were these little windows into another world – a couple of sheets of perspex, fitted together with space enough in between to fill with sand. In it you put ants, and watched as they built themselves a community, digging tunnels, creating the whole ecosystem they needed to survive, with a little help from the kid who had it, of course.'

'Sounds like fun, in a weird kind of way,' Mary said, 'but I prefer donkeys!'

'I can see why! But under the Nullarbor it's a bit like those ant farms – a massive labyrinth of underground caves. Imagine a cross-section and try to picture limestone instead of sand. That limestone has formed over millions of years, partly by the gradual build-up of marine fossils. Limestone dissolves in water, and tunnels have been created not by ants as they are in the ant farms but by heavy rains over thousands, *millions* of years. Some of these tunnels have pushed all the way through to the water table to create underground lakes with waters as pure as glacial ice, under limestone ceilings that drip like melting candle wax.'

'Sounds beautiful.'

Sounds fantastic.

'Cocklebiddy is one of the longest single-entrance underwater caves in the world – it extends more than six kilometres and is a playground for serious cave divers. Down there it's a world of silence and absolute wonder. Or so they tell me.'

I'd seen Clinton's quiet enthusiasm over the last few days as he was taking photos, but I hadn't seen how he was able to transfer it so beautifully to another person, a near stranger. He had us both hooked.

'Are you going down?' Mary asked eagerly.

'Me, no. I like to be able to see the sky above me, to feel the fresh air around me. I leave the diving to the others, but I'm heading out there to meet with the team, to take some photos.'

'How can you do that if you don't go down?'

'We fit a camera to a scooter that goes down with the divers. Part of my job is to take care of any technical issues that may crop up, make sure the camera is properly fitted before they go down, that sort of thing. The divers have enough to do without having to worry about that. But a lot can happen above ground too, with a team the size of the one they've got together this time, and I'll be there to record that. Ah, see that sign up ahead?'

'Aye.'

'That's the start of the Eyre Highway. This is where I'll be leaving you.'

No. Ask her to stay, Clinton. Don't let her go.

It had been only a few short hours, but I wanted them to stay together. *You can't just drop her off by the side of the road. Anyone could pick her up, and not everyone's as nice as you are. What if something happens to her?* Ugh. It was like talking to Sophie. I got nothing from

Clinton and knew there was no point in trying. I had to remind myself what I had a feeling Clinton already knew – that Mary was very much her own woman and was capable of making her own – and the right – choices along the way.

Clinton turned off the Coolgardie–Esperance Highway and drove towards Norseman's service station. Mary had become quiet – not even the bizarre corrugated iron camels that sauntered across the roundabout on the way into the small town brought a comment.

'Back in a minute,' he said. 'Just getting some petrol and a few supplies for the drive to Cocklebiddy.'

'Okay,' she said softly.

I went with him, and as he walked back towards the van I could tell he was lost in thought. Then I glanced at Mary, and she had that same look on her face. I wondered what they were both thinking – whether they were thinking the same thing. I wondered if Mary might've been anything like Wendy. She didn't look like the girl in that old Polaroid, but maybe they shared that same lust for life. Clinton pulled himself back in the van and started up the engine, then returned to the intersection where he'd be dropping her off.

Say it, Clinton. Say it, I quietly urged him, for what it was worth.

He switched off Morrie's ignition again and they sat for a few moments, first in silence and then they both spoke together.

'Thanks, Clint,' she said.

'Travel safely,' he said.

And then there was another brief moment of silence. *I'm going to burst!* I had such a strong feeling that Mary knew she was saying goodbye to someone she'd like to travel one of those parallel universes with.

'Here, take my number,' he said to her, handing her his card.

Noooo, I cried, to no-one.

'If you ever need anything, use it.'

They didn't say goodbye. It wasn't forthcoming, from either of them. There was another quiet moment as they looked at each other.

Last chance, you two.

Then Clinton leaned across and kissed Mary's forehead. She opened the door and was on her way. Just like that. He watched her as she walked off, and waved when she turned back to see him for the last time.

∞⌘

The road from Norseman is sealed and smooth, and a lot of it is as straight as those tracks I'd watched from the driver's cabin on the Indian Pacific. It was just me and Clinton again, and for a while he travelled in silence – no music in the cassette player, no singing along when there was a familiar chorus. He was again deep in thought, and I don't know where he might have been. Maybe with Mary. Perhaps Wendy. Wherever he was, I hoped he wasn't alone. Clinton was as capable a man as any I'd ever known, but I'd seen how he was able to shine in the presence of others and for some reason I needed to know he was okay.

There wasn't much of any scenic significance as we travelled from Norseman, or perhaps my heart wasn't in it. I was feeling more miserable than I'd felt after that bushwalk with Sophie. What was I good for? I didn't seem to make Sophie's life any better, and she was the only one I had even a remote chance with.

It's amazing how strangers can appear in your life without warning and then disappear almost as quickly, but in that time they manage to touch a part of you that had been sound asleep for some time, or that you never knew was there in the first place. I'd felt that. And I was sure there'd been some kind of spark between Clinton and Mary – maybe one he hadn't known since Wendy. I wanted so much for them to stay together, just as I'd wanted things to work out with Sophie and Jack. I wanted the comfort of knowing that the people I cared about were being cared about themselves. But I was powerless to bring people together. I was powerless, full stop.

Stop it Georgia. Self-pity isn't your thing.

It's true. I had to snap out of it. This was an epic road we were travelling. I needed to stop thinking about what had been going on inside the van and focus on what was happening outside.

∞⌘

As I watched the passing landscape it reminded me of a quote I'd read from a South Australian explorer, Richard Thelwell Maurice, about the Nullarbor. 'Any man who would travel this country for pleasure would go to Hell for a pastime.' I wasn't far into that trip myself and was beginning to wonder what I'd let myself in for. If Clinton were making notes, I thought words like melancholy, ghostly, hellish, unforgiving, monotonous, overwhelming, desolate, featureless, daunting, stark, repetitive, harsh and savage might have been emerging from the point of his pen. They were floating through my mind as I tried to picture this landscape before the road was built. Somehow it seemed a much more powerful and unfriendly environment from the intimacy of the van than it was from the train. Maybe it had something to do with us being on the road and being able to see so much more around us.

I felt so insignificant out here. But I was also ready to take it all in – it was starting to feel so real.

As the kilometres clicked over, and more and more road was being sucked beneath us, those gloomy words in my mind were starting to change. Others like incredible, endless, spectacular, timeless and fascinating began floating around me, and as I began to think more positively about the adventure that was only beginning to unfold, even those words were starting to give way to others that described a place of wonder and vibrancy – words like serene, mysterious, magic, beautiful, spiritual and even ethereal. I could feel myself being pulled further and further into something undefined and totally spellbinding.

I wondered what it would be like to walk this immense plain, as that explorer had done. That would have to stir up an altogether different set of feelings and emotions, and a far greater appreciation of the smaller stuff that you miss when you drive past at speed. But why would anyone do that? Why would anyone take on the task – the lonely, punishing, gruelling task – of walking in the steps of explorers who had regarded it as their worst nightmare. There's got to be an extreme adventure gene in the DNA of just a handful of people, I'm sure of it. I wanted adventure, but I wasn't crazy.

Crossing the Nullarbor is an adventure in itself, even if it's done from the comfort of a van. It's a big country, and doing a trip like this makes you see how really big it is. Between the Indian and Pacific oceans are such vast open spaces and long distances, and nondescript towns that are hours apart. And barely a soul to be seen.

The long distances are impossible to ignore. We'd passed no more than a handful of places where Clinton could buy food or petrol – a couple of hundred kilometres between them wasn't out of the ordinary – so planning a trip like this must've taken him some doing. Roadhouses and motels dotted the way, but when road trains thundered past I felt as though Clinton was no safer than a matchbox under a falling brick in the otherwise comfortable air-conditioned Morrie. But he was a capable driver, and I loved the huge 'whoosh' that rocked the van with every road train we safely passed, belting along in the opposite direction.

It made me think of Celia, and her fears for Sophie's safety whenever she was on the road. The trucks, more than anything, bothered her – road trains would terrify her. I tried to avoid those thoughts and instead looked out for the curlicues. It had always struck me as funny that the cabin doors of these big trucks were decorated with fancy calligraphic twists – the bigger the truck, the more delicate the curlicue. It was like dressing a sumo wrestler in a lace G-string.

I felt more alive than I had in a long time, yet more relaxed, but I didn't know whether these feelings were good or not. I was thinking ahead to the Nullarbor, beneath which – according to Clinton – lay one of the world's largest and most phenomenal underwater cave networks. Out the window was this vast limestone plateau, but this gigantic slab of limestone was hard to fathom. I could follow the logic surrounding the formation of the caves below the surface – it all made perfect sense. What I couldn't do, however, was picture those caves. The two things seemed worlds apart as we crossed the deceptively dry landscape.

PART TWO

Cocklebiddy

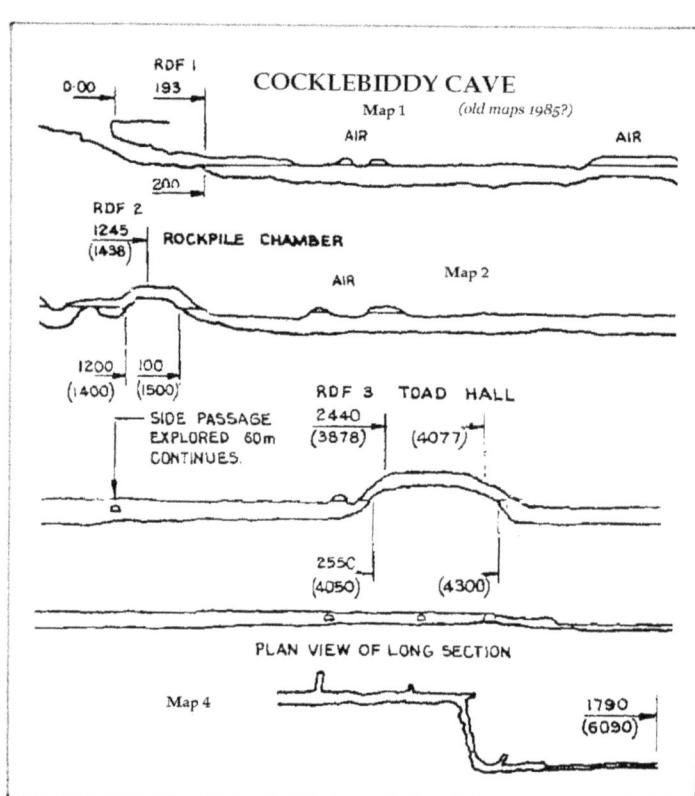
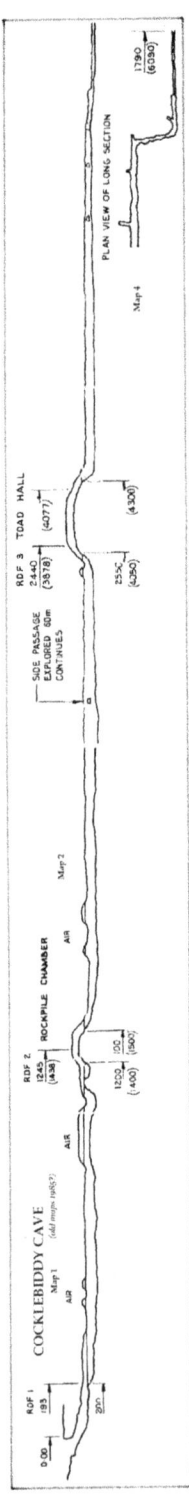

Drawn by: ROBYN COUNSELL

Arriving

Clinton arrived in Balladonia and pulled up at the petrol station. There was a museum attached to it, so I wasn't sure if this stop was for him to fill up and stretch his legs or whether he was going in for a look around. I wasn't left wondering for long.

'Is the museum open?' he asked as he paid for his fuel. 'I was hoping to see Gary.'

'Nah, it's been closed for a while, but Gary's around somewhere. I'll see if I can find him for you. What's your name, mate?'

'Clinton West. Thanks.'

Clinton waited outside, and it was only when I followed him out and started looking around that I noticed the enormous piece of space junk fixed above the museum's roof. The word 'Skylab' was clearly visible on the side, but it was minus the curve of the 'b'. Must've torn off when the spacecraft crashed. Geez, that would've made a massive hole in the ground, somewhere. I remember Sophie learned about Skylab at school, but never in a million years would I have thought back then that I'd be out here someday, seeing part of it. I was thinking how weird this all was when a voice interrupted the quiet.

'Clint! G'day.' The voice came from behind, arm outstretched.

'Gary,' he replied as they shook hands.

'It's been too long, good to see you.'

'And you. What's going on here? I was hoping to have a look around.'

'Come in – I'll take you through.'

Gary was an average-looking bloke, thin, around Clinton's age. He was completely bald, but grey stubble grew on his chin. His jeans were well-worn, and his Marvin the Martian T-shirt wasn't one he'd bought last week either. He walked with a bit of a limp, hoisting up his jeans every now and then, and his hands were rough and grubby.

Clinton and I followed Gary back into the store and then beyond it. We passed the door visitors would go through had the museum been open, then entered the museum by the 'Employees only' door.

'Been working on the place a bit,' Gary said. 'It was shabby and cluttered, and people were nicking stuff. There's still a lot to do but we're getting there.'

Wow. This was it. My first real taste of what we were heading towards. I was surrounded by an amazing display of stuff – not only space junk from that notorious Skylab crash but also heaps of photos from deep within the Nullarbor caves, and more information than I had a hope of digesting while we were here. It was fantastic though, and gave me a glimpse into this other world. It also taught me a new word – speleologist. Seems the caves under the Nullarbor are a speleologist's paradise. These people must have that extreme adventure gene, because from what I was quickly learning they were prepared to risk life and limb as they swam waters that were incredibly clear, but could also be disgustingly murky. They'd crawl among rocks that were often precariously positioned and they'd squeeze through unbelievably tight passageways. Then I noticed a chart with the heading 'Why do they do it?'

'It has been referred to as the "Star Trek Syndrome" – going where no man has gone before', it read. Wow. The risk was enormous, but if you're born with that extreme adventure gene, you live for moments of great risk. I was so excited, but not enough to want to do it. That fear of water, for one thing. Plus they needed enormous skill and nerves of steel. I'm not sure I had either of those things.

It was the thrill of the unexpected, the idea that they may be the first person to ever explore a particular passage, or even just a small bit of one, that could be millions of years old. To discover how far it might go, and what's at the end of it. That all sounded awesome to me.

To do this, I read on, they had to assess every inch of the dive, recalculating when necessary. The equipment they needed for each stage was an unknown until they reached that stage. And every dive was a new challenge. But there was no guaranteed outcome for them. Instead, several possibilities – and not all of them good.

I read that dozens of lives had been lost cave diving in the past, and with each one came an increase in public hysteria. But the chart also said that the sport enjoyed a much better safety record these days, and that the usual fears associated with diving – lack of air, drowning, claustrophobia, and simply being trapped – were taken in a diver's stride.

Thing is, no-one ever expects to die. If they knew what it meant to be dead they might have second thoughts.

'Technology,' I heard Gary saying as I returned to their conversation, 'it's moving so fast, especially for us way out here. Every dive means another story, which means more and more documentation, and we need to keep on top of it.' He looked around at the mess in the museum. 'Life's never dull,' he sighed. 'But what brings you here Clint – the dive in a couple of days?'

'Yeah.'

'Terry passed through here yesterday.'

'Yeah, I spoke to him last week. He's really drawn to this place, isn't he? I could hear it in his voice.'

So *that's* who Clinton was talking to back at Margaret River. I thought about that call, and the disturbed night Clinton had after it.

'Sounds like he's got a good team with him this time,' Gary said. 'Big, but good.'

Clinton laughed. 'It always amazes me how that works, you know. I've seen it with other groups as well – not just divers. They come together from all over the place, often never having met before and nearly always having nothing in common except their thirst for adventure. But it seems to work. They get so absorbed by the challenge – they have to. Nothing else comes into it.'

'Yeah, they're trusting each other with their lives out there,' Gary said.

'I always imagined ego might play a big part,' Clinton continued.

'I suppose it does sometimes.'

'That's the thing though. I've never seen it. Maybe I've been lucky not to. But you know, their enthusiasm is infectious, and this place –'

'It's got an almighty power, hasn't it? Draws people in. It got to me the first time I came out here. Never left! How are you going to shoot it this time, mate? You haven't started diving yourself, have you?'

'Not a chance,' Clinton said. 'I'll be above ground, same as before.

There's a guy going down who does some photography – Malcolm Davies. Know him?'

Gary scratched at the stubble on his chin, making that creepy fingernail-on-sandpaper sound that made me shudder.

'Heard the name, that's all.'

'We'll fix a camera to one of the scooters and he'll take over from there. I'm staying above ground. Just there to help, if I can, with any problems Mal might have, and record the story from above with the journo.'

'Have you gone digital yet?'

'Reluctantly, yes. I still use film when I can, but there was no escaping digital, not if I wanted to keep working. They're getting some high-quality digital records in the caves now – I'm sure you've seen them – but things are improving all the time. Tell me mate, you know Nathan Richards, don't you? The journalist?'

'Nate Richards! Shit yeah, I know Nate. Is he still around?'

Clinton laughed. 'Yeah, he's still around. You haven't seen him come through this way, have you? I was expecting a call from him.'

'No, haven't seen him. He might be there but it's more likely he's running late. Nate Richards,' Gary sighed. 'I haven't heard his name in years. He was always such a flake. Hard to believe the success he's had.'

'Yeah, he's one of a kind. Anyway, I should get going. Just wanted to say g'day on my way through.'

'Send me some photos for the museum, won't you?'

'You bet. See you next time.'

As he turned to leave, Gary called him back.

'Clint?'

'Yeah, mate.'

'I was sorry to hear about Wendy.'

'Thanks, Gary.'

My turn to sigh. Just the mention of Wendy's name made me sad. If there are others out at the cave who know Clinton and haven't seen him since before Wendy's death, I expect there might be a bit more sadness to come. Does it ever go away, when someone so close isn't with you anymore?

ಸಿಂಡ

There was a slight bend in the road not far out of Balladonia, and then we passed a sign that read '90 Mile Straight'. We'd reached one of the world's longest straight stretches of highway, which was also the western end of the drive across the Nullarbor. One hundred and forty-six kilometres of straight road lay ahead of us. Far out. How does a driver not lose concentration in that time? Especially on his own. I hope Clinton keeps the music playing. And loud!

And then I thought about what we were driving above. Cocklebiddy is at the heart of some of the Nullarbor's most interesting caving country – I read that back in the museum – and yet as we made our way towards it, a few bushes and clumps of tumbleweed bouncing in the wind were all I could see for miles – for ever. A lot of the passing traffic was probably unaware of what was underneath them, because the idea that there was a massive network of caves down there – largely flooded – seemed inconceivable to me. The idea that this desert was once an inland sea was hard to get my head around, too.

More than anything else it was dry and dusty – overcast skies produced winds that were fitting for such a desolate environment. I could almost feel the wind pushing Morrie as his tyres gripped the road. I was becoming more aware of the bird life too – those wedge-tailed eagles looked magnificent, but menacing, and so much at home out here. For a brief moment that's where I wanted to be – at home. With Sophie. What was I thinking? Setting off without her like this. It looked so harsh. Cruel. But then I remembered Clinton telling Mary how unpredictable it could be, and that made me excited all over again. I wanted this adventure – a bit of unpredictability might be fun.

The sound of Morrie's indicator meant we'd arrived. *This is it. We're here!* Clinton pulled into the roadhouse over on the right, and any thoughts I'd had of wanting to be back home were forgotten by the time he'd switched off the engine. When Clinton opened the van's door it didn't feel as hellish as I'd expected. It was windy, but the earth didn't open up and suck us in, and we weren't lifted off the ground by some freakishly large wedge-tailed eagle with nothing but the meal of his life in mind. It was pretty nice for the middle of winter.

Cocklebiddy looked to be no more than the roadhouse, but its sloping red roof and the motel rooms with their matching red doors gave the Wedgetail Inn the feel of a welcome outback retreat in an instant. There were a few other four-wheel-drives parked out front, pulling trailers heavily weighed down with what I assumed was diving gear, as well as a couple of trucks and a road train, and when Clinton stepped inside to the reception desk and rang the bell on the counter, a rotund woman with a smile as welcoming as her roadhouse appeared from a back room to greet him. I liked her straightaway.

'G'day love, what can I do for you?' she asked Clinton.

This grandmotherly figure gave the immediate impression that what she lacked in height she made up for in good nature. Her long grey hair was tied back in a scarf and she wore a grease-stained apron over a brightly coloured knitted jumper.

'I'm meeting a guy called Terry James here – he's with the dive team headed for the cave. My name's Clint. Clinton West.'

'Terry's at the bar with some of the others, love. I know he's expecting you. Come on through. My name's Beryl, by the way. I'm the owner of this grand estate.'

'Good to meet you, Beryl.'

Beryl took Clinton through the cafeteria to the bar where a small group was gathered and clearly having a good time. I couldn't see Jack there, but in a matter of only seconds, a man who could've been Terry caught Clinton's eye and came towards him with an outstretched hand.

He was a tall, thin man, clean-shaven with a big smile and a kind face. But maybe it wasn't Terry, because he looked younger than the level of caving experience someone would need to lead a group like this suggested.

'Clinton, you made it, my friend,' he said as he hugged my travelling companion. 'Come in and meet the team.'

'Terry. Good to see you.'

It *is* Terry. Must be older than he looks!

'Ah Nathan, you're here. That's good.'

'Hey Clint, long time.' They both reached forward to shake hands. 'Sorry I didn't call. Lost your number, then I lost my phone. Man, it'll be my mind next.'

Good grief, I thought. And I wasn't the only one. Terry and Clinton glanced at one another with warm, knowing smiles.

Terry might have been thin, but Nathan was scrawny, with long scruffy hair he had tied back in a ponytail and an untidy, sparse beard. He wore a faded flannel shirt over a tie-dyed T-shirt, old blue jeans with a hole in one knee, and a pair of well-worn sneakers with no laces. I'd thought Clinton looked like a throwback from the '60s, but I had to admit he was looking pretty normal alongside Nathan.

The noise in the bar hadn't faltered much, but there was a respectful drop in volume as Terry made the various introductions.

'Okay, first up here is Ek, then there's Stefano, Tobias – he's the guy we all hope we won't need, but he's got the first-aid skills if we do, Jules – uh, sorry, Julie – she hates me calling her Jules! You know Mal's wife, Darcy, she'll be keeping us well fed out here. Next is Bob – our service technician, and Mal's over at the pool table with my boy Alex. Jude finally let him come out here with me. As you know, he's been at us for a long time!'

A confusion of handshakes and a mumble of hellos, g'days and how you goin' mates followed.

It was an assorted bunch, which wasn't so strange, but so many new faces all at once. How was I going to remember them all? Darcy and Julie would be easy. Darcy looked to be in her mid- to late-forties. She had shoulder-length blonde hair, a sweet round face, and a figure that suggested she not only enjoyed cooking food, she also enjoyed eating it. Julie, on the other hand, was athletic. Not at all cuddly, like Darcy. She didn't look that friendly, either. But attractive, yes. Very short, with a deep tan and long brown hair. She'd have to be one of the divers.

Ek was Asian – that's as specific as I could be. He also looked athletic and had a beautifully gentle face. Tobias – first aid. He was older, in his fifties maybe. That's good! Lots of experience! His hair was almost entirely grey, and he wore glasses, but he looked incredibly fit.

Bob – perfect name for a service technician! Maybe it wasn't going to be so hard to remember them after all. Bob looked about the same age as Tobias but wasn't in the same physical condition. He carried the early stages of a beer gut, and as well as having a little grey through his dark brown hair, he had a grey moustache. Then there was Stefano. He'd moved across to Julie and put his arm across her shoulder, whispered something in her ear. Maybe they're together. I would find out soon enough. He looked Italian – olive skin, dark hair, fit, and handsome, in a Mediterranean kind of way.

Everyone was getting along well, but Jack wasn't there. Maybe he's not coming after all. If only I could ask Terry where he is. This is so frustrating. It was easy with Clinton, and when I'm with Sophie, she always seems to find out the things I want to know.

'We're still waiting on a few others,' Terry continued. 'Jack, Mark, John, and a young guy by the name of Tee who's joining us to help out and learn. They're all expected tomorrow.'

Yes! Jack *is* coming! It'll be good to see him again, find out what's happening in his life.

'Great,' said Clinton. 'Good to meet you all.'

'How about a drink?' Terry asked him. 'We were about to head out to set up camp when we had a call from Gary over in Balladonia to let us know you weren't far off, so thought we'd wait. A good excuse for one more, before the hard work begins.'

'Yeah.' Clinton looked distracted as he glanced over to the pool table. 'Is that really Alex? How old is he now?'

'Eleven.'

'Eleven,' Clinton sighed. 'How about that.'

Alex was a cutie. Thin like his dad, just shorter. He had fair hair and a big happy smile, freckles on his nose, scabs on his knees and he'd obviously held a pool cue before.

'What'll it be then?'

'Oh, Coke, thanks mate.'

As Terry waited at the bar, Clinton headed for the pool table to see Alex, who he knew but hadn't seen for some time, and to say g'day to Mal.

'Alex, how's things?'

The unexpected greeting made Alex miss his shot, and I wished I was able to distract people like that. I could have a lot of fun!

'Clint! Hey wow, this is great. Dad didn't tell me you'd be here.'

'Nor me you. Shouldn't you be at school?'

'Yeah, but Mum let me miss a week. It's school camp anyway. I won't miss anything.'

Clinton said hello to Mal – seems they'd seen each other more recently – then chatted for a while with Alex.

'You're playing pool now. Are you any good?'

'I can beat Dad sometimes.' Alex seemed pleased with himself.

'You must be good then, your dad's a champion! So what class are you in at school?'

'Sixth. High school next year.'

'High school. Geez, it doesn't seem that long since you started primary school.'

'It does to me.'

I liked Alex. He'd be fun.

'So, do you think you'll follow in your dad's footsteps – I should say flippers! – and start diving some day?'

'Yeah, as soon as Dad lets me. I can't wait.'

'Well you should be able to learn a lot while you're out here. More than at some boring old school camp, right?'

'Dad says I *have* to. That's the only reason he let me come.'

Terry had returned with Clint's drink and raised an inquisitive eyebrow.

'Dad says you have to what?'

'Learn stuff while I'm here.'

'Too right you do. That's the only way his mum would let him come with me,' he told Clint. 'He's going to keep a diary while he's here, so she can read what he's been up to each day.'

'*Da-aad*. Do I have to?'

'That's what she said, buddy. And that's what your classmates are doing on camp.'

Mal had joined the conversation. He was perhaps about fifty. Seemed a quiet man. Maybe that's common among photographers. So he was Darcy's husband. Looked like he enjoyed her cooking, too. Nice couple.

But then all these people seemed nice, and fun, which would be normal at this stage of the dive, before it gets too serious. I was getting more and more excited and hoped they'd leave soon for the cave. I was busting to see it.

'I've heard,' Clinton said to Alex, 'that cave diving is different to something like mountaineering in that the aim isn't necessarily to reach the end of the cave, as it is the top of a mountain.'

'Not for me,' said Alex. 'I want to reach the very end of every cave under the Nullarbor.'

'*All* of them?'

'We'll see!' said Terry. 'You've got to finish primary school first! Come on. We should make tracks.'

Yes! I was outside again faster than any of them. *Come on, guys.*

It was getting cooler out there. The sun had started to drop slowly towards the horizon, and as everyone emerged from the roadhouse I watched as their shadows stretched out like figures distorted by mirrors in a fun park. I also noticed the 'Ambulance' sign beneath another one that directed weary travellers off the highway and across the road to the roadhouse. Hopefully we won't be needing that.

Everyone made their way to their vehicles. Morrie didn't fit the mould when it came to divers' transportation, and Nathan had come in an old campervan that looked like it had travelled to the end of the world and back again, much like Nathan himself. It was only the accumulation of mud and dust that provided some kind of link among this unlikely convoy.

One by one they all turned west back on to the Eyre Highway and, for about ten minutes, Morrie was driving us in the direction we'd come. But indicators were flicked to turn right and in a moment we'd left behind the smooth black bitumen of the highway. It was a rough track out to the cave, one that headed gradually north but meandered a lot, becoming very wide in places and splitting in others – obviously paths taken according to weather conditions. Terry had said it was only about another ten kilometres to the cave's entrance, but it seemed a lot longer.

Ahead of me was nothing but a vast and empty landscape. It didn't offer any reason for the nervous excitement I was feeling. Maybe it was the sign that had done it. I'd seen it not far off the highway. 'Danger!' it read. 'Cocklebiddy Cave closed until further notice.' Recent heavy rain had destabilised the cave's entrance and anyone venturing out there was warned not to approach the entrance or enter the cave. All the people in Terry's group must've seen the sign – *Terry* must've seen the sign – which had been put there only months earlier, yet they'd driven right past it. *Are they crazy?* They didn't appear to be, but my heart was thumping.

Off the highway, I felt as though I was truly on the Nullarbor Plain.

It was a lot greener than I'd expected, although heavy rains tend to have that effect on a landscape. And it was seriously flat – unbelievably so. Out of the van I could turn a full 360° and see the edge of the earth, uninterrupted all the way round. I was captivated. I don't know why, but I felt I was in the real Australia, and yet at the same time it felt foreign. It was almost pretty, but that word was wrong.

Then I saw it. At first I thought we were approaching a dip in the ground – a big dip – but then I realised what it was. It was the cave. The dip grew and grew the closer we got, and eventually looked more like a canyon. The hole in the ground must've been the size of a football stadium. One side, the far side, was a sheer drop, straight down. I don't know how far – I'll explore later. The side closest to us was a long slope, littered with rubble and boulders, some larger than the vehicles we'd all arrived in. The slope led down to the cave's entrance, where it met the base of the vertical drop we were facing.

All the vehicles pulled up a short walk from the cave and straightaway began to set up camp on the barren, dusty plateau. Without hesitating, I was out of Morrie and heading across to that hole in the ground. I expected it to be big, but I never imagined it to be *this* big. When I reached the edge where the ground sloped away, I saw another sign. 'Cocklebiddy Cave', it read, in case visitors were in any doubt. Nailed to that sign was another, erected by the Department of Conservation and Land Management, which repeated the warning I'd seen just off the highway. I was puzzled, because these guys weren't troublemakers. They must've had some kind of permit to enter and dive.

Now I was so close, I could guess at the length of the slope – it went gently down and inwards, northward for a few hundred metres. They'd be able to walk to the cave's entrance, but they'd have to be careful. I was thinking how easy it would be to slip and sprain or break an ankle when Clinton appeared next to me.

He had his camera, so he was treading carefully, but even so he was a confident man and didn't hesitate to go right down to the cave's entrance. I followed him.

The entrance itself was pitch-black and sort of oval in shape. It gave no hint as to what was behind it. That part of this adventure would have to remain a mystery to me. No way was I going in. And that's where

Clinton stopped, too. There was fencing and protection tape from one side of the constricted entry to the other. It might've stopped Clinton, but I wondered whether it was enough to stop anyone who had ignored all the other signs so far.

Clinton looked up and I followed his gaze. He was looking at that sheer drop – the one on the northern edge of the hole in the ground. It was now immediately above us, and it must've been about fifty metres from where we were, up to ground level. I heard voices approaching, and Clinton turned.

'He wouldn't have slept tonight if I hadn't brought him down to see the entrance before dark,' Terry said, once they were a few feet away.

'What do you think, mate?' Clinton asked Alex.

'Awesome. But you can't go in. There's tape.'

'That's okay, buddy. We've got permission,' Terry said. 'The signs are for tourists who just come out for a look.'

'Can you drive down here, Dad?'

'Not a chance.'

'Then how will you get all your stuff down? Do you have to carry it all?'

'We'll carry some, but the ground is tricky enough to walk down when you've got both hands free. It'd be near-impossible, and foolish, to carry a lot of the heavy equipment down here. See up there.'

Terry pointed up to the sheer long drop. Alex looked too, his mouth falling open at the same time.

'We lower a lot of it from up there, you'll see it all happen tomorrow. But we should head back to camp, it's getting dark.'

As dusk was settling in, I was hoping that no-one in the team was prone to sleepwalking. Strangely, Nathan sprang to mind. It was fantastic out here. Not a picture postcard at all, but apart from the hole in the ground, nothing much looked strange. I don't know what made me think it might. It was the Nullarbor after all – a landscape void of shadows, a sprawling desert of almost pure wilderness. We weren't here for a quick stop on our way through from Perth to Sydney. This was Cocklebiddy, on the Nullarbor Plain, and I was ready to devour all of it – at least the sounds and the sights, if not the cave.

෨෬

The deep colours of the night emerged as the evening sky squeezed the last of the light from the day, and the campsite was alive with activity. Nathan had brought a guitar, and was strumming away while everyone else was pitching their tents. It was lovely, and unexpected. I heard voices around me, nearly spilling with a restrained excitement, and conversations that were full of cautious optimism. I already loved Darcy. She was very maternal and knew what she was doing – must've done this before, many times. Her mobile kitchen was sending out wonderful aromas before I even realised she'd set everything up.

There were little fridges and gas stoves and pots and pans that looked as though they'd been around for camping adventures that had spanned decades; and there were containers full of supplies to last for days on end. There were tea towels and hand towels hanging from the support beams, paper towels and napkins. There were cartons of beer and boxes of Coke, bottles of wine and plenty of water. There were bags for garbage and there were plastic utensils, can openers, bottle openers – this kitchen had it all, even a sink.

Clinton, who would be sleeping in his van, was helping in the kitchen, getting a few tables set up, and unfolding chairs for everyone. The kitchen would be the centre of above-ground activity during the expedition – it was where they'd have their informal meetings to check on progress, much like every kitchen.

I was happy to hang around with them during dinner. There was a lovely relaxed atmosphere as they were all getting to know one another, and I wanted to learn as much as I could – about them and about the dive.

Gary had been right – they seemed to make a good team, in these early stages at least, and it's true to say that a good feed never hurt when it came to keeping spirits up. Those who hadn't arrived for dinner with an extra layer or two soon returned to their tents or vehicles to get something that would keep them warm. It had become cold. I'd read that the nights could be around zero at this time of year, but the food and the camaraderie combined to create a warmth that no amount of cold seemed able to penetrate.

I learned that Julie was French, Stefano was Italian and, as I'd thought, they were a couple. I learned that Ek, and Tee who would be arriving tomorrow, were both from Thailand, and I learned that Alex, apart from being Terry's son, was also Darcy's godson.

I was so happy, being here. The air was clean and the sky clear. The cloud cover from earlier in the afternoon had passed and the wind had dropped. But if I'd thought Sydney's weather could be changeable I was learning fast that out here it could be even more so. We weren't all that far from the coast – a little over thirty kilometres – and it wasn't any old stretch of Australian coastline. This was the Great Australian Bight. Violent storms and strong winds were to be expected, just as day follows night. It could be savage, it could be placid. Tonight, however, all was calm on the ground, and above us the sky was like black velvet, sprinkled with angel dust and shimmering with secrets.

ഇൽ

Once the meal was out of the way and a few of the men had helped to clear things away and clean up, everyone gathered again for a run-down on the following day's activities.

'First up,' Terry began, 'we'll need to check all the equipment one last time before it goes down. I'm not sure what time the others will be here, but it should be before lunch, so let's take the morning to get that done. Enjoy the daylight while you can – you'll be a few days without it.'

I hadn't expected that they'd be staying underground overnight, in a cave that was ninety percent flooded. Ugh. My sense of adventure clearly didn't extend as far as I thought. And that was just the beginning. From what I could gather, equipment failure was always one of their main concerns, so the time they would spend above ground checking it all over tomorrow would be invaluable, and no-one would be taking that task lightly.

I listened with enormous interest and genuine admiration as I learned, on this still winter's night – and thanks largely to Alex – more about this extreme sport.

'How is it all sounding?' Julie asked Alex. Her voice was gentler than I'd expected it to be, and her accent was beautiful.

'Really good,' he replied. 'I wish I could go down with you.'

'Well, I look forward to diving with you some day, young man.'

Alex looked both shy and thrilled.

'One step at a time, buddy,' Terry said. 'Okay guys, tomorrow.

You're all responsible for your own equipment and what you do down there, but we're a team, so we help each other every step of the way.'

Terry was a natural, with a no-nonsense approach that was neither condescending nor arrogant. He'd planned this expedition to minimise risk. He had to. As the team's leader his responsibilities went beyond his own safety. 'Questions?'

'How far are you going?' asked Alex.

Terry had a diagram of the cave spread out on the table where, not long ago, they'd all been enjoying dinner.

'Mal, Ek, Jack and I plan to go as far as Toad Hall?'

'Why do they call it Toad Hall?' asked Alex.

'One day you'll get there, and you'll find out then.'

'Oh Da-aad, that's not fair.'

'Sorry, buddy, that's the way it is.'

'Do you know, Julie?' Alex tried.

'No, Alex. No-one will tell me either.'

'Will you find out tomorrow?'

'Stefano and I are only going as far as Rockpile Chamber – see, here.' She pointed to the map. 'And maybe a few pushes into some of the side passages. I'm not sure about the others. What are their names again, Terry?'

'John and Mark. Like you, they're going as far as Rockpile Chamber, and Tee will be helping us get everything down and then sorted in the entrance chamber.'

'Why don't you all stay together, and go all the way in?'

'Different levels of experience,' said Ek. 'There are cave-rated divers, but Cocklebiddy is rated a "cave and penetration" site, which puts a much bigger restriction on who can go where.'

'He's right,' Terry continued. 'To be a penetration diver means you have to train four or five years, even longer for Cocklebiddy. Only once you've reached that level are you good enough to pass through the Rockpile Chamber at the end of the first sump.'

'What's a sump?'

I was glad Alex asked that one.

'As far as caves go, I suppose it's a bit like an underground lake – a depression in the cave's floor where water collects.'

'Then what?'

'Well, to go any further you need additional equipment and a really big supply of gas, and that requires special training too.'

Gas. Ugh. That fills me with dread.

'What if it explodes?'

Well done Alex! Asking all the questions I'd like to ask.

'That's why preparation is so important, buddy. We have to be prepared for the worst, to be self-sufficient and to know how to deal with emergencies.'

'Like a gas explosion?'

'Well, yes, but that won't happen if we prepare ourselves.'

'So what else might happen?'

Darcy looked concerned. She was trying to attract Terry's attention, perhaps to suggest he tone it down a bit for Alex, but he didn't see her.

'Loss of air supply is a big one, equipment failure, even being blinded by the silt that gets disturbed as we push through really tight passages.'

'Sounds scary, don't you think, Alex?' said Julie.

'Sounds awesome,' he replied, wide-eyed. Darcy just shrugged. 'But yeah, scary too,' Alex added.

I knew what he meant. It did sound awesome, but there must be some element of fear for them at the same time. I suppose they wouldn't get out of it all that they do if they were entirely fearless. And as Terry explained, they've all undergone extensive training. They understood the dangers and they'd make sure they anticipated all the problems. But could they ever be absolutely sure what might happen once they're down there? It's an extreme sport, so the whole idea is that they can't be.

Just as I was starting to wonder if I would've had it in me to cave dive, had I survived – and not had this fear of water – the conversation ended and they decided to call it a night, except Clinton, Terry and Nathan, who lingered a while.

'Beats me why you do it, man,' Nathan said to Terry as they sat in the dimly lit kitchen, their hot drinks slowly cooling. 'Let me ask you this,' he continued. 'If someone told you that this dive would be your last, that this time something is going to go badly wrong and when Alex sees you off into the cave tomorrow, it will be the last you ever see of him – of anyone and anything – would you still do it?'

There was a silence.

'See, I don't think you would, man,' Nathan continued. 'If you knew.'

Shut up Nathan, I wanted to scream.

I looked at Terry and tried to imagine what he was thinking. Probably much the same as I was thinking. Clinton too. That, and how pleased he was that he'd be able to leave Nathan above ground tomorrow, and that he'd be out of earshot for the duration of the dive. This wasn't the time or the place – and it certainly wasn't the audience – for that sort of conversation. Guitar strumming aside, Nathan was irritating. He should've had more sense.

'Yeah, I have to admit, sometimes I don't get it either,' Clinton said, trying to lighten the mood, 'but isn't it good that we're all made so differently, with different interests, or everyone would end up being boring old journos and photographers like us, and we'd be out of a job!'

Go Clinton! Just like that, I could feel the tension that had been building ease.

'So Terry, man, what got you interested in cave diving?'

'It was so long ago I barely remember. I suppose, like so many of us, I started out scuba diving. I've surfed since I was a kid – Clinton and I go way back, don't we mate? It was the ocean – I've always felt like I belong out there.' He paused for a moment. 'That's right – it was a guy I met through scuba diving. He dived in caves. I was curious and couldn't wait to give it a go. And once I'd started, that was it. I couldn't get enough.'

'You'd never get me down there.'

'No, I don't suppose we would,' Terry said, breathing a quiet sigh of relief.

'Crazy, man,' he muttered to himself. 'Well, that's it for me,' Nathan said as he pulled himself up and reached for his guitar. 'See you both in the morning.'

'Do you need a hand with anything, Nate?' Clinton asked.

'No, it's cool.'

'See you in the morning then.'

Clinton and Terry stayed up a while longer. I liked both these men, and was curious about their past, so I hung around a while longer, too. Once Nathan had gone they looked at each other and laughed.

'Is he always that tactful?' Terry asked.

'Yeah, he is.'

'I've long since given up trying to explain to people why I dive. Especially people like Nathan.'

'It's such an unusual thing to do though, mate,' Clinton said. 'People are curious, and maybe a little jealous that they don't have what it takes to do it themselves. Who knows, maybe Nate's afraid of the dark. You know it's not where I'd choose to be.'

'Yeah, but people like him, they don't understand it at all, and what gets me is that they usually don't even want to *try* to understand it. I'm used to people's reactions to cave diving now, but it still irks me.'

'I can see that!'

'It's funny, you know, telling anyone you're a cave diver is a real conversation stopper, but if I were climbing Mount Everest like every other mid-life crisis guy with a stack of money to pay sherpas they'd all think it was great, and that I was normal. But this is exciting stuff, Clint. These caves – they're part of the planet too, and many of them haven't yet been fully explored or documented. People like Nathan – there's no getting through to them. It'll be interesting to see what kind of story he puts together.'

'It'll be great Terry – despite everything else, he's good.'

Terry paused, then said, 'I've heard a bit about him, heard he lived in a drug-induced haze in the '70s, that he's not as sharp as he likes to think he is.'

'But somehow he survived,' Clint said. 'Even pulled himself together enough to carve out a name for himself in journalism. I don't know how he does it, but he is good.'

They were both quiet for a moment.

'I guess we were all more experimental with things back then,' Terry admitted. 'Those old surfing days seem a lifetime ago, don't they mate?' he lamented.

'Yeah, but they were the best, weren't they?'

'Pasta Point certainly was. I wonder if old Davo's still over there in the Maldives? Ever hear from him?'

'Nah, he never spoke to me again after Wendy and I got together. I always felt bad about that, but me and Wendy, we just –'

Clinton stopped.

'Some people are meant to be together, Clint, others aren't. The two of them weren't going to last anyway, whether you'd turned up or not. And he and Casey got together soon after that anyway.' Terry sighed. 'Those were the days, eh?'

I couldn't help thinking that Sophie and Jack were meant to be together, too, and I wished they had been, if only to avoid having to see her so sad for so long.

Clinton hadn't responded, and Terry paused for a moment before he spoke again. 'So how are things? Are you doing okay, really?'

'Not too bad, mate. Nightmares occasionally, but not as many as before. Apart from that, I just miss her. Every day.'

'She was beautiful.'

'Yeah, she was. We had such a great time together, right from the beginning – not many couples can honestly say that. I feel so lucky to have had the time with her that I did. She taught me the beauty to be found in solitude and the gift that we have in true companionship. I'm only haunted by the pain I know she must have felt at the end.'

Terry didn't know what to say. With all the words in the English language, sometimes there still aren't enough.

The silence in the kitchen was now filled with memories of Wendy. Nothing more needed to be said. But as I watched them both, dreaming a little of their younger days, a bizarre scream came from the direction of Nathan's campervan.

'Arrrggghhh!!!'

The two men looked at each other and made a move to see what had happened, but before they'd got to their feet, I caught a glimpse of Nathan jumping frantically from his van. His lanky body resembled a silhouetted, out-of-control marionette under the soft light of the Nullarbor moon. His arms were swinging wildly about him, and his legs were dancing some manic ritualistic move from a long-forgotten tribe of the era psychedelia, and soon he had the attention of every Cocklebiddy camper.

He had mine. I was in hysterics!

Heads had started to appear from the scattered tents, and concern had momentarily filled every pair of weary eyes, until they realised who was making the racket.

'Scorpion! There's a scorpion in my van!' Nathan yelled as he stumbled and then tripped on a tent peg, falling with a thud on the hard earth. But the fall wasn't enough to silence him, and his screaming continued.

'Get it out! Someone get it out of my van! It could've killed me!'

Tobias, Clinton and Terry were the only ones to make a move to help. The others seemed to dismiss him and his alleged scorpion and returned to the warmth of their sleeping bags. I was riveted. Without any TV out here, I'd been missing a little light entertainment!

'Settle down, mate,' Tobias said. 'If it was a scorpion, the Aussie ones aren't lethal. The worst he can do is make the next few hours a little painful for you.'

'I don't care, get it out of there,' Nathan persisted.

While Clinton tried to offer some comfort to this insane over-reacting, Tobias grabbed a torch and went into Nathan's van. I went with him – I'd never seen a scorpion – and the first thing we both noticed was the smell. Nathan had been smoking grass. *No wonder he's acting so weird.* After he'd sniffed the air, Tobias chose to ignore it and searched Nathan's van for the culprit. He was about to give up, mumbling that either Nathan imagined it or the scorpion had found its way out, when he saw movement in the body of Nathan's guitar.

'Aha! Gotcha!' Tobias said quietly as he picked up the guitar and lifted it from the van.

'Got it, Nate. You can sleep in peace tonight. I'll take him for a walk and he won't bother you again.'

Tobias wandered off with the critter still in the guitar until he thought it was a safe enough distance from the campsite, then shook the scorpion free from the guitar's hollow body and returned to where Nathan sat fidgeting. Clinton was attempting to calm his nerves with a cup of hot milk.

'He's gone now, mate,' Tobias reassured him. 'Won't be bothering any of us again tonight.'

'Yeah, you say that, but what if he does, man – how am I supposed to get any sleep out here?'

'I'm sure he won't be coming anywhere near you again, Nate. You've scared the little bugger half to death.'

'Okay, so *he's* gone, but there's got to be other things out here that could kill me in my sleep.'

'And if one of them doesn't, I just might,' I heard Mal mutter to Darcy as they snuggled up and tried to get back to sleep.

It took a while, but Clinton and Tobias eventually convinced Nathan to return to his van, although not before they had to check it completely for anything that might've crept in while they weren't looking. It was the only way Nathan would calm down and get back in. Once he was in, I watched as he made sure the windows were shut tight and the doors locked.

Tobias and Terry slipped back quietly into their tents. Clinton had already returned to Morrie, but I stayed outside for a while longer.

Eventually, calm returned to the campsite. And the silence to be heard a short time later, once everyone had at last, and again, bunked down for the night, seemed larger than the Nullarbor itself – larger still when the eerie sounds of desert wildlife came into play. It had been a difficult night, with so much new information to digest – exciting, frightening information – and a near-empty world right in front of me. I wasn't sure how I felt – it was like I'd experienced a total sensory overload that I wasn't as well equipped to deal with as I thought. But as I made myself comfortable up on Morrie's roof, I glanced out at the stars and thought of Jack. I was sorry he hadn't been around today, but tomorrow isn't far off. And with that thought I drifted off.

Thursday

It wasn't Clinton groaning as he reached for a tin of pineapple that woke me – although that followed soon after – but when the morning wildlife shift took over from their nocturnal friends. I'd stayed on Morrie's roof all night but now dawn was sketching a day full of promise, and the first creatures to know it were the birds. I'd become convinced over the past week that there wasn't a more beautiful time than the moment when everything starts to awaken and breathe life into a new day – when the slightest ripple gently breaks the still of the night and the uncertainty of what lies ahead hasn't yet sunk in. There's a purity in the unknown, an optimism in all its possibilities, and a wonder in the means we use to find them. I would've been a morning person. There were times at night when I found myself consumed by darkness and all that's wrong with the world – me not being a real part of it, for starters.

Sophie was the same. I remembered her first and only long stretch overseas, on her own and away from family and friends and all else that was precious to her. The only time I knew her to feel a strong pang of homesickness came, like clockwork, at the end of each day. She might have been reading, or writing a postcard or a journal entry, but she was always in bed, and when it was time to go to sleep it was that moment as she reached across to turn out the light when a sting of loneliness hit her. Just for a split second, but I knew she always wished there'd been someone with her – not just to enjoy every new experience that travelling in foreign countries presented but to hold her as she fell asleep. That was when I'd done my best work, but she didn't know it was me. She just thought she was tired. The good things in life can often go unnoticed, and she only seemed to know I was there when I was annoying her.

My thoughts were interrupted by a tap on the window, and when I looked down I saw Terry by Morrie's open door.

I couldn't get over how young he looked, especially now. He was wearing a baseball cap. Funny – add a beard, look ten years older, but a baseball cap somehow took years off. But Clinton and Terry seemed to have known each other forever, so I had to assume they were about the same age.

Terry was also smiling. I'd only seen that once yesterday – when Clinton arrived at the roadhouse. Maybe if I encountered him under different circumstances he'd be smiling more, but his smile was there now, and it was easy to picture him as a young boy, because Alex was so much like him. As the leader of this expedition, however, Terry was carrying an enormous responsibility. He was a calm man, organised and entirely professional, but this morning he was enjoying a light moment with Clinton.

'Still keeping those pineapple plantations in business, I see,' he said.

'Everyone's got to do their bit,' Clinton responded with a smile. 'How's it all looking this morning?'

'Looks like a great day. Lots to do before we go down tomorrow, but we should have plenty of time. Will you come down to the entrance chamber with us?'

Clinton gave Terry a sideways glance, raised one eyebrow and said, 'Yeah sure.'

'I'm serious, mate. We've got easily a hundred loads to move before we go down. It would be a big help, and you'd get a first-hand glimpse into the cave. Mal's great, and I'm sure his photos will be too, but the more the better.'

'Well, yeah, maybe,' Clinton said. I could tell he was trying to end this line of conversation. He paused for a moment, and Terry wasn't about to push him.

'No, probably not, eh? But if you change your mind –'

Just then, Alex unzipped the tent he was sharing with Terry and came to join them.

'G'day, Dad. Hi, Clint.'

'Hi.'

'Dad, do you think Darcy would mind if I got some breakfast? I'm starving.'

'Why don't you ask her yourself, she's right behind you.'

Darcy had appeared from the side of the van. 'Ask me what?'

'Is it okay if I get some toast?'

'Sure, help yourself, but I'll be there in a sec to set things up for everyone if you'd rather wait a few minutes and join us. They all seem to be stirring. Good sleep, guys?'

'It sure was,' Terry replied. 'Well, once Nathan got himself settled.'

'Can you believe that guy?' Darcy laughed. 'Our kids wouldn't carry on like that! Come on, Alex,' she said as they went to the makeshift kitchen. 'I'll show you where everything's kept so you can help yourself if I'm not around.'

'How about you, Clint?' Terry said. 'Come and join us – man cannot live on pineapple alone.'

'You go ahead, mate. I'll be right behind you.'

ಶಃ

They were early risers. Within half an hour, and seduced by the smell of toast and brewing coffee, all but one of the campers had emerged, some more bleary-eyed than others but all ready for the day ahead. They were a capable but relaxed group, which could only work in their favour. When situations become tense – as they must in any extreme sport – and as the numbers involved increase, the last thing anyone wants is to have to deal with high-maintenance or up-tight personalities.

Maybe it was this place though. Maybe being stripped of just about everything that makes life comfortable, a person is forced to rely on their innate survival skills. Not just the physical. Getting along with people can be every bit as challenging, and when the two are combined it can create all the ingredients for a volatile situation. It was still early in this expedition, and Nathan, who hadn't yet risen, had already irritated everyone. But he wouldn't be diving, and I gathered that the others had decided it was best to ignore him. By doing that, they should be able to minimise any conflict.

Maybe, too, it was their ages. Apart from Alex and Tee, they must have all been between their mid-thirties and mid-fifties, and I could only think of Sophie and how it wasn't so long ago she'd felt the impact of some kind of turning point in her life, one for the better. A definite shift comes with middle age. I suppose it's because, by then, most people have seen how tough life can be, and realise it's not worth wasting time and emotional energy on the little things. When they're young, everyone seems to want it all, and they think that having it all will secure their happiness, but it doesn't work like that.

As they all tucked into breakfast, the morning chatter of the desert camp faded to a background hum as I thought about Jack, on his way. It had taken a few years and another failed relationship for Sophie to get her head together after she and Jack had stopped seeing each other, but she did it and I had to hand it to her – these days she was enjoying life more than I'd ever known her to. It was weird, like something had swept right over her and sprinkled some kind of magic. Like an epiphany. And it happened around the time she got Cujo. I don't like to admit that he may've succeeded in a way I never have, but he *had* made a huge difference. All the things that had darkened her world for so many years suddenly lifted, and none of it seemed to matter anymore. She started looking at her life for what it was rather than what she'd hoped it would be, and what she saw she couldn't argue with. Life was good. There was nothing she could honestly say she wanted, or wanted to change. It was that simple.

I have to admit I didn't believe it could possibly be that simple, which is why I've been hanging around so long, still trying to push her in directions I'm finally beginning to understand she seriously doesn't want – doesn't need – to go.

ಬಂಚ

As breakfast was being cleared away, the sound of a vehicle approaching the campsite made heads turn. I hoped it was Jack. It wasn't.

'Looks like John and Mark,' Terry said. 'Excellent.'

He wandered over to meet their four-wheel-drive and extended his hand to greet each of the men as they stepped out.

'Good to see you, John. You're earlier than I'd expected.'

'G'day, Terry. Yeah, we arrived in Cocklebiddy late last night and thought it easier to grab a room at the roadhouse and make our way over this morning. You know Mark, don't you?'

John and Mark could've almost been twins themselves, and while they were a little more solid than Terry, the three of them all looked about the same age. I'm guessing they *were* mid-thirties though. They were strong looking men. Mark had gingery blond hair, John's was fair and a bit curly, but both were blessed with particularly friendly and strangely similar faces and, like all the others, they were dressed for the occasion, with one small difference. Mark wore a faded black T-shirt with 'Shit happens' emblazoned across the front.

'Sure do. G'day, Mark. I hope it doesn't!'

Mark looked puzzled.

'Your T-shirt. You guys hungry? You could still grab something for breakfast if you haven't eaten already. I'll introduce you to Darcy – she'll fix you up with something.'

'Thanks, but we showered and ate back at the roadhouse,' Mark said. 'You can put us straight to work.'

'Great! Come and I'll introduce you to everyone. We're just about to get all the gear out and sorted.'

༄༅༄

I watched in amazement as all the equipment was brought out. I'd been wondering how they could possibly fill in a day, even more, getting this stuff from their vehicles down to the cave, but until Terry had mentioned gas, I hadn't thought much beyond a pair of flippers for each of the divers.

Now I thought about it, there *had* been a lot of equipment in the photos on display at the museum in Balladonia, and Clinton had talked to Gary about fixing a camera to a scooter. When I stopped to think about it, the photos had looked like they could've been stills from some big-budget science fiction movie, but with the space junk from Skylab it was easy to let my mind wander, and I hadn't taken as much notice of the diving display as I should've. It was fast becoming real and deadly serious, and I was glad Clinton wasn't planning on going down. Right now he was looking sane among a group of what I suspect might be a bunch of crazy people.

Alex was with all the divers, helping if he could, but so much of the equipment would've been too heavy for him and they couldn't risk the possibility of any damage.

'What's that, Dad?'

'It's called an A-frame. Before anything can be lowered down to the cave's entrance, we need to fix it in place and make sure it's secure.'

'What about that sign?'

Just metres from Terry, a third sign warned of the cave's potential danger. 'CAVE UNSAFE' it said. 'DANGER! ENTRY PROHIBITED.' I wondered what a sign would have to say before these guys changed their minds about going down.

'It's okay, buddy. Like I said yesterday, we're okay to go.'

'How do you know the frame won't fall?'

'We use these fixtures, see, in the rocks?' Alex peered closer. 'Other divers who have been here before us put them in place.'

The frame looked flimsy to me, positioned precariously as it was, just an arm's length from that fifty-metre drop, and at no point on the northern arc of that enormous hole would you want to drop anything, especially yourself – only rocks would break your fall. But Terry assured Alex it was secure.

'But what if it does?' Alex persisted.

'It'll be fine, Alex. I'll make sure it is.'

'How does it work?'

'See this swing-out arm? We secure the equipment to this, then ease it over the edge and lower it slowly down. One of the guys will be down there waiting for it. Then later on, we'll use a flying fox to move the gear from down at the cave's entrance to the entrance chamber. It all gets methodically sorted and stacked from there.'

'How long will it take?'

'We'll be doing this all day and well into the night. Each of us will have to make a few trips down and back before everything we need for the next three days is there and ready to go.'

Three days! This was amazing. Like Alex, I was completely spellbound, and decided I wasn't going anywhere today. I'd hang out with Terry. This was like nothing I'd ever seen before and I wanted to watch it all.

'Dad?'

'Yeah, buddy?'

'What if you fall?'

Terry laughed. 'I won't fall, bud – that's why I'm wearing this harness.'

Terry's harness was attached to the A-frame, and I could see how important it was as, one by one, the others were bringing load after load for Terry to rope up and gently lower down. They all handled the equipment with such care, and there wasn't a lot of joking around, but it wasn't a job done entirely without humour. While Terry worked at ground level, Mal was down at the cave's entrance, receiving all the equipment at the other end of the pulley, and unstrapping it as it arrived. As the hours passed and his appetite was building, he placed his lunch order from fifty metres below, over a walkie-talkie.

'You there, mate?' I heard his voice crackle from something attached to Terry's waistband.

'Hearing you loud and clear,' Terry said.

'I'd like a ham and cheese toasted sandwich thanks – with butter, not margarine. Oh, and a chocolate milkshake.'

Terry smiled. Alex lit up. 'Can I get a chocolate milkshake too, Dad?'

'Not out here, buddy,' Terry said as he brushed his hand across Alex's head. 'He might as well have asked for lobster and champagne.'

Alex's smile faded as Terry grabbed his walkie-talkie and responded to Mal.

'No worries, mate – we'll get that down to you, along with some sunscreen.'

೭੦੦੩

The morning seemed to slip away with all the activity, but it was fantastic. I spent my time with Alex and Terry, watching the equipment pass by. Sometimes I went down with it, riding on the flying fox. Funny name. It doesn't look anything like a fox, and a real flying fox would have been heaps more fun!

Darcy was over in the kitchen getting lunch prepared when the second last of the divers arrived. And this time it *was* Jack. Yay! He seemed to appear without anyone noticing – they were all so engrossed in their tasks – but when his four-wheel-drive was almost at the campsite, John yelled out, 'Car!'

Ha ha! I bet he had kids, or was still a big one himself. I remembered a road trip Celia had taken Sophie and her brothers on, when they'd try to pass the time with games. It wasn't 'Car' but 'Cow' on their list of things to look out for.

I felt a strange rush of nerves when I saw Jack pull up, but as soon as I heard his voice, all was good. Weird – that was more like Sophie than me. I'd love to have seen them together out here. He would've been so surprised if he'd pulled up and seen Soph. But I had to stop myself from thinking such thoughts – she wasn't here and it was better that way.

Jack got out of his vehicle and headed across to Terry as the others who were above ground made their way over to him as well.

'Terry, how are things?'

'Jack. About time you showed up! Good to see you, mate. How was the trip?'

'Long,' he said. 'Sorry I wasn't able to make it yesterday – I got away much later than I'd hoped.'

'No worries, we're just glad to have you here. Everything's okay I hope?'

Jack was non-committal. 'How's it all going?'

'So far so good,' said Terry. 'Ah look, here come our last pair of hands.'

Once Tee had parked his truck, he joined the others.

Terry pulled out his walkie-talkie. 'Come on up, guys. Jack and Tee are here, and lunch isn't far off.' Terry made a few introductions, the rest once the others were back. Jack had heard the names of some in the group but hadn't met any of them before. Same with Tee.

'Tee's going to be helping us get things to and from the entrance chamber. He's studying geology, in Thailand.'

'Good to meet you, Tee,' Jack said. 'Is this Alex?'

Alex grinned.

'Well hello stranger! You'll be as tall as your dad soon.'

'Hi, Jack,' Alex was beaming.

'Is Jude with you, mate?' Jack asked Terry.

'No, the two younger ones are still in school. It's a bit of a treat for Alex, being here.'

'Except I have to write a diary,' he groaned.

'And one day you'll be glad you did,' Terry said.

'Lunch is ready!' Darcy called from the kitchen.

'You've both arrived at the right time. Let's go!'

ଛଠ

Darcy had made so many sandwiches for everyone, and I couldn't believe how fast they disappeared. She didn't seem surprised – she'd seen it all before.

It was good, seeing Jack again, but he wasn't saying much. It was Tee who was doing most of the talking during lunch. Uni students – they're always happy to share their newly acquired knowledge with anyone who'll listen.

When I glanced over at Terry, I saw a hint of concern in his eyes as he looked towards Jack. I hoped everything was okay.

'It's surprisingly fragile under the ground,' Tee was saying. 'These limestone formations are so easily damaged, even destroyed if people don't know what they're doing down there. Which I'm sure you all do,' he hurried to add.

'It's beautiful down there,' Julie said. 'The limestone formations are pure white under the water, and the walls become dappled cream and white with the light –'

'The sensation of diving,' Stefano added, 'it's amazing. The saline waters give you neutral buoyancy, so you feel like an astronaut, floating in outer space.'

'What's saline, Dad?' Alex asked.

'Salty, and they're right. It's another world down there, and that sensation of floating is heightened by how crystal clear the water is. Not all the way through the cave, but in parts.'

'It does sound amazing,' Clinton said.

'Will you be going down?' Tee asked him.

'No, I hate to admit it, but I hate dark, confined spaces. I'd be wanting a few more air chambers than Cocklebiddy has – some skylights would be good too. And I don't want to be getting in the way of all you experts – you don't need that sort of distraction down there.'

After lunch was finished and cleared away, the diagram from last night was returned to the table. It helped me to understand what it was like down there, and with all the talk that was going on, I was feeling a lot less clueless than I was when we first arrived. Cocklebiddy Cave is a long straight tunnel, most of which is flooded, but it has two dry air chambers – Rockpile Chamber and Toad Hall. They'd been talking about those yesterday. That's where the divers can stop for a while and breathe normally. *Just as well.*

'Those air chambers aren't such a good thing for us, mate,' Terry continued from where they'd left off. 'It would be much easier to just swim through from start to finish, without having to worry about the air chambers in the middle.'

'Why?' Alex asked.

'Because of all the heavy gear we have with us. We have to carry a lot of that, like you would a backpack – it's on a harness over our wet-suits. So all of that has to go across the rockpiles, which is hard enough at the best of times, but these rockpiles are unstable and hazardous.'

'The areas you might think would be the easiest, because it's dry, are actually the hardest part of the dive,' Tee said.

'What got you interested in geology, Tee?' Terry asked. 'And diving?'

'I have a fascination with the deep – the deep layers of history in the rocks, whether they're above or below ground. I can't wait to get enough training under my belt to go cave diving. It's got to be surreal.'

'That's true, but it's no picnic! A lot of it is just bloody difficult!'

I liked Terry. For a guy in charge of a group like this, with so much responsibility, plus having his son out here, he had just the right way of getting a message across. I learned at lunch time that he was a university lecturer. *I should've guessed.* He'd be a great teacher – he's got so much knowledge. I couldn't imagine him ever coming down hard on his students, or making them feel inadequate, and I was sure he'd be the kind of teacher his students would respect, but could also think of as a mate. He seemed a natural leader, the kind of man you wanted heading a team like this one, and I liked his gentle humour. It was perfect for easing any pre-dive tension that may've been building.

'You should find plenty of inspiration out here, Tee. Everyone does,' said Clinton.

'Yeah, it's like that, isn't it?' said Jack.

I didn't think Clinton had been listening to the conversation, so I was surprised when he spoke. He'd spent a lot of the lunch break at one end of the kitchen, deep in conversation with Mal, who would be photographing the actual dive. *That'd be hard, handing the job over*, but their roles were clearly defined, and they both seemed fine with it.

'Okay everyone, let's get back to work,' Terry said.

Having seen the preparations that were going on this morning, and heard everything at lunchtime, I was starting to look at the cave's entrance as not just a great big hole in the ground, but more like some strange doorway into another world – one I'd become very curious about. Damn my water phobia. Despite the potential dangers, there was a sense of calm about the team as they busily prepared for the days ahead. I was itching to go down. Maybe you'd have to be at least as far as the cave's entrance chamber, watching as they all swapped their overalls and boots for wetsuits and fins, and disappeared into who knew where, before the sense of danger really kicked in. Or maybe it's one of those weird things where, because it's so calm underground, the dangers are camouflaged.

There was no doubt in my mind that what they were doing was enormously risky, but without that level of risk they'd never be sure how far they could push themselves.

That's where I started to question so much about this sort of adventure though – when reality kicked in for me. Risk and pushing yourself to that extent might be a fine concept for them, but in my mind, it had one significant flaw. Surely once you reached that point where it was too far, it was also too late. Lights out. Time's up. Show's over. Another wife left without her husband, kids without their dad. Sure, you've taken yourself that little bit further, but is it worth it? I know Sophie's dad – my dad – would've given anything to be able to see his children grow up, to be part of their lives all the way. It's bad enough when we have no control over a life taken too soon, but it does seem to be madness flirting with death the way these people do.

It must've been Jack's arrival that started me thinking like that. And it was because I knew him. I wasn't close to the others, but I knew each of them would've meant the world to someone – a family of someones. Did they think about that. Did they care? I had to assume that the chances of disaster were far outweighed by the likelihood of a successful dive, and I knew they'd say that there's more risk getting into your car in the morning and going to work. Probably true. I also had to tell myself that rather than the divers being the selfish ones, selfishness was on both sides. Isn't that just the way everyone's made?

Living your dreams, that's what it's all about, and no-one should have to settle for a life that doesn't allow them to explore those dreams.

⊰⊱

It was a beautiful day – not a cloud in the sky and a gentle breeze helping to keep everyone fairly cool as they worked up a sweat. I can't imagine how unbearable the heat out here would be in the summer, although I don't suppose anyone would be foolish enough to do this sort of thing then. It was a little over twenty degrees, according to the thermometer Darcy had hanging in the kitchen – perhaps a bit more out in the early afternoon sun – but when Nathan had come to talk to Terry this morning, Terry said that once they were down in the cave, the temperature would be stable. It is year-round. He said it's around nineteen degrees in the water, and a degree or two warmer out, although the further in you go, the warmer it gets.

I wanted to hang out with Clinton and Nathan this afternoon, but not until I'd spent a bit more time with Terry, because he and Jack were making their way over to the A-frame to start moving some more heavy loads down that hole, and I thought the two of them might talk. They did.

'Is everything okay, mate?' Terry asked.

'It will be,' Jack replied.

Terry's tone was hesitant. 'Not Charlie?'

'No, not Charlie. He's doing great.' Jack paused. 'Diane and I have split up.'

Oh. My. Goodness.

'Oh mate, I'm sorry to hear that.'

Not me, this could be fantastic news for Sophie!

'Would've happened a long time ago if Charlie hadn't been so sick. We've just grown apart over the years.'

'Are you okay?'

'Yeah, but she was at me again when I went to see the kids before I left – you know she never liked me diving – and that upset them. I just needed to make sure they were okay before I left home, so I stayed that extra night.'

'And they are?'

'Yeah, they settled down. It took a while, but they're okay.'

'How about you, Jack? Are you up to the dive – because if you don't think you are, or you'd rather not, you only have to say the word?'

'Wouldn't be here if I wasn't up for it, mate. It's when I feel most alive, when I'm diving. Let's get back to work.'

Had they been two women, that particular conversation would've lasted a couple of hours rather than a couple of minutes, but Jack and Terry were moving the equipment in the next breath, as though nothing had been said.

Mind racing, I left them and went to find Clinton and Nathan. I wanted to tell Sophie that Jack had split from his wife. She wouldn't know yet, I'm sure of it, but I was powerless. Ugh. Sometimes being me is the most frustrating thing in the universe. But then even if I'd been with her, I wouldn't have been able to convince her. The most I could've done was try to talk her into calling him. That was some consolation, and I know she'll find out soon enough. The old gossip-line will be onto it in no time.

Clinton had been shooting all morning while I was with Terry at the edge of that hole, and he was doing more of the same this afternoon. He was so unobtrusive, capturing these busy hours without getting in anyone's way, which had been interesting to watch. A few days ago I would've thought he was better on his own, shooting nothing but nature, but his talent extended beyond that. I should've known this man could turn his hand in whatever direction he needed to, without fuss, and with truckloads of skill. Well, except going down into a dark, flooded cave. I never imagined he'd have that kind of fear, but I was with him on that!

I was amazed by Clinton's ability to not get in the way. There were times I don't think the divers even realised he was hovering, sometimes within just feet of them. It helped that they were so busy. He shot their faces, he also shot hands. Lots of hands, hard at work. He was looking for patterns when equipment was being laid out, and he always found interesting angles. He paid particular attention to composition, as well as light and shadows. Out here in the middle of nowhere the light was unique.

Then there was Nathan, whose approach was harder to describe – Nathan-like was perhaps the best I could come up with. After last night, word had spread around camp that his social skills didn't live up to the standard of his writing. But everyone was prepared to start fresh again today – to forget the blunders of last night and give Nathan a chance to do the job he'd been sent out here to do.

He'd be tolerated, just, but only for the sake of the article. And I knew that for some, even that was going to be an effort. He seemed harmless enough, and well-meaning, but he did say what was on his mind before he thought too much about it, or who he was saying it to. Out here, on the Nullarbor with a team of divers, that wasn't real smart.

These two men, Clinton and Nathan, had both lived a good half of their lives, and it showed on their faces, particularly out here under the glare of the desert sun, where shadows caught the lines that made older faces so interesting. That was one of the beautiful things about the ageing process – the lyrics of people's lives become etched on their faces as the years pass. Those who let it, that is. I've never been able to understand why anyone would want to erase all that.

Like Clinton, Nathan had been working since he'd arrived, but unlike Clinton, he fell short on subtlety. He was all over the camp, asking questions of the divers and participating in their conversations, but mostly he just hung around, taking it all in, trying not to get in the way but often failing miserably. He kept one pen in his ponytail, and he carried another on him, sometimes between his teeth, but most of the time it was sticking out of his shirt pocket with a note pad that he would pull out from time to time.

Nathan also tried to lend a hand where he thought he might be able to help, but he wasn't asked to much. He tried to engage with members of the team in conversation that I could only assume he was gearing towards his story. He asked so many questions, most of them intelligent and all of which, eventually, resulted in an outpouring not only of facts about diving, Cocklebiddy and the Nullarbor, but also about what drives these people to such an obscure pastime.

'So Jules –' Nathan began.

'Julie, please,' she replied.

'Sorry, Julie. I notice you're the only female diver out here. What are there, eight of you going down? Is that normal?'

'Yes, it is. Not just here in Australia but the world over. Extreme adventure sports attract more men than women, although it's changing.'

'Why do you think that is?'

'I don't know, maybe the answer lies in that Y chromosome.'

'Well, what made you start diving?'

'That would be Stefano!' she said. 'We've been together many years. We met when we were scuba diving off the coast of Malta. We talked about a lot of things, as people do when they're getting to know each other, and he'd just started to cave dive. He made it sound so wonderful, and I knew if I did it too, we could spend more time together. But there are many reasons why people like to dive. Like Tee, who is studying geology.'

'Ah yes.'

'I have seen how very beautiful it is in parts of the caves,' Julie continued, 'and the feeling of weightlessness, as Terry was saying last night. It's indescribable.'

'It did sound pretty cool,' Nathan admitted, 'but you could have been an astronaut if you wanted to float in space.'

'Well yes, and maybe if Stefano had been doing that, I would have too. But that's not the way it happened for me.'

'Are you and Stefano competitive?'

Julie laughed. 'No, not at all, at least not with each other! Some people are and maybe that's what draws them to dive. Everyone has their own reason.'

'Ah yes, the desire to go further than anyone else has ever been.'

'Oui, and many are just fascinated with the deep. It's hard to explain to someone who doesn't do it, but the rewards are enormous. But I need to go now, Nathan. Will you excuse me?'

'Oh, yeah, sure Jules – uh, sorry, Julie. Thanks!'

Julie had caught sight of the others converging at the campsite. Stefano, Mark and John were getting their things together, ready to make their way down the slope and into the cave, where Mal and Ek were waiting. They were all collecting their backpacks. Stefano handed Julie hers, and I hopped on board.

Darcy and Alex were coming across from the kitchen, Bob and Tobias a few steps behind.

'Are they about to go down?' asked Alex.

'I think they might be,' replied Darcy.

'Wish I was going,' he said.

I felt the same. It *was* getting exciting. *So what's stopping you?* Right then, I didn't have a good answer for myself, not if I went just as far as the entrance chamber. I could do that.

Nathan offered to help them for this initial land-based descent into the cave, and although the uncertainty of whether or not they should accept his offer was clear on their faces, they knew that the more hands they had the better. Clinton stayed to help Terry and Jack until the last of the heavy stuff had made it safely down, then Terry gave Alex a hug before he, Jack, Nathan and Tee were on their way.

'This is it,' Nathan said to Clinton as they reached the edge of the slope. The others kept walking. 'Down they go. You know I read that swallows gather around the entrance to the cave – they dig the coolness of the cavern at dusk.'

'Is that right?' Clinton said.

'Yeah, and at the same time they stir up the bats who hang around in there, which makes them go crazy and take off. Maybe I'll see them when I get down there, bursting into the evening sky.'

'If you do, and they come out, I'll be ready to shoot them,' Clinton said.

Nathan looked alarmed and was about to speak when he realised what Clinton meant. 'Oh, I get it! Shoot. Camera. You got me there, Clint!'

And when I listened, I could hear them. The birds. Bats too. Wow. Just as well Cujo isn't here. But I wondered if they'd be a problem for the divers, whipping in and out like that. I suppose not, or they might've talked about it.

Without having to carry anything, the track down to the entrance wouldn't have been too hard to walk down. And it was a breeze for me. But they'd all taken some of the lighter equipment with them, as well as their packs, and had to be super careful. A little way in, a whole lot of uneven steps and boulders down a ten-metre drop were both helpful and hazardous, but once they'd passed that section, it was much easier for them to navigate their way down.

About three hundred metres later, they reached an extensive cavern, a sloping mud bank.

'This is it, guys! Welcome to Cocklebiddy,' Terry said. 'This is the entrance chamber. This is where we'll be preparing all our gear.'

And at that point, I went back up and outside.

The afternoon light had an eerie glow, although maybe I was imagining it. With most of the group underground, I was starting to feel a bit uneasy. What Nathan said hadn't helped. Ever since I'd watched that Hitchcock movie with Sophie, years ago, birds in big numbers had given me the creeps.

ஐஜ

'How's that diary coming along, Alex?' Darcy asked from the kitchen. I was in there with her, sitting on her shoulder.

Nathan and Tee were both back up after helping the divers, and Darcy had started preparing dinner for the few remaining above-ground campers. She'd organised all the food the team needed to take down into the cave with them well in advance – tonight they'd be having tinned spaghetti in the entrance chamber, where they'd be sleeping – and seemed relieved that this day was almost behind them. Tonight she could relax, although until Mal was back with her I didn't think she'd be sleeping too soundly.

'It's not,' Alex said as he slouched at the table.

'Well you'd better get started. What's stopping you?'

'I don't know what to write.'

'Alex James, that's the most pathetic excuse I've ever heard! I bet your classmates would be wishing they had as much to write about as you do right now. Come on, I'll help you. Where's your diary?'

'In the tent.'

'Then go and get it and we can work on it together while I get dinner.'

Alex returned with his diary, and Clinton.

'Looks like we've got some homework to do!' Clinton said to Darcy.

'Oh good, I'm glad you're here. Would you peel these potatoes please?'

'Sure, I can do two things at once,' he winked at Alex. 'Let's get you started here.'

'But that's the thing, I don't know how to start.'

'Well, it's a diary,' said Darcy, 'so start with the date.'

Alex did as he was told.

'All you have to do next is write what you've been doing today. Easy.'

Alex got going, but after a few minutes he stopped.

'What's up?' Clinton asked.

'I want to write down all the stuff I saw Dad sending down into the cave, but I can't remember it all.'

'What have you got so far?'

'Um, oxygen tanks and lots of air cylinders – more than I could be bothered counting – twin and single …'

Terry had been explaining to Nathan earlier in the day that the risk of air failure once they were inside the cave was one they couldn't ignore. Divers always pushed in pairs, and each diver needed to save at least two-thirds of his total air supply for the return journey, in case his partner's tank failed. The further a diver pushed into a cave, the longer he'd be spending underwater, and so the more air tanks were going to be needed. Made sense to me, but that was just the beginning.

'Sledges …'

To help them carry these extra air cylinders they either needed more divers – who in turn needed more air – or more sledges. The sledges would prove invaluable when it came to carrying the enormous amounts of air that were required. It all became a very cumbersome exercise.

'Regulators, harnesses, plates, and something else, um, was it a wing?'

'Yep, good boy,' Darcy said. 'And the wing is used as a –?'

'A buoyancy condensator.'

'Com*pen*sator. Well done! What else?'

'Um, computers?'

'You bet! No self-respecting twenty-first century expedition of this scale would be complete without computers! What do they use them for?'

'To show depth and time.'

'And?'

'I can't remember.'

Tobias joined in. 'Decompression. Cocklebiddy's shallow as far as underwater caves go – the water's less than fifteen metres in most places, so decompression isn't a serious threat but, like everything else, it needs to be factored in to the long list of possibilities. What else is there?'

Alex was quiet.

'What was your dad using to lower everything down?'

'Oh, flying foxes and abseiling equipment, and ladders.'

The logistics of it all were becoming mind blowing. I could only try to imagine how much more stuff, and divers, might have been required if Terry or any of the others had been planning on going *all* the way to the end of the cave. Cocklebiddy was over six kilometres long, so the pyramid of support that they'd need to reach the end, in human and technical input, would've been huge.

'Okay, what about the smaller stuff? What did each of the divers need for themselves?'

'A wetsuit.'

'Yep, what else?'

'A safety helmet with a strong torch at the front, a mask, heavy-duty gloves, um, knee pads, climbing boots –'

'You're on a roll Alex, keep going!'

'Extra clothes, just in case. Space blankets to sleep under. Spare torches, spare batteries, spare everything in case their equipment failed.'

'See, this isn't so hard. Any more?'

'Lights. They had heaps of lights.'

'That's right,' Clinton said. 'They had LED lights, HID lights and standard light heads, as well as lamps they could use out of the water. Sounds like overkill, doesn't it!'

'It might sound that way, but it's not,' said Darcy. 'Down there it's a world of complete darkness. If anyone were to get lost, underground or underwater, not having any light would make even the bravest of them learn the true meaning of fear.'

You could, I was learning, never have too many torches.

'What about if they get dehydrated? Heat can be a problem and they can't drink the water in the cave,' Tobias added.

'Oh I know,' remembered Alex. 'They had lots of bottled water. And they needed those tube thingies to keep things dry. Their food and tools.'

'What about if guidelines weren't already down there from other divers, to help guide them back to the entrance chamber?'

'Oh yeah, they needed to take guidelines.'

It was a bit like Hansel and Gretel.

'Did you get the big stuff?' asked Tobias. He glanced down at Alex's list and saw he'd missed a few things. 'Remember they took down half a dozen scooters – long- and short-bodied – to propel them through the water.'

Scooters? Far out, was this list ever going to end? I had to admit, scooters were definitely a far more sophisticated means of travel than flippers.

'What were they for, did anyone tell you?'

'Yeah,' Alex was looking pleased with himself for remembering. 'They use them to tow the underwater sledges. Oh, I just remembered something else,' said Alex. 'They took containers for their wee and poo!' he giggled.

'That's one part of it all that I don't like to think about!' said Darcy. 'Especially while I'm getting dinner. How are those potatoes coming along, Clint?'

'Almost done, Darce.'

'All their waste in fact,' added Bob, who until now had been quietly doing a crossword. 'Cave divers know to take nothing but pictures and leave nothing but bubbles.'

Alex giggled again and wrote that down. 'Is that enough?' he asked.

'I think that'll do,' Darcy said. 'Dinner's almost ready. You can put your diary back in your tent and wash your hands. That goes for all of you.'

ಸಾಂಛ

It was a lovely, still evening. After dinner, and once the mess had been cleared away, Tee took his tent from his truck and set about organising his sleeping quarters. Nathan focused his attention on Bob and Tobias, and the roles they had to play in all this, while Clinton seemed content just being there with this small group of people in the still of the Nullarbor night. I was too.

A little later, it was Darcy's turn to tell the others as much as she knew about Cocklebiddy, the cave, and what the few days ahead would be like for the divers. She was getting on beautifully with Clinton – whether or not that was because they were both such easy-going people

I wasn't sure. Maybe it had something to do with the fact that, along with Nathan (who, with the others safely underground, wasn't creating so much tension), they were roughly the same age and so shared a lot of generational stuff. Whatever it was, there was an enormous amount of laughter in the kitchen. Recollections of songs they all knew – many of which they would sing as Nathan strummed softly on his guitar – of what it was like growing up where and when they did, and a good many stories left Alex and Tee wondering if life really was as good back then as they were making it sound.

Friday

It was another beautifully tranquil dawn as I awoke and found myself reflecting on the night before and the day that was. It had been a good night, a peaceful night, most of which I'd spent awake, on top of Morrie again, thinking about Jack. And Sophie. And the possibilities. Or not. Maybe he'd met someone else. And even if he hadn't, that didn't mean he'd try again with Sophie. Or that she'd even want him to. She seemed to have moved on and maybe she wouldn't be interested in going down that path now.

All was quiet at the campsite. There'd been a lot of subdued anxiety around here in the past twenty-four hours, but it had vanished entirely – either that or it went down underground with the others. Darcy was lovely – as supportive of Mal's adventures as any wife could be, short of joining him in the bowels of the earth, and more supportive than Jack's wife had obviously been. But also concerned, again as any wife would be, every time he disappeared below ground level. And as Alex's godmother, she'd be concerned for him and Terry, as well. Perhaps it was the softness in her voice combined with an authoritative and matter-of-fact approach to her storytelling that made everything seem so relaxed last night, but I thought a lot of it probably had to do with the absence of all the equipment that had filled the campsite before it was moved out of sight.

Life on the surface might've seemed relatively blissful at this point, but there were still things that needed ongoing attention. Once everyone was up and finished with breakfast, they all lingered a while in the kitchen with Darcy, talking about all sorts of things – the cave, the divers and themselves – before they set to work.

'Do you think they'd all be awake yet?' Alex asked Darcy.

I had assumed that, just as the others were waking up for the start of a new day, so too, deep underground, would be the divers. Alex and I were on the same wavelength a lot of the time. I wondered how they'd all slept. What it was really like down in Cocklebiddy Cave, where day and night were indistinguishable and there was no such thing as climate change, or even much of a fluctuation in temperature.

'They would've been up for a while, Alex.'

'I wish I had a magic camera that could see down into the cave, so we could watch what they were doing.'

Clinton laughed. 'That *would* be something, wouldn't it?'

'I'd say they're about to start making their way into that flooded tunnel as we speak,' said Bob.

'That'd be cool, watching them disappear into the black,' Nathan said.

'Except it won't be black,' Darcy stressed, trying to reassure Alex – herself too – and get a point across to Nathan. 'Don't forget the number of torches they took down there with them. It might be brighter down there than it is up here.'

I wondered about that. The tunnel they were heading into was huge – some thirty metres across – and I wasn't convinced that their torches could light the cave up as much as Darcy suggested, but she would've known a lot more than I did. I couldn't help thinking, though, light is life.

'And hotter,' added Nathan.

'Yeah, but they all know what to expect, Nathan. You couldn't get a better prepared group of people.'

'Is it hot down there?' Alex asked.

'It can be hot for them, while they're busy, but then it can get cold when they stop,' Darcy said. 'That's why they have the special blankets with them.'

'How long between when they start diving and when they can stop?' he asked.

'Well, they have to make lots of return trips through that first sump to Rockpile Chamber – that's about a one-kilometre swim. They stockpile the air cylinders there, and the other equipment they'll need to go any further,' Darcy told him.

'That's a lot of labour,' Bob added. 'It'll take them the best part of today to do that.'

'The whole day! But it's just a kilometre,' Alex said.

'Yep,' said Bob. 'It wouldn't take that long if you were just wearing your togs, but remember all the equipment they took down? A lot of that has to be strapped to their bodies, which makes it tough-going for them. And they have to do it again and again, to get everything across to the chamber.'

'Still think you want to be a diver?' Darcy asked Alex.

'You bet! I wish I was down there now, then I could help them. What happens once they get to Rockpile Chamber?'

'Well, it's a good place for them all to stop for a while. Rockpile Chamber is their base camp,' Darcy told him. 'It's fairly comfortable – with good air for them. That's where they'll be spending tonight.'

'It's also a good place for a rest day,' said Bob.'

'A rest day? What will they do for a whole day?' Alex asked.

'Rest!' said Tobias. 'They're all incredibly efficient, but think about all the effort involved in getting everything from the campsite to the entrance chamber, and then to base camp. That was all done on top of the long drive just to get out here to Cocklebiddy.'

'And a flight for some of them,' said Tee. 'Jetlag!'

'They need the day tomorrow before Terry and the other push divers continue to Toad Hall on Sunday. It's tiring work, and dangerous, so they have to be well rested.'

Terry had been saying at dinner the night before last that they'd been preparing for this dive for eighteen months, and that no-one was out to break any records. They were lured by the vision of a world virtually untouched, an environment that was older than any of us could fathom. He was ideal to lead the team at Cocklebiddy, having been many times before, and I'd seen how much he loved it. Jack too.

'It'll give Mal a chance to take some photos,' said Clinton. 'He said he was hoping to experiment with panoramic shots in the two air chambers.'

'And Stefano was saying he's into fossils,' said Bob. 'They'll have plenty to do for the day, but most of all they'll be taking it easy. You know for most cave divers, Cocklebiddy is on their list of must-do dives, so no-one wants it to be over in a hurry. They're happy taking their time down there.'

As Sophie opened her blinds she was greeted by gloomy skies, and within moments the rain had started up again, albeit lightly. She and Cujo managed a short walk before Sophie left for work, but both arrived home a little damper than they'd been before they left. Sophie dried Cujo off with a towel – he loved it when she did that – and then went for a shower.

She'd been thinking about Jack ever since she'd woken up. It was impossible not to, knowing he was out on the Nullarbor where she was now convinced Georgia had also gone. *If it weren't for Cujo being a little more subdued than usual, I'd have to say I've been feeling really good these past few days. Like I don't have to explain myself all the time, and I'm not doubting myself so much either. Something's different. Georgia has gone, I'm sure of it, and Cujo knows it too.*

What's wrong with you, Sophie? she wondered. *You know Georgia's not real.*

The days of dwelling on Jack had passed, but she was curious about his diving, knowing he was at Cocklebiddy, and tried to picture it out there in the middle of nowhere, down in that cave.

Sophie had decided to take Cujo in to work with her, as she was enjoying a fairly relaxed couple of days in at Gedup'n'go. The long weekend was approaching and many of her workmates had taken the opportunity to have an even longer break, leaving the office quiet and the workload not at all demanding.

The weather had been improving over the last couple of days, too. Although everyone knew how desperately Sydney needed the rain, it never took all that long once it did start raining for people to crave a little sunshine again.

But the rain was getting heavier as Sophie drove to Gedup'n'go with Cujo. She walked quickly through the courtyard on her way in, but not so quickly that she missed the ducks. She always went in past the ducks. It was perfect weather for them, and the tranquil flowing waters of the little pond in the courtyard, as they spilled over rocks from the top deck to the pool below, were not only a calming influence on the staff but an invitation to the local ducks when they felt like a dip. Watching them as they splashed down the tiny waterfall and then waddled back up, only to go through it all again, always made for a good start to the working day.

The ducks were there, playing as usual. Sophie and Cujo could've watched them for ages, but she didn't linger. She went straight to her desk. It was situated, as most of them were, alongside a wall of glass that looked out onto bush. Some mornings, when she arrived after heavy rains the night before, she would walk in and see a picture of calm and exquisite beauty before her – trees with branches weighed down by innumerable water droplets that sparkled as the early morning sun cast its rays upon them. Trunks that had been blackened by the rainfall a stark contrast to the ethereal mist that floated weightlessly through every twist and curve on every tree. But not this morning. There were no rays coming in from the sun today.

It was a quiet morning in the office, and when it was time for lunch Sophie grabbed a cup of tea, her sandwich and a treat for Cujo, and took them across to Gedup'n'go's library where she found herself a book on the Nullarbor, sat down and started to read.

꽁꺼

The morning passed surprisingly quickly once the campers dragged themselves away from the kitchen. I watched on as Bob made sure the additional air tanks for the divers were kept full – it was a never-ending job. Generators and compressors needed a constant watch, too. The flow of air and electricity to the divers had to be maintained from the surface, something that was done through an extensive maze of cables and pipes.

Before anyone realised, midday had been and gone. Tee lifted his head from a geology book he'd been immersed in, saw Darcy and asked her what was for lunch.

'What do you feel like making?' she replied. She was a gem! Heart of gold and willing to be there for them all, but clearly not prepared to be taken for granted.

Tee smiled. 'Point taken. Who's for a sandwich?'

'We'll need bread,' Darcy said. 'Someone will have to go to the roadhouse. Water, too.'

'There's lots of water back here,' Alex said.

'Thanks, hun, but we'll need a lot more than that over the next week or so. With fifteen of us, that's not going to last us long.'

One of the most important jobs for the above-ground crew while the others were out of sight was to drive back to the Wedgetail Inn for supplies – fresh fruit and veggies, and water. They'd each been advised to start with forty litres, but water was scarce out on the Nullarbor – as much a necessity underground as it was on top.

'I'll go on across,' said Clinton, who appeared out of nowhere. 'I need to get some cigarettes. Anyone want to join me?'

I did.

'Can I come?' Alex asked.

'Sure you can. Does anyone want anything?'

I went to Cocklebiddy with the two of them and realised, once I was back there again, that the roadhouse *is* Cocklebiddy! The town had a population of eight, and a good feel to it. There wasn't much to see or do there, not for anyone who stayed close to the Eyre Highway, but there was an aviary out the front of the roadhouse, which was good for those who enjoyed a little effortless birdwatching.

I followed Clinton and Alex into the roadhouse. I'm sure it had everything anyone could want – anyone who was simply passing through and unlikely to stay more than one night, that is. Basic accommodation, a caravan park, a restaurant, cafe, pub, pool table and a service station, as well as that ambulance out back, and an airstrip for the Royal Flying Doctor Service. I thought it would be neat to be able to see one of them in action, but I quickly changed my mind. If that happened, it would mean someone was in trouble. With my new friends not far away, that was the last thing I wanted.

'G'day Beryl,' Clinton said as he walked in.

'Well hello again, Clinton. And hello to you, too, young Alex.'

'Hi Beryl.'

'How's it going out there?'

'All good so far, the divers have gone down. We just need a few things.'

Alex was looking around while Clinton found what they needed.

'What's up here?'

Alex was pointing at a map, at the area north of the Nullarbor.

'That's Western Australia's sheep-grazing belt,' Beryl told him. 'Some of the stations up there are bigger than many European countries.'

'Wow.' Alex was clearly impressed.

'And you know that not far south of here – not by outback standards I should say – is the Great Australian Bight. Those cliffs are spectacular. If you haven't seen them, get your dad to stop and show you on your way home.'

Clinton appeared at the counter. 'Did you find everything you need, love?' Beryl asked him.

'Yep, we're good to go,' Clinton said as he paid for his shopping. 'You ready, Alex?'

Alex left the poster he'd been reading.

'Hey Clinton, did you know that Cocklebiddy started as an aboriginal mission. All that's left are some stone foundations.'

'No, that's something I didn't know – a good thing to write in your diary tonight, eh? Do you know where they are – the foundations? We could try to find them.'

'That'd be great. Can we?'

'I don't see why not. You'll have to check with Darcy though.'

By the time they returned to the campsite everyone was ready to eat. Darcy had taken out the sandwich fillers and it was on for one and all. No-one hesitated as each of them grabbed what they wanted, and there was no waiting to start eating once they had it all thrown together. A strong wind had picked up after Clinton and Alex had left for the roadhouse, and that, combined with the desert heat, turned their soft fresh bread hard and crusty in almost no time at all, but none of them seemed to care, or even notice.

'I thought I might head out again after lunch,' Clinton said to Darcy. 'Alex found out that the remains of an old aboriginal mission are out there somewhere. If it's okay with you, I can take him with me, drive around a bit to see if we can find them.'

'Sounds great, and fine with me.'

'Tee, want to join us?'

'Nah, I'll stay here. I've got some reading to do.'

Although there was no line of communication between the divers and the crew up top, Bob and Tobias were still on call, and had to stay at camp. Darcy wanted to stay close by, too. They didn't seem to mind – Tobias had brought along his chess board and he and Bob had been challenging each other to a game ever since they'd arrived.

Nathan seemed at last to have found his place at camp. After he finished eating he pulled out his laptop and started typing up his research, while Darcy made a start on tonight's meal. Last night she made lasagne. Tonight, judging by the ingredients she was pulling together, some kind of chicken curry. But I wasn't staying to watch. I wanted to go with Clinton.

It was a fun afternoon, driving around with him and Alex. The two of them got on well, and I was enjoying watching the dust fly as they drove around the Nullarbor, looking for those stone foundations. Clinton was also showing Alex how to take photos with his camera, which was amazing. He must've trusted him, because I didn't think he'd let too many people even touch his camera.

'It's really heavy,' Alex said to Clinton when he first held it.

'My dad made that camera for me, a long time ago. I don't think he would've believed that one day everyone would be taking photos from their phones, and that those phones were carried around in people's pockets.'

'Where did you carry them?' Alex asked, and I laughed.

'We didn't. They weren't made to be carried. Most people would have their phone sitting on a table at home. They'd have to be plugged into the wall, and it wasn't to charge them.'

I imagined Alex might have a lot to add to his diary tonight.

They drove all over the place, discovering other caves and sinkholes, but nothing that resembled the remains of an aboriginal mission. It didn't matter. Alex had been having a great time. Me too.

When we arrived back, the chess tournament was still going, but Nathan and Tee had joined them all, having put their work aside for the day.

'Dinner smells fabulous,' Tobias said. Darcy whispered a thank-you to him.

Their conversation soon turned to the divers, as everyone wondered how they were doing.

'What are the others having for dinner tonight, Darce?' Tobias said as he checkmated Bob. 'Another game?'

'Baked beans,' she said. 'Not much choice for them down there – just tinned spaghetti and beans – things they can eat cold.'

'With snack bars and glucose tablets to keep their energy levels up,' added Tobias. 'And no wine with their dinner, or hot coffee to finish the meal with – that will have to wait.'

'Sounds like a form of torture to me,' said Nathan.

'I wonder if they're keeping to schedule,' Tee asked. 'As much as is ever possible underground.'

'I'm sure they are,' Darcy said, 'and no news is good news, as they say. Chess board away, fellas, and help me get things ready for dinner.' She opened a bottle of red, poured herself a glass and when the table was set, they all settled in for another quiet night at camp.

༄༅༅

When Sophie had left work for the long weekend, she borrowed the Nullarbor book she'd been reading at lunch time, and another couple she found on cave diving. She had learned a little from Jack all those years ago, but there was a lot more to it. She read into the night. The more she read the more intriguing it became, and the more concerned she was feeling. All the things that could go wrong. But she couldn't put the books down.

Saturday

Saturday was a rest day underground, and for those of us above ground, another day much like yesterday was on the cards. More chess, more reading, writing and photography, more cooking, eating and drinking. More talking. Nathan went for a game of snooker back at the roadhouse with Tee – they were both getting restless. Clinton stayed at the campsite, and I stayed with him. The sky out here is huge. I could never tire of it, especially when it's the backdrop to days like today. Not a whisper of a cloud in sight, and just a hint of a breeze. I was feeling particularly mellow.

That is, until I thought of Sophie. I started to feel so guilty, because I hadn't been thinking much about her at all. There was so much else going on. I wondered what she was doing over the long weekend. Then I remembered she'd be seeing Paul and Emma.

ಸಿ಼ಐ

When Sophie woke up that morning, the cave diving book she'd fallen asleep with was on the floor. She picked it up, found the page she was up to and started reading again. It was mid-winter, and it was cold and wet outside – just the right sort of day to snuggle up with a book and lose all track of time, which she did until her phone rang.

'Hello.'

'Hello,' Paul said, the happy bounce in his voice instantly recognisable. 'How are things?'

Oh shit, I'd forgotten all about today.

'Hey, Paul – good thing you rang. I've had my head stuck in a book and had completely forgotten about this afternoon. Are we still on?'

'Yeah, that's what I'm ringing about. What are you reading?'

'Ah, just something about diving – I grabbed it from work before I left yesterday. Long story.'

'Diving? That doesn't sound like you!'

Sophie laughed.

'Well, you can tell me all about it when I see you. Listen, would you mind coming over here rather than go somewhere else for coffee. I've got Ben with me and I'd rather not take him out in this weather. I've checked with Em and she's okay.'

'Yeah sure, that's fine. Same time?'

'Yeah, about three.'

'Great, I'll see you then.'

These June long weekends meant memories, and if the three of them were all in Sydney, they made a point of getting together. Admittedly it hadn't happened all that often, as both Emma and Paul had spent so much of the past twenty years either living in or travelling to faraway places. But when it happened, it was a chance for a bit of childhood nostalgia.

Emma and Sophie had been in primary school together, and back then Paul had been Emma's neighbour. The Queen's Birthday weekend had been the best, because it meant bonfire night, and after Sophie hung up the phone she thought back to that time when they were all so much younger.

Emma's family lived on the edge of the bush, with a huge backyard that tilted slowly down to a creek that was, by day, a great place to go exploring but by night, it could be plain scary. Her dad, who could only be described as eccentric, had built all sorts of weird and wonderful playthings for his children in their backyard, which all the other neighbourhood kids were happy to take advantage of. It was like they had their own adventure park right there on their doorstep.

The Saturday night of the long weekend, however, was the biggest night of the year for the street. Emma's dad, along with a lot of other local dads (they lived in a sociable street with many of the families having young children), would build a huge bonfire down near the creek, and people from all over the neighbourhood would gather there. Dressed for the cold in thick jumpers, beanies and scarves, the night would start with a barbecue.

After they'd eaten, Guy Fawkes, whose effigy was positioned on top of the bonfire, would be burned and fireworks would, one by one, be spectacularly spent, and then the parents would all disappear indoors for coffee. The kids lingered around the bonfire as it continued to burn, rugged up against the mid-winter's night air in their many layers, the older ones telling ghost stories until the little ones became too scared and went up to their parents who would say it was time they were all going home anyway. It had been a wonderful tradition.

They all relived those days when they met at Paul's that afternoon. Just like it had been at the reunion, and apart from the inevitable physical changes in those old friends that could take a while to come to grips with, it was always so easy to slip back to a time that was well over twenty years ago, a time when none of them worried about anything at all, except not getting in trouble from their parents for doing something wrong. That was about as bad as life got back then, although that had seemed bad enough.

What a difference time and age make. Fireworks had long since been made illegal, Emma had enjoyed countless experiences in more exotic places than Sophie could ever begin to imagine, and Paul had lived for almost a decade in a foreign country before returning home with his wife-to-be and starting a family. And then there was Sophie – not a lot had changed. But having been to their school reunion the previous weekend, she knew she was okay with that. Her life *had* been every bit as full and rewarding, as Kelly had said. Just different.

When Sophie returned home later that evening, she fixed herself some dinner as she thought more about those days before they all morphed into teenagers and then adults, and then she picked up the caving book she had put down when the phone rang earlier that day, and read until her eyes would stay open no longer.

෩෬

Darcy had decided on a barbecue for tonight, which the chess players seemed particularly happy about for a couple of reasons, the first being that they were up for the task themselves, and the other, well, in their eyes food didn't come much better than those big sizzling steaks cooked on a barbie. They packed away the chess set and, while Darcy put the others to work making salads and buttering bread rolls, Tobias and Bob started to prepare the meat. Darcy poured drinks for them all and put her feet up as she watched on, contentment in her eyes and, I suspect, Mal in her thoughts. I stayed there with her, on the tip of her shoes, and lost myself in my own thoughts for a while, too.

The mood over dinner was light, the conversation spirited.

'They should be back here with us this time tomorrow,' said Bob. 'Celebratory dinner?'

Darcy just smiled. She was looking forward to their safe exit from the cave as much as anyone. Alex too.

'Lots to do once they're back,' he continued. 'Enjoy tonight while you can.'

'What do you have to do when they're back?' Alex asked.

'Much the same as we did to get them down there,' Tobias said, 'but in reverse. Lots of trips in and out of the cave again to bring all the equipment back up. But before the big clean-up, they'll have a rest day up here.'

'They sure do a lot of resting,' Nathan said.

Tobias looked almost ready to thump him, but didn't. 'The clean-up dives take a lot of time and effort, just as the set-up did, but fatigue will have started to kick in, and even if they brought the barest minimum out with them, the journey would be challenging enough. This rest day is crucial for them.'

'I can't wait to see Dad again,' said Alex.

'Yep, me too,' said Darcy, 'but now it's time for you to get to bed.'

'Okay. Night, Darcy. Night, everyone.'

After Alex had left them, the conversation returned to tomorrow.

'They're not finished down there yet,' said Darcy. 'The push to Toad Hall is scheduled for the morning. I hate this part.'

'Ah yes,' Nathan spoke. 'Some of them are pushing even further into the abyss. What happens if someone falls and needs medical attention? You can't do much from up here, can you Bob?'

I'd been wondering that myself, but although curious, was glad it hadn't come up.

'That's when things get really difficult, Nate. Those rockpiles can be steep and dangerous, and unstable.'

I was glad Alex had gone to bed.

'Cocklebiddy is about a hundred metres below the surface,' Bob continued, illustrating his points by showing Nathan on the diagram. 'It's not only long – it's massive. Three main sumps are separated by the two rock-filled air chambers, between which are a number of side passages. The first air chamber, Rockpile Chamber –'

'Someone got creative with that name,' Nathan said, laughing to himself.

'– and then Toad Hall, present a high level of danger. It would be all too easy for one of the divers to lose their footing and fall, or drop equipment, if their attention wavered for even a split second.'

'Yeah, we know all that, Bob. But what do they do if someone falls?' Nathan pressed for more.

I was watching Darcy. She poured herself another glass of wine.

'Mate, the effort that would be required to move a diver who had sprained an ankle or broken a leg would be huge. No-one can help but the people who are down there already, and exhaustion kicks in after a while, even when everything is going well. If an accident like that happened beyond Toad Hall, few people would be capable of having any chance of reaching the diver in trouble – no-one in the rescue services, or the police or navy, would be able to help. And unless they were there at the time, the diver would have taken his last breath long before help arrived.'

Sunday

'Can *you* tell me why they call it Toad Hall?' Alex asked Tee at breakfast.

'Wish I could. It's a geological wonderland down there – could be anything. But it's an unspoken rule among Cocklebiddy divers – only the privileged few who make it that far will ever know. One day I hope to find out.'

'Me too.'

They're a weird mob, I was thinking.

৪১০৪

Toad Hall, like Rockpile Chamber, came about as a result of the cave roof collapsing, Sophie started to read on this miserable Sunday morning once she'd made herself some hot chocolate and gone back to bed.

This is sounding good, she thought.

Divers tend to stay in these chambers for twenty-four hours if they intend swimming beyond them, to allow their bodies to adjust to the surrounding environment. While the air in Toad Hall is good, it is warm and humid for the divers, and the effort involved in crossing these small mountains of rocks while carrying all the equipment they would, or might, need was hard going. The further into the cave they went, the more difficult it was for them to breathe, the hotter it became and the more lethargic they would feel. Headaches were likely, tempers could be short.

Yep, that's my idea of a good time, not.

But at the same time, the further in they went, the more exciting it became …

Yeah right.

… as they penetrated the endless dark and left the safety of the world outside them even further behind.

It was when Sophie reached the part about the Nullarbor's

unpredictable weather, and how freak storms passed through from time to time, that she shut the book hard and went to play with Cujo.

Too much. I don't want to know.

ಲ‌ೞ

'Big day for the four going to Toad Hall today,' said Clinton, as he met up with Bob on the way to the kitchen for breakfast.

'Yes, it is. It must be strange, with no sense of time down in the cave, but let's hope they all slept well after their rest day.'

'How much further is it for them?' Clinton asked.

'Another two and a half kilometres,' Bob said, 'which is a long stretch of water with no air space. It'll take them a couple of hours each way, so it'll be physically and psychologically difficult. Then it's no bed of roses once they reach Toad Hall.'

'And they're still loaded up with their gear at that stage, aren't they?'

Bob and Clinton paused outside the kitchen.

'Yep,' Bob said, 'and it starts to feel heavier and more cumbersome down that end of the cave. They can expect headaches and nausea.'

'I can't imagine anything much worse, you know,' Clinton said.

'Honestly, I'm with you. But these guys are capable. Terry's done Cocklebiddy many times, and Mal's been down a couple.'

'What about the others who aren't going to Toad Hall?' Clinton asked.

'They'll be staying around base camp, ready to meet them when they get back. And they'll be getting extra gear ready for retrieval after their rest day here with us.'

Bob sniffed the air. 'Let's go in, that coffee smells too good to let go cold.'

ಲ‌ೞ

Most of the day at the campsite passed by much as the previous couple of days had, and everyone was looking forward to seeing the divers again later in the evening. I couldn't wait to see them, and to hear how everything went down there.

In the short time I'd known Clinton, he never seemed to be wishing he was anywhere but exactly where he was. The others, however, not so much. They'd all been getting along well enough, but their conversation had ebbed and flowed at times, and was slowing down between meals. As for the chess players, Bob was yet to beat Tobias and so was losing his enthusiasm for the game.

But it was Nathan who was getting particularly restless. I got the feeling that he didn't like being in the one place for too long, and he was still uptight about the scorpion incident. No-one minded his paranoia at first – they ignored him – but now he was starting to get on their nerves. Always on edge – too many of those weird cigarettes, I figured – his eyes forever darting about him. He couldn't relax for a moment and I knew it wouldn't take much to bring him undone. Not only that, but every time he picked up his guitar his anxiety was obvious – he had to shake it for a good few minutes before he could be convinced nothing nasty was lurking inside it. And although Nathan's playing was something we'd all been enjoying, his song list wasn't great and his tunes were becoming repetitive.

ಸಂಆ

'The four push divers should've reached Toad Hall by now,' Bob said, breaking the silence in the kitchen where they'd all congregated for lunch, and then stayed into the afternoon. 'It would've been a long hard dive, but I bet they'd be feeling good to have got that far.'

'Dad told me how frustrating it is to get so close to the end of the cave,' Alex said. 'He said he wants to go all the way some day.'

'He said that? Then I'm sure he will, but not too many divers have gone beyond the third sump. The dangers escalate enormously up that end of the cave.'

I'd heard Terry telling Jack, as they were getting the equipment down the other day, that he'd like to do a solo dive beyond Toad Hall, but that it was a pipe dream. He acknowledged he'd need a dive buddy to help get the gear to and across Toad Hall, but because he'd been that far already, he knew he'd be mentally prepared to enjoy the experience a lot more on his own. Jack seemed to understand what he meant. Another diver, Jack said, was always a distraction from the dive itself, and the surroundings.

As they'd been talking, I thought how both of them were so in tune with the secrets the cave would reveal to only a few. And a little bit crazy. But there was no question, Terry would never dive solo. Nobody would. A dive buddy is critical, not just for a diver's safety but for their sanity.

I'd grown to like Jack even more out here in such a different environment, and it was hard to stop myself from wondering if he and Sophie might have a chance together. I wish I knew if she knew he'd split from his wife, and if she did know, what she might be thinking. But I didn't have a chance of hearing anything that was going on in her head from way out here.

ഌ

Sophie had spent the rest of the day with her mum. They braved the cold and the wet and went out for lunch together, then took themselves off to see a movie. Something light-hearted – Celia always preferred to see movies that made her feel good. What was the point, she would say, of going out to make yourself miserable – there's already too much sadness and aggression in the world without going out and looking for more. It was late afternoon when they emerged from the cinema, but even so it was prematurely dark and the bad weather had worsened. They made a dash for the car and drove home in silence. Celia knew Sophie would need to concentrate in what were fast becoming treacherous conditions. The wind had picked up and was so fierce they could feel it trying to pull the car. The wipers were doing little to clear the rain that pounded the windscreen, and the headlights of oncoming cars were all but lost in the mist that was engulfing everything around them.

ഌ

'But they think it's worth it, and in a way I can understand it,' Bob was saying. 'Mind you, seeing Mal's photos will be enough for me!'

I thought about the photos I'd seen back at Balladonia. The divers' headlamps had lit up the limestone walls of the cave like spotlights on a darkened stage. And in that light, the build-up of rocks and the patterns in the walls were every bit as clear below the surface of the water as they were above it. These men *could* have been floating through air, it was that clear. So one thing that would've made those next couple of kilometres particularly tempting, I imagined as I tried to look at it all in a more positive light, was that the further in the divers went, the clearer the water became. They'd be floating like free spirits, and I know what an amazing sensation that is! But it also became increasingly warm up there – 'toasty' was how Terry described it.

'Mal's told me how clean and pure the walls are down there,' said Darcy.

'Yes, they've been spared the external forces of nature, and any pollutants introduced by man,' Tee added. 'It's so clear, the shadows of the divers can resemble frogs sometimes –'

'Frogs!' Alex laughed.

'It does sound incredible,' Nathan agreed. The image of these guys as frogmen made him laugh, too, and I hadn't seen him laugh before.

'Well, yes, despite the scooters that reach out ahead of them, and the air tanks strapped to their backs, they can look like frogs.'

'How will they be back tonight?' Alex asked.

'They don't stay at Toad Hall for long, Alex,' Tobias said. 'Once the four of them emerge from the water there, it will be oppressively hot and humid. Ek and Jack will find it particularly so, having not experienced it before.'

'They're made of stronger stuff than me,' said Clinton. 'I could never do it.'

'And what's the bet that within days, Mal will be talking about doing it all again, and soon!' Darcy said.

A few moments of silence passed before Clinton spoke.

'Hasn't been much of a day up here today,' he said, noticing the absence of a lovely sunset.

It had been overcast most of the day, so the change from afternoon to dusk wasn't as pronounced as it might've been. But this was the Nullarbor, and the sudden and deafening sound of hundreds, maybe thousands of birds overhead had captured the crew's collective attention in a heartbeat. Just as quickly, I saw Clinton get to his feet, grab his camera and begin shooting – this was the sort of moment a photographer dreamed of, and could make a lot of money from. It was an incredible thing, being there. I'd never seen so many birds nor heard such a frightening noise. Everyone was speechless, frozen in time, looking skyward with mouths agape. But Clinton was in his element.

And at that moment I became so scared for everyone. Birds seem to be able to read the weather well ahead of humans, and this display was more sinister than I believed possible.

☙❧

Clinton, through the eye of his lens, was the first to notice the sudden change in the massive cloud behind us. The others, who'd been following the path of the birds as they flew overhead in a mass of frenzied feathers, first knew of it when they heard Clinton's deep and hollow gasp at the same time as the birds were blending into the grey of the distant Nullarbor sky. I watched as they turned in fear, the deathly sting of the savage wind penetrating them as it swept through the campsite. The reactions of the support crew were immediate – they moved to put everything that wasn't fixed firmly to the ground away, but in no time they could see their efforts were futile. Tents were being lifted from the ground like dandelions in a summer breeze. Darcy's kitchen and everything in it was picked up before it came crashing straight back down.

'Get in!' Clinton shouted as he slid open Morrie's side door. But even once they were in, it wasn't the calm refuge they hoped for. Nor was Tee's truck, where the others had gone, but all they could do was sit it out.

I was in Morrie, where Alex, Darcy and Nathan were all sitting in stunned and horrified silence as they watched the enormous and menacing cloud Clinton had reacted to, only minutes earlier, descend over the campsite area and turn late afternoon almost as black as it would have been underground. There was a terrifying clap of thunder – louder than any I'd ever heard, which was saying something because Sydney had suffered many severe storms of its own over the years, with thunderclaps that I thought might be the last thing any of us ever heard.

I wasn't the only one who would've been thinking about the others in the cave, and I'd never felt as frustrated as I felt right then. I knew there was nothing I could do, but I had to go. I needed to know they were okay.

Just as I was leaving Clinton and the others, the rain came. A deluge of rain. More rain than I would've believed possible. I watched as the campsite, which only moments before had been almost torn to shreds, filled up with water, and I was terrified by the thought that they could all be swept away, cruising the Nullarbor as might have been possible millions of years earlier. I pictured them all in those two vehicles, huddled together, fearful for their lives and numb with unspoken thoughts of the others down in the cave.

☙❧

I was so scared.
> *You can do it, Georgia.*
> *I don't know that I can.*
> *You can! What've you got to lose? You're dead already.*
> *But all that water ...*

So much water was cascading into that hole in the ground as I made my way down to the cave's entrance, and there was only one place it could go. Same place I was going. Part of me wanted to turn around and go back out again – I was terrified of all the water, terrified for what I might find – but something I never knew I had in me was pushing me on.

Then I saw them. All of them. I was so relieved, so incredibly relieved. They were just this side of the entrance chamber, making their way out.

But as I watched them carefully negotiating the climb back up to the surface, deafening rumblings came from above and they all stopped still. I was sure I could feel the thud of their collective heartbeats as they realised things were about to go dreadfully wrong. Then, with nothing more to warn them, the tremendous weight of the flood waters above came crashing through the cave's entrance, and with it an avalanche of boulders and rocks. I know they'd all trained for the unexpected, but I didn't think anyone could ever be prepared for this.

I watched as they all turned back. They needed to get back down to the entrance chamber, and they could waste no time getting there.

Terry was the first to get back down to an area of relative safety – I could only guess that, as the team's leader, he'd been the last to start heading out. Ek and Stefano were right behind him. They watched anxiously as the others tried to find secure footing that would lead them down to the chamber before tonnes of water and falling rocks caught up with them and knocked them off their feet. But the rocks had begun tumbling down closer to their pathway, and the divers still to reach the chamber knew they had to work with greater urgency. In his haste, John took a fall but was back on his feet and scrambling down with Mark right on his heels.

Shit really does happen, I thought as I looked at Mark and remembered his T-shirt.

They clambered past a boulder that had been balancing precariously since it had taken the full force of the initial downpour. It was the size of a small car but would've weighed much more, and I was relieved when I saw John and Mark had moved away from it and its possible pathway, should it tumble.

But then the worst happened.

That boulder was shoved from above by another as it fell through the cave. This one was much smaller, but weighty enough to dislodge the massive boulder and send it crashing down, just missing Mal and Julie who had been the first out of the cave but were now not far behind Mark.

But Jack! Oh no. No, Jack, no.

Jack was directly in the path of the plummeting boulder and stood no chance as it pushed its way down at incredible speed, bringing with it everything it touched. I looked in horror, then the world went silent as I felt the pain of his children, his wife. Sophie. The other divers. The support crew at the campsite. Sophie. Sophie. The lives of every one of them had just changed forever. Jack. Oh Jack.

Mal and Julie were moving as fast as they could in the wake of the boulder. They had to get down, and fast, but it meant passing Jack's motionless and broken body. Seeing their new friend like that would make their descent even more of a psychological challenge than it had begun. They might not be thinking about it now, but they would be. It could have been them. And it still could. They had to get down to the entrance chamber.

The anxiety in the faces of those already down there, as they watched the two figures negotiate the fractured innards of the cave, was excruciating. For Julie and Mal it must have been beyond frightening. But they made it, and the moment their feet were again on the stable cave floor with the others, Julie's knees gave way and her legs crumbled beneath her. Stefano was there to catch her, and he held her tight. She wasn't physically hurt, just shaken at the sight of Jack's body. They were all down at the entrance chamber again, and for now there wasn't anything they could do but wait – wait until the rock fall had stopped and some calm had returned to the cave. I had to get out of there. I couldn't stay to look at Jack like that any longer.

ಸಂಬಿ

Within half an hour of the storm's first drops of rain, the last had fallen. I was back at the campsite, or what was left of it. Everything was still again outside and the crew who had taken refuge in their vehicles had emerged in a silent daze. The sun had almost set but it did shine brightly for a few minutes before it was swallowed up entirely in the jaws of this monstrous afternoon. It was cruel that it should appear like that – its cascading brilliance bringing with it a sense of hope – and then disappear almost as quickly.

'The ambulance will be on its way,' Bob assured Darcy. She'd been unable to speak, her thoughts with Mal and whether she'd ever see him alive again. I desperately wanted to tell her he was okay. To tell Alex his dad was okay.

'The call would've been made to the RFDS, too,' he continued. 'They'd be straight onto it after a freak storm like that. No waiting for someone to call for help. They'll be here real soon, love, real soon.' And quietly, he hoped he was right. He held Darcy close and tried to comfort her that little bit more by telling her what she already knew – that this was a highly experienced, skilled and careful team down there. That if anyone could have survived such a storm, they could. What he didn't say, but what I suspect his churning gut would've been feeling, was that sometimes all the experience and skill in the world just aren't enough.

Alex was shaken. Clinton was his comfort, wanting to say something that was going to help, but nothing would. There wasn't much any of them could do now.

On the way out here a few days ago I'd wondered about the pattern of the tracks Morrie had driven along once we were off the highway. Now

I could see how fast that rough dry track could turn to thick, slippery, impenetrable mud. Four-wheel-drives could mostly make it through where other vehicles wouldn't have a chance, but even they would struggle in extreme conditions like this. I hoped the ambulance could make it through, and quickly.

☙❧

My mind was all over the place. Even above ground, I couldn't escape that vision of Jack, or the look of terror on Julie's face. I couldn't keep still, and all I wanted to do was to go back down.

I couldn't believe I was feeling that way, but I was. They'd have to focus on their own survival until help arrived, but I was sure Terry would be worried about Alex and the devastation up at the campsite. He and Mal would want to get a message up to Darcy, but he knew better than I did that there was no chance of communication between the two worlds at the moment. He'd also know the emergency call would've been made and help would arrive soon.

But the situation remained critical. Everyone knew that.

☙❧

The ambulance team arrived at what had been, only hours before, a highly organised campsite.

The paramedics were met by the sight of seven dishevelled people – six adults and a child – huddled together in and alongside a blue Kombi van that also looked worse for wear. Darcy was in shock, resting on Clinton's mattress as he sat beside her, gently stroking her forehead.

One of the ambos attended to Darcy while the others made sure everyone else at the campsite was okay, then it was time to organise the divers' rescue.

Beryl and Ted arrived a few minutes later. I was amazed how fast they'd all made it here. She started unloading blankets and food.

'We've left a couple of the guests back at the roadhouse to make up some rooms, and get some more meals prepared for everyone. You'll all need a good feed and a warm bed once tonight's over.'

Thank goodness for people like Beryl. No-one might want to leave the campsite to go back with them to the roadhouse tonight, but it was good to know they would be safe and warm there if they did.

'The police rescue are on their way,' Beryl said. 'They've got further to come, but they shouldn't be too much longer. Here, love, put this over you.' She reached across Darcy with another soft thick blanket and wrapped her arm around her. 'Ted'll get you something to drink, won't you, love? We brought as much hot food and drinks as we could, and we've got plenty of blankets. Are you warm enough, love?'

'Here, get this into you, darlin'.' Ted offered Darcy a cup of steaming hot chocolate and then poured more for the others.

'The track from the roadhouse is like the road to hell at the moment. You're lucky the ambulance made it through. Don't suppose you've heard anything?' Beryl asked.

'Not a word,' said Tobias. 'Once police rescue arrives we can set up some lighting and try to communicate somehow, but until then there's nothing we can do. All our equipment has been smashed.'

'It won't be long,' Beryl muttered as she started fussing over Alex.

And she was right. Coffees and hot chocolates had barely been sipped when the flashing lights from the police rescue squad appeared in the distance and they heard the sound of the flying doctor approaching. It seemed to take an eternity for them to reach the campsite, but there was some relief when they did.

And that's when I went back down into the cave.

ಸಂಬ

Much of the divers' equipment was buried under small mountains of rock and mud, but that would've been the least of their concerns. They needed to get out, and Terry was talking to them about that as I reached the entrance chamber.

'Further rockfall is our biggest problem,' he was saying. 'The path we came in by –'

That's the one they were using to get out when the floodwaters came pounding into the cave.

'– is now impossible to follow back up. We need to establish a new exit route, and here the danger is twofold: the rockpile we have to cross over will be unstable, and the cave roof could fall at any moment.'

I was so scared for them all. Getting out of the cave wasn't something they could rush, not if they were to all stay alive.

The water that had been pouring into the cave when I was here earlier had started to ease up. That was something. There was more discussion, then they decided that someone had to go up before they all attempted their exit. They needed to let the support crew know that seven of the eight of them were okay.

Seven of the eight. Jack. I can't believe it. I could tell Terry was not only devastated, but torn. It's going to be a difficult and risky climb, he'd said, and as expedition leader, he'd wanted to do it himself, but he also knew his place was with the others until every last one of them was safely out.

'I want to go,' said Mal. 'Darcy –'

'That's why you're not going,' said Terry. 'You need to stay until we work out a safer exit plan.'

'I'll go,' volunteered Stefano.

'No, please,' Julie begged. 'Stay with me.'

'I'll go,' said John.

'I'll go with him,' followed Mark.

'Okay, good.'

Once John and Mark had started on their way, Terry made his next decision.

'All going well with their exit,' he said, 'and as long as this stillness holds, we'll follow the path they take up through the mouth of the cave, one by one. All the equipment stays here. What we need now is a whole lot of concentration. A little luck won't go astray either.'

ଓଙ୍କ

I watched the two men as they began their painfully slow climb out of the cave. The potential for disaster was enormous. Every step they took could've been their first into a world far darker than the one they were trying to get out of, and unlike Cocklebiddy Cave, it was a world they wouldn't be so keen to explore. Their feet were critical in guiding them out. I couldn't move as I watched them test the ground beneath them, stepping onto only those rocks they believed wouldn't move from under them. It was excruciating for the five watching from below, too. All they would've been able to see were two little headlamps, getting smaller and smaller as they moved slowly up towards the surface. I wished with all my heart that no-one would have to see those headlamps stumble and plummet back down, like fireflies struck by some nocturnal predator. I could tell how unstable and slippery the rocks were. Those men's lives were depending on every step they took. I was willing to bet this was the hardest climb either of them would ever have to do.

❦

It was approaching midnight and, under blinding floodlights that had turned night into day as I once again emerged at ground level, the emergency crew was preparing to go down when a headlight appeared in the mouth of the cave. Then another. John and Mark were met with cheers from the small crowd who had gathered to help with the rescue, or watch as it unfolded. Not Darcy though. As the two men made their way onto stable ground, her hand reached for her mouth and tears fell from her eyes, but when John was safely up he wasted no time in going first to her.

'He's okay, Darcy. Mal's okay.' He held her tight as she sobbed with relief – Mal wasn't out yet but he was alive.

Mark had gone to Alex. 'Your dad's fine, mate,' he said as they hugged each other.

'The others?' Tobias asked.

'The others are fine too. But Jack,' he continued, 'Jack –'

'Oh God,' Darcy whimpered.

This was unbearable. I'd never encountered the kind of emotion that was surrounding me tonight. It was heartbreaking, and I wanted to be with Sophie. This time *I* needed comforting.

The emergency services had set up ropes as far into the cave as they considered it safe to go, and were about to send one of their guys down when they saw the rope vibrating and then another headlight. It was Mal.

Darcy ran over to him as we all watched on. Seeing them reunited after such a hellish ordeal was an emotion-charged moment for everyone.

'It's good to see you, Darce,' he said quietly as she wept.

By sunrise, Julie and Stefano had both surfaced to cheers and applause from the crew. One by one they were examined by the ambulance staff who treated minor cuts and abrasions while Beryl, who was making sure they were kept warm and comfortable, had sent Ted back to the roadhouse for more hot food and drinks.

It was around seven when Ek appeared. 'It's good to be out,' he said as he took the hand of one of the police rescue officers who had been waiting for him at the top. 'Thanks, mate.'

He glanced over to Alex who had been so patient throughout the night, knowing his dad would be the last to come up and praying with the safe exit of each of the other divers that Terry would make it out safely too.

'He's coming up, Alex. Your dad'll be here soon.'

And so he was. Fourteen hours after the storm had hit, Terry and Alex were reunited, but the euphoria that was felt in the camp once the seven of them were safely up was short-lived. All it took was the realisation that eight had gone down only a few days earlier. Jack had to be brought up. Terry had been able to confirm Jack's death as he passed his body on the way out. Now his wife had to be informed.

Monday

It was close to sunset again before Jack's body was retrieved. An additional police rescue team had arrived to help, as had a helicopter, and the divers and above-ground crew had all stayed on to offer what support they could. They were all physically and mentally drained, but there was no way anyone – not even Beryl – could convince them to get some rest at the roadhouse until the last of the divers was back up. It didn't seem so daunting a task by the light of day, now that the rain had stopped and things were drying out. But they were aware of how fragile the ground still was, and so every move they made had to be a carefully calculated one.

Terry was able to lead the way in with two of the rescue officers and a stretcher they'd fixed to a pulley system during the morning. It's part of the job for those in rescue professions to be in potentially life-threatening situations, and they're familiar with death and the myriad ways it presents itself, but for Terry this was a devastatingly hard task. It had been his team. Not only that, but Jack was a good friend. A good man. A man whose only crime had been to follow a dream and become one of the best. They all knew the risks, but they went ahead anyway because it made them feel so alive.

I was hoping to feel like that when I left Sophie almost two weeks ago. And I did. It had started out so well. I had to go in with them, one last time.

When they reached Jack's body, Terry cried a respectful and silent tear before the three men carefully lifted him from the place he had come to rest and strapped him to the stretcher.

I was struggling, confronted by death as it is for just about everyone. There's nothing more for Jack. Ever. His life is over. I could only think how incredibly lucky I've been to have had a second chance.

Once Jack was secure they pulled on the rope to let the ground crew know he was ready to be lifted, and as he was slowly manoeuvred out of the cave, the men followed carefully and silently behind. I left the cave with them, knowing that even if some of those people returned here one day, I never would. I felt completely deflated. Lost. Unsure what I thought about life, and death. And now myself.

ಬಿಚ್ಚ

Sophie turned on the evening news as the last few hours of the long weekend were slipping away. It was the usual run of depressing stories. There was no surer way to spoil the end of a good weekend – even just a good day – than to turn on the news. She often wondered why she bothered. *What's wrong with us all?* she would think. *Why do we do this to each other?*

And then she felt a sudden and overwhelming weight crash to the pit of her stomach. The graphic that appeared behind the newsreader was emblazoned with the words 'Nullarbor Tragedy', and then his report began. 'A flash flood in the small town of Cocklebiddy on the Nullarbor Plain has claimed the life of one man, diving at the time with a team in Cocklebiddy Cave.'

The report continued.

> A freak storm dumped almost two years' worth of rain in less than half an hour last night on the tiny settlement of Cocklebiddy on the Eyre Highway in Western Australia. Winds of up to one hundred and eighty-five kilometres an hour ripped through the area and in the space of six hours, an estimated hundred and fifty million litres of water poured into the cave where a team of divers had descended a few days earlier. Hundreds of tonnes of rocks were believed to have avalanched into the cave. Miraculously, most of the divers made it out safely. One, however, did not.

And then his face appeared on the screen.

'Jack Murphy,' the newsreader said, 'was pulled from the cave late this afternoon. He leaves behind a wife and two young children.'

'No,' she said softly as tears welled up in her eyes and spilled down her cheeks. Sophie pulled her knees up to her chest and held herself tight. 'Jack, no.'

Hours passed but Sophie didn't – couldn't – move. The news was over. Opening songs had been sung and credits had marked the end of countless other programs before she came to and realised how long she'd been sitting there. She switched off the TV and crawled into bed, where she curled up under the covers and cried until she finally fell asleep.

ಸಿಂ

As they were lifting Jack into the helicopter I saw his wallet fall from his pocket. And in that brief moment before it was noticed and picked up, as it lay there open in the mud, I saw Sophie's spider-web photo. I knew by the end of today she would've heard news of Jack's death, and I wished desperately I could be with her – not that I could do anything, except try to send a gentle message to her that she would be okay. Having seen her photograph, however, I wanted so much to tell her he'd kept it close to him all this time. It would've meant so much to her to know that. But she never would.

The beds that had been made at the roadhouse the previous night were about to be put to good use. No-one had wanted to begin the long journey home last night or before Jack's body had been retrieved, but now they all shared the desire to get away from the campsite and were grateful for a hot shower and a warm, soft, safe bed. I went with Clinton. They'd all agreed to stay for a good breakfast in the morning, then return to the campsite to collect whatever they could, and go home.

Tuesday

The words of the newsreader were playing over and over in Sophie's head when she woke up the following morning. 'He died doing what he loved,' he'd said.

Sophie hated hearing that, and knew she'd be hearing it again and again in relation to Jack's death. It was one of those clichés that was used so much when death was discussed – a certain kind of death anyway. To her, the comment seemed no more than a way of trying to justify the loss of what was generally a young life, a life that was most likely lost doing something that to most people seemed crazy. In Sophie's eyes, you climb mountains, you might die. You dive in caves, you might die. You take on any of these extreme adventure sports and you might die. It was that simple, and she could see no sense in that sort of death.

Several years earlier, Jack had been telling Sophie about a series of lectures he was giving on diving. He was an inspirational man, something that had always come across so clearly when he spoke. Jack talked about getting kids outside and off their screens. About encouraging them to explore, allowing them to fall over, and being there to help them find the courage and the confidence they might need to pick themselves up and try again. This, he stressed, all helped prepare them for life's challenges – and apart from that, an adventurous spirit was fun.

But now Sophie wondered about the people he had inspired over the years. Many of them were very young, children even, whose dreams up to that point were still only that – dreams. Having listened to him they might have taken that next step in pushing their personal boundaries and pursuing those dreams. How would those people be feeling today? Cocklebiddy was an isolated place, the Nullarbor an outwardly calm yet deceptively wild environment. This was a timeless land. She had secrets she was never going to give away.

Jack had known of the ever-present risks associated with diving and was always careful. He had a great respect for the dangers of the underworld. And he'd learned so much about life through avenues that most people never explore, but he'd paid the ultimate price, and Sophie wasn't sure anymore how inspirational that was.

Jack was dead. Not because of something beyond his control, as is often the case, but because he'd followed a dream. No matter how hard she tried, she couldn't come to grips with that. This had been within his control. He didn't have to do it. He could still be here.

But at the same time she knew, deep down, that there was truth in what the newsreader had said, and in all Jack had said in those lectures. Jack had only recently turned forty-five and yet she knew he wouldn't have been happy living twice that long if it had meant living in someone else's shoes. This was all he'd wanted. It became his purpose when the rest of his life failed to satisfy him. His involvement in such a pursuit was the way he not only *wanted* to live his life, it had become the only way he *could* live it. Forty-five years, and at last he'd been able to spend them being the person he wanted to be. Surely that was better than a hundred years living a life of quiet desperation. And then Sophie got to thinking about old age, and the great sadness and discomfort associated with it when it's combined with severe physical and mental decline. Was it really worse to go the way Jack did than to have to endure the pain of growing old?

ಸಿಂಅ

The morning was slipping away and Sophie was still in bed when she felt the warmth of Cujo's breath on her face, saw his tail wagging, then realised someone was at her front door. She dragged herself out of bed, pulled her doona around her and went over to open the door. It was Celia.

'You left your coat beh– Sophie darling, what's wrong?' Celia asked when she saw Sophie's swollen red eyes. 'You've been crying.'

As soon as Celia said that, Sophie's tears spilled over and she started crying all over again.

'Oh darling,' Celia held her daughter tight for a few moments. 'Come and sit down, tell me what's wrong.'

Sophie wiped her face.

'Did you see the news last night?' Sophie asked her mum once she was able to string a few words together.

'No.' Celia looked concerned.

'It's Jack. He's dead.'

'Jack? Jack Murphy? Your Jack?'

Sophie nodded.

'But how?'

'He was diving. There was a flash flood.'

'Oh Sophie,' Celia pulled her daughter close, holding her until Sophie was ready to tell her more. Once she'd heard as much as Sophie knew, she spoke again.

'Come and spend the day with me. I don't have anything on today.'

'Thanks, Mum, but I said I'd go in to Gedup'n'go today.'

Celia looked concerned. 'I'm sure they'd understand if you called in,' she said.

'Yeah, they would, but I should go in. I need to see Peggy and go over last week with her.' Sophie looked at the clock on her wall.

'Oh shit, I've slept in.'

'It won't matter, darling. Let me make you a cup of tea.'

'Thanks, Mum, but I should get ready and go. I'll get something in there.'

Sophie kissed her mum goodbye, thanked her for bringing in her coat, and said she'd call her through the day.

ಸಂ

When Sophie arrived at Gedup'n'go later that morning she walked into a place with a sombre air. She'd considered not going in – spending the day instead with her mum – but decided that being there might prevent her from slipping too deeply into her own cavernous grief. Now she wasn't so sure. It was too still, too quiet. Everyone was conscientiously going about their work. Any early morning chit-chat there might have been was over, and barely a head turned to say hello as she walked through. Even the ducks hadn't been playing in their waterfall. But that suited Sophie just fine. Despite having been up for a while now, and having had a shower, her eyes still looked swollen from the tears she'd cried the night before, and she wanted nothing more than to make it uninterrupted to her desk where she, too, could sit and be alone to get on with her work.

But as she walked past Cath's office she saw her friend standing alongside the scanner with images of Jack around her, and scraps of paper towel in the palm of her hand – scraps she was using to catch her own tears before they slid down her cheeks.

Sophie approached her. 'Are you okay?'

Cath nodded.

Sophie moved in closer and held Cath's free hand. She was preparing a photographic tribute for Jack to put up on the Gedup'n'go website. It was safe to assume, too, that one of the writers she'd passed on her way in was working on the accompanying text. As Cath clicked slowly on one image after another, she talked a little about the last time she'd seen him. Sophie had no idea they even knew each other, but then apart from Cath, the staff at Gedup'n'go probably had no idea she and Jack knew each other either. Why would they?

Cath told Sophie she'd been to his home, a few weeks earlier. They were doing a piece on the preparations for the expedition to Cocklebiddy – a boxed section to go with the story of the dive itself once it had been and gone. This would form part of an even bigger article on cave diving. As Terry lived over in Geraldton, Jack said he'd be happy to talk to them, and to have all his equipment available for photographing should that sort of thing be required. And so the photo shoot had been done at his Sydney home.

'I met his kids,' she told Sophie. 'They were lovely. One of them had cancer some years back – he's doing great now though. Beautiful children. It's been a tough time for them though. He told me he'd just split from his wife.'

Sophie felt faint.

'He didn't say as much,' Cath continued, although Sophie wasn't hearing anything much she was saying now, 'but it was pretty clear she'd given him a hard time about all the diving he was doing. She wanted him at home more, to spend more time with her and the kids.' Cath paused and dabbed her eye with the paper towel. 'Which photo do you think we should use?'

Nothing.

'Sophie?' Cath turned her head to look at Sophie.

'Sorry. That one,' Sophie said quickly, pointing to a photo. It had been all she could do to contain her own tears, and her shock at learning Jack and his wife had separated.

'I'd better get to work,' she said to Cath as she turned away. But as she approached the kitchen to make herself a cup of tea, she walked straight into Frank.

'Oh Frank, I'm so sorry,' Sophie said, trying to avoid looking at him.'

'Sophie?' he said gently as he put his hands on her arms. 'What's wrong?'

Frank's comforting, fatherly voice was all it took. Sophie couldn't hold back her tears any longer.

'Come and sit down, pet. I'll make your tea.'

When Frank returned with two cups, he sat beside her at her desk until she was ready to talk.

'Damn,' Sophie said. 'I can't seem to stop crying.'

'It's okay, Soph.'

'Remember what we talked about on our way back from Melbourne?' Sophie said to him. Frank nodded. 'I told you there had been someone, but it wasn't meant to be.'

'Yes, of course' Frank said.

'That was Jack Murphy.'

ဢ☾

The divers and their support team all met one last time at the campsite. There was little that had survived the storm intact, but they took anything they thought they could salvage. They did what they could, too, to clean up the scattered mess the storm had left.

'What about everything that's still down in the cave?' Alex asked his dad.

'It'll have to stay there, buddy. The next group of divers to come along will be able to get anything we left in the entrance chamber, but a lot of it's been buried. That stuff will have to stay there indefinitely.'

'It's likely the cave will be closed – seriously closed – for some time,' Tobias added.

'The diving community's a small one,' Terry added. 'The cave will reopen again someday, and when it does, whoever collects what's down there will get it back to us.'

But Jack will never be back with you. With anyone. Like everyone who dies – everyone except me – that was it for him. For the first time I wished it had been like that for me all those years ago. I tried to understand why it hadn't been. Why was my journey so different? I always thought I was the lucky one, having that second chance. But I'm not so sure. This grief thing. It's an overwhelming, almost suffocating feeling.

I saw Nathan, about to get in his car and drive off. He'd surprised everyone by not shooting through as soon as the weather had calmed. But he was a journalist, and he had quite a story to tell. It wouldn't be the one he came out here expecting to write, but I hoped he'd make it a story Jack would've been happy to read.

'Nate, got a minute before you go?' Terry called out. Everyone was packed and ready to leave, but Terry pulled them together one last time. This last gathering was a more solemn moment than I'd ever known. Terry spoke a few words, they said a silent prayer for Jack, then after hugs all round that left me aching with sadness, they all turned and were on their way, back on the road again, this time going home.

ऴଓ

As so often happens in life, the worst of events can bring out the best in human kindness, and in the actions of this group, and all the others who came in to help from the moment the storm hit until the last vehicle had left the campsite, I'd seen it. But when Clinton turned on the ignition I felt a gigantic sense of relief. I wanted to get away from there. When I set out to join him, almost two weeks ago, I expected adventure – I wasn't prepared for tragedy. But whoever is? Life's a bit like that. Celia knew it. Sophie knew it, too.

So what do you do? Tackle it all head on and hope for the best, like Jack did, or take a step back and enjoy what's there without flirting with danger, Sophie style? I think I get it now. Who's to say? Certainly not me. I'd been out of line. There's no right or wrong – everyone needs to work that one out for themselves.

Clinton made one last stop in at the roadhouse to see Beryl and Ted, and thank them for all they'd done – not just for him but for everyone.

'You're very welcome, love,' Beryl said. 'Will you be alright? You're on your own, aren't you?'

'Yeah, I'm fine, thanks. It's what I'm used to.'

'If you're passing through here again sometime, stop by and see us, won't you?'

'Without a doubt. Thanks Beryl, Ted.'

'You take care, son,' Ted said as they shook hands. And then Beryl wrapped her arms around Clinton and squeezed him with a warmth that radiated love and kindness, as well as genuine concern. I thought I was seeing more than just a reaction from the sadness of the events at the cave the day before, such was the strength, the tenderness and the apprehension in her embrace. And I wondered at that moment what Beryl and Ted's story might've been. They'd surely have one. Everyone does. Clinton knew that, too. He was a man who let people be themselves without feeling in any way judged or alienated – something that made him as instantly likeable as he'd proven himself to be. It was a gift, one of many. Here, through Clinton, Beryl was saying goodbye to everyone who had been part of Terry's dive team – above and below the ground – Jack included.

The couple from the Wedgetail Inn watched as Morrie turned on to the Eyre Highway and disappeared towards the Pacific.

೫)ఴ

It was a strikingly beautiful day, or it would've been if that dark cloud hadn't been hovering immediately above our heads. But I had a feeling that particular cloud would be with us all for a while longer – for some who'd been at Cocklebiddy, maybe even forever. The good bit was that we were on the road again. Just me and Clinton. Heading home. To Sophie. I needed to know how she was, and my return to her couldn't come soon enough. I wished my own dark cloud would burst and rain down like confetti, to be swept up, tossed away and forgotten.

But it would never be forgotten.

Clinton would've expected to be at Cocklebiddy several days longer than he was, so maybe he was in no hurry to arrive in Sydney. But I was.

In the last couple of days I'd wanted more than anything to be with Sophie again, to make sure she was okay. This was part of it though – the whole letting go thing I was working so hard on – and I knew Celia was there if she needed someone. I wanted to be back home for me, too. I wanted the comfort that comes with all that's familiar. Home, Sophie and Cujo. And Celia.

The morning's drive was nice. 'Nice'. That was the best I could do. All the way it was impossible not to notice the many sobering reminders of the dangers of long distance driving – 'Take a break', 'Stop if tired', 'Stop, revive, survive', 'Fatigue is fatal' and, most sombre of all, 'Drowsy drivers die.' *Everyone dies,* I thought. *Jack died. I died.*

As we inched our way closer to the coast, and as Morrie was wheeling it up the Eucla Pass, I realised we were only a few kilometres from the coast itself.

By the time we got there, I was feeling torn. I wanted to see Eucla, to see the old jetty that was on a calendar Sophie once had. I loved jetties, particularly those that are either mind-bogglingly long, like the one back in Busselton, or incredibly old and run down, but somehow still standing, like the one here at Eucla. But I also wanted Clinton to keep driving, to drive without stopping until he reached Sydney. That wasn't going to happen, I knew that. He had more sense, and was in no hurry. At least we were only kilometres away from the South Australian border, and that sounded reassuringly closer to home than Western Australia.

Clinton pulled into Eucla's roadhouse for a bite to eat, then when he returned to Morrie he drove back to a turn-off that led us towards the jetty. It was a few kilometres down a rough and at times steep road to the old telegraph station, which was no more than a few remaining foundations, largely buried in the drifting sand.

Clinton stopped and parked right there. It was as far as any vehicle could go. He took his camera from the front seat, then walked another kilometre or so to the ocean's edge. As he walked, I floated above the dunes, carried by the sea breeze, and felt better than I had done since, well, I didn't want to think about that.

And there it was. I felt a hint of the joy I'd been feeling on the drive between Perth and Cocklebiddy, which was good, but somehow it felt wrong to be even a little bit happy. I couldn't help it though. We were here, and there wasn't another soul to be seen. And it was extraordinary. We'd walked right into the photograph that had been hanging in Sophie's kitchen for a month all those years ago. At no other beach I'd been to here in Australia in my entire life – well, my entire existence – did I get the sense that I was right on the edge of the country, but here that sensation was overpowering. Maybe it was because there was no-one else in sight, no-one else within earshot, and for a moment it was like Clinton was all that existed in the world, all that existed for me. Cocklebiddy was still there, haunting me, but it almost didn't seem real. And in that moment I was miles away. In a world so heavily populated, it was hard to imagine even seven other people out there, let alone seven billion.

In my mind I saw a map of Australia – its form so beautifully balanced – and I saw Clinton, standing there, a micro-dot on the southern coastline. A wave of insignificance splashed right over me, its contradictory force more powerful than the ocean from which it had leapt. What was I, really? I came up blank. I'd been kidding myself that I meant something to Sophie.

There wasn't too much of the jetty left. Not enough for Clinton to safely walk along. And today, the beach itself was a bit of a mess. Seaweed had washed up on shore and was now being swept back to sea as the afternoon tide snuck in, creating a vignette of blues and greens and browns that blended like some strange oceanic cocktail. The ocean itself was oddly beautiful. The jetty occupied the focal point of this captivating scene, disappearing into the distance as the theory of perspective said it must. Wooden beams that had once all connected to form a carefully constructed jetty – one built to withstand the pounding of the surf at its ankles – were no more than beams bleached by the sun, worn partly away by time and yet standing resolutely where they were first erected.

I watched Clinton as he started weaving his way in and out of the jetty's legs. I watched as he waded out as far as he could safely go without risking any damage to his camera, observing and then capturing the interesting shapes, both positive and negative, created by the centipede-like structure, as well as the shadows it cast. I watched as he shot the gentle waves lapping the shore, and the distant dunes that gripped the far curve of the coastline. It oozed beauty, and his pictures, I knew, would do it justice.

It was then I understood what Sophie had meant about wanting someone with her to share it all when she was travelling, because as captivating as it was, I wanted her here. It was too easy to feel the events at Cocklebiddy slipping away, but it was less than forty-eight hours ago. I felt pangs of guilt every time I caught myself thinking of something else, and I wondered if Clinton was going through the same thing. It was hard to tell with him. He was on his own again, and who really knows what's going through anyone's head except them. Okay, so I'm the exception, with Sophie, but something tells me that this trip is going to end up being more significant – for me – than I'd ever imagined.

Like me, Clinton had known loss, a loss that was far closer to him than the one back at the cave. Perhaps that made Jack's death easier for him to accept and deal with. From the moment we're given life, we have to expect death. But I also knew that his own loss would've made him more sensitive to the pain the others close to Jack would've been experiencing, so I assumed – in those moments when I watched him and saw his eyes looking like they were a million miles away – he was thinking of Jack's family and friends and hoping they could see even now that although things would never be the same, they would be okay, with time.

We left the jetty and were soon back on the bumpy old road up to the highway. In no time at all we were passing the agricultural checkpoint on the border into South Australia, and for the rest of the day we drove along the weather-battered Great Australian Bight.

It was such a quiet day, and a sad day for the most part. In the silent hours as Morrie's wheels transported us – too slowly – towards the comfort of home, I had so much time to think about Sophie. I was concerned about her. She was such a sensitive soul, and although she'd managed to accept that she and Jack were over, she still loved him. We both knew she always would. She'd be feeling the sadness of his death as much as anyone. I'd seen her broken when her relationships ended, but this was different. This was death. There'd be no more lunches, no conversations, no looks of love and longing pass between them anymore.

One thing I was sure of though – Celia would be there for her. I'd never known anything like the love those two shared. It was more than just mother and daughter, more than best friends. It was an unspoken and unconditional caring, and I wasn't – could never be – part of that.

Robert's death had precipitated a relationship that neither of them could ever have foreseen. They just grew into it. I felt unexpectedly lost, not just in my thoughts but with my own purpose in this world, as I heard Morrie's indicator.

Clinton was turning right, and I only just caught sight of the sign – Head of Bight, turn right, 300m – before he passed through a gate, then followed a road that meandered south for another twelve kilometres to the edge of this almighty continent.

We'd left the desert landscape and were now on what had to be one of Australia's most sublime and theatrical platforms. The only sound breaking the enormous stillness that extended across here from the heart of the Nullarbor was the ferocious crashing of the waves below us as they beat the limestone cliffs on which Clinton now stood. It hadn't seemed that far from Eucla – perhaps only a couple of hundred kilometres – but back there you could simply slide your foot along the sand and transport yourself from land to ocean. How was it possible that it could all change so dramatically, so quickly. Here Australia just dropped away. I could float above solid ground, then move only a fraction and it was gone. For anyone else, sliding a foot to feel the water lick their toes here would mean certain death, after a spectacular freefall.

Signs all around said to approach with caution. 'The actual edge of the cliff is not readily seen,' they said, and a little diagram of a figure falling head-first from the cliff's edge as it crumbled away beneath him made it clear for anyone who hadn't already got the message. These soaring, majestic cliffs fall dead straight into the wild and foaming waters of the Southern Ocean. It's a stark, grand vista that stands in such contrast to the endless bluebush plain immediately behind it, and yet both of them echo tales of a part of this country that remain incredibly feral and thankfully untouched.

I'd seen heaps of people when we arrived, but hadn't been paying them any attention as the afternoon slipped away. Clinton and I had both been in our own private worlds. I couldn't blame him for losing track of time – I suspect this long hard journey of his had started almost five years ago, when Wendy died. Sooner if she'd been ill for a while. And maybe there were times he could see no end. I wanted to keep moving, but was in no position to rush this man.

It was when the sound of a thumping bass that had been a steadily increasing noise in the distance became a pounding interference in a place generally devoid of that sort of intrusion that Clinton made a move. By the time the car full of kids pulled in, he'd pulled out and we were on our way again.

It wasn't for long though. Clinton's next stop was at a place called Twin Rocks, and he stayed there until the sun was completely snuffed out. I doubt whether he could've dragged himself away from there before then even if he'd wanted to – and I wasn't sure I could either, despite wishing he'd drive through the night. The colours that were filling the late afternoon sky had been lovely, but against the backdrop of the Bunda Cliffs they were magical.

The water below us was choppy and as I watched Clinton fix a huge lens to his camera I caught a glimpse of why. Whales. There were seven of them, right in front of us – one a mother with her calf – and I could see another pod out in the distance. I watched as they cruised gracefully beneath us, and thought about going out to join them. I wanted to. It was an opportunity I'd never get again. I could stay with Clinton and Morrie, and drown in the sadness I was just managing to keep on top of, or I could go down and kill some of this excruciating time having some fun. Maybe I was wrong to do it, but I went anyway. This was their natural breeding environment and it was my chance to be with them for an unforgettable experience.

I hung out with the calf, just a breath away from the others who were, in turn, bursting out of the sea until they were almost entirely airborne, then slamming spectacularly back into the waves. I watched as they surfaced, blowing spray with such force I almost thought I was going to be plunged into the ocean with it. If that didn't do it, the slapping of their perfectly curvaceous tails might, but I didn't care. If this was how the curtain was going to fall on The Life of Georgia, Take Two, so be it. I was ready. Seeing these giants of the sea rolling about belly-up was the most fun I'd had since the dolphins back in Esperance, and so much had happened since then. Until now I'd never understood people's reactions when they saw brief glimpses of the back of a whale, way off in the distance, when to me it looked like no more than a floating mound. This, however, this had been unbelievable.

But playtime was soon over. I had to get back up to Clinton and I was feeling tired. A little weak. I managed to get up there, but it had felt an awfully long way, even for me. Something was happening, draining me of the unlimited energy I'd always possessed. It was a relief to settle down again with Clinton. The light had started to fade and the cliffs could almost have been on fire as light radiating from the setting sun created tones of gold and rust that lit the craggy limestone face and left it burning before our eyes. It was like seeing fireworks caught in a freeze-frame – a magnetic natural lightshow and the best possible way to end a day that had started so painfully, and continued to grip us with its darkness, despite the joy of the whales.

A distinct chill soon settled around Morrie, every bit as comfortably as the stars that studded and sparkled in the night sky. Clinton grabbed a book from the front of the van and climbed in the back, propped up his pillow, wrapped his blanket around him and started to read. I made myself comfortable on the pillow beside his head, where I felt so cosy and safe, more so than I'd felt since I left Sophie. Never before had I felt I *needed* anything, or anyone. Tonight I did.

I was able to think so clearly out here. About Sophie. About me. Ever since I'd seen Jack's body, lying broken on those fallen boulders, something wasn't right. It almost felt like the life was slowly being sucked out of me. That's why I went to play with the whales. It wasn't just to have some fun – I needed to see if I *could*. I was beginning to think I was on this trip for a reason far greater than the one I'd convinced myself of.

Clinton didn't slide the door shut, and it wasn't long before I understood why. It was eerie at first, in the black of night, but when I realised the peculiar sound out there was the whales communicating, it became not an eerie noise but a haunting song – one that was more beautiful and soothing than any I could remember.

Wednesday

Clinton hadn't been reading for long last night when he put his book down, sent a text message, switched off the light, had one last cigarette for the day and then fallen deeply asleep. I hadn't seen him send any text messages before then, but watched over his shoulder as his fingers typed. It was to Cath, at Gedup'n'go.

'Should be in Syd Fri pm. Will try to get in 2CU. CW.'

With the exception of the whales and the sound of the waves crashing against the cliffs below, it had been a still and quiet night, one I knew I'd remember forever – I just wasn't at all sure how long forever might be. It didn't seem all that long before the veil of dawn was lifting on a new day. Sunrise was every bit as peaceful as the night had been, although a few passing motorists – most of whom had come from the east – pulled into Twin Rocks to soak in the aura of the Southern Ocean as they began their own journeys across the Nullarbor. I wondered what their plans were. Being away and on the road like this, it's so easy to forget that the world continues to exist in its own way for billions of people. I'd discovered that one of the real joys of travel is that it's a great escape. But these people who were sharing Twin Rocks, admiring our view, were such a strong reminder not only of where we were going but where we'd been, and suddenly the numbing sting of reality clouded everything in my sight and I wanted, more than ever, to just get home.

Clinton stirred with the arrival of these strangers. He sat up, lit a cigarette and looked out to the ocean. When I watched him like this, I wanted so much to know what he was thinking. I wanted his wisdom. But no-one could do anything for me. I was alone in this world. Even when I was with Sophie, I was alone.

It was still early, but Clinton must've wanted to make an early start because after only about ten minutes he'd emptied the contents of his last tin of pineapple, pulled on his jeans and a sweatshirt and taken to the wheel. In no time we were back on the Eyre Highway.

The road took us a little way inland again where the harshness of the Nullarbor slowly tapered away, its cruel face a fading image in the rear-view mirror.

ಬಿಜ

Sophie's phone rang.

'Hi Sophie, it's Peggy.'

'Hi Peggy, how are things in there? I missed you yesterday.'

'Yes, sorry about that. I was caught up all day in meetings. It's been a difficult few days for a lot of the staff. Quite a few of them knew Jack Murphy, some of them well.'

'Yeah, he was an old friend of mine too. We'd worked together many years ago.'

'Oh, Sophie. I'm sorry.'

'Would you like me to come in today?'

'No, that won't be necessary, but I had a couple of things I wanted to ask you.'

They went over details of a few loose ends from the previous week and decided it would be good if Sophie could go in for an hour or two tomorrow, then Peggy asked Sophie if she'd be able to go up on Friday afternoon as well.

'Cath's expecting one of our photographers to stop by sometime – he was out on the Nullarbor, at the cave, and with the way everyone's been feeling these last couple of days we've decided to break early for drinks – say around four.'

'Sure, I'd like that. Thanks, Peggy.'

Sophie hung up the phone, took a deep breath and told herself it would be okay. Time, that was all.

ಬಿಜ

As we drove further and further away from the cave site, I thought more and more about Sophie. I'd be back home with her soon. She would've been thinking of little else but Jack, and I wondered how much she knew. Would she have heard that he'd split from his wife? Probably by now. That would've made news of his death so much harder. All the 'what ifs'.

Getting involved with Jack was something she'd told herself she'd never do, and although I could understand why, there was always something about the two of them that made me so sure they should've been together. That's why I never discouraged their relationship. Not until I saw how much pain she was in, trying to make the most of it while knowing how wrong it was.

In a sense I wished Sophie had been on this trip, to get to know Clinton and to have learned a little of his life with Wendy. Or Jim and Clare, from back on the train. Maybe that would've done some good in restoring her faith. It had mine. But knowing how even those she believed would never lead such a deceptive path, herself included, could be drawn so easily into situations that had potentially devastating repercussions was disturbing, to say the least. Getting involved with a married man should've been easy for Sophie to avoid, and yet she'd done it. It hadn't been so easy after all.

I'd observed so much of relationships, Sophie's and those of others around her. Emotions play such a huge part – love, joy, sorrow, fear, hate – they're so often responsible for people getting caught up in the moment, and in some cases tangled up in its messy, complicated and at times heart-wrenching aftermath. It should've been as simple as two people staying away from each other, but neither of them had wanted to do that.

Jack had been Sophie's friend before anything else and she couldn't see the point in losing a friend simply because they'd become closer – that seemed crazy and she thought she was stronger than that. Thought they both were. They both wanted things to be the same as they had been, before they got so close, and I had to hand it to them. It hadn't been easy – temptation is all too powerful at times – but they'd done it. And that's when I knew that the feelings they had for each other were never going to fade. They weren't just in love, and it was more than just loving each other. They genuinely *liked* each other, too. I don't think I ever really believed they might end up together, not until a few days ago when I heard of his separation. I'd been so excited by the possibility.

Then I saw her spider-web photo in his wallet.

The sadness I was feeling was overwhelming. Like everything had gone so completely wrong and was slowly suffocating me. Jack. Sophie would never see him again. It was inconceivable, even to me.

ଛଔ

Clinton stopped at a little store in Ceduna where he bought a couple more tins of pineapple, and when he returned to Morrie I noticed a certain pain had crept into his eyes. It was almost like he was just going through the motions now, getting from here to there.

Ceduna, I read, was the gateway to the Nullarbor. Well, it would be if you were heading west, but for us it was the back door we'd now closed behind us.

In knowing that, there was also a very real sense that we were edging closer to home. It felt like it, too, with so many more people and the amount of traffic we were now seeing. We were leaving the wide-open spaces behind us and re-entering places that were actually populated. Ceduna was the biggest town between Norseman, where we'd left Mary back in Western Australia, and Port Augusta here in South Australia, and from here, New South Wales isn't far away.

The countryside we were passing through was comparatively lush and rural. Quite suddenly there were things to look at, as opposed to the vast emptiness I'd become so used to. This was a good thing – more to be distracted by. It was wheat country – silos stood tall at regular intervals along the highway, and sheep were grazing on land that was far more fertile than any we'd seen in about a week. The roads had become smaller, too. Bendy and even hilly – which sounds absurd because they weren't in the least bit hilly, but even a gentle incline is like a hill after days on the Nullarbor.

It had been a desperately quiet afternoon. There'd been no singing – not even any music playing – and Clinton was withdrawn. He made several stops during the afternoon, and with each one I wanted to scream at him and tell him 'Please, just get me home!'

Most of the stops he made had involved no more than simply pulling off the highway. With Morrie parked on the gravel, he'd get out to photograph the many abandoned farm vehicles that dotted the rural landscape. If he needed to jump the fence for a better shot, and was able to, he did. But I couldn't be bothered. Not until he reached a place called Iron Knob. It, too, was home to more than a few of these caricatures of farm machinery, but they weren't his motivation for stopping this time.

Iron Knob – I could hear Mary's laughter on learning that name – wasn't much more than an abandoned shell of a place. Just a kilometre or two off the highway, it was stained with a certain melancholy, having lost the spirit – the people – who so many years ago when it was a flourishing mining town would've given it great character and warmth. It looked like a town that was still adjusting to its newly acquired ghost town status, and it mirrored Clinton's melancholic mood. Mine too. Clinton pulled up on a wide, empty street, alongside a neglected old church.

Sophie had never been a religious person, so it was a rare thing for me to go inside a church, but she did love churches, some of them anyway. They could be extraordinarily beautiful.

The church at Iron Knob, however, was little more than four corrugated iron walls and a corrugated iron roof. I adored it instantly. Painted an inoffensive custard yellow with a distinct white cross fixed like a warning to the front wall, it stood on dry patchy earth on a street corner with a cluster of boulders curiously deposited inside the front gate. To the left and supported by wooden posts was a tiny A-frame roof, a large bell hanging silently underneath. On each side wall of the little church were three long narrow windows. No stained glass here, this was a simple town.

I was trying to imagine Sunday mornings in Iron Knob's more prosperous days – the bell would be ringing as residents strolled the short distance from their own front doors to the door of God where they would enter and give thanks for the good fortune that had blessed their tiny town.

But today the church, like the rest of the town, was empty, and that was perhaps why Clinton pushed opened the stiff gate and made his way along the short and well-worn path to the side of this house of God. He stopped by one of the windows, cupped his hands around his eyes and peered in through the dirty glass before apprehensively turning the rusted and creaky door handle and silently walking inside. I was right beside him. Clinton hadn't struck me as the church-going type, but even if he wasn't, we all do things from time to time that we don't normally do in order to experience the full spectrum of life, and with the events of the past few days I knew he would be needing to find solace in whatever way he could. Maybe surfing isn't always enough.

I wanted to stay with Clinton, and I did, but I wasn't comfortable in the little church, not at all. The feeling of suffocation I'd been experiencing was even stronger in there. I know the reality of life is tough for everyone from time to time, and we all need something to help us through the bad patches, a way to process life, to try and make some sense of it when at times there seems no sense at all. But religion wasn't for me.

It was only the warmth of Clinton's solitary soul that soaked up the emptiness inside this quaint little church, a church that seemed even smaller from the inside than it had out. He sat down on one of the eight stark pews and buried his face in his hands. For several minutes he sat as still as the air in the Nullarbor had been, moments before the storm, but after a while he began to sob and I could feel my heart breaking. I'd grown to love this man, and to see him in this kind of pain with no-one by his side to hold him was unbearable.

Everyone struggles with pain, and there are always going to be times when the weight of the sadness becomes overwhelming, like now. But Clinton would be okay. I didn't see him as someone to dwell on things – not outwardly anyway – but I believed that Jack's death must have echoed Wendy's in ways I could never know. Losing her must've been the toughest thing he'd ever had to deal with, and Cocklebiddy had seen him relive a nightmare. Clinton would never forget Wendy, never forget the joy she brought to his world, but life goes on, and I was sure he, as much as anyone, knew of the beauty to be found all around us if we take the time – and in some cases find the strength – to look for it.

As he got up to leave, and I made a move to follow him, something made me stop for a split second. It was Sophie's voice. I know it was. It was so faint, but I knew it like my own.

'I'm okay, Georgia,' she said. 'It's all okay.'

I was completely thrown and, despite her words of reassurance, now even more anxious to get home.

It was dark outside. Clinton went straight to Morrie and started up the engine, leaving Iron Knob's little church and the emptiness of the town behind him. Within an hour we were in Port Augusta, where he stopped to pick up some take-away from a Chinese restaurant along the main street before driving a short distance out of town to a quiet little spot that was to be home for the night. He'd been looking tired, and he slept undisturbed.

Thursday

I didn't sleep at all, but Clinton must've needed the rest because he didn't stir after he dropped off to sleep last night. Morrie was parked on the southern edge of the Flinders Ranges, a little way out of Port Augusta itself, and although we were a long way from their beating heart, it was still easy to feel their mesmerising presence. I'd left Morrie to watch the sun rise – needed to get out into the open air – but the strength I had just days ago had abandoned me.

The sun had risen gently – like a helium-filled balloon – above the plains and over wheat fields that seemed to stretch on endlessly, or at least until they touched the heels of those hazy purple mountains I could just make out. I didn't drift far – partly because I knew it would be exhausting, but also because I didn't want Clinton to leave without me. But there was something beautifully mysterious about this landscape, and I could see how artists like Hans Heysen had been seduced by it. An unsuspecting ripple in the land north of Port Augusta would've caught their eye, and I pictured them tracing its path as it blossomed into an enchanting mountain range – a wonderland that had been sculpted over millions of years for people to enjoy today. From the dusty quiet of this sun-soaked morning, I tried to reach Sophie, but without succeeding. And I thought about Clinton as I floated about, hoping the darkness of his yesterday may have subsided.

When I returned to Morrie it was hard to tell how he might be feeling, but the sadness that had engulfed him yesterday – the emptiness that had taken over the warmth of his eyes – seemed to have lifted, at least a little. He checked the map. I checked the map. Sydney was getting closer all the time, but we still had a long way to go. A sharp increase in the amount of traffic on the roads meant we were getting closer and closer to the big towns and cities. Adelaide wasn't that far away, relatively speaking. We hadn't been among this much traffic since Perth.

We passed through lots of small agricultural towns, but it was one called Ororoo that brought a smile to Clinton's face and a change in his mood.

'Ororoo. Now what might Mary think of that?' he mumbled quietly to himself. She was a hard lady to forget, and I wondered whether she'd met up with her friend in Kalgoorlie, and where she might be now. I wondered whether the man she'd met in Broome had left there to join her on her travels. Then I realised that our encounter with Mary had been just over a week ago. So much had happened in that time and it was more than likely she was still in Kalgoorlie.

The smile that had reappeared on Clinton's face, even if it had been no more than a small one, was reassuring. He'd be okay. And if I was hearing properly last night as we left the church in Iron Knob, Sophie was okay too. So why wasn't I feeling better than I was?

I watched Clinton reach for his box of cassettes, pull one out at random and slip it into the player, and I knew he was back, for the moment anyway. It wasn't long before he even started to sing.

It was pastoral country out here, with breezy wheat fields and other grain crops growing at every turn. It was also an area steeped in railway history, and for the next few hundred kilometres the road and the train tracks ran side by side. The longer we followed those tracks, however, the more distressed I was feeling because it seemed we were edging closer and closer to nowhere. *Of course, this is the outback,* I reminded myself. Broken Hill is the next big town, and although Clinton was more like his old self, I was getting agitated. We crossed the border into New South Wales at Cockburn and from there it was less than an hour to Broken Hill. Coming across on the train I would've given anything to be able to spend more time there, but now I was hoping Clinton would drive right through.

But when we reached Broken Hill, he took the turn-off to Silverton, another twenty-five kilometres north-west. Shit, Clinton. No.

It was a bizarre little town. A small cluster of colonial buildings remained standing to entice visitors, although to call it a cluster suggested they were positioned close to one another, and the first thing I noticed as we drove into Silverton was how scattered the few remaining buildings were. Crumbling remains of other buildings existed nearby. Clinton pulled up in front of the hotel, got out and went in. The bar sat squarely in the centre of the cluttered room that, to me, seemed more like a milk bar than a pub. Movie memorabilia filled every spare inch of wall and ceiling space while tacky souvenirs sat waiting to be purchased in the same breath as a beer from the counter.

Clinton wandered through, ordering a Coke as he went, and sat himself down in the beer garden while I lingered inside the main part of this small, cramped establishment. Faded photographs from movies like *Mad Max* and the TV mini-series *A Town Like Alice* lined the walls, giving an insight into what life was like during the production of these iconic Aussie films. Others chronicled the extreme weather conditions that can change the appearance of a town like this in no time at all. Thoughts of Cocklebiddy flashed through my mind and I had to get out. I went to join Clinton in the beer garden.

Just as I did, a voice loomed large behind me.

'Clint!' it beamed with warm recognition. 'I thought it looked like your old Kombi out the front. How are you, mate? Can I buy you another drink – Coke?'

'G'day, Dave,' Clint said as he stood and shook this man's hand. 'Yeah, thanks mate.' The big voice disappeared into the pub and returned a couple of minutes later with two schooners of Coke.

'So tell me, how are things? What brings you out here?'

'Been out on the Nullarbor, doing a job at the caves.'

'You weren't at Cocklebiddy were–'

'Yeah. That was us.'

'Geez mate, I'm sorry. We saw it on the news. Talk about bad luck.'

'Yeah, one of those things. Nothing anyone could do. I'm heading across to Sydney. Just thought I'd detour on my way through – always did love it out here. The place is looking great.'

'Stay and have some lunch, mate. Our burgers are still the best.'

'That'd be great, thanks.'

As Dave was heading back into the pub to organise lunch for the two of them, one of the many donkeys I'd seen as we came into Silverton had sauntered over to the beer garden. He was gorgeous, and had a dark band across his shoulders, just like Mary had said. He was happy to hang around Clinton. Maybe he knew that if someone was out there, food was on its way.

Dave brought burgers out for them both, but in the time it took to scoff them down and catch up on things, neither of them returned to the events at Cocklebiddy.

I hadn't wanted Clinton to make this detour, but I was glad he'd stopped in to see an old friend. I was beginning to think he had old friends all over the country, perhaps even scattered round the world. He would wander in and out of their lives with great irregularity but he seemed to have these people's love and respect wherever he went. He was a calm and gentle soul with a big heart and a fierce independence. I don't think he'd ever let himself be a burden to anyone.

გოყ

In at Gedup'n'go, the mood was still grey but it had lifted marginally since Tuesday. Sophie was still feeling a little numb and talk of Jack and the Nullarbor tragedy continued – it would until after the service – but she tried to block it out, to keep her head down and to concentrate on the work she had to do.

გოყ

We left Silverton and passed back through Broken Hill, heading east once more.

We had a long drive ahead of us. The Barrier Highway was supposedly the most direct route through to Sydney, but it still seemed an awfully long way. Or maybe I was simply wasn't coping. I wanted to be home, and anyone knows that when that feeling starts to kick in, you want it to happen, quickly. It was never going to be quick, though. Wilcannia was the next town we stopped at, a couple of hundred kilometres beyond Broken Hill.

From what I could see, not a lot was happening in Wilcannia. Everywhere except the service centre looked to be bolted shut. As Clinton pulled in, he grabbed his phone to make a call, only to find the battery dead. Tossing it aside, he opened Morrie's door and wandered into the store to buy a few supplies, and on his way out he stopped by the pay phone to make his call. I strained to hear.

'Terry. Clint.'

'Clint. How are you, mate?'

'Good, thanks. Just wondering how you and Alex are doing. I guess you're back home?'

'Yeah, got in late Tuesday,' Terry said. 'Alex is having a rough time – he was doing well until we got back. Seeing his mum again and talking to her about it must've made it all sink in, but we're home and he'll be okay.'

'How about you?'

'Honestly, mate, not that great. I spoke to Jack's wife when we got in – that was hard.'

'How's she doing?'

'She's not too bad,' Terry said. 'She'd always hated him diving, had wanted him to stop. Said something about knowing it was going to end badly.'

Clinton listened, silently.

'They'd split up not that long ago, too, so the kids are having a tough time – Jack moving out was one thing, but now this. They're old enough to know he won't be coming home at all, and that's the hardest part. I can't imagine how those kids must be doing.'

'They'll be okay. I don't know how, but they will,' Clinton said. 'If there's anything I can do, let me know.'

'Thanks Clint. When are you due in Sydney?'

'Should be there sometime tomorrow afternoon. I've lined up a visit to Gedup'n'go if I arrive early enough. I haven't been in there before, so thought I'd stop by to meet Cath and some of the others.'

'Sounds good. Give her my best – she's a treasure. Had a bit to do with Jack so I imagine she'll be feeling the loss too.'

'I'll do that. Don't suppose you know when the service will be?' Clinton asked.

'Looks like Monday. Will you still be around?'

'I doubt it, but you never know.'

'Okay, bye mate. Keep in touch.'

Terry was the last person to ever speak to Clinton. We'd been driving towards Cobar as the afternoon slipped away, listening to a selection of fabulous music. Clinton, despite the difficult nature of the call he'd made to Terry, was in good spirits again and seemed relaxed. Out of Morrie's window the countryside resembled a canvas of earthy tones, gradually melting into one another as the stark rays of the sun gave in to the softness of the late afternoon.

I watched as hundreds of beautiful galahs took flight, their full pink breasts splashing colour in a dimming sky. I could make out kangaroos on the ranges on either side of the highway, and thought how wonderful it was to be seeing them in their natural environment. The only ones we'd seen for days had been dead on the side of the road, providing a feast for the crows that would flock to the roadkill, tearing warm flesh from the carcass. The second before a passing vehicle was upon them, the ravenous birds would take off, only to be back feeding the moment any threat had passed. Then there were the wedge-tailed eagles, impressive in their strength and size, and their dominance when it came to feeding time. I'd been surprised, too, by the number of goats we were seeing, and still many emus that, while camouflaged against the parched land and low scrub, could be spotted without too much trouble if they were on the move. There seemed, suddenly, to be so much life all around us. But then just as suddenly it was all over.

Clinton was about an hour out of Cobar. Springsteen was belting out the last verse of 'Born to Run' – the lyrics suddenly touching a raw nerve. His singing stopped. As the sun was going down on our last day together, the driver of a semi heading west along the Barrier Highway rounded a bend and veered on to the wrong side of the road, blinded by the setting sun. Clinton never knew what hit him, something for which I would be forever grateful.

ಐಂಡ

I'd managed to slip out of Morrie's window a split second before impact, but descended into some kind of momentary haze because it was now twilight and I could hear sirens blaring in the distance. The closer they came the more devastatingly real the situation was feeling, but it was the smell of smoke and burning rubber in the air that brought me back to the shock of the moment. The smell wasn't just smoke and rubber – it was also the smell of death, and I didn't want to have to look at the tangled mass of blue that had been my home for the last ten days, nor to think of Clinton inside it. It was an excruciatingly painful image, one that left me aching all over.

Then something else hit me as rescue vehicles began to pull up alongside the wreckage – something every bit as powerful. Sophie could've been in that van with Clinton. If she'd listened to me, she would've been.

Part of me wanted to stay. I knew there was no way Clinton could've survived, but part of me needed to see him before I could believe it. I couldn't, though. Losing Jack had been awful enough, but I'd never known this feeling of absolute despair and what I most wanted to do was to get away from it all, to be with Sophie again and to never leave her side. The idea of hitching a ride with one of those monstrous trucks made me feel ill, but I knew it would be my quickest way home. The police and rescue teams had arrived at the crash site and floodlights were being erected. It was surreal – this strange commotion around a stillness that held not even a breath of life. I had to go. Passing traffic was being directed slowly around the wreckage, and I grabbed the opportunity to jump on board a truck heading east.

This new and not at all comforting feeling of being so completely alone, my sadness for the man I'd left behind just out of Cobar and my longing for home was combined with enormous frustration as my truckie stopped in Nyngan for dinner and then again to refuel. It was good he was stopping, I tried to tell myself – these guys need to take breaks and eat well – but I hadn't been thinking properly and assumed he'd be flying through. I could hop on another truck, sure, but that wouldn't get me there any quicker. I needed to be patient, so I sat it out in the cabin of the truck until he returned.

He did, eventually. But before he left he made himself comfortable and took a nap. *Ugh. I wish I could fall asleep that easily, and be oblivious to this next stretch of our journey,* but I knew that wouldn't happen. He was out for an hour or so and in that time I tried so hard not to think about Clinton and the accident, but it was impossible. The country music station this guy was tuned into was playing softly as he slept. If anything it offered some kind of sweet distraction – without it I might gently slip away to a place that was so dark I might never find my way out again – but I was restless and couldn't wait to move on, and was thankful for a caller to the station whose big laugh in the still of the night made my companion stir and then get going again.

The Central West was one part of New South Wales, apart from Sydney, that I was a little bit familiar with. Sophie used to go out there a lot after she'd finished school, staying with an old friend who took her all over the place – not just exploring the area but taking part in its unique night life. I made myself think back to those times as we drove through the night. Anything to distract me.

The truck was driving so slowly. Okay, so it wasn't, but that's how it felt. As we passed through Dubbo, I remembered our trips out to the zoo. Orange, and my thoughts turned to Celia. Bathurst – I wondered how the diabetic from the train was going. Had she been able to continue her trip somehow, or was she back home, all holiday plans a lingering and disappointing memory? I tried to think of everything but Clinton. But try as I might, he was never far away.

And neither were Sophie and Celia. Maybe Celia would hear about the accident out of Cobar, but probably not. Accidents like this often made the news but they seemed to happen with frightening regularity and I'm sure there were far more of them than we ever heard about. And if she did hear about it, to her it would be no more than another terrible crash involving a big truck, and her fear of being out on the road – or of Sophie being out on the road – would escalate that little bit more. I knew Sophie would never tell her the significance of this particular fatality.

ഩര

Sophie called in to see her mum when she arrived home later that day.

'How are things in there?' Celia asked her daughter.

'Getting better. The service is on Monday.'

'Will you go?'

'I don't think so.' Cujo appeared at the door. 'Hi, Cujo.' Sophie smiled as he nuzzled in for a cuddle. 'How's he been today?' she asked her mum.

'Good,' said Celia. 'Whatever might've been troubling him seems to have passed. Are you sure, Soph? About the service?'

Sophie nodded. She'd decided against going to Jack's service. She had every reason *to* go – they'd been close – but although she was convinced some people enjoyed going to funerals, she hated them, and this would be a hard one. Under the circumstances it was also perhaps better if she wasn't there. And he was dead. Her being at the funeral wasn't going to bring him back, nor was hearing about him going to make her feel any better. *He* certainly wouldn't be hearing any of what would be said about him. She'd struggled with life's complexities on so many levels. Speeches at funerals were one of them. It was too late to tell the deceased how you felt about them. Sure, everyone else could hear it, but what good was that? Was it simply an attempt for the mourners to ease their own pain? So many people seemed to end up living with sadness – and often guilt, and regret – because of the things they'd left unsaid. Jack knew how Sophie had felt about him. There was no more she could do.

'I've got some friends coming to dinner on Saturday night,' Sophie said to her mum. 'Want to join us?'

'Oh, Soph. Thanks, but you don't want me there with you all.'

'Why not?'

'I'd cramp your style.'

Sophie laughed. 'I don't have any style!'

'No,' Celia said, 'but your friends might.'

Sophie laughed again.

'It's good to see you smiling, Soph,' her mum said.

Sophie got up to leave, kissed her mum and said, 'If you change your mind, you know you're welcome.'

Home

There was nothing in particular about this truck driver I found endearing, but in all fairness that would've had as much to do with my frame of mind as it did him. It had been the longest night I can ever remember, although the one back in Cocklebiddy had come close. This trip should've been the adventure of a lifetime, not the nightmare it had turned into.

And yet the more I thought about it, the more I realised that in many ways it *was* the adventure I'd hoped it would be. I'd seen so much of Australia – seen it with a man who had opened my eyes and touched my soul and I knew that a part of Clinton would be with me, always.

I was, however, surprisingly saddened by the loss of all the images he'd taken while I'd been with him. Not too many people had the kind of patience he did, and I'd seen how that patience had allowed him to develop an incredible rapport with the world around him. I'd seen him anticipate nature's ever-changing moods – the whimsy of the baby emus back at Margaret River, the power of the storm at Cocklebiddy, the colours of Australia's outback, and everything in between – and I knew he understood and respected her unpredictability. The beauty he was able to capture in the conditions she'd confront him with would, I know, have resulted in images that would take someone as close to a place as they could go without actually being there. With every release of the shutter – and I knew I would think of him every time I heard that gentle sound – he was soaking up the poetry of life. Photography had made him a rich man in the sense that it had taken him places where he could develop a deep appreciation for life. I could only assume that part of his reason for doing what he did was to try to instil in all those who enjoyed his photographs an equally rich appreciation for a world that at times failed to deliver all they hoped it might.

I'd been miles away and barely realised where we were when the truck I was in pulled up at a service centre in Mount Lambie. Breakfast.

Inside were men whose own trucks had pulled up outside, tucking into greasy and oversized meals under flickering fluorescent lights. I'd been trying to think about anything but Clinton, but it hadn't been working. Everything came back to him.

The sunrise was dull without him. If I'd been able to, I would've acknowledged that it was a beautiful mid-winter's morning. And if I'd been able to, I would've helped my own truckie get through his steaming calorie-laden breakfast faster, but all I could do was wish he'd hurry up as I thought of Clinton, and Sophie – who was almost within reach again – and how close I'd come to losing them both.

This drive back home, since Cobar especially but really it had started at Cocklebiddy, had given me more time to think than I'd both expected and wanted. When I heard Sophie's voice back at Iron Knob I had a feeling my fate had been sealed. I was meant to come on this journey, just as Sophie *wasn't* meant to. I'd never wanted to acknowledge that she could survive perfectly well without me, and I suspect that's why I stayed with her so long. She needed me, I'd convinced myself. Needed my guidance. But this trip – Clinton – had taught me so much about people, and about life. I'd been wrong all along. *I* needed Sophie.

But Sophie can't give me anything. She doesn't even know who I am. I wasn't meant to find a way out of that birth canal, but I did. I'd found my second chance.

I need to get back home and see her again, but I know it will be brief. I'm tired. So tired. I just want to sleep.

ಶಃఴ

Dawn's lacklustre overture had long since finished when my truckie turned off the M4 into Homebush Bay Drive and continued towards the northern beaches, but it was Friday morning and we were in the thick of peak hour traffic as we drove through Ryde and its neighbouring suburbs. I hoped Sophie would be working from home today. I knew I didn't have much time left. The sun was blinding me in a way it never had before, and it hurt. It didn't help being in all this traffic, either. Having just come from the immense openness of the outback, this squeezing of my soul, this greater force, was willing me to relinquish the life I'd had with Sophie faster than I was prepared for.

The driver I'd spent the night with had passed through the worst of the traffic and was now hurtling towards the northern suburbs way faster than he should've been, but I didn't care. The faster the better. He'd be driving right past Sophie's house – I couldn't have picked a better truck. I wasn't sure if I could do it, but I knew if I was going to see Sophie one last time I had to jump out. I stumbled. Felt sick. He hadn't been expecting to have to stop around that bend. *It's no wonder there are so many accidents along here.*

It was all I could do to push myself home. My life was slipping away so fast now. And then I saw her. Sophie. She was outside with Cujo.

ಐಂಚ

That was close, Sophie thought as she heard a truck screeching to a stop just along the road.

ಐಂಚ

Home. I made it. I snuggled in with Sophie, where I'd always felt I belonged, and then I looked at her. I looked long and hard. Even that was exhausting.

She looked so sad, but then I expected that. I stayed quiet. Even if I'd had the strength to speak I wasn't going to. But I watched on as she sat out there with Cujo. He was so excited, dancing around in circles, and I wondered if he knew I was there. He wanted to play. He kept bringing his toys over to Sophie, one by one, hoping she'd get up and have some fun with him, but after a while he knew she wasn't going to and he sat quietly by her side. She was worlds away, but then she was often like that and I couldn't have dug any deeper at this stage even if I'd wanted to. Maybe things weren't as bad as they looked.

She snapped out of it when her phone rang, and I was relieved to hear her voice. It was strong and sounded happy.

It was Kelly.

'Sorry to call so early, Soph,' she said. 'Just checking about tomorrow night. Are you still expecting us?'

'Sure am. About seven.'

Sophie had organised a dinner party for a handful of her old school friends, a kind of post-reunion catch-up. None of them knew Jack, or knew that she'd known him.

I was pleased to know she hadn't cancelled her plans. It would've been easy to, but it would take her mind off Jack and the service on Monday. Just as she was getting up to go inside and work out what she'd make for dinner tomorrow night, Celia appeared with two cups of tea.

Celia. How I loved her.

'How are you feeling, darling?'

'Thanks, Mum. Pretty good. Surprisingly good.'

That's how she looked, too, and I suddenly felt a contentment I'd never known. Being here with Sophie and Celia, and Cujo. They were okay. Sophie didn't need me at all, and I would've been no good to her anyway. Not now. My time was almost up, but I was okay, too.

'I'm going to the shops a bit later. Can I get you anything?' Sophie asked her mum as she finished her tea. 'Or would you like to come?'

By the time Sophie and Celia had returned home from the shops, where they'd stayed to have some lunch together, it was mid-afternoon. Sophie made a dessert for tomorrow night before she left for Gedup'n'go to join the others for drinks. She felt a little unsettled as she arrived. By now, word would have spread that she and Jack once worked together and had been good friends, and if that were the case, she could expect everyone to be especially nice to her. She didn't want that. It would only make it harder.

Frank was the first person she saw as she walked into an office filled with food and drinks, and a lot of laughter.

'Frank, hi!' she said.

'Sophie, how are you?'

'Good. I'm good, but please don't be too nice to me or you'll make me cry.'

It was good for Sophie to get out, to mingle a little. The mood in the office had lifted considerably since earlier in the week. A normal pre-weekend anticipation filled the air, but amid much laughter, no-one but Cath seemed to notice that Clinton West hadn't appeared.

൦൦

It was Saturday night, and Sophie was hearing a lot of laughter coming from her lounge room as she prepared dinner. The others were reliving the reunion, talking about a time that seemed a lifetime ago, and for the first time in almost a week, she was feeling happy.

She was almost ready to serve up the meal when Stu appeared in the kitchen.

'It's smelling good, Soph.'

'Thanks, Stu. Is everyone right with a drink out there?'

He stuck his head around the corner to check. 'Yep, how about you?'

'Got mine right here.'

Maybe he'd been happy to take a break from the reminiscing in the other room, or maybe he just wanted to see how she was going out there. Sophie thought it was probably both.

'How are you Soph, really?'

'I'm good, thanks,' but when she looked up, she saw his eyes searching hers. He knew she was holding something back.

'Well, okay. I've been better,' she admitted.

'Yeah, I thought so. What's up?'

Sophie was touched by his concern.

'An old friend of mine died a few days ago, but I don't want to talk about it tonight, okay?'

Stu looked so sad for her. He walked across, gave her a cuddle, put his hands on either side of her face and kissed her forehead, then stepped back and said with renewed energy, 'Okay, what can I do?'

Sophie wiped a tear from her eye and put him to work.

'Is your mum joining us?' Stu said.

'I asked her to, but she said she'd cramp our style!'

Stu laughed. 'We don't have any style!'

'That's what I told her.'

'I'm going to get her. Be right back.'

Sophie laughed at how easily he'd wormed his way out of helping in the kitchen. But that was fine.

No more was said about Jack, much to Sophie's relief, but Stu's concern had been lovely. Some people, she thought, know exactly what to do.

And the only other tears shed that night were tears of laughter. Even Cujo was back to his usual happy, playful self again.

Life Goes On

When Sophie arrived at Gedup'n'go on Monday morning she knew it was going to be another difficult day. What she wasn't prepared for, however, was news of another death. There was an air of disbelief as she walked through the building that morning, and when she went to see Peggy to ask what was going on, she was told that Clinton West, the photographer they'd sent out to cover the dive at Cocklebiddy, the one who had been going to join them for drinks on Friday afternoon, had been killed in a car accident on Thursday night.

Cath had received the news from Terry over the weekend. She'd assumed Clinton had been held up somewhere. There'd been no firm arrangement for Friday afternoon and so when he hadn't stopped by, or even called, she wasn't concerned. It was the nature of the work with these guys out on the road.

Sophie sat in silence, stunned by what she was hearing. The more Peggy talked, the more her voice became a distant hum and the gravity of what had happened was sinking in. She could have died in that crash with him. It was all too much. First Jack, and now the photographer – a man she didn't even know but one she was never going to forget.

As many of her workmates were starting to leave mid-morning for the funeral, Sophie stayed behind and did all she could to keep her mind on her work. It wasn't working though. A funeral made a death so real. A lot of colour had drained out of her life since Jack's death, but she'd been coping better than she expected. Clinton's death on top of that though – and what it meant – it was too much. She needed to get outside, on her own, and so when her lunch break came she went for a long walk and did what she could to clear her head.

It had helped. Walking always did, even without Cujo and Georgia – especially without Georgia – and before the end of the day she'd been able to find a new way of looking at it all. She had to, she told herself. In

Clinton's death – in what could have been her own death – she saw another reason why it's so important to treasure every day, every moment. There's no way any of us can know which day is going to be our last. Sophie had known that – she just hadn't been seeing it this past week. And in looking at Clinton's death that way, she was able to find another way of looking at Jack's death. They had both died doing what they loved. At last, she thought, she would be able to find that inner peace again. Every day brought with it new opportunities, new possibilities, new dreams.

Two months later

Weeks had passed and Sydney's erratic weather had returned. After what seemed like days of non-stop rain, Sophie and Cujo finally made it out again for a walk. They'd both been keen to get going, because although the sun was doing its best to shine through the lingering dark clouds, it didn't look as though it was going to succeed in pushing them away completely, and Sophie thought the big wet was likely to return before too much longer.

They hadn't gone too far from home along the main road when Cujo stopped to sniff something, as he often did – reading his pee-mail, someone had once suggested – and Sophie's attention was drawn behind her to a rainbow that stretched towards her from a place somewhere off in the distance. She stood frozen as she stared at this rainbow that was glowing in a sky that wasn't sure what it was doing, this rainbow whose end she could actually see – something she had, until now, not believed possible. The end of a rainbow had always seemed a mythical thing. People would talk about the pot of gold they all hoped to find if only they could get there, but they never could. Yet there it was.

As she stood there, thinking how beautiful it was, the clouds opened, drenching her and Cujo with another downpour.

'Come on, Cujo. Let's go home.'

৩০Ω

I'd managed to stay with Sophie all those years ago, not just for the duration of that most amazing, moist and dark nine-month journey, but until now. I stayed because I loved her, because I saw it as my second chance at life, and also because I thought I knew better. I can see now I did little more than create a world of quiet desperation for her. That was never my intention.

I thought if I was loud enough, and persistent enough, she'd change, make her life the sort of life *I* thought would make her happier. But it wasn't up to me to determine Sophie's path. She was more than capable of doing that herself.

Sophie will be forty soon, and she's fine. She and Celia are both fine.

Who says it has to be a certain way? A lot of people seem to think that for a person to be content, for a life to be complete, there needs to be a partner, as well as huge experiences. That's what I thought. But I understand now that true contentment must come from within, before the rest of it has even a chance of falling into place.

Fears, insecurities and problems haunt everyone – they just present themselves differently. Sophie had been working herself out. I'd just chosen to ignore it. But they're content, Sophie and Celia. Clinton was too. They knew there were always going to be hard times – that everyone struggles with life from time to time – but the hard times help make the good times that much better.

Sophie's a dreamer, but everyone needs to dream. For some people, like Jack, those dreams don't get much bigger. For others, like Sophie, dreams are only small but they mean just as much. I remembered the words Clinton spoke to Mary when she was questioning life on the short drive they had together. 'People can get great pleasure out of very simple dreams.'

Sweet dreams to you, Sophie.

Epilogue

I know you'll be wondering what happened to everyone, so …

Mary returned to Ireland, and to Patrick. She'd read about Clinton's death in the *Outback Times* while she was still in Kalgoorlie with her friend Angie, and told her about the short time they'd spent together – how learning from and about Clinton, his life and his death, had made her realise how much she loved and was missing Patrick, her ex. She could see she'd let something precious slip away.

Angie had in turn contacted Patrick to see how he was doing. She encouraged him to come Down Under for a while, which he did, and after he and Mary had spent some time together seeing more of Western Australia, they returned home to Ireland with a new appreciation for each other and their individual needs.

In the years that followed, Sophie's treasured friend slipped inexplicably out of her life. Kelly just closed the door on that one – shut Sophie out of her life, and was noticeably absent from all the good times, the difficult times and the sad times in Sophie's. Some years later, when Sophie saw her and asked what had happened, Kelly simply shrugged her shoulders and said, 'We drifted apart.'

Kelly's heart was still beating, but it was cold.

Sometimes there are no answers.

The man in the broad-brimmed hat and Sophie eventually met, in very wet circumstances. He'd been in his ute, stopped at traffic lights the day she was out walking with Cujo and they'd been caught in a downpour as Sophie stood dreaming about rainbows. When he saw them he'd honked his horn and reached across to open the front passenger door.

'What's with you and getting caught in the rain?!' he'd said with a sparkle in his eyes. 'Hop in. I'll give you a ride.' Sophie and Cujo hadn't hesitated. It had been a little cramped in there with the two big dogs, but she didn't notice. And then he'd asked her what her name was, *before* asking about Cujo's. It was the start of an unexpected and very lovely but short-lived friendship. After a while she learned he had a girlfriend, one he left his wife for some time later. Bullet dodged.

Cujo died. Sophie's sadness was cradled by Celia's love, but ultimately a death – any death – is a sadness we carry alone. Without a word, dogs find their way into our hearts and souls and stay there forever, even when their bodies find somewhere else they need to be. Losing them hurts.

Celia also died, creating a very different sadness in Sophie. In losing Celia she'd lost more than just her mum, she'd lost part of herself. But her life had been blessed and enriched by the presence of such a selfless and gentle soul, by Celia's love, and by their unbreakable friendship.

Sophie is doing well. She'd tried for too long to unravel the meaning of life, but knew she was never going to and it was pointless trying. She felt liberated without Georgia constantly in her head but, as the years passed, she put her increasing contentment down to one of the advantages of getting older. That, and Izzi.

Sophie remained largely clueless about people and eventually got another dog – another Golden Retriever, because their smiles and their enthusiasm can brighten even the darkest day. Izzi is completely different but every bit as adorable as Cujo was, and provides the kind of company and comfort that somehow only dogs and mums can provide. And Izzi is a mum – over and over again. Sophie moved to acreage in nearby Terrey Hills, did all she needed to do to become a breeder, and hooked up with a lovely couple who provided the male Retriever, Gunner. Hectic? Absolutely, but joy by the litter-load!

There is, of course, no replacing Celia. That's a sadness Sophie will live with forever.

And Georgia? Your guess is as good as mine.

Acknowledgements

My sincere thanks go to ...

Tony Richardson, who so generously and willingly offered me his time and abundant knowledge when I first began this story and my research into cave diving. Tony's contributions extended throughout the writing process and onto the Nullarbor Plain, and I can't thank him enough for his kindness.

The other guys we met at Cocklebiddy in April 2007 – Mark Pain and Brian Brumley – who allowed us to glimpse this extraordinary other life of theirs. And Barrie Heard who was also on the team at Cocklebiddy – sadly Barrie died some nine months later. He wasn't diving at the time.

Kelvyn Steggles, who shared the dream and the driving as we crossed this vast and incredible country.

John Cleasby for the map of Australia, and Robyn Counsell for the diagram of Cocklebiddy Cave.

Sue Fear, whose untimely death in Nepal, May 2006, made me question so much about life and death and the path each of us takes as we journey through one towards the other.

The many people who, over many years, took the time to read one of my many drafts. My heartfelt appreciation goes to each one of you for your willingness and your input. It's been so long in the making, I'm sure I'd forget someone if I started to list names, but particular mention to Christine Pelosi and Adrienne Roydhouse for their ongoing encouragement, and to Stewart d'Archy for planting the seed.

Pamela Freeman (Hart) and my classmates at the Australian Writers' Centre (2018-19) who managed, in ways both subtle and not, to make me see what I'd written from such different perspectives. It was an inspiring and fun six months with them all.

Jenny Mosher, Ally and Astrid at IndieMosh, who were all an absolute pleasure to work with during the publishing process.

Cujo and Lucy, for providing so much sunshine.

My family. I don't believe in a lot of things but I believe in the strength and love of family, and I'm lucky to have (and have had) the best.

And lastly Chris and Bob Vaillant. I don't know Chris and Bob, but they posted a YouTube clip from their own trip to Cocklebiddy and it's an awesome three minutes with a brilliant soundtrack from Crowded House. Go and watch it now!

https://www.youtube.com/watch?v=vG_5KLX6o-c

Lightning Source UK Ltd.
Milton Keynes UK
UKHW010721091020
371301UK00001B/44